SAVAGE LANDS

SAVAGE LANDS BOOK ONE

STACEY MARIE BROWN

Published by: Twisted Fairy Publishing Inc.
Layout by Judi Fennell (www.formatting4U.com)
Cover by: Jay Aheer (www.simplydefinedart.com)
Edited by Hollie (www.hollietheeditor.com)
Edited by Mo Siren's Call Author Services
(mo@thescarletsiren.com)
Jordan Rosenfeld at Write Livelihood, Developmental Editor
(http://jordanrosenfeld.net)

ALSO BY STACEY MARIE BROWN

Contemporary Romance

Buried Alive

Blinded Love Series
Shattered Love (#1)
Pezzi di me (Shattered Love)—Italian
Broken Love (#2)
Twisted Love (#3)

The Unlucky Ones
(Má Sorte—Portuguese)

Royal Watch Series
Royal Watch (#1)
Royal Command (#2)

Smug Bastard

Paranormal Romance

Darkness Series
Darkness of Light (#1)
(L'oscurita Della Luce—Italian)
Fire in the Darkness (#2)
Beast in the Darkness (An Elighan Dragen Novelette)
Dwellers of Darkness (#3)
Blood Beyond Darkness (#4)
West (A Darkness Series Novel)

Collector Series
City in Embers (#1)
The Barrier Between (#2)
Across the Divide (#3)
From Burning Ashes (#4)

Lightness Saga
The Crown of Light (#1)
Lightness Falling (#2)
The Fall of the King (#3)
Rise from the Embers (#4)

A Winterland Tale
Descending into Madness (#1)
Ascending from Madness (#2)
Beauty in Her Madness (#3)
Beast in His Madness (#4)

Savage Lands Series
Savage Lands (#1)
Wild Lands (#2)
Dead Lands (#3)
Bad Lands (#4)
Blood Lands (#5)
Shadow Lands (#6)

Devil In The Deep Blue Sea
Silver Tongue Devil (#1)

To Jason Momoa:
If I can’t have you in real life,
at least I can have you as my book boyfriend.

Chapter 1

The terrain shuddered with an outgoing train, the spine-chilling howl of the whistle signaling its departure from the eastern banks of Budapest. The eastern side, Pest, could not have been more suitably named as that was exactly how the Buda/Fae side felt about us humans.

Pests.

Vermin.

Nuisances.

The squeal of the tracks shrieked through the dark, coating my skin with goosebumps. The night was unseasonably cold for late spring, causing a lacy fog to climb up the rails of the bridge, like the dead crawling up from their graves, slinking across the ground in hunt for life. The thick atmosphere pillowed the air raging through my lungs. My heart thumped in a tandem of fear and excitement, covering my tongue with the bitterness of adrenaline. Headlights glowed through the mist with an eerie luminosity in the deep witching hours. The conductor's tall, willowy frame was outlined in the window, giving the impression the Grim Reaper was driving, his course set firmly ahead. It was his mission to cross the bridge without casualty.

The Margaret Bridge was split in half by an invisible border. The humans controlled the Pest side of Margaret Island; the fae owned the Buda side. But the bridge was not guarded, making it prime for raids. The train operators knew to be on alert thanks to people like me.

Thieves.

I was the worst kind. I didn't do it to save my family from poverty or because I needed the money. I did it because I could. For the thrill. To confirm how good I was at it. Some might say I was a Robin Hood of sorts, taking profit from the rich fae and humans, who used the poor and desperate as their labor horses. That was complete bullshit. I did it because I loved the high, the danger it brought my controlled world. I was exceptional at sneaking quickly through the night, which filled me with something I never got a lot at home. Pride.

The night trains were partially used for travelers journeying to other towns and countries. The other part held cargo picked up in the neutral zone before heading to Prague, where the goods would be traded or sold, the money going straight into the pockets of the already exceedingly wealthy.

"In ten," I whispered to Caden, his tall form hunched next to me behind a dilapidated souvenir shop. It had been years since tourists came here, back when Budapest flourished with foreign money and travelers. That all ended the day I was born. My birth not only killed my mother but had also marked the deaths of millions of humans, the world as they knew it, and was the beginning of the end for this country.

I carried that weight every day.

"In eight." Similar to a lion creeping up on its prey, I slunk closer, my dark clothes hiding me in the shadows, my long black hair tucked back into my beanie. I pulled down my balaclava, covering my face, only eyes and mouth visible. A knife was strapped to my side. I had yet to use it or even pull it out on any runs. My talent was not robbing head-on but slipping in and out like a ghost. The conductors didn't even realize they had been robbed until I was long gone and back in my bed.

I was the top fighter in my class because of my talent for sneaking up on people, even if they knew I was there. Caden was always in awe of this ability. I was average height, but years of training had my figure fit and slight, able to slink in and out of tiny places like a reedy cat.

"Five," I whispered, leaning on my toes, ready to pounce.

"Brex," he murmured my nickname in my ear, casting shivers down the back of my neck. Instead of the train, my focus turned to the proximity of his mouth, my gaze sliding down to his lips and jaw as he pulled down his face mask.

Clearing my throat, I turned forward.

"Can't back out now, Markos." I used his last name, forcing back the butterflies in my stomach determined to upset the fragile balance between my best friend and me. We had been inseparable since we were children, when the differences between boys and girls were *far* less, and when I didn't want to find out how his lips felt on mine or feel his hands on my body. "Not like you haven't done this before."

"I know, but if we ever got caught… My father..." He shook his head. The ski mask covered most of his gorgeous features and silky brown hair. In the sun, it looked like rich, warm soil, the kind you'd find in a desert, with sparks of reddish-brown I longed to run my fingers through.

The train curved on the track, heading for the Margaret Bridge. End to end, it was two minutes and twenty seconds. We had to be off before it reached the other side.

The fae side.

My heart rapped against my ribs, telling me in code I was an idiot. I was good, remarkable even, but if something happened and we were caught by the fae? Tossing out the thought, I primed my legs, seeing the last few cars coming up the track.

"Now!" Keeping low, I scurried for the back of the train, my legs kicking back, picking up speed. The traveling coaches were the first ones, leaving the back ones holding cargo. Easier to unhook in Prague while the front carriages continued on their journey.

Leaping for the step, I landed soundlessly and skipped up, leaving the stair clear for Caden to jump on.

His boots clanked against the metal, his hands gripping the handles as sweat dripped from under his mask. My concentration faltered as I pulled out my favorite fae device—a very high-tech lock pick, which I pinched from our impound room at headquarters. The magic easily unlatched any kind of locks, which made it illegal and only found on the black market.

Caden climbed up, all six feet of him moving beside me as I stood, stuffing the device back in my pocket. He pulled at the door handle, opening the entrance to the carriage.

This was the fifth time we had raided a train. Caden tried to hide the fact that my kind of fun terrified the hell out of him. He never backed down or tried to dissuade me, but his taut expression when I brought it up told me he did not enjoy it at all. But Caden Markos would be the last person to admit fear, to ever back down from a challenge.

His father did not allow weakness.

He peered down at his wrist, tapping his watch. "You have a minute forty. Clock is on. Go."

I nodded, slipping into the car, knowing exactly where to head. The laborers loading the carts weren't creative and probably didn't care what happened to the cargo once it left the warehouses. They would never see a quarter of the money these products earned.

Blood rushed into my ears as I beelined for the crates most likely loaded with magic-infused pharmaceutical and recreational drugs. Hard drugs were illegal in most of the Western world—the Unified Nations it was now called—the countries under the rule of Lars, the Unseelie King, and Kennedy, the Seelie Queen. But here, if it could make money, it was fair game. This shit sold on the black market for millions, and the richest, most powerful people here were profiting off it.

My connection at HDF—Human Defense Forces—helped me put a nugget of it back in the hands of the individuals who worked in labor shops. Let them sell it on the streets and earn extra money to get the medicine for their child's illness or pay rent for their run-down homes. Some thought the mysterious hero who robbed the trains, giving back to the poor, was some kind of vigilante—one of them.

I wasn't.

I was one of the elite, one of those humans who lived within the protected walls of the area called Leopold, a twelve-block section between the bridges going out to the old Bajcsy-Zsilinszky road, where HDF had taken up residence in the old parliament building on the Pest side. Stuffed with military and the rich, the HDF's main goal was to gain power over the fae, which was a daily struggle against their magic and supremacy, fueling an impending war between the two sides.

Neither side cared about the place where the poor, thieves, murderers, druggies, and mixed-species dwelled. Both sides ignored the lawless land, the terrain where the "savages" lived, which consumed most of the Pest side like the black plague.

My fingers dug into a crate and ripped off the top, finding huge uncut blocks of fairy dust, cocaine laced with fae magic, which got fae high but had humans so addicted and desperate for it that it contributed to most of the murder and suicide rates.

Outside the window, HDF headquarters flashed by, the gorgeous, gothic-revival, white stone building stretching sharply up to the sky, all but glowing with the lights. The palace was a symbol of this city's grand past.

Right now the train was midway at the sliver of land set in the middle of the river, Margaret's Island, and entering enemy territory.

"Twenty seconds," Caden hissed from the door, swiveling his head and nervously tapping his hand against his leg.

I nodded, stuffing the pack on my shoulder with the narcotics, filling my bag, about to move on to the next crate.

"Brexley," Caden hissed. "We don't have time. Come on!" He pranced by the exit, the end of the bridge barely seconds away.

"Shit." I jolted, realizing how much time I had wasted.

"Hey!" A voice boomed from the opposite door, a train guard stepping into the car, his gaze raking over me and my loaded bag. "Stop!" He reached for the weapon in his holster.

Having a gun pulled out was bad, but recognizing the guard as someone you've seen around HDF was another level of awkward. And he would definitely know us. Especially Caden. Our faces were covered, but it felt like cellophane, as if my name were scrolled across my tight black sweater in neon.

In a blink, I darted for Caden, sprinting for the exit.

"Stop!" the guard yelled as we leaped out the door. The wind whistled against my covered ears and whipped at my clothes, my skin temporarily numb to the chill I knew was seeping through the fabric.

"Shit!" Caden exclaimed.

Panic gripped me as we passed the place where we could safely jump.

"Stop, or I will shoot!" The short, stocky blond guard came barreling for us, one hand on his gun, the other reaching for his walkie-talkie.

Fear tugged at my lungs. In a few seconds, we would be stopping. The fae toll-and-customs border was a few yards ahead.

Stealing was punished on both sides. Severely.

"What are we going to do?" Caden's voice bubbled with alarm, his head darting back to the sentinel. "We missed our jump. There's nowhere to hide."

"Fuck." My head twisted back and forth, the train slowing, preparing to stop. The guard stood just a yard from us. I knew there was only one option.

"Jump!"

"What?" Caden's voice pitched.

I gave him no time to contemplate my plan. Grabbing his hand, I pitched us off the moving train. My bones crunched as we hit the pavement, rolling over the concrete, my skin and muscles burning as my body skidded roughly on the hard surface.

"Stop! Thieves!" the guard yelled, his voice carrying to the fae sentinels standing at the platform up ahead, their weapons already primed at their sides. They whipped around, hearing the calls from the guard.

"Come on!" I grabbed for Caden, pulling him up.

Bang! Bang!

Bullets from the fae whizzed by our heads as we darted the opposite way, but the bridge was far too long for us to run. Even in the dark, we were exposed. They would have no problem gunning down thieves where they stood.

"Caden." I twisted to my friend, holding out my hand to him again. "Do you trust me?"

"Uh." He ducked as another bullet pinged off the metal railing. "Yeah. Sure."

"Then…" I grabbed the railing, swinging my leg over. "Jump."

He turned a shade of white, but as more shots rushed past our heads, he scrambled over the railing.

"Just so you know, Brex," he peered down at the dark, freezing, swirling river below, "I pick the activity next time."

"Fair enough."

Pop!

A bullet smashed into the pole right by our heads.

"Now!" I cried out as I let go, plunging into the icy depths below, disappearing in the inky blackness of neutral waters.

Chapter 2

Shivers stomped up and down my spine, making me jerk and twitch, my arms hugging close to my body as we made our way back to headquarters. My jaw was locked tight to keep my chattering teeth from rattling out of my mouth.

Saving our lives meant losing all the product I took. My backpack slipped into a watery grave. It was all for naught, which did nothing for Caden's already prickly mood.

"Seriously, if going to jail wouldn't put a serious dent in my placement after graduation, I'm pretty sure I'd kill you right now." Caden curled his shoulders against the cold, our saturated clothes only enticing the chilly air to nuzzle against us. Technically, summer was encroaching on spring's territory, but it was taking its sweet time. Like the rest of Hungary, even the seasons lived by their own rules now.

"It would make the holidays very awkward."

"One less present I'd have to buy."

"Buy? You'd have to make me something since you'd be in jail." I nudged his arm. Caden was always serious, making it my mission to get him to laugh. Relax a little. Have some fun. "So, what would you make me during those long, lonely hours in prison?"

"I wouldn't. You'd be dead." His wet boots slapped against the pavement.

"Not the point."

"Totally the point. That's why I'd be in jail."

"I survived." My arm brushed up against him, causing the butterflies in my stomach to take flight.

"You would. Just to annoy me, huh?" A slight smile quirked up his mouth, and he elbowed me back.

"Now, what would you make for me? Sculpture made from locks of your chest hair?"

"Gross."

"But I'd love it. It came from your heart. And chest."

He shook his head, chuckling. "You are weird."

"It's why you love me."

His steps faltered, his eyes finding mine for a moment, a pause in the air. Nerves fluttered in my stomach, hope vaulting up my throat. Caden and I had danced around each other since I turned fifteen, the platonic relationship shifting with our awareness of the opposite sex. As we'd grown, we both realized at the same time that our bodies had changed and were far more intriguing now.

Many girls at the academy longed for him. He was tall, gorgeous, fit from years of training, with deep brown eyes, a slight scruff, silky brown hair, and lips you couldn't help but stare at.

Girls always questioned me about us, asking if we were together and cooing about how hot he was. It wasn't until Lilla, a fellow trainee, tried to stake a claim on him that I realized I didn't want any other girl to touch him. Too scared to lose our friendship, I stayed quiet, hoping he'd give me a sign he felt the same.

He stared at me a lot. Teased and touched me but never enough for me to grasp if it was just friendly or there was more. His compliments were very guarded and general.

I knew I was different from most girls around here. My Russian and Irish roots gave me pale skin, but extremely dark and sharp features. "Unique" and "stunning" were words I heard the most, along with "intimidating." I had a lot of male attention and interest, but most guys stayed away, like an invisible line had been drawn around me. Either they were scared of me or didn't want to cross the most formidable cadet at the school. Caden Markos was the son of the highest-ranking general at HDF, Istvan Markos, the leader of the humans.

Now Caden's attention drifted down my body and back up. I didn't move, afraid even a twitch would stop him from saying what I wanted to hear for so long. "Brex," he uttered, his eyes dipping down to my mouth, close enough I could feel his heat colliding with my damp clothes.

I bit my bottom lip, my lungs hitching. His gaze stayed on my mouth, the feel of his breath tickling warmly over my skin. The need to push up on my toes and take what I had craved for so long throbbed through me. He watched me for another beat before he jerked his head, taking a step back.

"The guards change in two minutes. We better hurry." He nodded toward the wall barricading the old parliament building and surrounding area, resembling a fortress. Stone loomed tall and thick around the military human section, securing the reign of man on this side of the river.

To the fae, our walled city was probably mere decoration, a barrier to keep out the very people we were supposed to be guarding, and one of the places the rich bought their way into. The military and the wealthy were condensed into this walled section of Pest, where the streets were spotless and laws still applied.

Guarded at all times, I had learned where I could get in and out without notice. I knew Caden was torn between the two parts of himself: the soldier who wanted to reveal weakness in their human defense so he could be the hero in his father's eyes, and the boy who used to love to pretend to escape beyond the wall with me when we were young. The more Caden advanced through the ranks, the more that boy disappeared. He used rules and laws as excuses more and more.

"Yeah." I nodded, my lungs deflating with disappointment. I could take any guy down in a fight, which was one of the reasons many found me intimidating, but Caden left me so twisted up and confused I wanted to cry.

"I meant it, Brex. This is the last time," he shot back at me, anger tingeing his words. "It's far too dangerous, not to mention illegal. I'll be graduating from the academy soon, and you are not far behind. We need to be soldiers, not criminals."

"We're stealing from the fae. Thought you put that in the 'saving humans' category."

"There are other ways. *Legal* ways."

I snorted, not believing his wishful idealism of truth and justice. I was much more pessimistic.

For nineteen years, all my life, this country had been in turmoil and constant war. I never knew the old world. I only knew a world of walls, death, and fear.

The fae ruled the west side of the river, where they set themselves up in the castle, taking all the land on the Buda side. Humans ruled a speck of territory on the northeast side. Less than half of a district. As if a scar slashed through the land, most of the Pest side hemorrhaged with people, disease, murder, starvation, prostitution, drugs, poverty, and half-breeds. It was called "the Wild West of the East."

The Savage Lands.

"Brex, come on." Caden's voice brought me back to the present. He turned for the hidden gate near a small park, which had turned into a cemetery after the last "confrontation" with the fae almost five years ago.

My boots sloshed as I ran across the road to the ancient iron gate hidden behind overgrown bushes and weeds. It was the least guarded place along the wall, the gate not even detectible from either side. I found it one afternoon years ago when Caden and I were playing hide-and-seek.

Slithering through the bars, I unlatched the rickety gate. It opened just enough for Caden to shove his body through. Barely. One more gym session and he wouldn't fit.

The fog clung low to the vegetation as we weaved through the cemetery, the stars bright in the night sky. Caden cut through another fence, popping us out onto the street. A dull yellow light glowed from a streetlight down the boulevard, shadowing the crumbling pavement and chipped paint. Even within the walls of wealthy *Lipótváros*, which was now called Leopold, the English version, if you looked hard enough, you could see the effects of the dying city bleeding in. The plaster trying to cover up holes in buildings, shoddy paint trying to refresh the facades, the potholes growing with wear and tear. Only a dozen lamps around the walled city were lit at night, the council deciding the money used there could be better spent on more weapons or igniting every inch of HDF in a sea of glorious light, to show the enemy our hold was strong.

Growing up, my dad told me tales of what Budapest was like before the wall fell. After it was relieved of communism control, the country became prosperous with tourism, museums, theater, and art.

"Kicsim, you could freely walk the streets without fear." Father tucked my stuffed dog, Sarkis, in next to me, a gift from my dad's best friend, Uncle Andris. Andris told me it was a shepherd to watch over and keep me safe when they were gone. Which was often. I knew he wasn't my real uncle, but it didn't matter to me. He was my father's right-hand man in

battle. Close as brothers. They said that made us more than family.

"No walls, no laws saying you couldn't walk around. You could go wherever you wanted." Still in his uniform, his day far from over, Dad always took time to tuck me into bed, telling me stories. I always wanted to hear more, to picture this fairy-tale place he spoke of. "Then you could go to the Buda side and stroll the castle grounds. Hang out in cafes, bars, restaurants, and party until dawn if you wanted to. Families went on picnics and to markets without the need to carry a weapon. It was glorious. Can you imagine?"

"No." I wiggled my head against my pillow, tucking Sarkis into my chest. "But I want to go on a picnic with you, Daddy. And you don't have to work ever again."

"Oh, Edesem." Grief cut across his face. "I want that too. Let's hope someday. Someday you will know a life without war and hate, but one with freedom and acceptance. Where both sides can work in harmony. I'm trying to do this. It's why I work so much, so you have a chance at that. Where you can live without threat."

It sounded like paradise. Something my mind couldn't even fathom. None of it was left. Now culture, language, and traditions were mostly lost, replaced by fae customs and the new wave of Westerners who thought this would be utopia without a ruling monarchy, pushing their ideals and culture on this eastern part of the country, blending and changing it into a confused hodgepodge of cultures.

Fae had been living among us since the beginning of time. Once leaders of Earth, they had to go into hiding for centuries, living in a realm called the Otherworld until a bitter old fae queen changed that, shredding the veil between the worlds, meshing them together. As children, we were taught Queen Aneira was a pitiless queen of the Otherworld, no longer wanting the fae scurrying around beneath the humans. Hiding. She waged a war that dissolved the barrier between the realms. Almost twenty years ago, the day of my birth, the wall between the fae world and Earth fell. History books told us the good guys won. And maybe to the Unified Nations, they did. But from Hungary east to Ukraine, we had split off from the rule of a Druid queen and an Unseelie king, becoming our own leaders.

The Hungarian fae nobles at the time thought being independent would be in the best interest of the people.

They were wrong.

When HDF came into view, my lips parted with awe. Basking in light, the gothic towers shot up dramatically like they were trying to skewer the stars in the sky, both beautiful and threatening. Growing up here didn't anesthetize me to the effects this building had on me.

Dozens of guards patrolled the palace, another tier of defense more for keeping out the "savages" than protecting us from fae.

Caden and I went around the side to a private entrance with fewer sentinels. A guard stood by the door, nodding at us. They might frown at us being out here this time of night, but since we were safe inside Leopold city, they couldn't do anything. And no one would ever tattle on Caden. No one would utter a word against the "prince" of Leopold.

"Sergeant." Caden nodded to the man as he opened the door for us.

"Out late, sir," the man responded, his gaze assessing our wet clothes and hair.

Caden put a hand on my back, rushing me through the entrance. My squeaky boots quieted when they hit the long, deep red rugs stretched down the huge hallway. The place had the ugly name of HDF, but it was a palace. Ornamental arched ceilings were painted with beautiful designs and frescos.

Staircases showcased ornate detail and golden lampposts. Sculptures, paintings, and tapestries had been done by world-renowned artists, long gone from this world. One of the most famous rooms was a hexadecagon, the sixteen-sided central hall. Most of the building was decorated in gold-leaf paint, marble, and rich fabrics. The decadence of this place was beyond belief, especially compared to the poverty I heard about on the other side of the wall.

The smallest wing held private living quarters for those high enough in ranking to live here. It included a pool, bowling alley, movie theater, and two massive kitchens. The servants resided in the basement rooms below ours. The rest of the palace served for business and to impress. It boasted grand rooms, theaters, offices, training facilities, cafes—really anything you could wish for. It was a city within itself. My maid, Maja, loved to brag about the magnificence of the building, boasting about the ten courtyards, twenty-nine staircases, and 691 rooms.

Night guards watched Caden and me move down the halls toward the living quarters. Their expressions were blank, but I swore I could hear their internal sighs. As usual, Brexley Kovacs was leading their perfect prince into temptation and trouble.

Yeah, okay, I did that. A lot. But he needed a little excitement in his orderly life. Soon he wouldn't be able to sneak out with me. It scared me that our time to be free like this was vanishing before my eyes. In a few weeks, he would graduate from the academy and become Lieutenant Caden Markos with his life laid out for him.

He'd no longer have time for me.

As we crept toward our residency, our boots harmonized in their high-pitched squeaking. I burst out laughing.

"Brex, be quiet," he hissed, but the odd melody merely

resounded more loudly through the hall, as did my giggles. He snapped his head to me, trying to glare at me, but humor divided his mouth, a chuckle tapping at his chest.

"I'm glad you find this so amusing," a deep voice boomed down the corridor. My stomach dropped like lead to my toes.

Fuck.

Standing before us was the leader of HDF, General Istvan Markos.

You could see where Caden inherited his looks. Tall and broad similar to his son, Istvan was still quite fit, with silvering hair cropped close to his head, a very trimmed beard covering his strong jaw, and steel blue eyes. Lines in his face showed the weight and stress of his position, but his handsome features and rank had women at his feet whenever he wanted. His wife's own beauty did nothing to keep him faithful. When I was fourteen, I found him screwing a Ukrainian princess in his office. He was forty-eight at the time; she was twenty.

Caden halted, stiffening next to me, standing tall with his chin up like we were in training. "Father."

"I am so deeply disappointed in you, Caden." His tone oozed with dissatisfaction and censure, and his stern face narrowed in on his son. "I keep thinking you have grown up and left this foolishness behind. It has been a long time since you have been a child. And yet…" He tilted his head, and his blue eyes darted to me, clearly identifying the true cause of his son's insolence. "You still act the same as one. As do you, my dear. Your father would expect more from you."

Ouch. I flinched. Straight through the heart. My gaze dropped to the rug.

Istvan sighed, tugging at his uniform, the blazer so decorated in badges, pins, and awards it could be used as a doorstop. The five-star general was beyond intimidating. Cold, calculating, and ruthless, there was a reason he reached the rank he had and stayed there.

Yet Istvan did have moments of kindness. He took me in when I had no one else, though it probably had more to do with his respect for my father. He always looked at me like I was dirt under his shoes, but when I became an orphan at fourteen, he and his wife, Rebeka, took over as my guardians. I had been such a fixture in their lives already not much changed, except my living quarters moved up a few floors, and I had to follow Istvan's rules. I did a crappy job of that. I was never good with rules.

"Do I dare ask?" Istvan motioned to our clothes, his lip twitching with disgust.

"We went swimming in the pool." Caden kept his head level, not flinching as the lie slid off his tongue as if it were the truth. The indoor pool was six floors down in the palace. It had been built for training purposes, but we used it year-round for fun.

"You went swimming?" His father's eyebrow curved up, not believing us for a moment. "At two o'clock in the morning, fully clothed?"

"I pushed him in." I shrugged, going with the fib. "He retaliated."

Istvan stared at us for a moment before he took a deep breath, rubbing his forehead. It was so close to something Caden and I would do I was pretty sure he believed our tale.

"I don't have time for this. I have actual emergencies to deal with. Lives on the line. But your mother found your room empty and called me, pulling me from *real* work as you two play like five-year-olds." He pinched his nose, every word stabbing into me exactly as he wanted them to. "Go to bed. I will deal with you two in the morning."

The general inhaled and took off for the door leading out of the residency, probably heading back to his office. He was not a man who rested much.

"Father?" Caden's voice followed him down the hall. Istvan glanced back at his son. "I am sorry. It won't happen again."

"I would like to believe that." Istvan's accusing gaze briefly drifted to me again. "It's time you take your position seriously. Other trainees look up to you, follow you as a leader. Someday you will take over my position. Start acting like it. In sixteen hours, we will be entertaining presidents and rulers. I don't need to remind you how important this is. The Romanian leader will be here, and I need you both to be on your best behavior."

"I will do better."

"From where I stand, you will need to do more than better," he replied curtly, then walked out, shutting the door to the private wing.

Tension ping-ponged off the walls.

"I'm sorry, Caden." I twisted to my friend, reaching for his arm.

He jerked away from my touch, his face crunching with anger.

"You always *say* you're sorry, Brex," he said, his jaw twitching. "But I'm always the one who actually is." He snorted, twisted around, and walked away, leaving me staring after him, tears filling my eyes.

I slowly made my way to my room, shutting the door. Peeling off my wet jacket and tossing it in the laundry basket, a sting of disappointment slouched my shoulders. The only items filling it would be my clothes tonight. Just one person ever went through my dirty clothes, finding the items I stole: my maid, Maja. She helped get the product back to the Savage

Lands. Both her son and daughter worked in factories there, barely able to buy bread. She was the one who told me tales of the barbaric living conditions scarcely outside the walls of Leopold. Honored and grateful for her position here, she still tried to help her grown children and their families survive, to afford medicine and food.

Tonight was a failure on all fronts.

With a sigh, I strolled into my huge bathroom, showering the Danube off my skin, and crawled into bed, sinking into the soft mattress with sheets that felt like butter. In the dark, my mind drifted back to Caden. He was Istvan's only child. I knew the pressure Caden was under, the constant need to prove his worth to his father. But still, I pushed because I sensed the boy I loved was slipping through my fingers.

And he was all I had left.

Chapter 3

My spine struck the mat with a smack, a groan puffing out of my chest. I wanted to lay there for the rest of the day. Maybe take a little nap.

"Again, Kovacs," a voice boomed from the side of the mat. Sergeant Bakos clapped his hands together to get me moving. "You are off your game today."

I was more than off. Only two hours of sleep will do that to you. Plus, my bones were protesting the dive roll onto the pavement and the swan dive off the bridge last night. Because of the adrenaline, I didn't feel the impact at the time. Now everything hurt, and I moved much slower than normal.

Usually I would have pinned my opponent to the mat by now, my elbow in their throat. My skill was a sore spot with the other cadets, mainly the guys, though the girls were on a mission to drop me as well. But I could see their moves miles away.

The men really took it personally, proving sexism was still alive and well. Not just because I was a slim, petite-boned girl, but it seemed to piss the boys off that I was pretty too. As if that was the reason they lost their concentration. As if someone who looked as I did shouldn't be able to outmatch them.

Sometimes guys got turned on, laughing and thinking it was a game until I tossed them down like sacks of flour. Their little fragile egos couldn't handle it.

Aron Horvát was one of those. He flirted—a lot—when he wasn't threatening me.

"Right where you should be… on your back for me, Kovacs," Aron murmured, winking, his brown eyes rolling salaciously over me.

"Fuck you, Horvat," I snarled, getting to my feet, my joints protesting the movement. Adjusting my dark cargo pants, I brushed back a few strands of hair that strayed from my ponytail, sweat trailing down my back.

"What is wrong with you today, Kovacs?" Sergeant Bakos walked over to me, rubbing his dark brown buzzed head. A few salt-and-pepper hairs were sprinkled through, ones he didn't have when I joined the academy at fifteen. Five years of dealing with me did that to people.

He was the training instructor here, coaching the students over the years and turning them into soldiers. He was brutal and relentless, but I respected him, and he didn't care what gender or body type you had. He simply expected the best from you, teaching you how to use your limitations as positives.

At five foot five, he was a little shorter than me but built of solid, rippling muscle. No guy here, not even Caden, could outfight him. He showed us strategy and how your own flaws could be an asset in a fight.

He made me into the fighter I was today. He encouraged me to work harder. Do better. I hated disappointing him.

Like today.

"There's no excuse, sir." I lifted my head, pinning my arms behind my back in soldier stance.

"That's right." Bakos nodded. "Your enemy won't give

a shit you didn't sleep well the night before or have a tummy ache." He stepped back off the mat, speaking to the seven of us still left in this year's class. "They will kill you in seconds. Attack without warning. Slaughter you without thought or remorse in a blink of an eye."

"Like *The Wolf*," Hanna said in a spooky voice, her playfulness dropping the moment Bakos glared back at her. "What? We've all heard the tales. He will kill you without blinking… and he's so unbearably hot, you go willingly."

"Hanna." Bakos sighed in annoyance. "I'm here to train you guys for *real* enemies, not make-believe ones."

"My sister's boyfriend's father said he was very real," Hanna countered. "Saw him fight a dozen men at once in the Fae War."

"Did he tell you Santa Claus was real too?" Bakos clipped. "The Wolf is nothing but an exaggerated and glorified tale, inflated every time he is mentioned."

We all had grown up hearing about the legend of Warwick Farkas. Not fae or human, but a living ghost. His last name meant Wolf, which is how he got the moniker, not because he turned into one. His tale was told to candidates to make them wet the bed at night. The stories about him left you in awe and horror at how easily, and how many, he killed. Barehanded. Gutted, burned, tortured, skinned alive.

"Back to reality." Bakos clapped his hands. "The threat of another war is on our doorstep, and our enemy is stronger, faster, harder to kill, and can shift or disappear in front of our eyes. We must be faster, fight even harder, and become smarter than them." He pointed at me to get back into position. "You will not get a do-over out there, so I never want to see anyone giving me less than one hundred percent. You got it?"

"Yes, sir," we replied in unison.

I dropped down into a defense position, my eyes settling

on Aron. A smirk spread over his mouth. Aron could have been good-looking enough, and at one time, I even thought so, but his jealous nature and constant need to be better than everyone made him ugly to me now. He was average in everything, including fighting, with deep insecurity issues that made him overcompensate and fluff his ego to the point I looked forward to sparring with him in class.

Here I could punch the crap out of him and not get in trouble.

"If you wanted to be under me again so bad, Kovacs, all you had to do was ask. Clearly, Markos is not satisfying you… though I've heard he's giving it to Lilla really good."

I gritted my teeth, moving around him. *Don't let him get to you*, I chided myself. Aron loved finding people's Achilles heel and biting down on it.

"Unlike you, she's a real screamer."

Rage boiled through my chest, spreading up my esophagus.

Bakos allowed shit-talk and taunting. Nothing was off the table because what we'd face out there would be much worse. He wanted us prepared to handle it all.

"Does Markos know I was there first, popped your cherry?" He nodded down to my crotch. "How do you think he'd feel about that?"

I gritted my teeth in disgust and fury, my body vibrating with the need to pummel him, shut him up. At least I forgot my sore muscles and fatigue.

I had tried to pretend Caden and I were just friends, and I didn't like him any more than that. I didn't care if he was hooking up with Lilla or any of the girls before her. I tried to make it the truth so much that I did the stupidest thing ever.

I let this asshole in front of me take my virginity one night.

I was drunk, heartbroken, mad, and lonely, and Aron was the only one who had guts to pursue me. The rest of the guys were too scared of Caden's reaction. It was like he controlled who I dated, while he freely got to screw every girl who walked by.

It was the first anniversary of my father's death. Aron was there, showing me the attention I so desperately craved. Losing my father had left me grasping for something, anything, to anchor me and make me feel good. I'd sunk into the sludge of desperation, watching Caden hook up with girls right in front of me.

Regret started even before Aron was done—which, let me say—wasn't long.

Now my worst remorse and humiliation was in my face daily, taunting me.

"Come on, Kovacs." He flicked his wrists, motioning to himself. "I know you want it. You can play the uptight prude all you want, but *I* know how you enjoy it. Know how easy those legs open."

Hanna, the closest I had to a girlfriend, inhaled with shock, her mouth dropping open. Shit. If it wasn't humiliating enough that I'd ever allowed this piece of crap to touch me, now everyone in this room knew. They stared at me with disbelief and repulsion, and my cheeks heated with shame. I knew they thought I was stuck-up and prudish, not imagining I could possibly have slept with Aron of all people. Especially with how much I clearly hated him.

Turn your weakness and embarrassment into your favor, I told myself, trying to push away the stunned faces of my comrades.

Taking a step closer to Aron, my lips curled in a heated smile. He stood there, watching me, his eyes widening with lust.

"Honestly, you were so incompetent in bed, I'd be surprised if you can even get yourself off." My voice went low and husky.

There was a beat.

"Oooohhhh, dammmnnn!" A few guys laughed, covering their mouths in shock.

Aron's head jerked back, his lids narrowing, nose flaring. "You bitch!" he sneered, leaping for me. All emotion and no strategy.

Perfect.

Twisting my body, I snapped my elbow up, digging into his esophagus and knocking him back. Aron grabbed for his throat, stumbling back, hacking and gasping for air. I was taught never to let your opponent recover. It might be the only chance you have to live.

Spinning, I kicked out, jabbing at the tendon in his knee.

"Ah!" He cried out as my boot slammed into his chest, tossing him back on the mat. Jumping down, I pinned his arms with my knees, my elbow pressing into the soft curve of his neck. His expression pinched with pain while his eyes glared at me with rage, his lips curling in a snarl.

"You're right, Horvát." I leaned into him, digging in deeper. "You do know how I like it."

"All right, Kovacs. That's enough," Bakos yelled to me.

I winked at Aron, withdrawing, basking in smugness as I stepped from the mat.

My self-satisfaction was suddenly clipped like bird wings, plummeting me back to earth with a painful crunch the next moment. Caden leaned against the door, which he did frequently, watching my class spar. He'd later give me pointers, working on moves with me. But this time, he was not grinning at me. His arms were folded, his expression taut and cold, but his brown eyes *burned* into me, ripping through my soul and peeling back my skin. His chest puffed in and out as he took in air.

There was no doubt. He heard everything.

His mouth pinched together, his head shaking slightly, and pain flashed in his eyes before he snapped his head away from me and turned, striding down the hall.

Drowning in guilt and sadness, I pitched forward, wanting to run after him. But years of training held me in place, going against my instinct to follow him. To explain.

Settling back in my place next to Hanna, I bit down on my lip, holding back the emotions trying to leap from my heart that wanted to make me say and do something stupid.

"Damn, girl," Hanna whispered under her breath.

"He deserved it."

"Aron always does," she muttered, her head staying forward. "But that's not what I was talking about."

Oh. That. "It was a mistake." My jaw clenched, my chin hitching up again as I watched another pair move to the mat. "Don't want to talk about it."

"Oh, we will definitely be talking about it at the party tonight." She leaned in toward me.

Party?

Oh shit.

I had totally forgotten. Istvan enjoyed impressing people, being admired. The more noses up his ass, the happier he was. He threw parties all the time—galas, balls, festivals—to schmooze with the rich and powerful. There they made deals, forged alliances, and gained more influence and power.

Tonight was no different. General Markos wanted to greatly impress the Romanian leader. I had no idea why, but he kept reminding Caden and me about the importance of this night. Funny, I ended up completely forgetting about it. Again.

I wasn't the kind of girl who enjoyed getting dressed up in torturous outfits and shoes, and I was rarely on my best behavior with stuffy, boring people. I'd rather be in my cargo pants and tank hanging out with Caden, drinking palinka straight from the bottle at our favorite spot.

"But again, that's not what I meant."

I peered at Hanna. An impish smile wobbled on her mouth, her blonde eyebrows rising to wicked peaks.

"What?"

"You are so blind." She shook her head, then tipped her chin toward the door. "Ca-den…"

"What about him?" I swallowed, heat clogging my throat and spreading over my skin. Why was he so angry? Yeah, Aron was an asshole, but Caden had no say in who I slept with. He had screwed half the girls here, and now he acted as though I'd hurt him? How dare he.

Anger diluted the mix of other emotions.

"Did you not see his face?" she stressed. "You might as well have stabbed him in the heart."

"What? No. That wasn't it at all." *It was disgust.*

"Suuuree." She shook her head. "You two. Someone needs to smack you guys in the head." She leaned in closer, whispering, "Maybe flirting with Sergiu tonight will wake Caden up. I've heard he's gotten really cute."

"Sergiu?" I gagged. "Are you serious? Gross. Plus, haven't you heard the rumors about him?"

"His kink is beating up prostitutes he's screwing, and he won't date anyone because he thinks he's above everyone?" She shrugged. "Yeah, but think how riled up Caden would get if you flirted with him. Might finally get him to act. Because Sergiu would fall over his tongue to get to you. *All* men do."

"Hanna, you're up." Bakos waved to her.

"Ugh. I hope I don't get a black eye like I had at the last

ball. Doesn't match my dress." She sighed, tightening her blonde ponytail. "And rumor is the minister of Serbia loves blondes and is very kinky." Hanna wiggled her eyebrows at me before heading to the mat.

I barely registered the last part, my mind still whirling around what she said about Caden. Could there be a chance he felt the same way? I was scared to hope. I had lost so many people in my life. I didn't want to lose him either. Yet once he graduated, he would be moving up in the ranks, leaving this place to get field experience, stepping up in the role his father carved out for him.

Tonight might be my last chance to make him see me and what we had together. Or could have.

I would tell Caden how I felt.

For good or bad, tonight, everything would change.

Chapter 4

"Stop fidgeting. You look stunning." Rebeka patted my wrist, similar to the way someone would tap the nose of a misbehaving dog. "The dress is impeccable on you."

Compulsion moved my fingers back to the top of the dress, tugging at the material, which barely covered the sides of my breasts. Not that I needed much to cover the minimal boobs I had. Genes and years of training had left my body very trim and flat. So many women would gush over my slim build, saying how lucky I was for my "model" figure and looks, while I looked at their soft curves with jealousy. I was all hard angles and coolness, nothing inviting or warm.

Many older men had told me how "sensual" they found me. Even at a very young age, my confidence and appearance drew unwanted notice and touches. I wasn't oblivious to how I looked, the power it generated—I just didn't care. Men treated me more as something they wanted to conquer or possess, not truly love.

"You will turn many heads tonight, my dear." Rebeka smiled softly at me, a deep sadness filling her brown eyes. The same deep brown as her son's.

Rebeka was in her early forties and beautiful with her

silky auburn hair, deep brown eyes, and full lips. She was my height and trim, but she had the curves I always longed for, which were on display in her delicately ornate gown cinched around her small waist. The front was nearly transparent, with beads and jewels placed to catch the light and set perfectly to look glamorous and elegant instead of cheap. Navy tulle descended from her waist to the floor, and her hair was pulled up in an intricate bun, diamonds dripping off her ears.

As a young girl, I used to idolize her. Wanted to be identical to her.

The older I got, the more I realized her perfection was a prison. She was good at doing her duty as "queen" of Leopold. Smiling, charming leaders and their wives, throwing the best parties and being the beauty standing at her husband's side. She wasn't a silent partner, though; she could put at ease and relax even the most severe, bad-tempered person in the world. Rebeka and Istvan made a good team. When he couldn't get something from someone, she went in, and I had yet to see her fail, making me wonder how far she went to win. She wasn't clueless to her husband's infidelity, but she never spoke of it. Only in brief moments would I catch a vulnerability and sadness in her eyes. But from little things I had picked up over the years, she didn't let her bed grow cold either.

"You will do well tonight." She tucked her arm in mine, guiding us to the ballroom.

"Do well?" I peered at her through my dark lashes.

"Before our independence from the Unified Nations, things were better for women here. Young ladies could marry freely, be whatever they wanted. The war changed that, moving us backward here. I hope someday we will have freedom again, but until then, many of us women do not dare to strive above the brunt of duty and circumstance. We wield our power in more subtle ways."

Her fingers tightened on my arm, making me swallow over the growing lump in my throat. Where Istvan always criticized me, Rebeka was more caring. She wasn't someone who baked cookies or played games with you, but she treated me with kindness. Sometimes even acted as a friend.

"I don't understand."

She stopped before the large double doors of the ballroom, impeccably dressed guards ready to open them for us. She turned to me, and a sad smile softened her painted lips, her fingers swishing a strand of my long black hair over my shoulder. Normally, it was straight, hitting my lower back, but Maja had curled it in loose waves, adding a few tiny jewels within the locks.

"You will soon." Her lips pressed together. She shook her head slightly, rolling back her shoulders. "Now, lift up your beautiful face and show everyone in the room they can take nothing away from you. No matter what. Never apologize for how *others* react to *your* strength."

My lungs fluttered at her odd speech. Rebeka had never been one for sentimentality or inspiring speeches. And she had never walked into a party with me, usually entering on the general's arm.

Why tonight?

"Rebeka?" I searched her eyes, but they were walled up again, her pleasant hostess smile pinned on her face.

"It's time." She curved back, nodding at the guards. The doors split open, revealing the breathtaking circular room. Istvan used his sixteen-sided central hall as the "ballroom." The guests arrived at the front entrance that led them through the jaw-dropping grandeur of the main hall, highlighted by old plated staircases, huge ornately curved ceilings, stained-glass windows, and glass fire-bulbs flickering on the gold lampposts lining the room. Waiters and servants took coats and offered champagne while a small orchestra played on the upper landing, filling the room with music.

Then they were guided to the central hall, the gold starburst designed dome ceiling leaving the visitor stunned at the ostentatiousness of the room. A huge orchestra sat on an upper level, where several full bars and tables of decadent food stood. Tons of waitstaff mulled around with rich hors d'oeuvre and champagne. Magic-influenced fire-bulbs and twinkle lights cast the room in a seductive ambiance. It never ceased to leave me breathless.

Heads snapped in our direction; Rebeka always made a memorable entrance. Now her eyes drifted to me.

"You leave them speechless, my girl," she whispered to me. "Putty in your hands." She squeezed my arm before ambling toward her husband.

Hundreds of eyes homed in on me, and I was overcome by the urge to turn around, go back to my room, and dive into my bed with a good book.

Sucking in a breath, I lifted my head, directing myself straight for a waiter carrying champagne. Swiping one off the tray, I guzzled half of it back when I spotted Caden across the room, leaning against the bar, his eyes on me.

His gaze felt heavy on my skin. Serious, but filled with something I had always hoped for.

Longing.

I had seen him in a suit or tux many times, and he always made my heart thrust into my throat. Tonight was no different. Dressed in a black tailored tux that fit his body perfectly, a glass of whiskey in his hand, he looked so beautiful I was almost speechless.

Sparkling bubbles danced in my stomach along with my nerves, magnifying like soap suds, causing my breath to gurgle.

He didn't smile or move toward me, but similar to a magnet, I felt the tug between us. The spark in the atmosphere. A shift in our friendship.

Bodies moved all around me. Music and chatter weaved through the air. The smell of expensive perfumes and food reached my nose, but it all seemed far away.

Caden was all I saw.

I downed my glass of champagne, placed it on a passing tray, and moved toward him.

"Hey," I barely squeaked out the greeting, my throat tight.

"Hey." He set down his whiskey glass, his eyes still on mine, hazy with drink. Normally, Caden was too rigid in his training to drink much, wanting to always be at his best. So it was odd for him to get drunk.

Did this have to do with me? What he heard earlier?

My brain scrambled for something to say. I had always been able to talk to him. To tease and be myself around him. Was it because the connection was one-sided, and he only saw me as a friend? Standing before him now, my throat cinched up; no conversation came to my mind.

"You look amazing." He cleared his throat, his attention moving down the gown. The bare skin between my breasts tingled.

When I had returned to my room after training, this gown had been laid out for me, telling me exactly what I was supposed to wear tonight. Usually, I had a few choices of exquisite gowns. This time there was one.

The floor-length gown was sensual and elegant at the same time. Silvery translucent flowers decorated parts of the ultra-sheer champagne-colored fabric, leaving glimpses of skin everywhere. The material sparkled under the lights like glitter. The plunging neckline went to the base of my sternum and exposed my back, causing me to feel very bare, which was funny because I was practically naked in training all the time. You became very comfortable with being minimally dressed when working out with a small coed group. With genderless locker rooms, we had no room to be modest. I had no problem with my body. I could handle walking around in boy shorts and a sports bra when training and be completely comfortable.

Now I felt uncomfortable—on display like some dessert.

"Thank you." I grabbed the glass from his fingers, taking a sip, my gaze sliding to him. "Looking forward to when it comes off."

His head jerked up, his eyes widening slightly.

Chagrin swam in my cheeks with the realization of what I said. "I mean—I didn't—"

"I know." A grin drew up his lips. "You'd rather be in workout clothes and tossing someone's ass onto the mat, making them cry."

"Now that sounds like my kind of party." I smiled around the rim, taking another sip, the smoky flavor burning down my throat.

He snorted, shaking his head. "Guess I need to order another one for myself." He nodded toward my hand. "Always the little thief."

"You act as if you can't just go behind the bar and take the whole bottle." I rolled my eyes, motioning to the bartender.

"I could take *everything* here if I wanted." He leaned into me, his mouth close to my ear, and my breath stalled in my lungs.

My gaze jumped to him, but I forced my expression to stay blank.

He stared at me, his intent penetrating me.

Holyshitholyshitholyshit.

"The same again, sir?" The bartender's voice jolted me, and I sucked in sharply.

Caden nodded, holding up his fingers. "Two."

"Yes, sir." The guy bowed his head slightly, reaching for the private collection of whiskey. Imported from Scotland, it probably cost as much as my dress did, if not more. Everything from the West—from the Unified Nations—was expensive, which allowed only the rich to be able to procure these items.

We both stayed silent. Tension, which had never existed before, now dripped between us like heavy syrup. The bartender set down the glasses, his eyes darting between us with curiosity before he moved on to other guests.

"Caden…" I twisted to him.

"Don't, Brex." He stared down into his drink. "It is taking everything I have not to go over and beat the shit out of that *te geci*." *Motherfucker*. His hands rolled up into balls, his glower stretching across the space to where Aron and all the different classes of cadets hung out, drinking and enjoying the night. "The thought of you being with him..."

I turned to face the room, not knowing how to respond.

"I can't believe you slept with that guy. He *touched* you." Caden's Adam's apple bobbed, his jaw locking down. "He's such a douchebag, and you let him…"

"I know what I did," I snapped. Aron wasn't my finest moment, a regret that I had to relive daily. I hated that he was my first, that he had something no one else would. But it was done, and in all honesty, I barely remembered it.

But what I did was my choice. My mistake. Caden had no right to judge or condemn me for it.

"When?" he croaked.

"Does it matter? It was a long time ago." I slammed back a huge gulp of my drink, my eyes watering as it scorched down my throat.

"Brex."

"It's none of your business. And why do you care? Aren't you fucking Lilla?" I glowered at him. "You aren't my boyfriend. You have no say in what I do. Or *who* I do."

He flinched, bowing his head. Then his lips spoke words so low I barely captured them. "What if I wanted to be?"

Like I had taken a punch to the ribs, fear halted my breath—fear I was mistaking the meaning of his words. Heard them wrong. Twisting to him, my chest puffed with tension as his gaze landed heavily on me. With want. Desire.

"Want to be what?" I whispered.

His gaze rolled over my body as he leaned in. "Want to be—"

"There you two are." Istvan's deep voice sliced through our bubble, jerking both of us toward him.

His stern expression showed nothing, but his steel eyes went back and forth between us, assessing us like a predator. Also dressed in a tux, Istvan looked every bit the ruler he was. Handsome, charismatic, ruthless, and arrogant.

"I expect you two to mingle and greet our guests, not hang out with each other as you do every day." He spoke to us but continued nodding and shaking hands with admirers passing by who wanted to speak with the infamous leader. "I want you both to join me in welcoming Prime Minister Lazar."

I straightened to my full five-feet-seven height, my stomach already twisting at the thought of conversing with strangers. I learned to be good at it, but I hated it. Since becoming Istvan's ward, he expected me to play the part as a real daughter would. Using both Caden and me like chess pieces, he strategically moved us around the room.

"These are *very important* people. I need you on your best behavior."

"Then I probably should stay here." My hand went to my stomach, where the whiskey and champagne now clashed.

Istvan's gaze slid to me. "I believe I said *both* of you."

"Yes, sir." I nodded. The man could make a monster cower with that look.

Istvan took a breath and strode away.

My focus fell on Caden, longing for him to finish what he was going to say.

"Caden…"

"Not now, Brex." He shook his head.

Pinching my lips, I exhaled. This night already felt too long.

"After you." Caden motioned for me to go first.

All I wanted was to be alone with Caden. What was he going to say before his father cut him off? Did he want to be my boyfriend? Was he finally admitting there was something there?

Later, Brex, I chided myself. *Just get through this damn night.*

Drinking down the rest of my liquid courage, I rolled my shoulders back and followed Istvan, trying to shove away the gnawing urge to walk straight out the door.

Chapter 5

"Prime Minister Lazar, sorry to keep you waiting." Istvan dipped his head slightly to the man standing across from Rebeka, who was joined by his family. Alexandru Lazar was in his fifties, short, with an average build. His dark hair was short, silvering, and styled perfectly. He had dark brown eyes, a long narrow nose, and thin lips. His dress uniform, also laden in medals, flaunted his power. "You remember our son, Caden. And our ward, General Benet Kovacs's daughter, Brexley."

"I do, General Markos," he replied with a thick accent, slanting his head at Caden. "It is good to see you again, Caden."

"You too, sir." Caden shook his hand, their exchange formal and stiff.

"Brexley." Lazar took my hand, his thin wet lips brushing over my knuckles. Peering up at me, his eyes lingered over my body. "Exquisite as always. Truly a work of art. You become even more bewitching every time I see you."

It was no secret he loved women and thought taking lovers was a man's right. He had made it clear since I turned fifteen that he wanted me to be one of those women.

"Prime Minister." I curtsied with a smile, tugging my hand away, rubbing it inconspicuously in the folds of my dress. I had learned how to school my face into a pleasant smile while screaming on the inside. "A pleasure."

"I hope Rebeka kept you entertained." Istvan touched his wife's back, sharing a fake "we're so in love" smile between them.

"Your *lovely* wife could always entertain me in your absence. I enjoy her company much more than yours, Istvan." You couldn't mistake the innuendo drenching his sentiment. His stern face and eyes stared back at our leader.

Rebeka's eyes slid to her husband with unspoken words, but a false, sparkling smile still stretched her mouth as she swished her hand at the prime minister. "Always such the charmer, Alexandru."

Tensions were high between Romania and Hungary. Instead of coming together when they realized splitting off from the Unified Nations was in nobody's best interest, they doubled down, wanting to acquire more land from the other. It was a constant threat, a thin line of alliance, which at any time could crumble.

Budapest always had a turbulent past, being tossed from one dictator to another, finally coming out of it only to turn its back on the king and queen, reverting this land back to authoritarian rule with a penchant for war.

"She was just confirming our *cargo* would be heading out tonight," Lazar stated, a challenge in his voice.

Cargo? As far as I knew, Romania went through Ukraine to export their supplies. Another leader attending the party who walked the line between enemy and ally. The room was full of adversaries, all pretending they got along and wanted peace between us. You'd think fighting the fae would bring humans together, but it didn't. Instead, they bickered and fought amongst themselves, each trying to seize more power.

"Yes, though I don't think this is the place to discuss it."

Istvan shoved his shoulders back, the war of egos battling it out. It would have been more honest if they had drawn out their dicks and started using them as swords.

"Why?" Lazar lifted his eyebrow, motioning around the room. "Isn't this exactly why you invited me? The room is set to impress. I do hope I wasn't supposed to be daunted by your wealth and power, Istvan. That would be a shame."

I could recognize the clench of Istvan's jaw, the negligible twitch in his left eye. It was so slight no one would notice, but I had spent years pissing off Istvan.

"The items will be departing on the last night train before dawn. Without a hitch, I assure you."

"I am taking a great risk with you." Lazar took a sip of his champagne. "If President Ivanenko hears of our *deal*, let's just say the next time he comes here, it will be with troops."

Ivanenko was the Ukrainian "president." A ceremonial title. With the walls falling between the fae world and Earth twenty years ago, there really were no presidents or prime ministers anymore. They each got a piece of the city they shared with fae leaders. But they clung to the old titles like wailing children trying to hold on to a favorite toy as it got tossed into the fire.

Ivanenko's power was multiplying as he acquired more soldiers, money, and weapons. Rumors of him working with the fae to expand his influence over other human-ruled lands abounded. His threat to conquer their land loomed over both Hungary and Romania.

"It will make both our countries very wealthy." Istvan kept his voice low, his eyes sliding around the room, making sure no one overheard him. "Once it is out there. We will control the trade—become untouchable. Have power and unyielding armies at our fingertips. Trust me. What I have seen… There is no question it works."

What was he up to? The wealthy businessmen in Leopold owned all of the human factories in the Savage Lands, not Istvan. I wasn't naïve to think he didn't dabble in their dirty dealings or know what they were doing. He had to. It was the only way to survive in these times in the East. And as a ruler, he needed to know everything going on, but he mainly stayed away from trade, letting his fat friends get fatter.

This felt different. What deal had he made with Lazar? And what were they exporting out of here?

"However, let me stress again that this is not the time to discuss such matters." Istvan cleared his throat, his demeanor lightening as he grabbed a champagne flute from a tray, his eyes falling on me. "We have much more pleasant things to plan."

Like an icy finger scraping down my spine, I shivered, my stomach twisting with alarm at his heavy gaze.

"Yes. We do." Lazar twisted to peer behind him, flicking his head at the figures. His stunning wife, Sorina, stepped forward, silent and demure. She used to model, prostitute, and work in adult movies before he pulled her from the trenches and made her rich and pampered. He treated her similar to a second-class citizen, and probably reminded her at every turn he could send her back into poverty's cruel embrace. She smiled and did all the right things but was vacant and dead behind her eyes. I wanted to feel bad for her, but she made her own bed...

A man stepped up to Lazar's other side. Sergiu. I had met their son only twice, many years ago, and he rendered a very less-than-stellar impression on me. He had been uptight and difficult, tattling on Caden and me if we did anything he found inappropriate. Which was everything.

A year older than Caden, he still looked like a teenager. He was an inch taller than me, with a slim frame and the same cruel eyes his father had. His longer brown hair waved back as perfectly as Lazar's. His nose was more bubbled at the end, resembling his mother, Sorina. Some might think him good-looking enough, but I never did, especially because he was as interesting as a dry rag, and had an evil cruelty behind his stiff demeanor.

He might have grown in age and height, but his sour expression suggested he was still an uptight prick. The rumors about him made me dislike him more. The gossip was Sergiu wasn't only rough in bed but outside of it too. He treated women like punching bags to alleviate the rage he kept behind the unemotional facade.

"Sergiu, it's been a while." Istvan shook the boy's hand. Sergiu nodded, muttering something I couldn't understand.

Damn! This was the longest night ever. My head twisted, searching for a tray of alcohol, landing on Caden's face. He kept his expression pleasant and neutral, but I knew he was feeling the same way I was.

Kill me now. I let my eyes roll enough for him to see. His lips went white as he pinned them together, trying not to laugh.

"Brexley?" Istvan's stern voice drew my attention back to him.

"Yes?"

"You remember Sergiu, I am sure." Istvan tilted his head to the man in question, the intensity in his eyes making me feel like I missed something. Something very vital.

"Y-yes." I pulled my focus off Istvan to Sergiu, dampness coating the back of my neck. "It's nice to see you again."

He kept silent, bowing his head at my comment, though his eyes raked over me. Unlike his father, his stare was full of judgment.

And I came up short.

"There will be some time to get to know each other before the day."

Huh?

"Day?" I swallowed, a dot of sweat trickling down my back.

Caden jerked beside me, his form going rigid, his eyes locked on Istvan. "Father?"

The general ignored him, getting between Sergiu and me.

"Yes. Alexandru and I thought what better way to strengthen and solidify the new bond between our countries. The union between Brexley and Sergiu will stabilize and increase our reign in the Eastern Bloc."

I was a mountain on the outside, immobile, stoic, and silent, but a volcano inside, lavalike emotions scorching me alive. I couldn't move or breathe.

"What?" Caden's head whipped between them, anger rising his shoulders. "Are. You. Fucking. Kidding. Me?"

"No need for that tone," Istvan snapped. "This has nothing to do with you."

"N-nothing to do with me?" His voice pitched, sputtering over his words, his eyes going wild as they went to me and then back to his father. "Yes—she does—no—you can't do this."

"Caden is very protective of Brexley." Rebeka laughed, brushing off her son's reaction. "She's like a *sister* to him. You can understand; I mean, they practically grew up together."

Sister?

In one statement, she turned everything I felt for Caden and what I believed he felt for me into something wrong, dirty, making it sound that we were actually related. Making a relationship between us impossible.

"You are not selling her off like cattle." Caden stepped

up to his dad, his fists tight at his side. "You can't do this. I won't allow it."

"I can. Did. And *you will.*" Speaking so only Caden and I could hear, Istvan pushed into his son's frame. "Now stop embarrassing me in front of our guests."

How did I not see this coming? They had been grooming me for marriage since I became their ward. Now they would sell me to get more power and control. They would never have let me be with their son.

Rebeka's odd speech to me on the way in made sense. She knew what was going to happen tonight and decided handing me over to an abusive monster was something she could live with if it kept her world protected.

My black-eyed gaze lifted to Rebeka, betrayal and hate spilling from my eyes. She held my stare for a moment, a slight apology in her gaze before she bowed her head, turning back to Sorina.

"I have so many ideas for the wedding; we must get together before you leave." Rebeka acted as though Caden and Istvan weren't about to throw down.

I choked. Bile burned up the back of my throat, twisting my stomach.

"Father." Caden's chest pillowed, his tone filled with warning.

"Caden." Sharp. Cold. "Either you gather yourself together and act like the future leader or step out until you do. Let the grown-ups speak."

Caden jerked back, fury flaring his nose, reddening his cheeks. I could see the debate in his eyes: one part wanted to fight his father, and one part wanted to please him. For a moment, I hoped the first one would win, that I was worth the fight.

Caden stepped back, shaking his head in abhorrence,

then flipped around, stomping out of the room, leaving me. His departure made me feel he was throwing me to a pack of hyenas. Isolated. Alone.

"Brexley, I expect you will be more mature than my son." Istvan turned into my space, speaking directly to me. "You might not be my actual flesh and blood, but I feel you are my daughter. You are smart, savvy, capable, strong, and understand when sacrifice for the greater good is necessary."

Every word was set to flatter and control. I'd seen him use this tactic so many times.

"Do you understand the importance of this union?"

Disciplined to not show emotion, hiding the sobs building in my throat, my gaze slid over to Sergiu. His sour, annoyed, bored expression made me want to vomit. Elitist and traditionalist, much like his father, he treated women as if they were property. I felt repulsed at the thought of him touching me, thinking he had a right to my body because I was his wife.

Staring at him, I could see my future laid out. I would no longer do anything I loved, living a life in a cage the same as Sorina or even Rebeka. One you survived while you wished for death to take one of you.

I wasn't built for that.

"Brexley?" Istvan's voice drew my attention back to him. His eyes now held a bit of softness I had never seen. "I know this is not what you dreamed of. But you are far cleverer than him in everything. I taught both you and Caden the things you need to be great leaders someday. You will be the one to rule... *not him.*"

That was the real reason for this union. Through me, Istvan was hoping to gain Romania. I'm sure Lazar was planning for the opposite. I was much better suited for battle or running a country. It was well-known Sergiu had been pampered and spoiled his whole life. Even now, he stomped his foot and acted like a petulant child instead of a man who could rule, leading humans into the frontier against the fae.

I couldn't stomp my feet or cry. I couldn't throw a fit or tell them all to fuck off. He might say I was like a daughter to him, but I knew my place. I was their ward, owing them my obedience and loyalty for their kindness.

They could have turned me over to my criminal uncle I had never met, who ran off after the Fae War and hid out somewhere in Prague, or my hateful grandmother who banished her son because he fell in love with my mother. This woman saw me as an evil bastard child because my parents had never married. She thought my mother had been socially beneath my father.

The Markos family had fed, clothed, and loved me in their way. They weren't bad people; they had given me the best of everything. Istvan was strict, but not once had he laid a hand on me. He was the one who taught me chess, who pushed me to study history, languages, and economics. He encouraged me to train in the academy when Rebeka thought I should be behaving more like a lady. It was all to have a smarter, stronger chess piece go into their game. Istvan wanted to dominate Romania, probably the entire Eastern Bloc. He didn't want me to be a subservient wife. He wanted me as their queen.

His love had all been a loan.

And it was time for me to pay back my debt.

Chapter 6

"The ceremony should be here." Rebeka lifted her hand, motioning around the room. "How beautiful the wedding would be in this room."

"No." Lazar shook his head. "It should be in Bucharest. Our palace of parliament is much grander."

"Larger in size doesn't mean better." Istvan took a sip of his drink. "This building is the jewel of Eastern Europe, renowned and envied around the world. By far more beautiful. We will have the wedding here."

They continued to talk about my future and my wedding to the asshole who was staring blatantly at women's breasts near our group.

I glared at the floor, my fingers clutching the flute in my hand so tightly the glass cracked in protest. Except for the throbbing pain from my heels, I was numb. I wanted nothing more than to slip out of the torturous shoes and let myself bleed away into the shadows. I doubted they would even notice.

My brain zipped around, trying to compute all that happened in a short time. Caden's "almost" declaration had left me buzzing with possibility and excitement, but this untimely marriage proposal had shot me down from the sky, ripping away any hope and exhilaration I had. The bars of my gilded jail had been shrinking down on me so slowly, I didn't notice until they crushed me.

"We have a lot to go over. Let's meet after breakfast to go over the marriage contract. By then, the train should be in Prague." Istvan's words trickled into my head as the women discussed having two engagement parties, one in Bucharest and the other here.

"Prague?" Alexandru Lazar frowned, not looking pleased. "I hope you have extra security on it. I've heard Povstat is only getting bolder and stronger there."

"Povstat is nothing more than what Sarkis's army is here. Your own country has them. A bunch of thugs playing at a man's game."

Povstat the Rebels, and Sarkis the Protectors, were the most notable of the rebellion groups popping up, the ones fighting against both sides, gaining power with those in the middle ground between the pure fae and elite humans.

"They blew up two government buildings in the last two weeks there and four trains."

"I have full confidence in my trained soldiers compared to some hooligans with overinflated confidence." Istvan took a drink. "Now, can we get back to the union of your son and my daughter?"

Daughter?

My mind stopped on thoughts of my father and how different everything would be if he were still alive. I'd marry Sergiu a hundred times if it would bring him back. There wasn't a day I didn't miss him. His death was still an open wound. So many things I did now were for him, to make him proud. Although he was a tough, stern man with his troops, he had been fair and kind. He was the type you wanted to work harder to impress and to earn his esteem. I got to see his soft side, his kindness and warmth. I never questioned his love and pride in me. He defied his parents, falling in love with a woman they didn't deem worthy of his stature. She was poor. They never married, keeping their love a secret. I didn't even have a picture of her. Their love story was short, enough time for her to get pregnant and carry me to term, but fierce with passion. My Uncle Andris said my father was never the same after her death. Dad talked very little of her, but when he did, the reverence and love he felt for my mother was still obvious.

"Kicsim, your mother...she was so smart. I don't think I ever had a chance at winning any battle when it came to her. She was strong, funny, and her beauty... she could drop me to my knees with a smile." He brushed a piece of hair off my face. "You are so much like her. You have her black hair and eyes. You also have the same fierce nature. You don't even realize how special you are. Never accept anything less than your worth."

My father never moved on after her death, burning for her until his last breath.

He would *never* have wanted this for me.

Imaginary walls pressed into my chest, blocking the air to my lungs, panic crawling under my skin. The party around me grew hazy and distant. I had to get out of here. Every word they spoke about my impending fate crawled up my throat. The need to scream, to smash my goblet onto the ground, had me clutching my glass harder.

"Excuse me." I bowed my knees, turning before anyone could stop me, and hauled my ass toward the doors. Once out of sight, my walk evolved into a jog out of the room and down the passage.

Run. The demand shrieked at me over and over.

Tearing off my shoes, I chucked the heels down a hall as

I ran up the stairs, my bare feet padding over the rugs, going higher and higher until the carpet became stone. Clutching my dress, I felt like a version of a fairy tale I read about as a child, but instead of running away from the prince at midnight, I was running to him.

I was far past where any visitor was allowed, and everything here was unadorned and basic, the opulence saved for the guests far below. My thighs burned as I pushed them up more and more stairs, my body automatically set on its course, knowing the route by heart. Very few knew of this spot or cared to go there.

A gust of wind pummeled me as I shoved open the door. I stumbled back, goosebumps exploding over my skin. This high up, the chilly wind channeling off the river whipped around, tangling my hair into knots and burning inside my lungs.

Walking farther out into the night, the catwalk trailed along the burnt-red roof, weaving through the dramatic spires. My feet padded away from the massive dome, the room I just left, the festivities far below, filled with smiles and laughter, their lives not destroyed under the sparkling chandeliers.

Lights glowed from the bridges and the fae palace across the river, the Danube glistening, resembling the stars in the sky. Up here, everything felt possible. Problems were far away. It was beautiful. Peaceful.

As children, Caden and I used the roof as our playground. The older we got, we still found ourselves up here often, either sneaking a bottle of palinka or imported vodka from Istvan's private collection, needing a place to let go of the demands and strains of life. Here we had no responsibilities or pressures. We could just be. I came a lot when my father died.

Rolling my hair into a knot, strands still whipped at my

face as I strolled down the walk, my toes protesting at the freezing metal.

My heart fluttered, seeing what I hoped would be here.

A dark silhouette sat, legs dangling through the bars over a death drop. A bottle went to his lips, and he slammed back a gulp.

Silently, I strolled up to him, tucking up my dress so I could sit next to him and thread my legs through the bars. I gazed out at the breathtaking view, inhaling a deep breath. This was my favorite spot in the whole place. It made me feel life could be happy. Free. That both sides could find harmony.

Staring at the fae side, the beauty of the architecture across the water was breathtaking. For one moment, I could imagine this city being one. Freedom to go anywhere. No sides. No us versus them. A life where Caden and I could have a picnic in the park and walk hand in hand, laughing and loving.

"You found me," he muttered, handing me the bottle of palinka, the potency from the fruit-fermented brandy burning my nose from here. Growing up on this stuff had our tolerance for alcohol at unbelievable levels.

"I knew you'd be here." I took a swig, the alcohol sizzling the back of my throat, warming my muscles.

"Really?" He took it back.

"It's where we come when we want to fight the world." I curled my arms over a rail, perching my chin on it. "Plus, I know you."

"Yeah." He huffed through his nose, procuring another drink. "I guess you do. The only one who really does."

I looked over at him. He kept his gaze out, not meeting my eyes. He swallowed, letting silence fall between us, anger thrumming under his skin.

"Caden…" I croaked over his name, scared to push him, but I needed to know.

He twisted his head away from me, slightly shaking it.

"Talk to me."

"Why?" he snapped back to me. "We should probably start learning not to. You'll soon be confiding in your *husband*."

"Stop." My lip lifted in a grimace. "Don't even start that shit. You think I want this? You think this is what I dreamed of? The man I wanted to spend my life with?"

"Then refuse."

"Refuse?" A barked laugh tore at my throat. "Like it's so easy."

"Why not?"

"Don't make this sound as if it's simple. I have nothing, Caden. *Nothing*." When my father died, he didn't have much besides a few trinkets that were sentimental but had no real value. "Without your parents taking me in, I would have been on the streets. Just another worker in the Savage Lands trying to survive off a loaf of bread."

"It doesn't mean they own you. Can trade you like cattle."

"Would you say no if your father said you had to marry some Polish princess to secure Hungary?"

"Yes!"

I tilted my head, my gaze drilling into him. He huffed again, wiggling beneath the weight of his lie. He knew he wouldn't have a choice either. Our duty, defending our country, the human race, was in our DNA.

"Brex…" My name came out a choked whisper, thick with despair and frustration.

The tears I fought earlier returned full force, blurring my vision. Overwhelmed with grief, anger, heartbreak, and passion, I couldn't get my mouth to move, to tell him I'd been in love with him for so long. He was all I wanted and who I wished to grow old with.

"I don't want you to marry him," he said softly, his brown eyes finding mine.

"I don't either." I gulped over the lump in my throat. All I saw was misery before me. My tongue was sharp, my will too strong, but I wondered how long it would take before Sergiu broke it.

Caden watched me, his tongue sliding over his lip, drawing my gaze to his mouth. I wanted nothing more than to finally know what it felt like to taste him. To feel his lips on mine.

"Caden?" I bit my mouth. Despair waited for me downstairs. For one moment, I wanted to know pure happiness. To be able to think back to this when I wanted to escape and know I had one second of joy.

Leaning into him, the heat of his mouth was so close to mine. My heart hummed in my ears, making me forget all about the cold or grief.

Caden froze, not moving away, but not moving closer, his Adam's apple bobbing. "Brex, don't."

"Why?" Pain and desperation rang in the single word like a bell. "Don't you want to kiss me?"

His chest moved violently up and down. "More than you know."

"Then please, Caden."

Agony flinched his cheek. "I can't."

Rejection filled my eyes, shattering my chest as if ice cracking open.

He grabbed my cheek, his warm palm cupping my face, his eyes wild and desperate.

"Fuck, Brex. This is torture. I want nothing more than to kiss you. To lay you down up here, amongst the stars, the world at our feet, and show you how much I want you. How I've wanted you for a long time."

"What?" A gulped cry hiccupped up my throat. He had wanted me? I thought it was completely one-sided. I could only think about all the wasted time. Now it was almost too late.

"Gods, do you even know how beautiful you are? So breathtaking I can't think properly when you are around."

Really? He never acted like I interested him. "But—"

"That's why I can't." Both his hands slid along my jaw, drawing me closer to him, his mouth skimming mine. "Because if I get a taste of you, I will *never* be able to let you go. And seeing you with Sergiu… it will *destroy* me." He leaned his forehead into mine, torturing me with the proximity of his lips, his hot breath against my mouth.

"We'll have the memory. I can carry it forever, getting me through the darkest of nights." My hand drew up to his mouth, touching his lips. Begging. Needing. It felt like the one thing that would let me float above the woe.

He inhaled sharply, like I was breaking him down. His mouth skated over mine, landing on the corner of my lips, kissing me softly.

"I can't. Kissing you, being with you, will destroy me. I must do the right thing." He drew back, tearing my heart from my chest, gutting me, bleeding out my hope. "Ask anything else from me, and I will give it to you. But this I can't. I won't come back from it."

I'd spent so many years hiding my emotions, but now a sob pushed out of me. What I wanted was within grasp, and I couldn't have it.

The horn of a train floated from below, my eyes watching it curve onto the bridge, gliding across to the fae side.

"The items will be departing on the train before dawn. Without a hitch, I assure you."

"It will make both our countries very wealthy. Once it is out there, we will control the trade—become untouchable. Have power and unyielding armies at our fingertips. Trust me. What I have seen... there is no question it works."

My attention stayed on the train, the thought sprouting up like a geyser. It was the only thing I had left. To feel alive. Free. Every minute from now on, my life would whittle down to a point. The freedom I took for granted, I would only dream about later. Sergiu, Lazar, and Istvan would all control me in some way.

This would be my last opportunity. And giving them a big fuck you by going after something of theirs would be even better. Nothing to really hurt them, but enough to give back to the people they were abusing. Enough to notice. And I couldn't deny my curiosity about what they were exporting out of here. What would make them more powerful than Ukraine?

"You said ask you anything?" I watched the train pull away from the fae stop, heading off to its destination. I knew at four forty-five a.m., the last night train would be traveling back across the same bridge, stuffed full of cargo.

"No." Caden followed my eye line. "No, I told you, not again."

"You said anything, unless you changed your mind about kissing me." I hoped he would choose that option instead, lay me down and let me feel the stars explode inside.

Caden didn't respond, his gaze still on the tracks. He wouldn't give in. He was far too stubborn. Once he decided on something, he locked down on it. Crossing that line was a no-go for him. But this was still a maybe.

"Last time." I nudged him. "You know everything changes after this night. Let's have one last time being crazy. Being us. The Robin Hoods of Budapest."

He snorted, shaking his head. After a few beats, he let out a sigh, his shoulders dropping in surrender. "I can never say no to you."

Only when it came to having me as his.

"Last adventure." I held out my hand.

He clasped my hand in his, lacing our fingers, sorrow crinkling his eyebrows. "Last adventure."

Whatever lay in our future, we had this last night together. Caden and Brexley.

Our last night of being free.

Chapter 7

"I can't believe you talked me into this." Caden shifted beside me, tugging on the black beanie covering his ears. Every day it was getting warmer, but with the chilly breeze whipping off the Danube, it was hard to believe summer was close.

"You are graduating in a few weeks, and I'm…" I broke off, my throat strangling on the thought. I doubted they would even wait until I graduated to marry me off to Sergiu. I wouldn't be surprised if they were planning a summer wedding. The sooner they could merge our countries, the better for them.

And whatever was on the train leaving Budapest this morning would apparently create an even stronger bond of power.

I couldn't deny it was more my curiosity that brought me here, the desire to see what they were doing. How dirty was the world I was stepping into? It was only fair I understood what I was getting into since they were making this my circus. If Istvan wanted me to be the powerful one in this union, I needed to know everything going on.

Yes, I could have asked him. But I doubted he would have told me, and he fully deserved this hit. They both did for using their kids as chess pieces for their own power. The two leaders were about to make my life hell. It was time for a little payback.

"Two minutes." Caden glanced down at his watch, pulling his hat down around his face, his dark eyes glistening from the eyeholes. Both of us dressed in black, blending into the dark, but the air was crystal clear, which made us a little easier to see.

The vibration of the train coming down the tracks hummed beneath my feet. Right on time.

"Stay on point. Last time you cut it far too close." He moved closer to me, his body pressing against mine.

I nodded, pulling my mask over my face, nerves dancing along my limbs. Every breath, every beat of my heart, made me feel alive. Caden teased that I was an adrenaline junkie, getting off on the high. I couldn't argue. There was something about walking the line between right and wrong. Life and death. Getting caught or escaping.

Headlights from the train came into view, and my pulse pumped faster. The outline of the conductor became more solid the closer he got.

My ears thumped, my bones vibrating as the train passed us, slowing as the lead car turned for the bridge.

"Shit," Caden muttered under his breath. I didn't need to ask what he was looking at because my eyes were already on the guards lining a few of the doorways along the train, rifles at their sides. This was new. "We can't, Brex. It's too dangerous."

"No." I gritted my teeth; my resolve to go forward fought against any logic. Seeing the guards only made me want this more. Whatever they were shipping out was more than their normal trade. Istvan had involved me, my life. I would not be blind or ignorant to what was going on around me.

Darting forward to the final car, I heard Caden hiss my name. Ignoring him, I leaped on the steps of the last carriage. Silent. Keeping low, I scrambled up to the platform, my head snapping around.

Caden jumped up after me, his lids narrowed on me. "Brexley, don't be stupid."

"Too late." My words were almost lost between the wind and the squeal of the carriage curving along the track. We were on the bridge. The clock was on.

Crouching, I opened the door with my device, the lock unlatching with a click. My pulse and breath marked off the seconds, dragging more panic through my chest.

My eyes adjusted to the darkness, the magic-infused fire-bulbs on the bridge casting a dim glow through the windows. Many of the carriages utilized for cargo were once old passenger cars, the seats torn out to make room. Nothing in Budapest was trashed because products were a lot harder to get or make. We reused and adjusted things of old. New items cost money, and we were dependent on the fae for items fitting into this new world.

When the walls between the Otherworld and Earth fell, magic flooded in, crushing a lot of human-made objects that were not able to hold up against the weight of magic. Everything from bridges to laptops had to be redesigned for the new world, which was why so much of the old items had been pushed out. The king of the Unified Nations (UN) was constantly updating and changing technology, making the Seattle area of the United States the most advanced and prosperous place in the world.

Hungary lived decades behind the rest of the world and was not up on the latest gadgets. Our separation from the rest of the UN left us far in the dust. Only the uber-wealthy had luxurious items like computers or mobile devices.

The thick waves in the sky were normal to me, but anyone older than twenty told stories of when Earth held no magic, when fae hid in the shadows. A world with no fire lightbulbs, magical herbs, or fae doors was a result of the stress on Earth as the two worlds merged and caused thousands of tears in the atmosphere. I had never seen one, but I heard soldiers talk about them being out on the field. We lost people to them. A fae door, which was invisible to human eyes, was easy to step in by accident and never be seen again.

Making my way to the large crates, the tool was ready in my hand to rip them open. I peeled off the cover, but stuffing concealed the top layer. Tearing through it, my fingers hit metal.

Guns.

Sadly, it didn't surprise me—guns, drugs, and money were heavily trafficked through the country. A train full of rifles would not make Markos and Lazar invincible. Confused, I dug deeper, hitting another layer of guns before I found stacks of cash.

Bribe money?

This was nothing new either in the shady world I lived in. Stuffing the cash into my bag with one hand, I dug even deeper with the other, my knuckles rapping against a thin layer of plywood six inches from the bottom.

It was set to divide the contents or appear at a glance as the bottom.

A false bottom.

"Brex," Caden yelled, tapping his watch. "Thirty seconds!"

Forgoing any plans to move on to another box, I tore at the thin lumber, the wood ripping through my flesh as I dug deeper, landing on the product contained below.

I knew it.

In my gut, I knew this was the product Istvan was talking about. You didn't put guns and cash on top if you weren't trying to hide something more important underneath.

Picking up a clear baggie, my bloody grip smeared over the plastic. My gaze narrowed. This was different from anything I had ever seen. I flipped the bag filled with neon blue pills; it was almost like they were glowing. My eyes searched for a label, but it was blank—no medical instruction or ingredients.

"*Brexley*," Caden snapped, anxiety coiled through my name. Time was up, but I couldn't move, taking in the thousands of pills stuffed in the hundreds of bags at the bottom, all jammed in the long container.

Drugs. But what kind?

These hummed with magic, more than any I had ever felt, almost like each one had a pulse. Glowing blue powder swirled in the transparent pill cases. I plucked one out, cracking it open, sampling a bit with my tongue.

I couldn't taste anything, but I could feel the buzz of magic coat my tongue.

I knew this was not the ordinary cocaine, fairy dust, heroin, or meth that traveled through our walls.

What the hell were they? What made these different from the normal fae drugs snuck across borders?

"Brexley!"

My gaze drifted to another dozen or more crates stacked in the room, all identical to this one. Were they all packed the same?

"Brexley! Now!" Caden's hand came down on my arm, yanking me toward the door. Brakes squealed as the train slowed, preparing to stop. My head whipped around, watching the bridge recede in the distance as the train rolled into the fae station, stopping.

Oh. Holy. Shit.

I barely managed to stuff the evidence into my bag as Caden hauled me out. He paused at the platform and peered around. At least eight fae soldiers stepped up to the train, weapons hanging over their shoulders.

"Fuck. Fuck." Panic radiated from both of us. My heart slammed against my ribs.

Fuck was right. I had taken too long, pushed our escape past the brink.

"Dammit, Brex." Blame drenched every syllable. "I yelled at you over and over that it was time, but you had to push it, didn't you?"

Voices traveled down to us, guards from both sides conversing.

"Carriage three, clear," a voice yelled.

"Passenger car, check," another called out.

"*Az istenit*!" Caden's head darted back to the bridge and then to the fae moving closer to us, checking each carriage.

"We run for it." Hands shaking, I put my arms through the straps of my bag, securing it to me.

"Run?" He spat, motioning to the bridge. The water, where we could have jumped before and swam, was now at least a block behind us. A long way to run in the open without any place to hide. "We'll be killed before we even get halfway!"

"What else do you suggest?" I volleyed. "There is no alliance between the sides. *You* get caught, and it will be like Christmas to them. A normal thief is dead, but what do you think they'd do with the son of their enemy?"

"You don't think I fucking know that?" He gritted his teeth. His fear turned into fury at me, which I fully deserved. "We're gonna die here tonight."

"Guess you should have just kissed me earlier instead, huh?"

He glared at me.

"We run. And we don't stop until we make it." I tipped my chin up, challenging him. "You with me, Markos?"

He gritted his jaw but nodded as the voices grew closer to us.

"On my call." He peeked around the side, holding up his hand. The sound of boots banging up metal steps echoed in the air.

My pulse twitched at my throat, my toes ready to push off on his mark.

His hand swished down. "Go!"

We sprang off the top step, instantly leaping into a sprint. My focus locked on our destination, my legs stretching, my arms pumping, running faster than I ever had. Caden's long legs easily overtook mine.

"Hey! Stop!" a voice hollered.

Shiiiitt!

There was no second notice. Shots rang out from behind, the bullets outracing me, pinging off the poles and ground close to my boots. A yelp caught in my throat, my feet stumbling. Years of instruction kicked in, making me zigzag so they couldn't get a clear shot.

Caden's head swiveled around, searching for me.

"Come on! Hurry!" He waved me forward, slowing down.

Waiting for me.

"Don't stop!" I screamed as hollers and gunfire exploded close behind me, drowning my voice. "Go!" He was just a few yards away from being able to jump. To escape. If Caden was caught, the fae leader would hold him hostage. He'd use the only son of the HDF leader to shred the human side.

Or he would be killed and left on display for Istvan to see.

"Go!" I yelled again. "I'm right behind you."

He nodded, turned, and ran.

POP!

Like a blade through my back, excruciating pain spread across every nerve. My ribs felt as if they were bursting open, freezing my lungs in a stuttered gasp. My legs stumbled.

Oh no.

"Brexley!" Caden's cry sounded far away, like he was speaking through glass.

A cough hiccupped up my throat, blood sputtering down my chin onto the ground. I felt nothing as I stared at the dark liquid in utter horror. My limbs gave out, feeling what I could not, and I crashed to the ground, my sight hazing at the edges. Footsteps pounded the concrete, reaching me in a blink. Fae were faster than humans, and it took them only a few seconds to catch up with me.

"I got her. Go get the other one," a woman ordered. A set of boots rushed across my vision, yelling after Caden.

Hands grabbed for my weapon, holding down my arms. Lifting my head, my gaze landed on Caden, our eyes locking for a moment. He stared back at me in horror, fear, and love, his figure set on me, not his exit.

No. Goooo... I mouthed to him, my eyes pleading. *Save yourself.* There was no hope for me, but he could still get away.

I knew he understood me. The years of knowing each other, the bond of best friends, always linked us. Grief tore over his features, an unexpressed cry pinching his lips together.

A bullet nicked close to his temple, jolting him awake. His eyes met mine one last time before I watched him swivel around and leap over the railing, dropping into the watery darkness below. I knew they wouldn't be able to get him now. He was safe.

Relief heaved from my lungs, and my head dropped to the pavement.

The woman spoke to me, but I couldn't make out her words as darkness crept around me. Death beckoned me into its bed.

And my last thought was: *At least I won't have to marry Sergiu now*.

Chapter 8

"Wake up."

A sting zapped through my nerves like a thunderbolt, light crackling across my dark world. Recoiling, instinct told me to bury myself deeper into the blackness. The light was a trick. A sparkling lure dangling in the deep depths, and if I grabbed on, it would only lead me to death.

Wait. Wasn't I already dead?

Another surge of pain lit up the space around me, no longer letting me hide.

"I said wake up," someone ordered. The voice was sultry and alluring, but the intention was not. Weakly, I followed the order, not able to fight the demand.

Flinching at the glaring light in the room, I scrunched my lids back together, allowing one eye to partially open.

A woman who appeared to be in her twenties stared down at me. She was dressed in purple scrubs, which complemented her lavender eyes and long white-blonde hair. With high cheekbones and full lips, her expression resembled the bored, pouting models on the covers of magazines in the Unified Nations. A fairy, or fay, was the "highest" breed of fae if you still went by the old ideals, and one stood over me.

Fae was the umbrella term for all those with magic. But there were hundreds if not thousands of species, races, and types under that umbrella.

Fae weren't the sweet, tiny, winged creatures you saw in books from long past. Not even close. Full of lust, greed, wrath, and pride, some used their looks for hunting humans—a buffet the fae could feed on. They didn't even need to use their glamour because most fae were humanlike and so stunning you got caught in their web.

"Sit up." Her perfect upturned nose wrinkled, pushing down the railing that kept me in the bed.

"Where am I?" My voice barely came out a whisper, my brain swimming in confusion, groggy and slow. My gaze danced around the space. It was some kind of "healing" room with a handful of medical beds spaced evenly around the room. "What happened?"

"You were shot," she responded, her bluntness stirring a few memories of brown eyes staring into mine—pleading and heartbroken.

Fuck. Caden…

My head jerked up, lids squinted, trying to make out the forms in the beds across from me. Only two of them were filled. What looked like a troll and a human woman were chained to the beds, sound asleep. No Caden.

A gust of relief sighed from my lungs. *Please say he made it home. He's safe.*

My gaze drifted over the rest of the room, noticing some Western human medical equipment on the far wall and another wall full of shelves—magical serums and antidotes. The potions and healing techniques were a few of the fae things humans accepted without a problem. Funny, if it benefited us, we were fine with it, but if it didn't, then it was from the "vile fae" set out to destroy humankind.

"Get up." She grabbed my legs, swinging them over the side and sitting me up abruptly. I tried to move my arms, but they were yanked back with a metallic sound. My gaze shifted down to my hands, my brain slowly acknowledging the pair of handcuffs chaining me to the bed.

"Against all logic, you lived, healing faster than us healers thought." She picked up a needle, filling it with liquid. "That gunshot should have killed you in an instant." Her sculpted eyebrows curved up. "Too bad."

I looked down at my torso and touched my sternum, feeling the bandage under the gown's thin fabric. The memory of the bullet going through me dotted sweat along my brow. I had been *fatally* shot. How *was* I alive?

"How long have I been here?" I croaked, my throat dry and wobbly.

"Six days."

"What?" Six days? Since I had been shot in the back? Shouldn't it take months to heal? "How?"

Fae magic was good, but I didn't think it was that fast, not for wounds like mine.

"You seemed very determined to live. The fae bullet barely missed your spine. Hit your lungs." The healer stepped back to me, her voice clipped and unfriendly. "A large amount of blood filled them, which should've drowned you." Bedside manner she did not have. "You *really* should have died. I would have let you. One less human in this world."

My black eyes lifted to hers, but not one emotion showed in my expression. I'd been taught to keep my emotions in check, lock up any weakness behind a steel exterior.

"Thought that went against a healer's code of ethics?" My voice came out raspy and low.

"Are you dead?" She smirked, then stabbed my arm with the needle, injecting a serum into my system. "But let me say… you will wish you were. Where you are headed, death would have been a blessing."

My mouth parted to respond, but a jolt of adrenaline lurched through my body, swallowing the hazy sensation in a gulp. My eyes bolted open, air slamming into my lungs.

Alert.

Sound. Sight. Taste. My senses flamed to life, turned up so high I could hear the flames lick the glass in the bulbs above my head, footsteps squeaking down the hallway, the smell of floor cleaner, the chalky-stale taste coating my tongue. My brain seemed at full charge, and my limbs twitched and squirmed as though needing to be let off a leash.

"It will fade in a few hours, but they want you awake and fully aware of what's happening to you." A menacing smile ghosted her mouth.

"What do you mean fully aware? What's going to happen? Where am I?" Just as the final words spurted off my tongue, the door burst open. Three huge men stormed into the room dressed in all black, armed with swords and rifles, wearing fae bulletproof vests over their shirts. The fae leader's insignia was emblazoned on their chests: two intertwined, detailed circles with a sword cutting through the middle, the blade and handle engraved with Celtic symbols and blazing with light. It symbolized the Sword of Nuada, an old-world treasure of theirs, which was said to have been destroyed in the Fae War. But some conspirators believed it made it out and was hidden.

To me, the crest represented fear and death.

Terror gripped my throat, my instincts kicking in. Leaping off the bed in defense, my wrist restraint yanking me back to the bed.

"Hey, Sloane." The healer tilted her head, smiling at the largest guard, her eyes glistening with lust, not really looking at the other two guys. Sloane had a patch on his arm signifying him as the highest-ranking soldier in the room. His caramel-colored hair was brushed back from his face, revealing eyes even more purple than the healer's. He was from a noble fairy line, at least at one time. In the new world, lineage didn't matter as much. The fae ruler here only cared if you were pureblood and could fight.

I guess the human side wasn't much different in our prerequisites.

Half-breeds weren't accepted on either side, living in the shadows of the Savage Lands with the rest of the degenerates.

"The captive ready for pick up?" He didn't even look at her, his attention falling on me. He was solidly built. Tall, wide, and ripped like he was carved from stone.

"Yes. Seems pointless to have the *elite team* on her." Her gaze drifted over to me, running down my barely dressed figure. "A human. *I* could snap her in half without blinking."

"It's our job. Pick up and transfer safely." A blond guard peered at me, a snarl of disgust hitching his lip. Another pretty guy who looked similar to all the rest to me. "Though she looks like a bunny-shifter could handle her."

Looks could be deceiving, asshole. I kept my mouth shut. We were taught to say nothing, even under torture.

"Let's just get this last transfer done." Sloane stepped forward, pulling a set of cuffs off his belt, his buddies moving in around me. Weaponless, wounded, and chained to a bed, the odds were against me.

"No," I growled, shoving back into the bed away from their reach, the frame squealing over the tiled floor.

The blond guard on my left snorted, laughing at my attempt to resist. My brain told me logically I had no chance, to save my energy. But I knew in my gut where we were going. They wouldn't have gone to all the trouble to save my life to kill me. No. Where I was going was far worse.

The drug she pumped in my system gave me the strength to bounce on my toes, my back curling in defense.

"Save your energy and breath, human." The third guard on my right, a striking male with black hair, dark skin, and amber eyes, pulled out a handgun from his belt. "This is only going one way."

Baring my teeth, I glared at them, widening my stance.

The third guard shook his head. "All right. We warned you." He lurched for me.

A grunt tore from my lips as I yanked at my cuffed arm, skating and twisting the bed across the floor, blocking them from me. I shoved at the bed, the heels of my feet digging into the floor, and rammed into the two guards with all the force I could muster. Their large bodies stumbled back, falling like boulders and crashing to the ground.

Cries of protest and surprise bubbled out of them. I leaped back over the bed feet first, my heels slamming into the healer's stomach, knocking her over. Ignoring the throbbing pain from my body and the tug at my wrist, I jumped down on one of the guards, reaching for his gun, my brain clicking into survival mode.

Four shots to the heart or brain, and I could have a chance to get out of here. Escape.

I had killed only once before. It was part of our evaluation last year in class. To see if we could move up in training. Had what it took to be put in the field. They didn't want us to hesitate or not be able to handle death out in the world.

When they brought out the fae prisoners for us to gun down like rats in a cage, Istvan had chosen that day to come watch me. His gaze drilled into me, the weight of his pride or disappointment riding on my shoulders. I pulled the trigger, shooting the fae in the back of the head with a fae bullet, watching his head explode like a watermelon. I almost vomited.

But I couldn't deny a strange buzz I got—the energy in that moment between life and death. A morbid fascination. I thought a lot about that moment since.

Sergeant Bakos kept reminding us the fae wouldn't falter, would slaughter us without pause as they had done to my father and so many others.

My fingers wrapped around the handle of the weapon, the power of it bringing me back to the present, the gun heavy in my hand, my finger pulling the trigger on the blond guard.

Kill or be killed.

A figure slammed into mine, bones crunching. The main guard, Sloane, hurtled us over the bed, flipping it with a piercing crash. The metal scraped and skidded on the floor, sounding like an explosion. Sloane's bulk slammed down on me, yanking my body and arm in opposite directions. My wrist twisted, the cuff pulling my arm back up in the air from the rail of the bed. A cry whimpered in my throat as I tried to wiggle away from him.

"Don't. Move," the massive guard barked down at me, his eyes glowing with anger. He climbed off me, his head shaking. "Did you really think you could escape? You foolish idiot."

Roughly, he yanked me to my feet, his eyes moving over me. He took in my exposed figure, his nose flaring, his body reacting to mine. Aroused. Rumor was sex and being naked were natural to fae, as natural as breathing. Seemed the gossip was true.

"You're bleeding," he grumbled, his eyes still hot on me, while his brow furrowed. I felt the warm liquid trickle down my abdomen, where my wound had torn open in the fight.

Noticing my lack of movement, he twisted my gown around, covering me and pressing the fabric into the pooling blood. "Clean her up. Some will smell the fresh human blood and go crazy." Sloane rolled his shoulders back, nodding to the healer to come over, moving away from me.

She hadn't liked me before; now I knew she really wished she let me die.

"Vale." Sloane nodded at the blond fae, his lavender gaze sliding back to me sternly. "Keep tight. She is more skilled than they led us to believe."

"Yes, she is." Vale chuckled, stepping up to me. "Most grown men, fae or human, pee their pants when we show up." He pressed the gun I'd briefly held into my temple while the healer dressed my wounds. "You are a spirited one. Gave me a little rush, human."

I didn't respond. My torso was on fire as the healer crudely patched my injury again. It took my entire focus to keep conscious and standing. I clenched my teeth to wall off the vomit threatening to come up my throat. The shot she gave me made me feel the pain like a train tunneling through my veins.

Don't pass out. Don't throw up.

"Connor, let them know we're coming." Sloane nodded to the dark-haired soldier. He nodded and muttered into a handheld device, a cross between a walkie-talkie and mobile phone. Very high-tech, especially in these parts. Our soldiers only got them when they were out in the field, and ours were antiques and cheap compared to what these guys had.

The moment the healer was done, Sloane unlatched me from the bed and cuffed both my wrists behind my back, shoving me forward. My heart thumped, and my legs wobbled. Anger at myself bristled at the back of my neck. I had been so close. I had a chance, and I failed.

Hesitated.

I had no more energy left to fight, having burned it up in those few seconds. My chance to escape was gone. Burying the sob building in my throat, I let the three guards move me to the door.

"Human," the healer called out to me, my head twisting to her. A cruel grin curled up her face. "You aren't going to last a week, but every second you are going to wish I took pity on you and let you die."

A blur of exquisite details, carvings, and paintings covered every inch of the large space they moved me through, suggesting it had once been used as a church. All the symbols of the old human religion were gone. The fae believed in honoring all the gods and goddesses, which was a value quickly spreading to the human youth. Those who were older still held on to their beliefs of one god. I didn't buy into either. I believed in myself, my family, and my friends.

The men rushed me through the large wooden doors, the sun dipping behind the breathtaking courtyard we crossed. The air was warmer, the evening sun painting the clouds pink. Summer had decided to finally peek through the chilly spring. On a night like this, all the cadets would group together out on the patio at the HDF bar after training, getting tipsy, absorbing the balmy twilight, giggling, flirting, and having fun. Were they there now? Was I already a fading memory to them? A warning tale to tell the new recruits.

"Move it." Sloane yanked my arm through the *köztér,* the plaza, where shops, hotels, business, dwellings, and cafes lined the meticulous square as if life here never changed twenty years ago. It was still thriving in freedom and pleasures. Nicely dressed figures milled around, chatting and laughing, enjoying the beautiful evening, but going quiet when they caught sight of the four of us. This area didn't strike me as a place that saw a lot of bleeding, barely dressed humans escorted by an elite squad.

It was far nicer than Leopold, everywhere there were buildings maintained with new paint, pristine roads, and fresh flowers. Our side crumbled behind the patchwork façade we put up.

The fae guards directed me across the square. I knew exactly where I was, recognizing the buildings from so many years of staring at them from the other side of the river or from old books Istvan had me study. There was no mistaking the taste of my city; Budapest curled on my tongue like comfort food. Cool wind rolled over the ornate buildings, smelling like the Danube, like home.

Tense and alert, they hustled me around the corner. I gasped at the view, struck by the beauty of the whitewashed mini castles and walkways overlooking the river, seeing the true beauty this close.

I'd looked out at this view many times from my high perch on HDF. But I had stared at the fairy-tale-looking buildings across the water, the white dreamlike spires and turrets, romantic and beautiful, reminiscent of fables humans used to think of as fairy tales.

"Fairy" had a different connotation now, and it was nothing I wanted to be part of.

What used to be called Fishermen's Bastion was now coined Killian's Bastion, after the arrogant fae leader. The neo-Gothic-Romanesque terrace was situated high on the Buda bank, Killian's Castle a little distance away. Through the ornate towers, the lights of HDF glowed in its majestic beauty. I had never seen it from this side, the glorious building causing a sob to hitch my throat.

As the men shoved me forward, I kept my eyes on it. My home. My sanctuary. My heart.

Caden.

My soul screamed for him. For him to feel me. Somehow see me. Was he sitting up at our spot now? Thinking about me? Staring over, not even realizing I was right here? Did he know I was alive? Were they trying to get me back? Was Istvan trying to make a deal for me? Istvan was cold and tough, but I knew he cared about me. Caden certainly wouldn't let me go; he'd make Istvan fight for me. Maybe Rebeka would also.

A bit of hope buzzed inside me as the guards walked toward a black SUV. For a moment, I believed Istvan would be sitting inside, motioning for me to get in. My heart sank when they shoved me past it, keeping me close as we marched down the street.

"Where are we going?" Fear choked me. What was ahead of me? Maybe they were going to kill me after all.

"Your new home." Vale smirked, pressing his gun harder into my back.

About to turn down an alley, I yanked my head around, getting my last glimpse of the HDF's dome, my heart breaking into pieces. The historic building twinkled in the darkening sky, so familiar and lovely—my old friend.

This was the last time I would see my home, smell the musty scent of the Danube, feel the wind roll over my skin.

I understood where I was going.

The place feared by HDF soldiers more than death.

Halalház.

The fae prison was dubbed the House of Death for a reason.

Captives went in...and never came out.

Chapter 9

Since no one ever returned from the *Halalház*, no one could expose the location. Theories and speculation buzzed around HDF. Istvan sent out spies, but so far, those scouts either never came back or never located it. It wasn't at the top of our priority list compared to all the other things we had to worry about, so this feared place remained unknown to us.

Sloane pulled me down the cobbled streets, Vale behind me, Connor in front.

It was strange to think tourists used to stroll freely through this area at one time, while now only a handful of the older human soldiers could recall what this area had once looked like. If you were wealthy enough, you could try looking up pictures on the internet, but Killian had blocked most for security reasons, along with live-action maps.

Just as our side did.

I was getting to see what few had seen in person.

We were not very far from Killian Bastion or the castle when Sloane stopped us in front of a building. It appeared similar to an ordinary attached house, painted a buttery yellow with an arched metal door at the entrance. A single guard stood outside. He opened the door the moment he spotted Sloane, exposing a set of steep stairs leading down.

Connor greeted him without a pause, heading down the stairs, the rest of us following, my bare feet slapping against the cool cement steps. I flinched as the door slammed behind me, the sound of my fate, my heart thumping in my throat.

When we got to the bottom of the dark space, the temperature was chilly, the air musty, feeling like a cellar.

My gaze absorbed the low cave ceiling and arched passages. It was dark, dank, and windowless with various rooms and spaces everywhere. The suffocation of being trapped underground burrowed into my lungs, causing them to move in and out frantically. We passed fountains and statues, and one gated space painted with the gruesome image of a man on the back wall.

Vlad the Impaler.

Dracula.

"This is the Labyrinth?" It was something you heard about, our elders telling stories of its existence, but to my generation, it had become a story. History said it had been used for various things throughout the years, even to imprison the man whose picture hung on the wall. However, before our country was divided, at constant war between humans and fae, it was a cheesy tourist attraction.

The fae squad led me down more stairs hidden in a cove, away from the tourist area, going deeper into the Labyrinth. In the darkness, my lungs tightened, my pulse racing.

More soldiers greeted us at the bottom, where another gate was erected, blocking off what appeared to be a pitch-black tunnel. "Need entry through. Dropping off prisoner 85221."

"Yes, sir." A young woman bowed her head at Sloane. Pulling on gloves, she unlocked the gate—a sign the bars were made out of pure iron. Most fae species had a weakness, not that we had figured them all out, but to Fairies, one was pure iron.

I didn't think it was a coincidence the weakness for the highest ruling class of fae was widely known. It wasn't just humans who didn't like the fae pyramid and wouldn't mind seeing the fay topple from the peak.

The gate clanked and cracked open, jolting me back to my current situation, dipping my knees. Sloane gripped me harder, yanking me through. Fire-bulbs dotted the walls; motion sensors ignited the path a few yards in front of us as we continued to move. The gate slammed behind us, and my heart jumped into my throat.

Nothing about this made sense. "I don't understand. I thought we were going to the prison." I looked over at Vale.

"We are." A cruel grin parted his mouth, showing off his white teeth. "Just a little farther."

"What?" I gulped. We were right below the castle grounds, not where the infamous and terrifying legend of the *Halalház* should be. Istvan was convinced it was in the Zugliget area, near the Tündér Mountain quarry, which made sense. Out far enough from the city, but still close, with minimal population in the area. It was an ideal place for a prison.

Predictable.

We were idiots. What better place to hide your captives than in plain sight? We never even contemplated it was in the city. So many of our fighters, taken by fae, had been closer than we thought. Cruelly close. To be right under your army's nose and know no one would ever find you.

My teeth sawed into my bottom lip. I would not cry. I would not show emotion.

The tunnel went on for what seemed like hours, zigzagging deeper, going up, going down, other tunnels splintering off. Sloane didn't hesitate on his path while my brain locked on each change. Finally, we went up steep stairs, circling up until my thighs burned, reaching a small arched door at the top.

Sloane shoved at it, the door squeaking open. Vale rammed my head down, pushing me through the exit, stepping us out onto pavement into the cooling evening. Unlit and quiet. No guards keeping watch here.

I twisted my head, staring up at a statue I had looked at from across the river through binoculars. The Citadella on Gellért Hill. Different from what was taught in human school, the fae claimed this statue of a lady holding a feather secretly represented the hiding fae, a sign that their power would prevail once again.

We entered the area behind the statue and went through more carved arches.

Where everything changed.

Vines and weeds grew up the walls and hung overhead resembling a hidden garden. The pristine paths crumbled and broke under my bare feet. I was overcome by the sensation that we had stepped back into a different time. The fae king clearly wanted this place to look rundown and unused.

It took me a moment to realize we weren't alone. Wearing all black, some almost blending in with the walls like they were ghosts, silent and deadly, a dozen guards strolled the area. Weapons I had never seen before were in their hands or dangling from harnesses. Bars and gates closed off almost every opening, giving "visitors" one way in and one way out.

The atmosphere plucked at my skin as my eyes picked up more and more soldiers, lining stairs below and above. They covered every inch, but you'd never notice them from afar. This place was impregnable.

I gulped, feeling the thumping of my heart crank up, sweat dripping down my neck.

Most saw Sloane and stepped to the side, eyeing me with

speculation or boredom. We went down a set of stairs, descending into the mountain.

No escape. As good as being buried alive. Panic spun my head, and darkness edged my vision.

"Hey, Sloane." A breathtaking dark-haired man with a long, refined nose and eyelashes a girl would stab someone for greeted him. He reminded me of a show horse. Long, shiny hair and huge dark eyes. Probably a shape-shifter.

"Zander." Sloane nodded.

"I heard you were bringing us another prisoner." The man stopped, his gaze going over me.

"Your new guest," Vale replied, motioning to me.

"Her?" Zander's lids narrowed on me then went to the guys. "She did that?" He nodded to the bruise on Sloane's face.

"She's a feisty filly." Vale winked back at me.

"She got the drop on *you*?" Zander gapped at Sloane.

"Why the surprise?" I snipped. "Is it because I'm not male?"

"No." He snorted, sounding like a huff. "We aren't chauvinistic as you humans are. But for someone to do that, I'd expect them to actually be dangerous." He leaned close to me. "Man or woman."

"How do you know I'm not?"

"Been here far too long." He chuckled. "You are not dangerous."

"Hey, it's the big boy's club." Another man strolled out, a woman right at his side.

"Sloane." The woman nodded at my lead guard. "Vale. Connor." She addressed the other two.

"Jade. What's up, sweetheart? I can tell you've missed me." Vale winked at her. He seemed to be the more playful, cocky one of the group.

"This is her?" Her partner stepped back, laughing, his golden feline gaze roaming over my bare legs and bloody gown. Another shape-shifter, some kind of wildcat. "Really?"

"Don't let her scrawny ass fool you." Connor shook his head.

"Oh, what? Did this little waif of a human kick your ass, Connor?" The man was far smaller and less built than Connor, but his arrogance consumed the space, reminding me of Aron. He'd be fun to put in his place.

As if Connor could sense my thoughts, his hand clamped down on my shoulder. "I would love to see this girl spread you over the cement, but we need to transfer her. I'd rather get to the pub and see my woman."

"It's only been six days since her capture; she is still healing, but don't underestimate her," Sloane added, pushing me forward toward them.

The fae woman nodded. She was so stunning it hurt to look at her, but her strange reddish eyes told me she was a demon, what they used to consider "dark fae" or Unseelie. None of it mattered anymore, just like race/skin, color wasn't relevant among humans anymore. All that was important now was humans versus fae.

Fae came in every shape, size, and magical ability. From high fae to sub fae, the types varied far more than human races did now. In the last twenty years, the mixed species of half-human, half-fae exploded across the world, although a huge following of extremists on both sides fought to keep the bloodlines pure.

"Don't worry, boys; the babysitters are here. You can go back to your cushy jobs up there." The guy waved his hand in the direction of the castle.

"Watch yourself, Zion." Sloane stepped closer to him. "I *am* your superior, and if I killed you, no one would miss you."

Sloane flicked his head to the woman. "Not even Jade would shed a tear."

Zion snarled, his chest puffed out, and his eyes challenged Sloane.

"Zion, come on." Jade yanked him away, her fingers wrapping around my cuffs, tugging me away from Sloane. "We got this."

The guy huffed, stepping back.

I twisted to see my three captors. Was it strange to feel scared to leave them? They were all my enemies, but at least I felt they performed their jobs with respect. These two terrified me, especially Zion.

The pair hustled me forward, the door to the outside world slamming with a screech. My body jerked with fear, tears burning the back of my eyes, bile hovering in my throat.

Don't show weakness.

From now on, if one sliver of emotion escaped, I would be torn apart. Even faced with a life of misery and hell, your first instinct was to survive. Try to make it against all odds. But no one had ever been reported to endure this place.

My new guards led me downstairs, deep into the earth's crust through two more heavily guarded gates, finally reaching an unlit passage. My gaze latched on to an orangey glow shining at the end of the wide tunnel, displaying a massive chamber beyond. I was assaulted by smells and noises—shouting, banging, crying, screaming, chanting, along with smells of body odor, piss, shit, dirt, and things I had no name for.

I scrambled backward, tugging against the hold Zion and Jade had on me, trying to retreat from the onslaught of fear. Zion's fingers dug into my skin, dragging me out of the tunnel and onto a metal landing overlooking the space.

Fright skimmed oxygen through my lungs, dimming my

sight. My jaw locked down, a guttural scream wailing inside while everything on the outside froze.

Even after all my nightmares of what I imagined the House of Death to be like—and I had a very active imagination—nothing came close to what it really was.

"Yeah, girlie. Most piss their pants here. No shame. Happens to the best of them." Zion leaned into me with a cruel wink. "Welcome to your new abode, human."

Chapter 10

Bile seared my insides, coating my throat and tongue, while my legs crumpled. The stench overpowered me, along with the terror ripping through me. I couldn't catch my breath, my heart thrashing against my ribs as if it needed to escape the tightness of my chest, no matter the cost.

"Whoa, girl." Zion pushed me against the railing, keeping me upright. "Go ahead and throw up. All do at some point." He nodded toward the smooth ground far below my feet. Some level of my brain understood his words, took in the sights and sounds, but I couldn't really grasp any of it. It was like floating behind a glass wall between me and the world.

"You act like you won't enjoy it here." Zion motioned out to vast space, which felt small and confined. "I think you are just being picky. I mean, what more could you ask for?"

"Zion, don't be a dick." Jade rolled her eyes at him.

I couldn't respond, fighting the tears as I looked around the dimly lit prison. Fire-bulbs adorned the walls every three or four yards, giving off enough light to see by, but heavy shadows lingered and clustered together where the lights didn't reach. The darkness added to the sense of confinement—the sense of death waiting in the wings.

Would I ever see the sun again?

The underground prison was far bigger than I thought. Shaped in rectangular boxes, the cells lining the walls all faced each other. The metal catwalk I stood on was about midway, the ground far below, and the ceiling far above. Comparable to a stacked city I'd seen in pictures of the Far East, cages were packed vertically and horizontally, reaching floor to ceiling along all four walls. There were about twenty levels with catwalks. Some were just one large cell between floors, and other levels had three to four cages stacked on top of each other before the next walkway. The one way to get in or out of those would be to climb over the others. A few cages hung from the ceiling, only accessible if a guard brought them down. Everything was metal, vibrating with noise. There was no space, no air.

I felt claustrophobic. Trapped.

"Looky, looky! We caught a new fish. *Az istenit*, a pretty one too."

"I get dibs first."

"No, I'm gonna tear into that sweet pussy first."

Vulgar words and sentiments were hurled at me from the inmates inside their tiny barred homes, drawing more and more of them to the front of their cells. Movement and figures consumed my vision, forcing me to glance down at my feet, trying to ignore the more violent and disgusting threats.

Vomit pooled in my stomach again. It was all too much.

Guards and prisoners bustled through the place, their boots clicking on the catwalks, the sound mingling with an endless stream of talking, yelling, and banging. I could taste the foul air on my tongue, feel the shrill noise piercing my nerves.

"The commissary is down there." Jade pointed to a passageway located on the bottom floor. "And the pit—"

"Please." Zion cut her off. "We're not going to play tour

guide. She will have the rest of her short life to get acquainted with this place." Zion clutched the cuffs behind my back, yanking me to another corridor on this level. "Now it's time for your welcome party."

"You really are an asshole." Jade sighed, moving to the opposite side of me.

"Stop being an uptight bitch," he barked back. "You demons act like you're above everyone now."

"Not everyone. Just above douchebags."

He snarled, baring his sharp teeth at her, his eyes narrowing.

"Oh, so scary." She laughed. "Do you forget every time you can't shift in here? Remember, it's a magicless space, moron."

His lip rose again, but he shook his head.

Magicless space? It made sense to control the fae prisoners in here from using their gifts. A siren or incubus could seduce their way out of here in a moment. At least it put everyone on a more even playing field, though not much of one. No matter what level the fae were on, even the least powerful or half-breeds, they were tougher than humans—faster, immortal, and much harder to kill. All things humans would love to change.

My brain was a blur, not taking in much as Zion and Jade transferred me down a dank hallway, the screams and shrieks following me, sputtering panic into my system, my legs dipping as they shoved me to move faster. As they heaved me through a door, my lids tapered at the assault of sudden cool light. My gaze darted around, taking in the sterile room, noting the three marked rows where observation tables stood marked with: fae, human, half-breed. Fae dressed in similar outfits as the healer earlier milled around the room, their attention snapping to me the moment we stepped in.

"What the hell did you bring me?" A tall handsome-faced fae with honey-colored eyes snarled down at my bloody gown, an electronic pad in his hand.

"Human. Thief," Jade responded.

"And no longer our problem. All yours!" Zion saluted the man, already retreating from the room. "I'm off the clock."

Jade and the man watched him leave the room.

"What an asshole."

"Tell me about it." Jade handed over the keys to my cuffs. "Be lucky you aren't partnered with him." Jade didn't even look at me before she left as well.

The moment she did, the guy's demeanor shifted.

"Full human?" His lip curled, typing into his device.

I stared at him, my mind slow to understand.

"I asked you a question, 85221," he barked, driving up the anxiety swaying me on my feet.

His jaw locked down, his buttery eyes blazing. "Oh, you're one of those who think being silent shows you're strong? Resilient." He chuckled, getting into my face. "Just wait. This place will break you. Not a scrap of you will be left. You will die here, whether it's in a week or a month. I guarantee you won't make it very long." A cruel grin broke over his beautiful face as he muttered to himself. "Full human." His fingers typed in what he said, but his gaze peered into mine with speculation. I held his scrutiny.

"Age."

"Nineteen," I whispered.

"Date of birth."

"November first."

His chin clicked up, his lids narrowing. "You were born on Samhain? The day the barrier fell?"

"Yeah, lucky me." I was anything but—a bad omen. The

wall between worlds had crumbled as my mother delivered me—then she died.

His brows furrowed as he typed in the info, his shoulders rolling back like my birth personally pissed him off.

"Diseases?" He snorted, a dimple showing up in his left cheek. "What am I saying, you humans come filled with sickness and germs. Thankfully we don't catch things easily from your kind."

He tossed the computer pad onto a desk, fury bristling off him as he unlatched my cuffs. Blood rushed through my pinched veins, my muscles screaming with relief as prickles moved over my joints. Seizing my bicep, he yanked me into a back room that smelled of stale water and cheap disinfectant. My bare toes slid over the damp cement floors, my stomach dropping, terrified of what was next.

It wasn't until now I realized how lacking our training really was. They never trained us how to handle getting caught or what it might really be like on the inside, and if we did get captured, they wiped their hands of us. We were as good as dead.

A dozen cold cement stalls lined a wall with one large drain in the middle of the floor. Each of the three-sided showers was about four feet wide and twelve feet high.

"Strip," he barked, shoving me into a stall and picking up a hose hooked on the wall.

Emotion cluttered my throat, and I began to shiver.

"I said fucking strip," he bellowed. "Or I will do it, and believe me, you do not want that. I don't take kindly to having my time wasted."

I burned with fury and shame, and my eyes began to twitch as I tried to lift my gown.

"You have two seconds." He took a threatening step toward me.

Sucking in, I reached behind and untied the gown, the thin fabric sliding off my shoulders. There was a difference between being comfortable with your body and with being naked, and being stripped of humanity—of yourself.

"Undergarments." He pulled a trash can to the opening, nodding at it. My jaw strained as I clenched it painfully. Struggling to swallow, I pulled my underwear down my legs, trying not to sob, tossing them and the gown into the garbage. My stringy hair fell across my torso, giving me a bit of shelter.

A malicious smile curled up the sides of his face as he watched me undress. He was getting off on this, and it had nothing to do with my naked form but his power to depreciate and dehumanize me. He stepped up to me, a bottle in his hand, and squirted its cold contents over me; his lips turned up like he was pissing on a vile piece of crap. My nostrils burned with the antiseptic smell.

I was nothing more than a flea-infested animal. Humans were less than. Weaker.

"Rub it over all over you and through your hair." He nodded for me to step deeper into the stall. "Humans need to be thoroughly disinfected of all the little bugs and bacteria." His hand flicked on a wall switch.

The blast slammed my frame into the cold stone wall as icy water assaulted my skin feeling like a thousand knives, tearing the oxygen from my lungs. My hands went up to guard my face from the brutal onslaught. The pressure was so harsh. My cry drowned in my chest as the stream of water pummeled my flesh. The guard wanted to wash the human disgust off my bones as well. The force shredded my healing wounds, old and fresh blood trailing down my legs with the water.

Whipping around, my hands pressed against the wall, sobs hiccupping up my throat.

Naked. Shamed. Degraded.

"Scrub," he ordered, moving the attack down my legs and back up to my ass. I rubbed my hands through my hair, but every moment felt like moving through mud. My muscles failed, wanting to crumble to the floor.

"Turn around," he instructed, the water punching my stomach and moving lower. "Come on; I said wash."

My throat was thick with humiliation, trying to hold back the flood of sobs shaking my frame, quickly doing what he said.

The water turned off.

"See, you do as you're told, and things go a lot easier for you." He hooked the hose back up and motioned for me to follow.

Shivering violently, I wrapped my arms around my breasts, trailing after him, my snarled hair sticking to my back, my raw flesh pricking and throbbing. My wet feet slapped the icy floor as I ducked my chin low, curving into myself.

He took us into another room, which was a large storage room filled with prison uniforms, boots, and wool blankets. Red, gray, blue, and yellow outfits were stacked on the shelves. Unisex, but separated into small, medium, and large.

"Here." He picked up a set folded on the bench like they had been waiting for me, a pair of worn boots underneath. "Get dressed."

I picked up dull gray cotton pants, a matching top, socks, a sports bra, and beige granny-sized underwear. Quickly, I put on the items, noticing the number 85221 had been stenciled out on the back of the shirt, the numbers still damp from being recently painted on.

The material was cheap, but so worn it was at least soft. I didn't want to think how many others had used them before me, who had sweated, bled, and died in this outfit. The only thing on me new was the number on my back. My quaking bones didn't care; they sought the warmth of being clothed again. The boots were slightly big and reeked of disinfectant, but every layer made me feel a little better.

"This is your blanket and towel." The man showed my number stenciled at the bottom of them. "If you lose them, sell them, or they get taken, it's your problem. You get *one* blanket and towel. You have been warned, so no bitching if you 'lose' them."

I nodded, taking them from him.

"Your kit is replenished every six weeks. If you run out before, that's also your problem." He handed me a clear bag filled with toiletries: toothbrush, toothpaste, comb, and soap.

His words registered, but numbness left me blank of a response.

"You missed dinner." He whirled around and strutted for another door across the room, going through it, leading me out into a dim cave-type passage. "Wake up is at 06.30. Breakfast is at 07.00. Lunch at noon. Dinner at 18.00. Otherwise you are either in your cell, or you're working. The more you work and follow the rules, the more privileges you get. Like first in line for food or better jobs."

"What kind of work?"

"Cleaning. Cooking. Sewing." He paused. "This place runs like clockwork. All *humans* contribute here. Or you go into the pit." Leaning into me, he sneered. "And believe me, you don't want to go in there. You won't make it out of there. Not without wishing for death first."

I kept my face neutral, pretending his words didn't scare me.

The fae took me up a few flights of stairs, walking me past occupied cells.

"Hey, sweet thing. You can bunk and fuck me."

"Come here, fishy, fishy."

"Watch yourself, human." A woman spit at me.

"I'll fuckin' kill you."

"You will die chokin' on my dick." A huge, beefy guy grabbed his nuts, sneering at me.

Catcalls, insults, threats. They barreled at me, hitching my heart back up into my throat, my teeth sawing down on my lip. The roller coaster of emotions and the trauma my body had gone through made me feel like paper. Every slur tore at the house of cards I was standing on.

Against my will, my lip started to quiver. Dipping my head, my hair fell over my face, hiding my misery from their view.

Don't let them see any weakness. Keep it inside.

The fairy stopped in front of an empty cage. A six-by-eight-foot box, it was smaller than my shower back at HDF. No bed or any furniture, only a hole in the ground you could piss in.

The door squealed as he opened it, jackhammering my pulse, flooding my throat with acid, my feet stepping back. Fear had been with me every step of the way, but it wasn't until this moment that I understood true terror. I stepped into this cage, and my life was over.

My head started to shake back and forth, tears building behind my lids, fear convulsing down my limbs.

"Kicsim," my father's voice whispered in the back of my memory. "You don't get much say in the way you die, but you can choose how you do." His fingers brushed my chin up, his bright blue eyes staring down at my nine-year-old self, his face filled with adoration. "Always hold yourself with honor. Especially in death."

"Go," the guard's voice snapped, tearing me out of my reverie.

Lifting my head, I stepped across the threshold, the slam of the door behind me jolting through my entire body. I jerked around to face him.

"Welcome to the House of Death 85221." He winked at me, strolling away, slipping out of view. "*Sweet* dreams."

I stood there, hugging the scratchy wool blanket to my chest, the howls and screams echoing off the walls, cocooning me in distress.

Fear had wiggled deep into my stomach. There were so many words to describe what I felt: terror, shock, anger, panic, isolation, and heartbreaking loneliness. All I wanted was to go back to that night—stay up on the perch high above the world and make love to Caden.

Unrolling the blanket, I set it on the ground and curled up on it. I stared out at the other cells across the way and cried until my despair took me from the conscious world.

Chapter 11

Sleep held me for brief moments in its mouth before spitting me back out again, raw, chewed up, and brutalized from the nightmare inside and outside my head.

The cries, bangs, and movement never stopped. It would quiet down enough to let you fall into a false sense of sleep before something would jolt you awake with a gasp. The four sides of the building rebounded noise across the courtyard like a rubber ball bouncing off the ground, which was another level of torture, another way to break us down.

I wasn't the only one crying myself to sleep, but I tried to keep my grief tucked into my blanket, finally drifting off again before a shrill bell bolted my eyes open, my head jerking up. Panic puffed air through my lungs. Confusion swung my gaze through the bars. Across the way, I noticed inmates stirring, figures moving to their doors.

"That's the wake-up bell." A small voice came from the corner of my cell.

"*Az istenit!*" *Shit. Fuck!* I scrambled back, my spine smacking into the wall, my eyes searching the dark for the owner of the voice.

I thought I had been alone in my tiny cell.

"The door will be opening soon," the male voice said, making my gaze bob and weave around, trying to make out any shape in the corner. Was I already losing my mind?

"Show yourself." My back stayed pinned to the wall, my knees up to my chest.

"Hell, Bitzy, this one is demanding. Not even a please," he muttered.

A squeak responded to him. I slammed my head into the hard stone. What the hell was going on?

"Where are you?" My pulse thundered against my neck.

A deep shadow shifted in the corner, and a small man dragging a broom behind him stepped into the dim light streaming into my cell.

A sharp inhale burned up my throat as my eyes locked on the being. His huge nose was the first thing I noticed, dominating his heart-shaped face, his ears slightly pointed. Brown eyes, brown hair and beard, the man was less than a foot tall, wearing what appeared to be a large orange nylon pot scrubber as shorts or possibly a tutu, and a stitched sock for a shirt.

"Are you…" I gulped. "Y-you're a brownie, right?"

I had heard about them. Seen pictures, but had never seen one in person. Istvan made sure sub-fae were kept out of HDF by poisoning them like rats. Brownies inhabited houses and helped with tasks around the home. However, I heard they did not want to be seen and worked at night or when no one was around.

"Yes. And you are a human. Good thing we have that all cleared up." He rolled his eyes, peering over his shoulder at a figure nestled in a doll-sized backpack on his back. "The naiveté is strong with this one. Won't last long here."

"Oh, my gods." My hand went to my mouth, my gaze latching onto the tiny, hairless creature on his back. It somewhat resembled an aye-aye, with its bat ears and huge eyes. Less than four inches big, it had three long jointed fingers on each hand. It was both cute and scary. "What is that?"

"What is your deal, fish? You act like you've never seen a brownie or an imp before."

I hadn't. Here was another moment that made me realize how sheltered my life had been within the walls of Leopold. Fae dominated our world, but except for fairies and a few shape-shifters, my encounters with them had been minimal.

"Fish?"

"It's the term here for a newbie. You're a fish out of water. Fresh meat."

I'd been called worse things.

"Who will soon turn stinky, your corpse rotting and smelling up the joint."

Oh.

"This is Bitzy." He nodded at the thing on his back. The animal thing tilted his head at me, its lids narrowing. "Bitzy, this is Fishy."

Bitzy's huge eyes blinked at me, and it squeaked, then picked up its three-pronged hand, curling two of them down, leaving the middle one.

"Bitzy," the brownie exclaimed through a chuckle. "Sorry, Bitzy can be a bit of an asshole."

"And you are?"

"Oh, I'm totally an asshole."

The first smile tugged at my mouth. "I meant your name."

"Opie."

"I thought brownies didn't like being seen."

"Oh, good! I love stereotypes." Opie waved his arms around while Bitzy flipped me off with the other hand. "Sure, we're all the same. No individual personality, and next you're gonna say I should enjoy cleaning."

"Don't you?"

"For fuck's sake!" He stomped his foot. "Would you like washing up after people? All their shit—*literally*. And humans are the worst. Lazy. Selfish. Think everyone else should tidy up their mess for them. So don't for a moment think I will be cleaning after you."

"Then what are you doing?" I flicked my fingers at him, trying not to smile.

He glanced down, his arms dragging the broom back and forth across the floor.

"Damn it!" He chucked the sweeper to the floor. "I have anxiety issues, which makes me clean, but I hate cleaning, so then I get more stressed out, which starts the damn cycle over again."

I tried not to smile as he fidgeted with the scouring pad he wore as shorts.

He was anything but invisible, his outfit screaming for attention.

Boom!

The sound of all the prison doors opening at once thundered through the building, vaulting me up to my feet. People strode past my door, heading in the same direction.

"Breakfast, Fishy. Better hurry and wash up. They only make enough for one serving per person here. And some take what they want."

Meaning many didn't get to eat.

I looked back at Opie. "Why are you helping me?"

"Helping? I drew the short broomstick on who got the newbie's cage. Usually, it's full of vomit, piss, and tears." He snorted, his booted foot tapping at the broom. "And take what I said as a strong warning." He smirked as Bitzy took one of her long fingers and slid it across her throat.

Okay. Wow.

"Move it!" a guard yelled from below, scrambling me up onto my feet, heading out of the cell.

"Don't forget this. You will get a lashing if you forget it." Opie held up my toiletry kit.

"Thank you." I took it from his small hand, tucking it under my arm with the towel.

"Oh, you really are fresh meat." His brown eyes rounded on me with pity. "Like a baby bird."

"I'm tougher than you think."

"Oh, Fishy-Fish." He clicked his tongue. "You just *think* you are."

In the sweep of bodies, I was hustled down the catwalk. Across the courtyard, I could see other levels with prisoners all heading in the same direction wearing the various colored uniforms—gray, blue, yellow, and red mingled on each floor. I grew agitated at the stomping of feet, bodies shoving me from behind and whispering threats in my ears as they pushed past me.

All the prisoners on my level were led to a large lavatory down a corridor. I wondered if every level had their own, keeping numbers manageable in the space.

One side held rows of toilets, the other side open showers, and in the middle were sinks with unbreakable metal mirrors. Guards with guns, tasers, and several sets of cuffs stood at the entrance and exit.

Another realization hit me quickly—the bathroom was not only unisex, but everything was out in the open: no doors or our own space. Our training room had unisex restrooms, but we still had privacy—curtains on showers, doors on the bathrooms. And you could go back to your room if you didn't want to shower there. There were levels of cushion. Safety.

This had all been ripped away from me in a brutal blow. Standing there, watching the prisoners do their business, everything on display, made me feel totally exposed and vulnerable. Opie was right. I had thought myself so tough, but I had been sheltered at HDF.

Locking in my emotions, I tucked my head down, not wanting to make eye contact with anyone. My bladder ached, but my skin crawled at the thought of sitting on a seat so many had before me—dirty and pissed on. At HDF, I had a maid who kept everything pristine and a bathroom bigger than four of my prison cells.

"Come on, princess." An elbow knocked into my side. "You have to piss with us filthy fae eventually."

My head snapped to a petite-boned woman next to me dressed in a red uniform. About my height, the girl was gorgeous, around my age, with long blue hair braided down her back. She seemed confident and strong. I saw nothing soft in her pale navy-blue eyes, which changed like glitter in the light.

I stepped back.

Demon.

My muscles locked up, my body turning defensive. Demons were high on our kill list. You could decipher their level of power by their eye color. Red and navy meant great power but were not the most dangerous. Yellow-green marked the emperor of all the demons. The King of the Unified Nations had those, his power unequaled. All demons' eyes turned completely black when they were "on." Black soulless pits.

"Relax, human." She rolled her eyes, brushing a strand of blue hair off her face. "I can't hurt you in here." Her head turned to me with a wink. "Well, not in the fun way." Her gaze roamed over me. "Though it might be really fun to roll around with you."

"What?"

"Fuck. You are a little lamb." She shook her head, her voice gruff, contradicting her petite frame and pretty face. "Most humans who come through here are like offerings to a wild beast. A rack of lamb slathered in sauce."

"I'm not a lamb."

"Saying it doesn't make it true."

"Two minutes," a guard yelled out, causing me to jolt.

She burst out laughing at me.

"See you around, little lamb," she snickered, strolling away, heading for the toilets.

Anyone would be terrified in my position, being thrown in a place called the House of Death, knowing no one ever made it out. But no matter how scared I was, showing it meant weakness here. Blood in the water. And as the demon pointed out, it only made me nourishment for fae.

The mess hall was huge, allowing all the prisoners in the space at once. The cafeteria-style setup was along one wall, the line winding all the way around the room, guards stationed every few yards. Inmates already sat down and ate at tables in the middle.

"*Te geci!* Don't fuckin' cut in front of me!" A man bellowed to several people ahead of me, shoving another man in yellow crashing into a table. The shrill clatter of trays hitting the floor had me stepping back, sucking in sharply. Guards moved to stop them as other inmates raced to take their space in line, causing more squabbles to break out.

"Move!" Someone yelled behind me, jolting me forward, my nerves already a wreck. My stomach grumbled. The last thing I recalled eating was a few shrimp at the party, which was more than a week ago. Any nutrients since then had been through my veins or from magical herbs while I laid unconscious. But knots of stress and fear still twisted up into my throat, blocking my appetite.

The gala already felt like a lifetime ago, where my evening had gone from hope to grief to hell in a few hours. When I put on that gorgeous dress complaining about the stuffiness of the party, little did I know soon I would be wearing a used prison uniform and sleeping on the ground next to a urine hole in one of the most feared prisons in the East.

To go back and do it over. The notion tugged at my heart. But would I have traded one prison for another? Marriage to Sergiu would have been another level of hell. One I would have had to suffer through for years, breaking every part of my soul until I was an empty shell.

The line moved faster than I thought. As I inched closer to the food, the scents of shoddy coffee, burned toast, and hot cereal drifted up my nose. Nothing smelled good, but my stomach still grumbled with the need to fill it.

From my place in line, I could see the food dwindling to a few ladles of porridge.

Grabbing a tray, I set it on the rail and slid it down to the worker scooping out the food. A shoulder slammed into me, a wide frame cutting in before me, shoving me back. I stumbled into a body behind me.

"Hey!" I pushed back onto my feet, glaring at the guy in front of me.

The line cutter was several inches taller than me and built wide and thick in the chest. His torso barreled, tapering farther down, reminding me of a bull. He had deep olive skin, a broad nose, and skinny legs.

His nostrils flared, brown eyes almost the color of his pupils, his black hair flopping in one eye. "What did you say, human?" he snarled, tilting his head.

"I was next," I spurted back at him.

"Really?" He chuckled. "Looks like I am, and oh look, I get the last of the breakfast."

"No." My voice came out soft and pliable. "It's mine."

A nasty smile lifted his thin lips as he stepped up so close to me, his chest touched mine. "You're new, aren't you?" He leaned in, taking a deep whiff of me. "So fresh I can smell the disinfectant on you. No matter how much they douse you with decontaminator, you little human fuckers keep surviving… like cockroaches."

"Rodriguez." A man's voice sounded low but firm behind me. "Leave her be."

The bull-shifter's eyes flicked to the man standing behind me, his lids narrowing in a glare.

"What if I don't, old man?" he huffed, his foot pawing the ground like an animal's hoof.

"She didn't know. Let her be this time," the man said. Every word he spoke was like a warm bath. Soothing and calming.

Rodriguez snarled, his head wagging. "You take far too many liberties, Tadhgan. Someday you will see you aren't as untouchable as you think you are."

"Until then…" I felt the man step in close in behind me. "You will not touch this girl." His hands cuffed my arms, firm and powerful.

Rodriguez's glower moved from him to me, disgust curling his lips before he snorted and shoved his tray at the man behind the counter, taking the final cup of food before marching away.

Tension vibrated in my body, along with anger, fright, and disappointment. I had taken down men with his temperament many times, but this time fear crippled me. Maybe he couldn't shift into his bull form here, but his power pulsated under his skin. He could tear me apart.

If I'd thought the teachings at HDF were brutal and relentless, I now realized it hadn't been enough for real survival. How ill-prepared every soldier there was for a real battle against the fae.

Taking a deep breath, I curved around to look at the man behind me. Surprise curled down my throat, not ready for who stood behind me.

"Old man" was an understatement. His back was curved and twisted, hunching him over, far below my height. He held on to a cane, the stick assisting his thin legs. He had shoulder-length gray hair, left loose and knotted. His face was craggy; years and stories lined it with rich history. Skinny, his white uniform hung off his bones. It was the only white one I had seen.

His eyes widened, his body jerking back like he'd seen a ghost, his throat bobbing. But the emotion fluttered from him as fast as it came, making me believe I imagined it.

I stared at him, my brows furrowing with confusion.

The bull-shifter yielded to this old man? Frail and deformed.

"Not what you thought?" A soft smile grew on his worn face.

"No. I'm just… that's not it." My tongue stumbled over my lie.

His smile grew, his shaky hand reaching out to pat my shoulder. "Can't really lie to a Druid, girl." He clicked his tongue. "We tend to see through bullshit."

"Y-you're a druid." My mouth fell open as people brushed by us, claiming what little crumbs were left. Shock kept me in place. Druids were *rare*, especially in Hungary. The bigotry toward Druids in the Eastern Bloc had never receded. Fae still hated them, and humans mistrusted them.

The old Seelie queen had murdered millions, long before

my time, driving many of them underground to survive. But the current ruling queen was a Druid, and she'd drawn them back into the light, moving many to the Western world to live safely under her rule.

"They don't have me wearing white for nothing." His free hand motioned down his bent form, chuckling. "Not that looking at this ugly mug doesn't tell you I'm certainly not fae, but still far too pretty to be human." He winked playfully.

Confusion tugged at me. Why was this man teasing me? It put me on edge, wondering if something was going to come at me while he was lowering my guard.

"So distrustful." He stared into my eyes like he was peeling away my skin. "But at the same time so naïve."

My jaw locked down.

"Come." He squeezed my arm, hobbling past me. "Sit with me. Have some coffee, at least."

"I-I…"

"I need some company. Tired of muttering to myself." He went to a counter with large thermoses, pouring two coffees. I followed, not knowing if it was a mistake, but the draw to the Druid was too powerful to fight. Something about him felt familiar and comfortable.

Automatically, I picked up both cups while he tottered to a table in the back. Heads turned in my direction, glares and snarls following me to the back table.

"Nice to have more than myself to converse with. Not many willing to sit with an old Druid man." He grunted noisily as he sat down on the stool attached to the table. Everything here was bolted down or built in. Fewer items to be used as weapons. "I can give you a little rundown of this place."

"I don't need your help." I set down the coffee cups. Need meant weakness.

He snuffed in. "Do you smell that?" He took a deep breath. "Are you bathing in bullshit now, girl?"

"Excuse me?"

"You heard me. Now sit down." He nodded at the chair.

Stiffly, I perched on the stool, my eyes darting around.

"Good. Always be on guard in this place. Imagine this is the pride lands of Africa, and everything here is hunting you."

"Africa?" I snorted, taking a sip of the black goop they called coffee, cringing as the bitter taste lumped down my throat. Africa was a distant continent I knew from geography books, but it might as well be another universe. I knew very little about it. "What the hell do I know of that place?"

"Goddesses, this breaks my heart." He sighed. "Your generation lives its entire existence on a speck of dirt, where experience, education, and life are confined within walls because some nobles wanted to keep all the power and control. That's not a life."

"It is to me."

"Because you've never smelled the rich spices in India, seen a sunset in Greece, heard the rush of the water in Victoria Falls, tasted real coffee in Turkey. Your life is minuscule."

"Fuck you." I slammed down my cup and stood up.

"Sit back down." He grabbed my hand. "It's not your fault, girl. Freedom is something this area has not had a great friendship with." His blue eyes stared into me until I felt my ass hit the seat again.

He tilted his head, his gaze not wavering. "You are a strange one."

"I'm starting to see why you have no friends, *old man*."

A grin bloomed on his face. "Never take anything in here at face value." He shifted on the chair with a groan. "What's your name? What family do you reside from?" His sharp eyes peered at me on the last question.

I watched him over my cup, taking another sip, the lie slipping out easily. "Nagy," I said. "Laura Nagy." I gave him one of the most common names in this area. There had to be thousands of girls with this name. Kovacs was common, too, but Brexley Kovacs was not. My real name was very well-known by the fae. I didn't want anyone knowing my real identity.

"Sure it is." His grin turned into a chuckle, amusement creasing his already wrinkled face. "I'm Tadhgan. Call me Tad. I know my name is a mouthful."

"Okay, Tad," I replied dryly.

His gaze centered on me, making me feel he was trying to dig through and unearth my soul, find my secrets.

"What?" I grumbled.

He watched me for another beat before he shook his head. "Nothing. Simply mind tricks of an old, crumbling mind." He took a sip of coffee and gazed out at the other prisoners. "You need to quickly learn the hierarchy here if you want to live under the radar. Survive." His blue eyes met mine. There was surprising youth, but extensive knowledge also dancing in them. I knew Druids lived thousands of years longer than humans, one of their gifts given to them centuries ago by the fae gods and goddesses. "Though, I say nothing comes from being nothing."

"Shocking really, you don't have friends." I huffed into my cup.

"Okay." He nodded around the room. "Humans wear the gray uniforms, half-breeds blue, fae the yellow, demons red. Druids are in white, which is just me. The prison divides us by color on purpose—to keep the lines of hate strong between the groups. They want us to cling to our bigotry so we fight each other, not them. They want the constant reminder we are not all equal." He patted his chest, trying to get down the thick coffee. "And merely because you're human doesn't mean other humans are on your side. If they are still here, it means they've learned to survive and will stab your back if they need to." He nodded at the dotting of gray outfits scattered through the space. There were a few seated together, but most had wiggled in with yellow and blue uniforms. "Rodriguez and his group are what I call third-tier bullies. Mean, intimidating, the kind who beat up smaller people to show how big and powerful they are. Definitely a group to avoid, but there's a lot of prancing and pawing the ground if the second-tier steps in." Tadhgan gestured toward a table in the middle. All red.

The demons. The top of the food chain. And almost all women. In the group of eight, only three I could see were men, resembling lions resting on their rock. My attention moved over them, noticing the blue-haired demon I met in the bathroom sitting among them. Within the group, she seemed to be an island within herself. Drinking coffee and picking at breakfast, she didn't engage with the other demons.

But she was part of the second tier. Powerful.

"Wait. You said second tier?" I looked back at the Druid. "What's above *demons*?"

His gaze slowly slid to mine, lowering the mug from his lips.

"Him."

Chapter 12

"Him?" My brow furrowed, following the Druid's gaze. I curved in my seat, searching the room until my eyes landed on a figure in the far corner sitting by himself. Like a blow to my lungs, air caught in my chest, and I sat up straighter. How had I missed him? In the sea of color, the huge man dressed in all black was a drop of blood on white paper.

His long, dark hair was pulled back, heavy scruff cut along his strong jawline, displaying his full bottom lip. His unnerving aqua eyes slid slowly over the room like fingers caressing a body. The bright color against his olive skin and black hair and lashes made them pop out like laser beams set on you. With one foot on a bench seat, he leaned against the wall, his arm draped over his knee, a king watching over his domain, taking everything in.

Alpha. Brutal. Raw. Dangerous. Terrifying. Sensual.

Everything about him was severe. Even sitting, I could tell he had to be taller than six foot six. His tattoo-covered arms, shredded with muscles, exhibited physical strength. Even the loose V-neck uniform curved snugly around his biceps, chest, and pecs.

Intensity, power, dominance, and violence danced

around him as if they were the only things daring to be near him. He appeared at ease, but every touch of his gaze over the room suggested he could kill before the enemy even knew he moved.

Peering through his dark lashes, his gaze met mine, and making me feel I had been punched in the stomach, ripping the air from my lungs. My heart thumped against my ribs like it came to life or knew it was about to die, drumming the final chords in my life. Against the cotton, my nipples hardened, instantly reacting to the intense energy moving around me.

Fuck. Me.

It was too much, his stare ripping the clothes away from my body, peeling at my skin, and tearing through my flesh. The adrenaline rushed over me at seeing death head-on. Finally, his impassive gaze broke away, and I gasped in relief.

"Wha-what is he?" Heat still lit my cheeks on fire, my pulse tapping at my neck.

"No one knows."

"What?" My head jerked back to Tad. "He's fae, though. He has to be."

"Does he?"

"No human has that kind of power."

"As a Druid, I can see the energy of everyone in this room, their aura, sense what they are." Tad set down his cup, clearing his throat. "Everyone but him."

"You can't tell if he's human or fae?"

"There is nothing around him." Tad's attention pointed at me. "Or around you."

"What?" I straightened. "Me?"

"Your aura is void of both life and death. Nothing." Tad tilted his head. "Like him."

"What do you mean?"

"Means either you have gotten unbelievably good at

hiding your aura, or I've gotten so lonely I'm making up imaginary friends."

"Believe me, I wish I weren't actually here." I ran a hand through my hair, which the harsh disinfectant had made brittle and knotted. "How would someone hide their aura? Is that why you said I was strange?" It wasn't something I remember learning, but maybe I'd done so accidentally.

"I don't know. Besides him, never seen it happen to this degree."

"What do you mean?"

"Some people get good at hiding their energy, build up walls, but I usually still sense something."

My stomach rolled, a rush of icy heat coating my skin.

"Don't worry, girl. You're looking a little peaked there." He shifted uncomfortably on his backless seat, pain flickering through his features. "You are human. I'm guessing you've learned to protect yourself. Keep your guard up at all times."

My shoulders lowered. I felt oddly relieved. It made sense I had put fortification around myself living with Istvan. Every day, I was either a soldier in training or attending a party upstairs with a false smile on my face. Always on the defense and ready for whatever was thrown at me. Some days it was a fist, on other days, a forced husband.

"Why is he the only one wearing black?" I couldn't fight sneaking another glance at him. Even though he wasn't looking at me, I somehow knew he was aware of my attention on him. Without his eyes on me, he still was like the sun, too much to look at for long.

"Because he's in a league of his own. They don't know what to classify him under. I'm warning you to be careful of him. He has pull here that no one has gotten close to. Whatever he wants, he gets, and the guards look the other way. You are dead if he decides it. He's undefeated in the Games. He rules this place."

"Games?"

"Right. You're a fish." Tad's head bobbed, and he rubbed at his callused chin. "No words would accurately describe it. You will see for yourself tonight."

A bell sounded in the room, and a table filled with blue and yellow uniforms next to us jumped up, making me flinch. My senses and defenses were turned up so high being this close to a bunch of fae.

"Breakfast is over." Tad gestured to everyone heading for an exit. "It's been a pleasure, *Laura*." He winked at me, struggling to rise. "Work time."

I leaped up, helping him get off the seat.

"Damn this old twisted frame," he grumbled, his nails digging into my arms as he rose to his feet. "I preferred when the only thing twisted about me was my mind."

I laughed, watching him hobble away, picking up our cups to take to a bin.

A figure moved past me, and people leaped out of the way, knocking into me. My head lifted to see the man in black sauntering past, towering above most of the prisoners here. His presence sent a chemical reaction through me; heat flooded my chest and flushed my cheeks. His broad shoulders, torso, and ass were so taut anything would bounce right off.

Did he spend all day just working out?

Why did everyone bow down to this guy? Why was he so special? Even the demons moved out of his way.

"Don't think about it, little lamb." A familiar voice tsked in my ear, moving in next to me. The blue-haired demon smirked at me, her head shaking.

"What?"

"There is not a woman or man who hasn't tried." She wiggled her eyebrows at his fleeting figure. "They *bring* women in for him to fuck. He doesn't speak to or associate with anyone here. He killed someone for sneaking into his cell and trying to seduce him."

"Seriously? They bring in prostitutes for him?" I blinked at her.

"Prostitutes." She snorted. "These girls would pay *him.* All come willingly."

"Why? What's so special about him?"

"Besides the obvious?" She pulled on her braid, still staring at his ass before he disappeared from view.

"He could be human for all you guys know. I didn't think fae ever bowed down to humans. Aren't we less than? Scum that needs to be erased?"

She curved her head to me and assessed my body. "Aren't *we* to you?

Fair point.

"He doesn't care if you are female, male, old, young, fae, or human. You bother him? You're good as dead." She moved forward, glancing back at me. "Just a friendly warning from your local demon. Stay far away from Warwick Farkas."

The foam cups slipped from my fingers, splashing the leftover contents across the cement floor, spraying over my boots.

"What?" Fear wobbled my voice.

"I gather even the human side has heard of him." A sharp smile curled her mouth. "It's like finding out dragons still exist, huh? But you'll never get to tell anyone you've seen one in person. Heed my warning, lamb. Stay away." She turned back around and strolled out of the room.

Warwick Farkas?

Holy shit…

Hanna's mention of him the day in training came back into my head.

"We've all heard the tales. He will kill you without blinking... and he's so unbearably hot, you go willingly."

"I'm here to train you guys for real enemies, not make-believe ones."

"My sister's boyfriend's father said he was very real. Saw him fight a dozen men at once in the Fae War."

"Did he tell you Santa Claus was real too? The Wolf is nothing but an exaggerated and glorified tale, inflated every time he is mentioned."

But the man himself just walked by me. The stuff of myths and fables—ghost stories told around a campfire, setting fear in your blood. The rumor was he did not consider himself loyal to any side. No one knew anything about him personally, only that he moved like a ghost and killed in silence. A true enigma.

But he was real. Here.

The man whose last name meant "Wolf" ruled the House of Death.

"Prisoner 85221!" A gnarly voice coiled down the dark hallway, sounding similar to broken glass ground on pavement. A huge creature stepped into my path, and I sucked back a wheeze of fear. Not all fae were beautiful or had a sultry voice, luring in their prey. Some were scarier than nightmares.

Dressed in all black like the rest of the guards, with weapons hanging off its belt, a monster more than nine feet tall stomped up to me, the ground shaking under my feet. Patchy gray skin, scarred and cut, covered its thick muscles; the shirt was so tight against its chest it looked as if it had boobs. Its shoulders brushed either side of the corridor, and its head bowed to keep from scraping the top. It had teeth like a wild boar, and its nose was smashed in, forcing the thing to breathe out of its stinky mouth. It snarled down at me. I couldn't tell what sex it was, but I knew it was at least half ogre. I'd seen many pictures of them.

"Come with me." The mitt-sized hand clamped down on the back of my neck, shoving me forward like I was a little kitten, causing my feet to stumble. "Move it!"

The ogre's grip felt like it cracked the bones in the back of my neck, pain lashing down my spine. The guard rushed me down several corridors, finally reaching a room the size of a small warehouse, buzzing with the hum of sewing machines and dripping with fabric. Steam rose from one side of the room where dozens of people scrubbed clothes on washboards in huge barrel buckets, their faces beet red and twisted with misery. Another group hunched over old-fashioned sewing machines as guards walked up and down the aisles, whips in their hands.

"Prisoner 85221," the ogre grumbled to the guard closest to us. He was slight but alluring in a way I couldn't define but felt in my gut. Dark hair. Yellow eyes. Demon. A powerful one.

"Put her on the machines." He pointed toward the back at an empty spot.

The ogre pushed me hard, my body barely keeping upright as I slammed into a table of people hemming items by hand. They peered up at me, glaring at me as though the disruption was my fault.

"Get to your station." The demon pointed to the chair. "Don't dally."

I righted myself, looking at the machine with aversion. This was not a skill I had been taught. I could drop a man with a pinch of my finger or wield a spear, but sewing was not in my arsenal of talents.

"I don't sew."

The room went silent, everyone stopping what they were doing, eyes landing on me with shock. Their expressions of "oh shit" made my stomach sink to the ground and my neck tingle with fear.

"Excuse me?" The demon stepped up to me, tapping the switch in his hand against his palm. "Did I ask you if you could sew?"

My throat bobbed.

"Answer me, 85221." His voice sounded like spikes covered in chocolate—smooth, delicious, but dangerous underneath.

"No, sir." My response croaked over my lips.

Crack!

The whip sliced across my face without warning, and fiery pain burst from my eye to my chin. A scream pitched from my gut, my bones thumping to the ground from the force as I fell in a lump.

"Say 'I'm sorry, *Master*.'"

Not able to catch my breath from the agony throbbing through me, I couldn't respond. I cupped my cheek, blood gushing from my split skin, my face feeling like it had been lit on fire.

Crack!

The whip belted across my torso, striking my still tender gunshot wound, anguish clawing up my throat.

"Say it!"

The words barely escaped my mouth.

"I didn't hear you. I want this entire room to hear you." He cracked the switch against my ankle.

"I'm sorry, Master," I spit out, blood pooling on the floor.

"Get up," he yelled at me.

From head to toe, every muscle seemed to go limp, traumatized by the assault.

"I said get up, human." The demon whipped my legs,

forcing another yelp to get stuck in my throat. "Last time I ask *nicely.*"

Grinding down on my jaw, I staggered to my feet, wobbling, but lifted my chin. It trembled with agony, but I bit back my pain and emotion.

"Unless I ask you a question, you do not speak except to say yes. Understand me?"

"Yes, Master." The bitter taste of copper glided over my tongue as I spoke.

"Good." His yellow eyes glided down my figure. "You have a warning, 85221. Next one, you will end up in the hole. Now go to your spot."

My face throbbed, still leaking blood, but I turned around and went to the station, sitting down behind the sewing machine.

"Idiot," a girl in a gray/human uniform hissed at me from the station to my right. Keeping my head down, I ignored her. I had been beaten up many times in my life, bloody and bruised, with several stints in intensive care. This was different. There I felt powerful. Resilient. I could fight back. Here, I was deprived of humanity, robbed of anything that made me believe I was strong, leaving me feeling weak and defenseless.

Fumbling with the machine, I heard a small cough to my right. At the third cough, I glanced over. A petite Asian girl with dark, silky hair tied back past her shoulders wore a yellow uniform. Her large, dark eyes drilled into me with intention, her head bobbing slightly to her hands.

She moved slowly, with purpose, threading the machine, her delicate fingers tapping on things, subtly showing me how to do it.

Tracking her movements, I copied them step by step. She would guide me with slight smiles or a shake of the head, her gaze always darting to the guards, watching so we didn't get caught.

Every time one passed us, her head would snap back down to her work until they walked off, then she'd return to helping me.

The fact she was willing to risk punishment to help me, cared to assist a human, made my heart swell with gratitude, which confused me. A fae was helping me while the human on my other side spat and glared at me, leaving me for the wolves.

The room was a mix of sexes and species, though I noticed a bigger ratio of humans here. This was probably all they thought we were capable of. Servant work.

Hours went by, and I worked until my ass, fingers, and back throbbed along with my cheek and stomach. A healer had come in and crudely covered the reopened injury along my ribs and put cream on my face, bitching I was getting blood on the clothes I was mending.

While others munched on moldy cheese and bread and drank a small cup of water from a dirty communal bin for lunch, I had to keep working, only getting one bathroom break before the dinner bell rang. Because of the lack of food, crippling pain, and loss of blood, I could barely stand when we were free to leave.

"You all right?" A soft voice barely made it to my eardrums as I gripped the table, pushing myself up onto my legs, my body complaining and revolting against me. Turning my head, I spotted the girl who had helped me. She was no more than five foot two, her persona cautious and shy, probably hoping to dissolve into the walls. She didn't seem like someone who'd be at Halalház.

She nodded at my face. "Be careful of Hexxus." Her dark gaze slid to the demon who had beat the crap out of me. He must be the top dog in here by the way the other guards bowed to his word. He had whipped three more people by the end of the day. "He gets energy from torturing people. Thrives off it. He actively seeks it out. Try not to give him a reason."

"I wasn't trying to." I hobbled for the door.

"You won't have to." Her voice was so soft I barely heard her over the jabber and movement of people heading for the mess hall. "It will find you."

"Find me?"

"Yes." She nodded. "Danger and violence want you."

My head turned to the tiny girl who barely looked older than seventeen—not that you could tell a fae's age by looking at one.

"They hover around you." Her black eyes almost made her look like she had no irises. "And you welcome them."

A figure clipped my shoulder, causing me to stumble. "Get the fuck out of my way," a woman snarled, shoving past me. "Watch yourself, new fish."

It was the human woman who had sat next to me. Blinking, I watched her graying-blonde bun move through the throng, her brown eyes glaring at me. What the hell was her problem?

"See," the girl said next to me.

I sighed, turning back to my fae companion.

"I'm Laura," I lied.

"You can call me Lynx."

"Well, thank you, Lynx. For helping me."

"Don't die." She blinked at me, then turned and walked away.

"O-kay." I shook my head and let it go. My mind focused on actually getting food this time. If I didn't, I wouldn't last more than a week, and I had a feeling I had only experienced the fluffier side of prison life.

This was a game of survival, and winner took all.

Chapter 13

Cries, screams, chants, bellows, and stomping of feet boomed through the arena, ricocheting off the walls, creating a frenzy of noise in my head. I cringed against the smells of blood, piss, and sweat. Every sense was assaulted and overwhelmed, my eyes unable to take in all the commotion around me.

"Fight! Fight!" Shouts were joined by the thud of stamping boots against the metal floor. I peered down into the pit as two people were shoved into the middle: a man in gray, the human, and the other man was the one who bullied me in line this morning, the bull-shifter, Rodriguez, who was three times bigger than his human counterpart.

Rodriguez smacked his barrel chest, his nose flaring as the crowd cheered for him, his ego soaking up the attention, lapping at it like cream.

The crowd hollered even louder. Even from my position way up, I could see the human shaking, urine staining his pants as he searched the arena for some kind of weapon. Rodriguez rolled his head around, a flicker of the bull underneath rippling to the surface.

"My gods." My hand went to my mouth, the manic energy shivering my body. "I thought there was no magic in here."

"There isn't," Tad yelled in my ear. "But that doesn't stop their essence from showing. Underneath they are more beast than they are men."

"The human is already at a disadvantage. He has no chance against him."

"Exactly." A woman slid next to me, bumping my shoulder, her navy eyes flicking to me with an evil smile. "Eliminate prisoners, especially humans, while you entertain the crowds. Perfect way to keep down the population in here, all while we keep cheering for more. Welcome to the gladiator games of Halalház. Where two go in and only one comes out."

The pit was set up resembling pictures I'd seen of the old Colosseum in Rome. Layered stands circled a dirt arena, where men and animals fought to the death.

"Do the fae always fight humans?" Is this why there were so few left?

"Not all the time. It's survival of the fittest. Which usually means humans lose. The first fight is usually new fae versus human or human against human. But whoever wins moves up and fights the winner of the fight last week to the death. You keep winning, and you keep living, fae or human." The demon shrugged. "As I said, humans usually die first. Since I've been here, no human has moved up."

Because fae were stronger, faster, and harder to kill. Humans stood no chance.

"What brings you slumming with a Druid and human, Kek?" Tad asked, his attention on the match below.

Kek, in the old Hungarian language, meant "blue." Her hair and eyes were certainly that.

"It's my day of charity." She shrugged, her attention halting on a group of demons located near the middle of the stands, their red uniforms resembling a sea of blood. Why wasn't she with them? What was she after? Didn't take a genius to understand you didn't trust anyone here. Everyone was out for their own. "Plus, this girl is fucking hot. Nice to have some different eye candy around here."

Almost all fae were uninhibited sexually, not having limitations when it came to gender, but still could have a preference. Not something I had dealt with much in my walled world. Humans in my sphere had reverted to being very staunch about sex and sexuality.

"Or could it be no one likes you. Not even your own kind," Tad replied evenly.

"They like me the same as they like you, old man." She snorted. "People call me Kek, by the way." She flipped her braid to the other shoulder.

"Laura."

She burst out laughing. "Sure. *Laura*."

"What does that mean?"

"Lovely name. It's just not yours."

"And Kek is yours?"

It was Tad's turn to chuckle. "Touché."

"All right, human." Her eyes ran down me with appreciation. "You can play. I like it."

A bell chimed, directing my attention back to the floor. The human was darting around, panic controlling his actions. It was something they quickly drilled out of us in school, tossing us the first day into a mock situation. If you let fear control you, you "died" and failed the first level of training.

This human was not a fighter.

Bile burned at the back of my throat as Rodriguez moved in with self-assurance.

"How do they pick who goes in?"

"The first ones nominated are those who cause trouble. You get in the hole more than twice? Your name is up on the list. If you get on the wrong side of a guard, they can put up your name. If they run out of those, it's by a lottery system," Tad explained. "Some have even volunteered."

"Volunteered?" My mouth dropped open. "Why?"

"If you win, you live like a king until the next fight. You win again, you become worshipped and can get away with so much more than before. To humans knowing they will die here anyway, why not go with perks? To most fae winners? They start believing they're invincible. They think they can beat the top fighter. Rodriguez has won the last two times. His ego is impregnable. You keep working up to the top position. Fae after fae has died to achieve that spot, but only one has held it continually."

I glanced at the old man, his bushy eyebrows lifting.

"*Him.*" He pointed, a knowing indication in his tone. My gaze followed his hand, landing on the man he was motioning to. Air clipped in my lungs. In a cushy chair in the middle of the stands, in a place of power sat Warwick, an emperor on his throne. No one dared to get near him, but many hovered close, drawn to him. His expression warned you to run the opposite way, like you'd be burned up if you dared look in his direction. But at the same time, you couldn't stop from wanting to move closer, needing to be near him, even if it turned you to ash.

He will kill you without blinking... and he's so unbearably hot, you go willingly."

Once again, he sat with his legs parted, one up on the ledge, surveying his kingdom without moving his head. Dangerous and powerful didn't convey the magnetism of this man.

A cry from the pit drew my attention from him. The crowd repeated a word over and over as Rodriguez jumped down on the human. The man swung and scratched at the bull's face, scrambling behind a box to hide. I noticed a few items you could use as weapons were placed around the pit—wood poles, blocks, and rocks—but the human didn't seem to notice them.

The chants grew louder, blending into one drum.

"What are they saying?"

"Blooding," Kek replied. "It's when the crowd is ready for blood to spill, blooding the ground."

Rodriguez snapped a wood pole in half with his foot. Twirling it, he pointed the ragged end at the human. More urine soaked the human's pants as he tried to hide, his body rolling up in a ball.

"This is disgusting. Barbaric." My throat watered with acid. "This isn't a fight."

"Did you think the *House of Death* would be fair?" Kek's blue-tinted eyebrows curved up. "That it was actually unicorns and rainbows in here?"

"No." I glared at her, motioning out to the pit. "But at least make it a fair fight."

"Fair." Tad snorted. "You humans love to throw that word around."

"Bull. Bull. Bull!" The mob roared as Rodriguez went in to kill the human, the spikey edges of the broken pole getting within an inch of the man before he'd stop. Every time the crowd grew louder and more savage. His ego was drinking it up, loving the attention, playing the human like a toy.

The man sobbed, rolling up tighter.

My stomach squeezed at the sickness of this whole scene, the eager, excited faces in the crowd enjoying this cruelty.

After several more times of Rodriguez taunting them, they started to get restless, booing him. You could see it in his demeanor, the shift, realizing he was losing his fans. He glared at the crowd and roared.

With one last dramatic heave, the stick speared through the man's chest, twisting and shoving it deeper. Blood gushed as his body violently flopped, and a gutting bellow ripped from the dying man's throat.

I twisted my head away, grateful the thundering crowd absorbed most of the human's screams of death. Swallowing over and over, I forced back the bile trying to come from the depths of my stomach.

The crowd's chants of "Bull! Bull!" drew my attention back to the pit where a guard dragged the dead human out, a blood trail smearing the packed dirt. Rodriguez was up on a box with his arms open, rallying the crowd to chant his name. He would have probably stayed there until the last cheer, but two guards finally hauled him out of the arena.

I thought the excitement before was intense, but the second Rodriguez disappeared, the stomping began again, people screaming and wailing with a chilling verve, the air clotting with brutal energy.

"Now for the main act," Kek muttered into my ear, flicking her chin at a humongous beast-man ambling out into the pit; his bare feet were at least the length of my arm. He appeared part giant and part something else I couldn't identify. He was wide with huge hands and at least ten feet tall. He had tan skin and was hairless except for a long black beard, which accentuated beady black eyes. He wore a yellow outfit that had been sewn together from several uniforms.

A few select cheers rippled through the stands.

"They don't like this guy?"

"He once was a favorite." She folded her arms, sitting back on her heels. "But it's hard to get behind and cheer for a dead guy."

"Dead guy?" I exclaimed, looking back at the monster in the middle of the pit. "Who could kill him?"

Right then, the assembly went crazy, their booming chants zinging up my skin.

"War-wick! War-wick!"

The man himself strolled into the pit as if it were a sunny afternoon, and he had nowhere to be.

My attention flickered to the spot in the stands where I had seen him sitting a moment ago, which was now empty. Fuck. This guy really did move like a ghost.

His fans went ballistic, banging and thumping. The metal under my feet vibrated so violently it rumbled up my spine, wobbling my legs. None of it seemed to faze him. Not taking any notice of the crowd, he rolled his neck and shoulders, stretching as if he had recently woken up from a nap. The giant towered over Warwick, but strangely, it didn't minimize him at all. Where the giant took up the immediate space around him, Warwick Farkas took up the room, his presence shoving against my skin and down my throat.

Not an ounce of emotion fluttered over Warwick's face as he prepared to fight this creature.

A buzzer sounded through the room, the chants quieted down, and people watched the two men circle each other. The giant swung first, his movements quicker than I figured. Warwick didn't even try to make a move. Goliaths usually moved slower, making it possible for the Davids to win.

Not this one. The giant was swift and not at all clumsy with his actions, his large fist grazing Warwick's head as Warwick dropped to the ground, rolling away and jumping to his feet so smoothly it looked choreographed.

Warwick's actions were efficient and controlled. Standing right in front of the beast, he somehow slipped in closer, jabbing the brute in the gut. The giant looked confused, waving his arms around as if he was batting at a fly, allowing Warwick to slip around and kick him in the back of the knees.

The giant dropped to the ground, and the crowd sang with brutal enthusiasm.

The giant roared, his expression pinching with fury. He clamored to his feet, whirling back to Warwick. In a blink, the Wolf was already behind him again, fisting him in the back of his spine.

Crack!

His hand ricocheted off bone, and the giant bellowed again. He tumbled to the ground, his back curved in pain.

"Warwick, we love you," a woman screamed. For a second, his eyes darted to the stands, stopping on me. Or that's what it seemed like. I knew there was no way, but the fire in his aqua eyes tore through all the voices, people, and commotion to find mine.

My gaze dropped to see the giant reach for the stick Rodriguez had left on the ground, still coated in blood and matter, directing it toward his enemy.

Behind you! For a second, it felt as if I was down in the pit with him, yelling in his ear, but just as quickly it was gone.

Warwick swung around as though he heard something, but not fast enough. The spear drove deep into his hip.

Warwick's form jerked, but he made no noise, his muscles locking down as he tore the harpoon out of his flesh and tossed it to the side as the giant got back up. The giant was in pain, saliva dripping down his chin as he growled at Warwick.

The Wolf lowered his head in fury, rolling back his shoulders, done playing.

The giant leaped for him. Warwick dropped, cracking his arm against his knees, bending them the wrong way. With a cry, the beast toppled over, panic and pain on his face as he crashed onto the ground with force. Dirt sprayed up, clotting the air and spewing debris as if a bomb had gone off.

Warwick leaped onto the man's back, wrapping his arms and legs around his thick neck.

Shouts and cheers of excitement thundered through the stands.

"Blooding! Blooding!"

The giant rolled, thrashing against Warwick's hold, whipping them back and forth vehemently, smacking the Wolf against the dirt and slicing gashes into his face. Blood trickled down Warwick's temple, but like a boa constrictor, the legend coiled up tighter, his jaw locking as he tried to hold the massive man in place.

"War-wick!" People throughout the arena shouted for him.

The giant's bulk twitched and flopped as Warwick tightened his hold even more, crushing his windpipe, snapping his neck. The monster's body went instantly limp, sagging into Warwick. He held on a few more beats before Warwick released his arm, shimmying out from under the giant's weight.

The crowd went insane: jumping, screaming, chanting, and clapping. He stood up, wiping the blood off his face with his arm. He glanced up, and once again, I swore his gaze met mine through the throng of people, way up where I was seated. Unsettling aqua eyes burned up into the stands. It felt like they had the power to part the crowd and land exactly on me, ripping the oxygen from my lungs.

Then he jerked his head away, spun around, and strolled out of the pit in the same lazy, cocky manner he'd walked in. While Rodriguez fed off the crowd, Warwick seemed ambivalent to them. And they loved him more for it.

Four guards came in to drag the dead giant away, struggling to move him. It was then I realized Warwick didn't use a weapon, choosing to kill the monster with his bare hands. The bloody broken spear still lay right where he chucked it.

He never needed it.

"Wow," I muttered to myself in utter awe of this man.

"Told you." Tad slowly turned to me, grunting. His back curved farther over, his hand on his hip, a puff of pain coming from him. "You had to see this for yourself."

"Yeah." I inhaled. No one could have described this scene to me in a way that would have prepared me, with its deafening noises, assaulting smells, and violent energy. It was an onslaught of extreme emotions, thrilling and exhausting, which left a trail of acid burning in my stomach and throat.

A bell rang through the arena, sounding dim compared to the chants around me for the last hour.

"Curfew." Tad tilted his head at the sound of the bell. "Better get to your cell. You don't need any more lashings." He pointed to my face and exposed bruises, the evidence of my beating.

With Kek in the lead, the three of us made our way out of the pit and into the hallway.

"See you tomorrow, little lamb." Kek winked at me before slipping into a crowd heading down a corridor.

"I also bid you good night." Tad hobbled off in another direction, swept up in the throng of people.

The masses moved me along, bouncing and smashing into me like bumper cars as we all tried to file into the dim tunnel toward our cell level. The crowd thinned as more exited toward their block.

For that hour, I had forgotten about my aching body and torn flesh. Now exhaustion swallowed me, my eyes aching with the need to sleep, my shoulders heavy from the long, brutal day.

It was a moment—a stupid lapse in judgment. I had briefly let myself relax. Let my guard down.

It would be the last time.

Because when you lowered your defenses, that was when the monsters attacked.

Chapter 14

A fist smashed into my skull, and pain sliced across my vertebrae with a blast as my wounded face smacked the floor. My nerves lit up like fireworks as my bones thumped on the rough ground.

"Bitch!" A boot struck my torso, hitting the bullet wound. I jackknifed into a ball, forcing a groan from my lips. My head swirled with confusion, agony slowing down my thoughts, making it harder to understand what was going on.

"This *kurva* is already acting like she owns the place. Thinks her pretty face will get her everything as it did on the outside." A woman's voice spoke over me. I twisted my head to see the attacker. The blonde human from the laundry room stood over me, her unpleasant face scrunched with hate. Two other women in gray stood on each side. One was of what I guess to be Japanese descent, stocky with graying black short hair; the other appeared to be of more Slavic origins with weedy light brown hair in a tight braid.

"You think you're already a big fish here?" The blonde snarled down at me. "First day and getting in cozy with the Druid and a demon?" She snapped her fingers. "Girls. I think she needs to learn her place, don't you? Where she is on the totem pole here… where the stanky fish belong."

Her two minions nodded in agreement.

The brunette minion stepped up, her boot treading over my hand. Cartilage and bones cracked and popped under her weight. A scream bubbled in my throat, but I pinched my lips together, a grunt huffing through my nose. She looked to be in her forties, rough and worn. Leathery. She was very lean from lack of nutrients. Her sagging expression showed she had nothing left and nothing to lose.

"That's not how it works here," the blonde snarled, brutal energy dancing off her. Clearly, she loved the power trip, especially having her backup team. She wanted me to cower. "You earn your place here, fishy, and you have yet to earn anything."

"She looks fuckin' familiar." The brunette shoved her boot to my neck, leaning over, her lids squinted, trying to figure out where she knew me from. The fear I might be recognized locked up my expressions. Being in Istvan's world made me very known; images of Caden and me along with Istvan and Rebeka circulated in the society gossip magazines and papers in *Leopold Weekly*. I hoped with no dress or makeup, far from the elite world, no one would recognize me, not placing the charity princess in Halalház. But my unique features could be the very thing that outed me. "Doesn't she?" She peered over at the leader, her voice harsh and coarse.

"All privileged bitches look the same to me," Blondie snarled, cracking her boot into my stomach wound again.

I shoved down the unbelievable pain screaming over every inch of my body. This was the first time anybody had ever successfully snuck up on me. Ever. And it pissed me off that it was this common bitch.

Suddenly, my injuries, lashings, the fact I had only eaten a slice of bread for dinner, and my blood loss didn't matter.

Like Bakos had told us, enemies waited to attack when you were at your weakest. There was no excuse. I let my guard down. My mind circled the scenario, assessing all the places they had me at a disadvantage.

Use your weakness against them.

"I don't need to earn." My gaze met hers. "I. Take." I waited a second to let her absorb my intention. My fingers wrapped around the foot on my neck, and I yanked hard. Using the energy of her fall, I swung my legs up and kicked out, my boot cracking against the blonde's face, flinging her back into the rail.

"Mio, get her," the blonde screamed at her Asian friend.

As I tried to scramble back to my feet, Mio's stubby leg slammed into my gut, knocking my ass back to the ground with a gush of air. The lean chick leaped back on her feet and rushed me, kicking and scratching at me.

"You bitch!" I heard the blonde snarl, joining in with her friends.

Come on, Brex! Get up. I tried to conjure energy from the depths of my soul, knowing I could take these three, but it leaked out of me like a blown tire. The lesion from earlier had torn open again, spilling blood down my side and face. My gunshot wound burned as my skin tugged.

A kick to the gut curled me over with a cough, my brain shutting down. They continued to beat me until I was coughing blood.

From a distance, a whistle snapped off the metal, shrilling the air. "Stop!"

The three paused, looking down the walkway.

"Enough," a man's voice boomed down to us.

"Grab it," the blonde hissed to the brunette. She slunk past me into my cell.

Steady footsteps running down the metal catwalk vibrated beneath me.

"Come on, Dee." The blonde motioned to her friend, who was already running away.

Dee leaped over me, her arms filled with my blanket. The three of them bolted off. My lids fell closed, my body no longer able to fight the pain coursing through me.

I could hear the guards yell after them, their footsteps stopping when they got to me.

"Damn. They broke her good." The sultry voice reminded me of the guard on the front gate when I first arrived, the pretty one who resembled a horse-shifter.

"Human-on-human crime." Another one snorted. "Like we give a fuck. Just drag her in."

"She looks in need of a healer," the first man replied. "She came in with a bad injury. Looks like she's already been whipped and beaten since."

"Why do we give a shit? Just a human. One dies, we get ten more," the second one with a nasal voice huffed. "Just think of it as a test. She makes it through the night, then she's a survivor. She doesn't? Oh, well."

The sounds of the noisy prison echoed around me, but the first guy kept silent.

"Such a fuckin' bleeding heart, Zander," the second man snarled. "We had to hide for centuries because of humans. They deserve everything they get. Come on, help me drag her in."

I was in so much pain it all blended together as they dragged me in.

"Fuck. They took her blanket too." Zander's voice drifted over me softly.

"Not been a good day for the human. Tomorrow is not lookin' any better." Nasal laughter drifted from my cell, but every sound and feeling started to slip through my fingers, my body letting go, wrapping darkness around me. Right as I drifted off, I thought I felt a hand smooth across my temple, words drifting over me like a wisp of wind: "Fight. You need to survive."

"Dammit, Bitzy. Stop sticking your fingers up her nose." A yelled whisper fizzed in my ear, dragging me quickly to consciousness.

And agony.

The pain swept in instantly, forcing a groan from my lips before my eyelids even opened. Vomit pooled in my stomach, and I had to suck in slowly to keep it from coming up. I felt no central point of pain. It drenched every cell, every muscle, every nerve. My head pounded, sharp daggers piercing my brain every time my pulse thumped.

A chirp echoed in the cell, and I willed myself to open my eyes.

"Don't bitch at me. You're the one who woke her up."

Opie. My brain clasped on to awareness at the same time it wanted to shut back down and hibernate for months.

I licked my lips. All moisture had been sucked from my mouth, which tasted like I drank battery acid while something died in there. Forcing my lids open, the face of a brownie and an imp's two huge eyes took up my entire field of vision. I yelped.

"It's *a-live*!" Opie raised his arms, laughing crazily as if he was acting something out.

Don't vomit. Don't vomit. Cringing, I rolled onto my back, a loud whimper puffing from my lungs.

A chirp came from the imp.

"You enjoyed the movie too. Don't act like you don't." Opie sighed, waving his arms at her.

Chirp.

"Please, you could not do better," he replied.

Chirp.

"Okay, then go for it. I want to see you do it as well."

Chirp.

"Oh… well… that was pretty good."

There was so much talking—so much noise. I curled back into a ball.

"Clearly not a fan."

One eye peeked open at them. Bitzy glowered at me. Raising her hand, she flipped me off.

"Really, Bitz. Is that necessary? Don't be sore because she liked my performance better." He shook his head. "I mean, I am the true artist here."

Chirp.

"I am not a wannabe."

"Please," I grunted, the effort to speak zapping at my strength. "Stop talking."

"You really did the first day with gusto, didn't you, little fish?" Opie stepped back up to me, touching my face with a cloth he held in his hand. Gently, he wiped away the dried blood around my mouth and nose. The whiff of rubbing alcohol bled into my nostrils. "I mean, if you're going to do something, do it with flair. Am I right?"

My notice dropped down to the outfit he was wearing. He made a bikini top with steel pot scrubbers and cut leg holes in a pink scouring pad that he wore as briefs.

"What the hell are you wearing?" I croaked, trying to lift my head, my fingers pressing into my forehead as slowly I sat up.

"It's pool day." His smile lit up his grumpy face.

Chirp.

"Okay, fine. It's my day to scrub dishes in the sink." He touched his homemade outfit like Bitzy had burst his pretend bubble. "I enjoy having a little fun with it."

A grin inched up my face, but I flinched in pain.

"Yeah, I wouldn't smile, blink, move, or even breathe deeply for a bit." Opie motioned to all of me. "You are a mess, fishy. Looks like you got the advanced new fish orientation. What happened?"

"Bitches happened."

"You just described everyone here. Narrow it down."

"Three human bitches." I rolled my fingers into my temples. "Trying to show me my place in the hierarchy here."

"Ahh. Mio, Dee, and Tess." He nodded. "They love to think of themselves as the leaders of the humans, put anyone new in their place right away."

Chirp.

"I'm sure she fought hard."

"What did it say?" I glared at the imp who appeared to be smirking at me.

"You just became their bitch."

"I. Did. Not."

"You did lose your blankie to them." Opie shrugged, nodding to the empty floor.

Fuck those bitches. They will go down.

Just not today.

The harsh morning bell rang through the stacked city, reverberating off the metal like an out-of-tune violin. The doors to our cages slid open.

Sick to my stomach, exhausted, and in agony, I didn't want to leave my cell. I simply wanted to sleep the rest of the day. But it would be a victory for them if I didn't show up.

They'd think they broke me. Even three against one, I would not bow to them.

A guttural cry began in my gut as I used the wall to rise, wrapping my arm around my middle, my bruised ribs protesting every movement. My uniform was spotted with drying blood, dirt, and what looked like vomit, which probably happened in the middle of the night and didn't remember. I bent over, sucking in gulps of air, slamming my jaw together to keep the tears from spilling down my face.

Chirp.

My gaze went to the imp. "What?"

"She just said you're a fucking idiot, but hey, I say the show must go on. Good on ya, fishy." He fisted the air in encouragement.

Having no energy to fight with an asshole imp, I shut my eyes, conjuring all the strength I could muster. Inhaling, I opened my eyes and took a step toward the door and almost fainted. Grabbing the bars, I watched the flood of prisoners heading to the bathroom, filling up the walkway. Many peered in at me, as though surprised to see me standing. All of them either encouraged or ignored the beating outside the cells the night before.

Camaraderie didn't exist here. Everyone for themselves. Every alliance was as thin as tissue paper.

"Have a good day, little fish," Opie yelled to me as I pitched myself into the throng, heading to the toilets with the herd of sheep. Halfway there, I almost turned back around. Consequences be damned.

"You are like fire, Brex. People try to put you out, but you come back with a roar," Caden's voice whispered in my head, the image of him leaning against the hospital room door, watching me put on my boots, heading back to training after

a brutal session which had put me in the clinic for a night. *"You amaze me."*

At the time, I thought friendship filled the sentiment, but now I could recall the way his eyes tracked me, a softness in them. Longing.

How did I not see it? Why did I not ever tell him how I felt? Now I would never have the chance to be with him. All because fear and misunderstanding kept both of us silent to what we really wanted.

Don't give up on me, Caden. I'm out here. Can you feel I'm still alive?

The memories of him drove me forward. I made it to the restroom, grabbing my kit out of my locker.

"Well, well." A voice stilled my movements. "I didn't think we'd be seeing you today."

Fuck me. Tess, Mio, and Dee grouped around me, their arms folded, faces wrinkled with abhorrence. Perhaps they didn't like that after it had taken three of them to take me down, I still got up the next day.

"I knew you'd miss me too much," I cooed, trying to keep my smile from turning into a grimace. Even speaking was agonizing. "Girls night was fun, wasn't it? I really feel we bonded."

Tess, the blonde leader, shifted her feet, her expression tightening, her nose taped from where my boot struck her. "Shut the fuck up, fish," she hissed, her crew moving in closer to her. "We went light on you. Make no mistake; we won't again."

"Ohhhh." A voice emerged beside me. "I enjoy it rough."

The trio's heads jerked to the figure at my side. Kek leaned her arm on my shoulder like we were chums.

"Oh, you weren't talking to me? How embarrassing." She grinned at them, showing her teeth.

"This has nothing to do with you, demon." Tess's voice softened, her bully pose deflating before my eyes.

"See, that's the thing." Kek's fingers brushed knotted strands from my face. "I kind of have a thing for this one. What happens to her is *my* business." Her eyebrows lifted.

She'd laid a challenge at their feet.

Tess grappled for a response, as though not wanting to show her limitation, but she also understood she couldn't fight a demon.

"Walk away," Kek ordered, moving her arm off me, standing straight. "Touch my girl again, and you deal with me."

Tess's jaw began to twitch as though with fury, nose flaring, but she finally stepped back.

"Whatever… like she's worth anything." She turned, motioning for her girls to follow.

Kek laughed lowly, patting my shoulder. "What a bunch of toothless cunts."

I stared at the floor.

"You're welcome, by the way." Kek leaned back, her hands going to her hips. "Looks as if I saved your ass from another beating. I mean, what the fuck? You were in bad shape when I left you last night. Did you actively go seek another fight?"

Slowly, I turned to her. Staring.

"What?"

"I don't need your help. I am *not* a defenseless little lamb."

"I can sense that. Believe me, I do not get any kind of weak vibe off you, which is why she had to challenge you with her buddies." She leaned her weight on one foot. "But right now, you are not in the best condition. I don't think you could have taken another beating. You can't see yourself, but yeesh." She cringed, motioning around my face and down my hunched figure.

If I looked half as bad as I felt on the inside, the outside must have been a horror show.

I studied Kek for a moment. Was I exchanging one bully for another one?

"Why are you protecting me? What's in this for you?" The skin of my lip split at the tiny tug of my sneer. "You want me as *your* bitch? Is that it? Jump on the fresh meat, forcing me to become indebted to you?"

Kek folded her arms, tilting her head.

"Sexual favors? Slave? What is it?"

"I'm not against either one." A grin hinted on her mouth. "But it's not why."

"Then why?"

Her eyes slid to the side, her shoulders rolling back. "I guess I just like you."

"Like me?" I huffed. "You don't even know me."

"You seem cool." She shrugged a shoulder, not looking at me. "I don't have a lot of friends here."

"And you thought we could be friends?" I turned fully to face her. "A human and a demon?"

Her blue eyes snapped to me.

"If you haven't noticed, the normal rules don't apply in here. Outside these walls, we might hate each other, try to kill the other, but in here, survival comes first. Not species."

Trust was fragile, and I wanted to keep my walls up, but for some reason, I believed her. "Tad mentioned the other demons don't like you. Why?"

A knowing smile pursed her lips. "Seeing if I'm a smart association to have?"

"As you said… it's about survival in here."

She chuckled, bobbing her head. "Fuck, I like you, little lamb."

"So?"

"I find them tedious and boring." Her eyes leveled with mine. "All they talk about is the good ol' days. Lounging around resembling pampered royalty, living off the fear our kind can cause on the outside. They forget we are impotent in here."

My lids narrowed.

"And I don't like them." Her arms went out. "Demons don't usually tolerate each other. We don't hang out in clubs or enjoy being around each other. We're territorial with large egos. Here, all the rules are bent, forcing us together like a band that hates each other but still has to perform together. We aren't a pack kind of species. We want to be the lone wolves. Leaders."

"Way too many metaphors in your explanation."

"See?" She gestured to me. "You have some sass. They are dull as shit."

"But why don't they like you?"

"Because I don't care about reminiscing the old days before the wall fell. It's gone. Get over it. I'm an in-the-present kind of girl. Plus, I tell them they are dull as shit and cunts." She gripped the ends of her braid. "Not really a people person."

Yeah. Me neither.

"Don't worry; I won't sit with you at lunch or anything. I have appearances to keep up as well." She rolled her eyes as she traveled to the toilets. "And the sexual favors… they will only be once a week." She winked over her shoulder.

"Kek."

"Kidding." She laughed. "Though once you go demon…"

Hobbling after her, I didn't even hesitate a moment to use the toilet. Funny how fast your standards dropped away when survival becomes your number one priority.

Chapter 15

If food fell on the floor in the Markos' dining room, the idea of picking it up and eating it would be scandalous. Uncivilized. Here, hunger had made me do just that at breakfast. Even beat up, I was about to cut an asshole for toast.

All I got was a half-eaten slice of bread and lukewarm coffee, but it was a win in my book. Rodriguez, recently off his victory, took most of the food for himself and his fellow shape-shifting group.

"You want to talk about it?" Tad took a sip of his coffee, his slice of toast sitting in front of him, untouched.

Nibbling on mine, I sucked down coffee to soften the dry bread sticking in my throat. I needed nutrients, but it tasted like shit, and my stomach was dicey at best. Though the food here was utterly tasteless and too bland to upset anyone's stomach.

"Not really." I shifted on the stool uncomfortably, every muscle and nerve crying out for painkillers.

"Will you retaliate?"

"Yes." I snarled. That bitch stole my blankie.

I used to have trunks stuffed with blankets. Faux fur, silk, cashmere—all of them so soft you melted into them. I never thought twice about the mounds of comforters, pillows, and blankets piled on my bed. Now the possessiveness I felt for a scratchy, smelly blanket should have frightened me. When you had nothing, those items you did have were treasures, and someone stealing them from you was the ultimate crime.

Tess and her gang would find out soon what a bad idea it had been to take stuff from me.

"You look like hell."

"So I've been told." I chewed down the rest of my meal. "You two are making me feel so good about myself."

"Two?"

"Kek." I rubbed my head, a deeper pounding thumping at my skull.

At Tad's silence, I looked up at him.

"What?"

"Just be careful." His lips pressed together, his gaze drifting over to the demon table where I knew she sat. Three words and he validated my suspicion about why a demon had latched on to me. And not for sexual favors or a prison pet.

"I am." I brushed my hands free of crumbs and pushed myself up to stand, though it took a couple tries.

"You sound like me." Tad chuckled as I keened and hissed getting to my feet, wrapping my arm around my torso. "Moaning and groaning over there."

"At least *I* will heal, old man."

"Keep that fire, girl. You will need it here." He winked at me, laughing.

Biting my lip, I grabbed my empty coffee cup. I knew it would take me longer than usual to get to the laundry room and did not want to chance being late.

"Here." He shoved his toast to me. "You need it more than me."

"No." I shook my head. "You need to eat. You're old and decrepit, remember?"

"Exactly. It's wasted on me." The youthful glint in his eyes suggested he was far from his deathbed. "Just take it. Someday I might need kindness from you." He dipped his head at the bread. "Take it."

Cautious, I took his offering, giving him a nod of thanks. Then I limped across the cafeteria and dumped my cup in the bin.

Something changed in the room, like fog rolling over a mountain, licking your skin with its presence. My arms prickled with the sensation, the hairs standing on end. It was also when I noticed the early morning murmur had gone quiet. The room was holding its breath.

My heart thumped at a rabbit's pulse. Slower than normal, I twisted around, my body shrieking in response. But just as fast as the pain struck my nerves, it vanished. As if the figure before me was emanating a sedative, taking away all my discomfort.

I was eye level with a black shirt, the chest underneath massive, forcing me to crane back to look up at the beast of the man. My throat strangled the air in my lungs.

Holy shit. Warwick Farkas.

To be this close to a legend. An icon. My brain struggled to recognize that he was real.

He stood less than five inches away, staring down at me, his intense aqua eyes even more unnerving this close. His weighty gaze rolled over me with curiosity as his head slanted to the side, a touch of disgust creased his brow.

He probably saw me as no more than a bug pinned to a board.

I didn't back away, holding my chin up, swallowing audibly.

His attention trailed down the lash mark on my face, the swollen eye, and halted on my broken lip. Flames flared down my back in a burst, licking my skin with perspiration. I swiped my tongue nervously over my lower lip. A crease appeared between his eyebrows before he journeyed down to the dried bloodstain on my uniform, how I still cradled my wound, and the bruises and cuts over my exposed skin.

Then without warning or verdict of his findings, he brushed past me, his arm grazing my skin, sending an electric shock through my body. I gasped for breath I hadn't even realized I'd been holding. Shivering, my shoulders relaxed as if his gaze had been a palpable weight on me.

What the fuck was that?

I surveyed the room, seeing if the encounter held their focus. Every pair of eyes were on me. They were slack-jawed and silent. Assessing and curious. But also angry, as if me getting his attention affronted them somehow.

Feeling the impact of their wonder, I swiveled around, ignoring my pain, which had returned with a vengeance, and hobbled out of the room as fast as I could.

Not far from the laundry room, I heard a soft voice, "What did I say?" Lynx stepped out of the shadows, and I jolted with her appearance.

"Fuck, Lynx." I cringed, everything in me revolting at the sudden movement. "Warn a girl."

"Why?" Her black eyes didn't blink. "I want to disappear into the shadows. Not be seen until it's too late."

"Good job then."

"I warned you. Danger and violence like you," she said softly, melancholy weaving through her words like a song. "I fear there is no going back now."

"What are you talking about?" I resumed walking, the

laundry facility in sight. “Don’t tell me you’re clairvoyant or something. Do those powers still work in here?”

“No. Nothing like that.” She matched my slow steps. “It’s not hard to see you just invited the worst sort of trouble in. His attention on you is not good for you.”

Warwick.

“I didn’t really have a choice. He was kind of there. In my way.”

“He’s never done that. No one has ever drawn any bit of his notice. Not even the ones he kills.”

Her statement wrapped around my throat like a noose. “Again, not something I could control.” I brushed it off with a shrug.

“True or not, you have opened the door for trouble. Good or bad, he put a bullseye on your back without saying a word, and you can’t die,” she said nonchalantly, strolling into the room and to her workstation.

Confused by her last statement, I rubbed my forehead. She was right about one thing. By looking at me, Warwick had marked me. Many would try to figure out what had captured his interest in me, even as brief as it was.

This kind of attention was not a good thing. The others would want to find out what had caused the notorious Warwick Farkas to pause.

And then they would try to destroy it.

Over the next week, fellow inmates circled me like sharks trying to figure out the piece of meat in the water. I felt eyes on me from every angle.

Except his.

Warwick had gone back to acting as if I didn’t exist, which I thought would ebb the curiosity. It didn’t.

The first full week of my incarceration had been hell. By day I pretended I wasn't terrified, homesick, and utterly hopeless. By night I curled up in a ball, crying silently on the cold hard ground.

Daily assaults tore at my psyche: the smell of the relieving hole only steps from where I laid my head, sleeping on packed earth like some animal, and being left in the same bloody, grimy clothes. I knew I smelled bad, but mine was a drop in the sea of stench.

Torture and terror stripped away at my sense of self. I felt primal. My mind slipped from reality and what I used to understand as normal. I had lost weight from stress and the lack of food. Even in sleep, my body never fully let go of the tension, and constant screams and guttural sobs woke me throughout the night, as well as my own nightmares.

I looked forward to sleep, though, because it brought dreams of Caden—feeling warm and restful. Though it hurt like a bitch when I woke up realizing where I was and that I would never see him again. Most likely, he thought I was dead. The "what ifs" of our story were punishment enough, but everything here was set to break you, even your own mind.

There were times death sounded like a dream. One you were glad to not wake from.

"Level 13!" A deep female voice boomed right as the door to my cell slid open, jolting my head up. "Shower day."

Movement stirred on my level as sleepy prisoners in all colors of uniforms strolled by. Pushing myself up, I joined the zombie train, stumbling toward the washroom.

I'd accepted my lack of privacy to some degree, but showering in front of all these people was another slash at my comfort. At my sense of safety. How arrogantly I had acted at HDF, thinking I was so bold and comfortable with my body around others. I had been with my small *safe* group of friends.

"Come on," the same guard yelled. "You know the drill. Undress. Clean. And get out for the next. No funny business."

A few guards were stationed around the room, not hiding their glee at watching the prisoners disrobe. A giant laundry cart sat near the open showers along the wall, ones I'd be washing and mending later. A table was set up with clean uniforms, underwear, and towels with your number on display on the top of the pile.

Grabbing my kit, I watched as veteran prisoners leaped at the chance to be first. Some shared a showerhead.

"Come on, fish." A guard came up behind me, tugging at my soiled top. His nasal voice sounded vaguely familiar, reminding me of the night Tess and her group beat me up. "Can't be shy or modest here. Strip!"

My nose flared as I inhaled a shaky breath, my throat closing.

"Don't you love when they are fresh and new? Scared and horrified?" Another guard chuckled. "Never lasts long, but most of the time, neither do they."

Don't cry. Don't cry.

"Now!" the first guard bellowed. Getting a better grip, he ripped my shirt over my head, along with my sports bra. Ice filled my bones, my eyes burning as the violation poured down on me. Laughter from the prisoners at seeing me humiliated resounded in my ears.

"You want me to do the rest?" The guard rubbed his crotch roughly into my backside, tugging at my thin pants, his hand snaking down them. "I have no problem stripping you naked while everyone watches." He motioned out to the room, all eyes on me, burning into my bare skin.

Unable to respond, I shakily got undressed, tossing the rest of my clothes in the bin. My jaw clenched so hard to keep from crying, and it sent sharp pains up my face as I tugged off my underwear.

"You can join me, fish." Some called to me as I strode to a shower, keeping my head level and my gaze on the cascading water, my kit in my hands. The water hit my skin like needles, the cool temperature tensing my already taut muscles, and I gasped and cried out as it burned against my tender flesh.

Two people moved in next to me, and within seconds their grunts pulled my attention. Both figures faced the wall. A gorgeous male fae, his hands on the hips of the woman in front of him, pounded into her while his eyes remained fixed on me. His brown eyes glinted when our gazes met, and he thrust into the female harder.

My body reacted. It was human nature after all, but a swirl of disgust and heat passed over me. The spark of need throbbed between my thighs, to feel a moment of bliss for one second here.

"Yeah, you want me to fuck you next?" His gaze dragged down me, stopping on my breasts, my nipples hardening. "This turn you on, fish?"

"You can join us." The woman's eyes slid to me, her teeth biting into her lip, clearly enjoying that I was watching.

I turned away, though I could not block out their laughs and slapping noises. My other view was of two fae males going at it in the U-shaped stall. None of the guards were stopping any of them, as though this was their personal live porno.

I pulled out my shampoo, wanting to wash and get out quickly. Scrubbing my body and hair, the two next to me finally finished and left, allowing the next person to move in.

"Well, well, if it isn't the fish without her protector." A woman's voice came behind me. "Where's your wife, little fish?"

Dread filled my gut as I slowly cranked my head over my shoulder.

Tess, Mio, and Dee. The three bitches of terror block B stood behind me.

Their nudity seemed to shield them, while mine left me feeling vulnerable.

"What will you do without your girlfriend?" Tess crossed her arms over her saggy tits. Her skin was wrinkled and old.

My gaze darted over her shoulder to the guards. They stayed in position, either not concerned with us or too busy watching people have sex.

"Can I tell you how much I love having your blanket?" Tess smirked. "I use it to wipe my ass after I take a shit."

Not responding to her taunt, I tried to finish cleaning up.

"Don't fucking ignore me," she growled, drawing attention from people around me.

Silently, I got the rest of the shampoo from my hair.

"I said, don't ignore me, stupid bitch." Tess slammed a hand into my back, my face cracking into the tile wall. The blood tingled as it rushed out of my nose.

The taste of the copper substance ignited fire in my veins. Whirling around, my knuckles crunched straight into her nose, pain rippling through my hand and up my arm.

Tess hit the ground with a slap, blood spurting out of her nose. Her shrieks echoed off the walls.

Mio and Dee leaped for me.

All emotion shut down; the only thing left on was my survival mode. Anger, frustration, sadness, and grief tunneled together. I'd had enough. The primal instinct to end the constant threat, to protect myself, rushed down my limbs.

They snapped my last fuck.

I heard the feral cry burst out of me, felt the impact of

my fist breaking across Dee's cheek, then punching again into her neck. She dropped to the ground, her hand at her throat, wheezing for air. A punch burrowed into my side, which increased my anger. Flipping around, I rammed into Mio's stomach with my knee. Bending her over, my elbow slammed down into her spine, her face slapping against the wet tiled floor.

I saw the guards running for us, yells and whistles blending into white noise.

Tess leaped back up, coming for me. Rage like I had never known before roared up my throat as I barreled into her, taking her to the ground with a smack. I didn't hesitate as my knuckles broke across her face over and over, her blood turning the water beneath us a deep pink.

"Stop!" Two guards yanked me off her by my arms and pulled me to my feet.

Tess's head lay limply to the side. Only the slight lift of her ribs told me she was still alive.

I snarled, tugging my arms out of the guard's grip. Stunned, they watched me walk back to the shower, wash off the blood, and turn it off. Snatching up my kit, I took in a deep breath and twisted around, scanning the blur of faces observing me. The silence in the room teemed with tension and shock. Maybe a little fear.

Without a word, I lifted my chin and walked to the table. I grabbed my pile of fresh clothes, threw them on, and waited for what I knew would come.

The guards were right on me, clutching my arms again, marching me out of the washroom. I didn't wonder where I was going. I knew.

The notion that I was provoked didn't matter. "Fair" was not a known word here.

We headed farther down into the earth.

Lynx was right; danger and violence liked me.

And I welcomed it.

Darkness.

Endless night.

They soaked into your mind, driving anyone mad after a time, which wasn't the cruelty of the pit. Nor was being in isolation. Hell, that was a holiday in my book compared to being with the group upstairs. I actually thought I might be able to get rest in here. Sleep a whole night.

Funny.

It wasn't the gnawing pain of hunger or your brain tricking you in the pure blackness, the absence of understanding time or how long they would leave you.

No. It was the bouts of noises pounding relentlessly into the tiny space that drove you to the brink of madness. Then it would stop for a while, easing you into stress-induced sleep, just to drive you awake with more. Minutes passed like years in which I lost not only sense of time, but of space. There was no place to go, yet my body still knocked against the walls, my fingers clawing at the surface, trying to escape the torture.

They changed the sounds just enough you could never tune it out to doze off. They reduced me to a sniveling blob curled in the corner. I welcomed death, hoping it would finally give me peace. Finally, for a moment, quiet surrounded me, and I fell into a wearied sleep.

A loud creak sounded as light burned across my lids, popping them open.

Flinching, I scrambled away from the painful light in the same way a terrified animal would. My emotions were torn down to primal responses. Instinct shoved my back into the wall, where I curled myself into the tiniest ball as a looming figure outlined the doorway.

"Learned your lesson, 85221?"

My eyes squinted against the blaring glow, but I could make out the silhouette of a guard, the one who had stripped me in the washroom.

"Get up," he barked.

I couldn't move, my heart pattering against my ribs.

"I said." He reached down, grabbing me by the arms and tugging me up. "Get. Up." His closeness made my skin twitch. I had the urge to snarl and bite his hands.

"How did you enjoy three days in the hole?" His eyes glinted, a sneer upping his mouth. A deep white scar hooked up his top lip; otherwise, he was very nondescript for a fae. "Want three more?"

My fuzzy teeth clenched together.

"Answer me, 85221."

"No." The syllable croaked as if my vocal cords had completely lost the ability to make words.

"No, what?"

"No, sir." I boiled inside, my lids narrowing on him. This place had fostered hate within me; it was the primary emotion driving me now.

Prisons thrived on breaking people down and rebuilding them. Maybe it worked for others—bad people. But when you broke down good people, we didn't rise again as even nicer people. No. That's not how it worked. We rose like a dragon, one that would spew fire and burn everything to ash.

We became the depraved.

Chapter 16

Allowed a quick restroom break, I brushed my teeth, peed, and washed my face. The fae guard observed my every move with a perpetual sneer on his face. He enjoyed watching me, especially on the toilet.

I stared back at him, detached and unrelenting, like a creepy child in a horror movie.

He stirred on his feet as if he didn't anticipate my response. He expected me to be a lump of clay with my head lolling forward. A broken toy. Obedient. Debased.

"Hurry up," he barked, jerking away from me, heading for the door. "Breakfast is almost over, but if you hurry, I'm sure you can lick the crumbs off plates in the bin."

A flush of anger throbbed at the back of my neck, but I swallowed it down, getting up and washing my hands. My eyes lifted to the scratchy metal mirror above the sink.

My face was thinner, highlighting my already sharp features and making me look more severe and intimidating. Wounds still marred my lip and eye, but the swelling was gone, and only light bruises were left. My eyes were the most unsettling. The inky color resembled pools of death, and if you looked closely, you would fall into the flames of hell. The girl in the mirror was a stranger. Cold. Empty.

"Come on," he snarled, then stood up straighter when my eyes landed on him. He stalked out into the hallway, heading to the mess hall.

The space was abuzz with noise and activity, smelling of waterlogged oats and eggs, with a dusting of burned coffee. There were moments in the hole when my stomach ached so badly from hunger it clawed and tore at the seams, and the thought of even this garbage food sounded heavenly.

Now I felt nothing. I was past hunger, past exhaustion, past sanity. They wanted to rip the humanity out of me? I hoped they were ready for what they asked for.

I stood at the entrance, staring into the room. My return was whispered throughout the room, heads whipping toward me, voices dropping away. Tess, Mio, and Dee swiveled around, their faces still looking like used punching bags. Tess stood up, but Mio grabbed her arm, pulling her down again, shaking her head.

My gaze glossed over the crowd, catching on a face in the back. His turquoise eyes were a beacon in the night, drawing me in from a turbulent sea. Alone, sitting on his bench, his boot perched on the opposite seat, he leaned against the wall, arms crossed.

The bored king.

He didn't move or respond, but the heaviness of Warwick's eyes tried to pin me to the floor again. This time I shoved back with my own, one of my eyebrows lifting. Defying. The one thing I promised myself in the hole was no one would control me. They could beat me, starve me, torture me, but my mind and will were mine.

You may scare everyone and dominate this room, but you will not rule me.

As if he sensed my rebellion, his lip lifted, in a smirk or a threat, I could not tell. I didn't move, didn't look away.

Everyone else around us disappeared, becoming blurry images in my periphery. Heat licked at the base of my spine, fear and anger riding up.

He cocked his head to the side.

I copied his movement.

Like a cat stretching after a slumber in the sun, he took his time rising to his feet. Damn, I had forgotten how massive this guy was. Meeting him did not diminish the folklore. If anything, he amplified it, intensified everything we heard this man was capable of.

Prickles of panic danced along my shoulders, but I stood my ground. His boots lazily hit the floor as he moved toward me, pounding along with my heartbeat. His arms were so ripped they swung like carved tree branches, his dark hair down around his shoulders, rendering him feral and animalistic. Hunting his prey. A smirk twitched his lips as he moved up to me. The air swirled around, whispering in my ear to run.

The edges of his boots hit mine, halting his approach. Using his towering height, he peered down at me, his arms brushing my skin as he folded them.

I couldn't help the internal gasp at his touch, though I swallowed it back down, my jaw cinching together.

He smirked, clearly aware of how his power affected others.

Arrogant bastard.

He huffed out of his nose, a slight humored expression twitching his cheek. "How adorable," he rumbled.

Oh. Holy. Shit. I realized I had never heard him speak. His voice could have been used as a weapon in itself. It was gravelly, deep, seductive, and my body reacted to the timbre. It felt like swimming naked in a barrel of the best whiskey imported from Scotland. Smooth, sexy, stinging, and callused all at the same time. It licked my pussy, carved into my bones, and heated my skin.

Pain and pleasure, pulsing my core.

He had to be fae. No matter how good he was at hiding his aura, no human had this kind of allure. He was confident in tricking everyone, playing everyone for a fool, controlling us like subordinates, which had rage bounding up my shoulders.

He would not control me.

"Thank you." I cheekily winked back. "Though I can't say most would consider me *adorable*. But to each their own."

A nerve convulsed under his eye. "You think going into the hole for three days makes you tough and ruthless now? Can get lippy with me?" The words were so deep and low they vibrated through my bones.

Gods, please stop talking. I tried to put a barrier around me by wrapping my arms around my chest. I despised the way my body flushed.

"Try two months, *then* come challenge me."

Two months? He put up with that torture for two months and came out alive? I barely lasted three days. No doubt I would have found a way to end things if they left me longer.

"Know your place, fish." He leaned in even closer, his form looming over me. He could drive my blood in two opposing ways with the same intensity.

Exhilaration.

Animosity.

"This is my kingdom." He slanted his head, rolling his threat into my other ear. "You are *allowed* to live in it." He shoved his face into mine, forcing a wheeze of air to whistle up my nose. He then paused. I peered up at him, his eyes boring into mine.

Anger. Hate.

Confusion?

"Move. You're in my way." His nose flared, and in a blink, he was moving, his shoulder slamming into mine as he sauntered out of the room. I stumbled back, the bell ringing like he had it cued to his exit.

Gradually, noise and movement stirred in the room as prisoners headed toward their next location.

"Holy goddesses." Tad's hobbled up next to me; his curved back bent him far over today. "What is it about you?"

"What do you mean?"

"It's just interesting the two people who have no auras are drawn to each other."

"We are not drawn to each other," I retorted, snarling at the gray-haired man.

A smile arched his mouth.

"What?" I huffed.

"I didn't say if it was a good thing or a bad thing." His eyes slid to mine. "Lust. Hate. Those two are so hard to tell apart."

"Shut up, old man." I rubbed my head. The adrenaline rush that man created in me made me want to flee for higher ground. "Not in the mood for your cryptic Druid shit."

"Someone came out of the hole in a bad mood."

I shot a glare at him, and he smiled hugely.

"Glad to have you back in one piece. That you are okay." He patted my shoulder. "I actually missed you."

"You missed having someone to talk to."

"Is there a difference?" He bumped his hip into me, his hand sliding something in mine before he shuffled away.

Staring down at my hand, I blinked, tucking back the emotion.

A full piece of toast.

It was almost as though he knew I would be coming out today and saved it for me.

"85221." Hexxus's powerful voice crawled up the back of my neck, tightening the air leaking through my esophagus. "Is this all you've done?" He picked at the clothing pile on my station as if it were contaminated. "Your daily quota doesn't stop simply because you are not here."

"What?" I blanched. Did he mean I had three days plus today to catch up on?

Still trying to learn to use the machine, my fingers were raw, and my exhausted mind and body were moving much slower than others.

"Do you know what happens when you don't keep up on your quota?"

I stared up at him.

"Answer me!"

I figured it was more of a rhetorical question, sir.

Gasps simmered in the room, telling me I had said it out loud. *Shit.* My fatigued brain had just let my thoughts slip out.

Hexxus's entire form inched higher as fury filled him, his eyes turning black.

"What did you say to me?"

Coming out of torture just hours earlier with no rest or food, I had hit the part of the day when I had nothing left. I had eaten the extra piece of toast Tad gave me a long time ago, and my stomach gnawed on itself and wobbled with nausea. I flinched at every loud song or bang, leftover trauma from the hole.

"Stand up, 85221," he snarled. His voice touched the part of my brain that wanted to oblige for fear of what he might do and follow his every direction even as it took you over a cliff. Top demons and Druids were most powerful at turning your mind and body against you. There were rumors within HDF drugs were being made to help humans block their minds to the fae lure, to help our kind survive and fight back.

Even if full magic was blocked here, Hexxus still commanded power with his tone, making my teeth crunch together. My bones were slow to move, my muscles stretching to stand up.

"You like it, huh?" He stroked the whip on his belt. "Gets you off?"

"No, master."

"Good. I would rather they scream and fight me." He stepped closer, his height the same as mine, keeping his malicious eyes on me as he tugged the whip free. "More energy in fear."

My gaze tracked him, already preparing to tuck myself away, hide anything that still could be felt deep inside my mind.

The crack of the whip reverberated off the walls, the tail of it just snipping my chin. It burned down my neck, across my nerves, and made my eyes water. I wanted to believe myself strong enough to endure all this. I wasn't. A true hero would hold their chin up and take it. I was no hero.

My legs wobbled, a sob choking my throat. His arm went back to whip me again. His yellow eyes turned completely black, reflecting my hollow figure. I hated knowing my life would end like so many before me. Dying in Halalház… no one knowing I was within reach. To them, my story ended on that train platform weeks ago.

I wished it had ended with a final view of Caden.

Crack!

My knees drove to the floor, not even a squeak coming

from my lips as I shut down. My imperviousness to death seemed to irritate Hexxus more. Did he want me to fight, to scream in fear?

"No! Stop!" a soft voice shouted.

Everyone in the room, including Hexxus and me, jerked to the person in shock.

Lynx stood next to her machine, her hands in the air, wide-eyed, as though she couldn't believe what she had done.

"Excuse me?" Hexxus heaved back his shoulders. Silence doused the room. Everyone stood opened mouthed and staring, even the other guards.

"It's my fault." Lynx licked her lips. "I forgot…" Fear swallowed her words, her throat bobbing.

Hexxus stepped around my table to hers, Lynx's body trembling, her gaze dropping to her shoes.

What the hell was she thinking?

"She's caught up. I held her pile on my table." She tapped the piles on her station, her voice and hand shaking.

Hexxus stared at her, his black demon eyes showing no reaction. For what felt like minutes, he didn't reply, the threat of his retaliation hanging in every breath.

He took a step up to her table, his fingers sliding over the cloth, his voice low. "You are telling me this is all hers?"

"Yes, master." She dipped her head in perfect obedience.

"And where is yours then?"

"Right there." She nodded to another pile on the floor underneath her station.

My mouth parted in surprise, the warm blood from the slice under my chin dripping onto the floor. I tried to meet her gaze, but she kept her eyes locked on the ground.

Another guard stepped up, grabbing the pile, inspecting it. She gave a nod to Hexxus. He swung back to Lynx, shaking his head.

"You are claiming *she*"—he flicked his chin at me like I was dog shit left on the pavement— "finished her three days' quota just in the few hours she's been back? Are you sure about that, 84999?"

Her throat bobbed, but her chin stabbed at the air. "Yes, sir."

"Well… my mistake." Hexxus twisted to me, a smirk coiling his face. His eyes glowed yellow. "Seems you have *magically* become proficient in mending since coming out of the hole."

We all knew she was lying. Covering for me. Had she been working double the whole time I was gone? Doing my share as well? Why? Why was she covering for me?

"It's a miracle." He snickered. Like a snake, he slunk up to Lynx, sliding his fingers through her silky black hair, then tucking a lock behind her ear. His tongue skimmed over his lips. His palm caressed her cheek, and his body pressed into hers. "You are one of my favorites. Always a hard worker, keeping to yourself. And I respect your need to want to save your friend. To protect her. It's an honorable thing to do, my dear."

Smack!

His strike ricocheted over the space. With a cry, Lynx crumpled to the floor at his feet, her hand pressed to her face.

Her name was on the tip of my tongue, but I bit down, knowing my attention would only cause her more harm.

"You still need to be punished for lying and speaking out of turn." He nodded at two guards close to her. "Three lashings."

"No," I grunted.

"Should I add more for your disobedience as well?" He curved an eyebrow at me. "Every time you speak, she gets another. Actually…" Evil crept over his smug face. "You will be the one who delivers her punishment."

"What?" The question barely made it past my teeth.

"You will administer her lashings." He held out the whip for me. "And if you go easy, I will add four more."

Bile boiled in my stomach like a cauldron, emotion I didn't want out blurring my sight.

"Get up, 85221." He nodded to the switch in his hand. "Make them worthy of her foolish protection of you."

There was a truth to his statement, which stoked the rage inside me. Pressing my lips together, I rolled my fingers into balls. Anger rose off me. It wasn't just at Hexxus, but for Lynx. She *was* a fool. I would have taken my lashings and been done. Now, two of us would be punished. I didn't ask her to protect me, and now I was indebted to her. Her punishment lay at my feet. But her kindness was what destroyed me.

Rising, I wiped the blood from my chin, taking the whip from his hands.

My gaze went to Lynx. Her lips trembled; her eyes swam with tears, but she held up her chin in pride. Again, I wondered what had put her in here; she didn't seem like a criminal.

The two guards turned her around, pulling her shirt up, displaying her bare back to me.

Just three strikes, and this would be done.

Acid burned along my tongue, but I swallowed it back down. Cutting out my feelings, I regripped the switch in my hand and swung.

The crack of the whip sang, followed by her exploding wail. She fell into the wall, but the guards held her up. A long red line burst from her back, the skin splitting in some areas, blood bubbling angrily to the surface.

"A natural." Hexxus was at my side, a salacious smile on his mouth. "Not one bit of hesitation."

How badly I wanted to turn the whip on him, make him feel every bit of my hatred.

"You enjoy it, don't you?" He licked his mouth. "Don't

deny it. I can feel it on you. There is enormous power in the most depraved actions. Don't you feel it? The taste of her terror on your tongue, her grief and pain like blood pumping through your veins? Holding a life in your hands."

I snarled at him because somewhere deep down, I could feel the energy of my act.

Life and death.

I liked it.

He laughed. "Deep down, under society's rules, all the things they tell you to be, you enjoy the wickedness." He cranked his neck to look at me. For a moment, I could feel his sexual charge, the desire billowing off his skin like a snare, capturing me in his web.

Grinding my teeth, I faced Lynx, hearing him chuckle. "Again."

Crack!

Her gut-wrenching scream cut through the air as the whip drove over the open wounds of the first one, Lynx's sobs clotting in my throat. The guards fully moved in, holding her up as her legs dipped underneath her weight.

One more. Just be done with it.

Sucking in my own cry of grief, I lifted my hand and lashed out.

A noise I couldn't even describe as human gurgled from her throat before her head dropped forward, her body going limp.

"I'm impressed, 85221." Hexxus faced me, holding his hand out. Everything in me wanted to refuse, to whirl the whip until no one in this room was left standing.

Seething, I placed it back in his hand, his self-satisfaction itching my skin.

He reached out, sliding his finger under my jaw. Pulling it away coated in blood, he sucked the red liquid off. "Mmmm… even your blood tastes sinful. Feral. Full of life."

He grinned, his eyes glowing like an idea had come to him.

"Now for your punishment." My stomach dropped, a rush of alarm cooling my skin, as if thrashing my workmate hadn't been enough. "Flogging is not sufficient for you. Nor is the hole."

I swallowed.

"You, my pretty thing, are meant for more."

"What?"

He stared at me for a moment before his expression turned to a taunting sneer.

"I think you will do well. It's for the truly debauched."

"Do well? For what?"

"The Games, my pet." He smirked. "You are going to fight in the Games."

Chapter 17

"Wakey, wakey, fishy." My eyes fluttered open at the singsong voice. Brown eyes looked back at me only an inch away from my face. "Good morning. Glad to have you back."

"Oh gods," I muttered, taking him in before I tucked my face back into my arm.

Opie stood with his hands on his hips, wearing a pink loofah for shorts, two round scrubber brushes like a bra, and more cleaning pads for a hat and shoes, his beard braided with garbage ties. Bitzy was on Opie's back wearing a swimmer's cap, her large ears sticking out of it.

Chirp. Her middle finger sent me a good morning greeting.

"Yeah, good morning to you too," I grumbled.

Chirp.

Groaning, I pushed myself up to lean against the wall. Last night I had fallen into a deep sleep, but terror trotted so heavily through my dreams, Lynx's cries haunting my soul, I felt as though I hadn't slept at all.

"Against my principles," Opie motioned to the cell, "I swept it while you were gone. Can't you tell? It's so sparkly. I mean, I hate it, like *really* hate it, but you can't deny my skills."

I peered around, noticing not one bit of difference in the empty cage.

"Uh. Sure."

"It's in my genes, I guess." He shrugged, his fingers playing with his loofah shorts. "Can't fight perfection." He held up his hand. "Don't get all used to it. My soul almost died. It was a huge sacrifice. I mean, I *hate* cleaning."

"As you say." I rubbed my face, trying to wake up. "So… what's the outfit for today?"

"Shower scrubbing." He twirled around, grabbing onto his scrubber pad hat. "I made it last night."

"It's perfect." I raked my fingers through my hair, rolling it up in a topknot.

"I know, right?" He rubbed his hands in circles over the scrub brushes across his chest. "Master Finn, our head brownie, said I looked foolish, and I'm an embarrassment to our kind…" Opie stared at his covered feet, sadness wrinkling his forehead.

"Well, this Finn sounds like a dreary asshole." A wave of protectiveness soared through me at the thought of anyone taking Opie's happiness away because he didn't act the same as a typical brownie. "Miserable git. You just be you. The best-dressed brownie on the block."

Chirp!

Two middle fingers waved in the air like a hallelujah, Bitzy's head bobbing in agreement.

A smile grew on Opie's face, and his hips started to wiggle back and forth like a song was playing in his head. "That's right, baby. I make work more fun. I can tell they're all jealous of my costumes."

"Who wouldn't be?" I winked at him, watching him twirl in his loofah like a ballerina. "Maybe you can make me a warrior costume."

Chirp.

Opie stopped turning, his joyous expression falling.

"Oh, right." He nodded at Bitzy. "I heard—" *Whack.* Bitzy's fingers knocked him over the head. "Okay, okay… *Bitzy* heard," Opie muttered. "How could she not with those ears?"

Whack.

"Hey!" He rubbed his head as her chirps rattled off, widening my eyes. "Sorry." *Chirp.* "No, I mean it." *Chirp.* "I wouldn't say it unless I meant it." *Chirp.* "There is nothing wrong with my tone. I said it perfectly." *Chirp.* "I'm not a bad actor. How dare you!"

"Hey. Hey. Both of you calm down." I held up my hands. "Bitzy, I'm sure he meant his apology."

Chirp. Chirp. Double flip off in my face.

"Wow… in the nicest terms she just told you to fuc—"

"Yeah." I nodded, stopping him from continuing. "I think I understood that."

"So?" He faced me again, tugging up his pink loofah shorts. "Were you really put on the list?"

I tipped my head back against the cement, swallowing. "Yes."

"That's bad, fishy."

"So I've heard." And seen.

Since Hexxus's announcement, I had shut down, going into complete denial. A few weeks in and I had already been beaten up, had my blanket stolen—fuck that bitch—got attacked in the shower, put in the hole, had to flagellate another inmate who wanted to protect me, and now put in line for the Games.

Games in which no one survived for long.

Let's say my review of this place would be abysmal.

"There is no escape." Opie pulled on his hat nervously.

"Unless you live, but even the most successful fighter will lose eventually."

"You are not helping."

"You can't do this."

"I don't have a choice."

"You will die."

"I know." I exhaled violently through my mouth, and a deep terror brushed over my soul. Death itself had just walked across it.

The morning bell rang through the block, followed by the clanking of doors opening, drawing my attention to the outside, my mind wanting to think of anything other than my fate.

"Well, I better go. Showers will be emptying out soon." He shoved at the scrubbers like he was pushing up boobs. "Work time, Bitzy."

Chirp. With her finger up high in the air whirling like a cowboy on a bull, they slipped through the bars and vanished.

Heaving myself up, settling in with the herd, I made my way to the bathrooms, going through the motions, but not feeling present in my own body.

"The trouble you get in without me, little lamb." Kek jumped on the counter next to the sink I was using. "You can't seem to stay out of it, can you? I need to wrap caution tape around you."

I cupped cold water in my hands and splashed it on my face, trying to wake myself up. Peering to the side, I noticed Kek's blue hair was down and wet, her uniform clean.

"Oh look, Stanky Fish's bodyguard is on duty," a snide voice cut in, pulling my gaze to the metal reflection of the mirror. Tess and her gang stood behind me in their pyramid formation around her. "Move. I need the sink," Tess snarled, moving closer.

There were dozens of other sinks she could have waited to use, but she was trying to make another stand against me.

I sighed, not bothering turning around.

Kek let out a howling laugh. "It's as if you enjoy getting your ass pummeled, Tessie." She leaned back against the mirror, showing they were no threat. "It took three of you and a surprise attack to take her down the first time. The last fight? Well…" Kek motioned to their still deeply bruised faces.

"At least no one owns me. I don't need a demon to protect me in exchange for sexual favors," Tess sneered.

"If *this* girl was offering sexual favors for protection," Kek motioned to me as she sat up, leaning closer to them, threatening, "you'd be *dead* right now."

Tess swallowed nervously.

"I might do it anyway because you are really pissing me off, human."

"You have no power here. You can't do anything to me," Tess huffed.

Kek slid off the counter with a malicious leer. She was slight compared to them, but confidence and strength radiated from her.

"You are all talk," Tess snipped, but I could see her take a stunted breath.

"You want to *try* me?" She got in Tess's face, Tess's two friends lurching forward in defense.

"Whoa," I hissed, stepping between them, my eyes sliding to the guards who were watching us intently. Moving in, my chest bumped against Tess's. "Back. Down. Try throwing your weight around somewhere else. But wait, that's the problem, isn't it? You're losing your hold on the nonexistent position you pretend you have."

Her nose and mouth wrinkled, fury spitting off her.

"At the end of the day, you are nothing here. Another

human who will die with no fanfare or recognition. Disappear as if you never existed."

"You think you will be remembered?" she hissed, knocking back into me. "Your rich mommy and daddy crying over you?" Her eyes scanned me. "You came in here dripping with privilege. Painted nails, creamy skin, silky hair… I can smell money on everything you do. How you speak, hold yourself, your entitled arrogance… You never had to suffer a day in your life. I bet you've never even set foot in the Savage Lands. It's probably just a story that gets you rich people all excited with the possibility of danger. You never had to work eighteen grueling hours every day to put food on the table. Watch your child die because you couldn't get medicine." She stepped even closer. "This place is a holiday for me. So, come at me. I will show you how we survive there."

"Hey!" a guard yelled at us. "Step back, or you all end up in the hole."

Tess's lips hitched, but she retreated, glowering. "I can't wait to watch you die. No one can protect you in the Games."

The three of them sauntered away, her claims sticking to me like burrs. I *had* come from wealth and privilege, never stepping even close to the Savage Lands. While I had endured loss and sacrifice, I had no idea how it felt to watch a child die because you could not afford medication. To not have food on the table.

Istvan threw feasts with mounds of food for guests to impress them. So much of it was tossed out after or given to the livestock.

"Don't let her crawl into your psyche. We are all here, and there is no rich or poor inside these walls. We all ended up in Halalház, which makes us on even ground now."

"Even?" I snorted. "There is nothing even about this place."

She pinned her mouth, nodding. "Come on, little lamb. Let's go get food before it disappears."

Kek left my side the moment we entered the mess hall, heading to her demon group, where food already waited for her. Grabbing a tray, I scanned the space, landing on someone I wasn't sure how to deal with.

Lynx sat at a table with other fae, but her head twisted to the side, staring at me. Her muscles were rigid, as if just breathing inflicted tremendous pain. Underneath her top, I saw the extra layers of cloth wrapped around her, keeping her skin together along her spine. Her dark eyes watched me with no emotion.

Keeping my expression blank, I stared back at her. She deserved to hate me, no matter how it all started. I would always be the one who held the whip, who left the permanent marks on her back that would be a constant reminder of me. How could you even start to apologize for that?

I had learned at an early age to pick your battles. Know when to stand up and when it was smart to bend—because bending kept you from breaking.

I remained stumped at her decision to cover for me. I had been taught fae weren't nice simply to be nice. Kindness for humans was not in their nature, so her actions didn't settle well with me. I couldn't stop wondering what she was up to. Though Lynx seemed so innocent, not some deceptive manipulator. If anyone was out of water here, it was her. But weren't those always the ones to be careful of?

Lynx's lips rolled together, appearing like she was going to turn away from me, but instead she gave me a slight nod before returning her attention to her group. It was all I needed.

Forgiveness or maybe understanding. She must not entirely blame me, which was more of a relief than I expected.

I let out a gust of air I didn't know I was holding and

headed to my table with a half scoop of oatmeal and a mug of lukewarm coffee. Eyes fixed on me from every direction, watching the soon-to-be-dead human, the Games ticking down the minutes of my life, a clock hanging above my head. But only one pair of eyes sliced through all the curiosity, burrowing into me as if he projected himself right next to me, taunting me to turn and look at him. A sensation fluttered inside me like living bugs, and the need to peer back at him clawed at the back of my head. The impulse was so powerful my flesh broke out in shivers, my jaw locking together.

Don't look, Brex. Don't give him the satisfaction.

With every step, the need grew stronger, the sense of his presence right next to me. My eyes watered as I resisted, swimming upstream against the current. Finally making it to my table, I sat across from Tad, purposely putting my back to the enigmatic man across the room. Was it completely my imagination, or was he stalking me without even moving? I had no idea what piqued his interest, if it was anything besides boredom, but I couldn't deny an acute awareness of him, like a ghost rubbing up against me. The impression of him right next to me.

Tad snorted into his coffee cup, shaking his head.

"What?" I grumbled.

"A simple pebble can cause a tsunami."

"Are you taking your meds, old man?" I shoveled the oatmeal into my mouth, not even letting it settle on my tongue before swallowing. "And why aren't you sharing them?"

"You," he said, setting down his cup with a clink next to his toast, "weren't supposed to get on the list."

"Like I asked to be." I stabbed my spoon into the watery oats, sourness filling my stomach at the truth. I was going to die soon. And from what I'd seen at the Blooding… in a very painful, horrific way.

"Is there any way to get off it? Scrubbing toilets? Good behavior?"

"No." Tad tapped his fingers against the mug. "Once you're on it, it's final."

And final meant final.

"How many come before me? I mean, I have a while. Lots of people are on the list before me, right?" I gestured around, trying to swallow, fear closing in my throat.

"They go to a lottery system when they run out of marked people, which would have happened tonight for the Blooding tomorrow," Tad spoke softly, making every word feel like a boulder. "Rodriguez killed the last one on the list."

My nose sucked in a violent swig of air. "Which means?"

"You just got bumped to the top," he replied. "You will fight tomorrow night."

He said *fight*, but I knew what he actually meant.

You will *die* tomorrow night.

Chapter 18

The vibration of stomping feet, the blistering chants, and screams of the crowd raked down my nerves, squeezing my lungs in a death grip. The sharp smell of blood, sweat, urine, excitement, and utter terror lashed up my nose and coated my tongue.

"Fight! Fight!" The death chant echoed through the dark tunnel I was in, pounding against the sound of my heartbeat. Peering down, I watched my chest heaving for air as though my heart wanted to break through my ribs and save itself.

"It's time, 85221." A guard walked past me, heading to the locked gate where I waited.

Terror I couldn't even fathom rattled my bones, separating me from my body, protecting me from fully understanding the truth. I wasn't even aware of how violently I was shaking until I peered down at my figure. My muscles twitched and rattled as if they pulled me out of ice while sweat pooled in my palms and down my back, ripping all the moisture from my mouth.

"They'll have someone more your level for the first fight," Opie had told me the night before. Somehow knowing

I would not be able to sleep, he and Bitzy sat with me all night, keeping me company.

"The human man Rodriguez killed wasn't his level," I quipped.

"Trying to make you feel better, fishy. Stop ruining my 'this could be worse, brighter side' crap." He stomped his foot.

Chirp! Bitzy snarled at me, flipping her finger.

"Fine. Sorry." I motioned to him. "Go on."

"Thank you." He dipped his head theatrically, cleared his throat, then paused, screwing his face into a frown. "Yeah, I got nothing. You're screwed."

Laughter burst out of me. I needed a break from the fear and tension, and Opie and Bitzy's company helped me through the night without losing my mind, even letting me drift off for a moment.

That small comfort felt at least centuries ago now.

The pounding of feet in the stands drumming along with my pulse brought the harsh reality of what was going to happen to me. And how my death would have them cheering and clapping, then they wake up tomorrow and go on, just the same as usual. Nothing different to them.

Were these my final moments? Was this how my story ended? It seemed cruel and unnecessary that I lived through all of what I did just to die this way.

The healer's words returned to me with painful accuracy. "*Human, you will wish I let you. Where you are headed, death would have been a blessing. You aren't going to last a week, but every second, you are going to wish I took pity on you and let you die.*"

The harsh grating of the gate opening sounded through the arena. I could hear the mob's excited shrill in my ears as they clamored for someone's blood to make them feel more alive in this death hole.

"Are you ready?" The guard spoke softly. "They just picked the lotto number of the prisoner fighting you." I was the warmup act. I didn't even qualify to fight other winners.

My teeth dug into my bottom lip, a wisp of a whimper clotting my throat as I stepped forward.

"Give them glory in your death or in your killing." The guard's sentiment halted me for a moment, my gaze snapping to the fae. For the first time, I really noticed him.

The horse-shifter, Zander, stood there, his chocolate brown eyes staring into mine. "Let their energy and your fear feed you, not starve you." His gaze remained intensely on me. Meaningful. "Use your head, find weapons in anything. Be the one who prevails."

The breath of kindness was a shot of adrenaline, filling me with strength and focus.

I nodded, silently thanking him for his words. Inhaling, I rolled my shoulders back and walked out of the tunnel into the area, light and noise crashing down on me.

Use it.

Take it.

Don't let it take from you.

The figures in the stands blurred into a mass of waving arms and muted colors due to their uniforms. For a moment, it was only me standing like a drop of water in a desert full of thirsty savages.

The slamming of metal jerked my head to the tunnel across from me where a person stepped out. Today's lottery pick. My gaze snapped to the figure, recognition registering in my brain.

Blinking, I took in her short, stocky figure and pinched face.

Mio.

A sneer lifted her lips, showing off yellowish teeth and

a missing incisor in her open mouth. "Come on, fishy," she taunted as she moved closer, as if she forgot I had recently kicked her ass.

It was better to overinflate your opponent's skills than underestimate them. That was another trick of mine, while many of the male recruits tended to do the opposite. I was good. Top in my class, because I always went in at 100%, believing they could outmaneuver me this time. Plus, I was really good at being sneaky and fast.

The only certain thing today was just one of us would be walking out of here.

She swiped out for me, her knuckles brushing my chin as I twirled away, the throng of people crooning at our first contact. Mio was a lot faster than she looked, her movements precise and controlled. She was much better than Tess or Dee, and by her actions, I could tell martial arts was something she was very familiar with.

The two of us circled each other, adrenaline from the crowd dancing over my skin, pumping into my veins. Mio shuffled forward, her jaw set, her leg kicking out at me, which I easily dodged. The crowd disliked our feeble attempts.

"Kill. Kill. Kill!"

"Blood. Blood. Blood!"

I twisted, using the angle to make my first strike, my knuckles cracking into her ribs. She stumbled back, and the crowd cheered with excitement, happy the fight was finally in motion.

Mio's short frame darted at me, her hand striking across my cheek, pain exploding through my face. My eye felt like it wanted to pop out of my head. She took advantage of my moment of hesitation and slammed her fist into my upper lip and nose, cracking the cartilage in my nostrils, bursting my blood vessels. Blood poured out, sliding down my mouth.

Before I could right myself, she kicked me in the stomach, tossing me back onto the dirt with a groan.

"Mio! Mio!" the crowd sang, bets passing between hands.

Leaping for me on the ground, she staggered when I rolled to the side, missing me. Jumping up, I spun, dropping my elbow into her vertebrae. She howled, her back arching at the impact, but she kept on her feet, her arm whacking my already bleeding cheek.

I tottered back, feeling rage climb up my throat and wrap around my muscles. I was better than this. I could drop trained soldiers to the floor.

Mio came for me as my leg swept in a roundhouse kick, hurtling into her gut. She hit the dirt with a thud. Stomping up, my feelings shut off. I kicked her in the ribs with an audible crack, forcing a cry to volley from her lips.

The part of me that didn't want to kill anyone was smothered in pure adrenaline and survival instinct; it was kill or be killed. I did not want to die—not tonight.

A guttural cry tore from her as she shoved against my onslaught, crawling away from me, her hand wrapping around a post stuck in the ground like Excalibur. With all the strength she could muster, she heaved it out of its hold, twirling it in her hands while limping back for me, blood trailing down her face. She was a lot stronger and more formidable than she appeared.

She dug her boot into the dirt, kicking up debris in my face.

"Ahh…" My hands went to my burning eyes, giving her time and free rein.

With a war cry, she plunged the stick toward me. Lurching back, I had no time to clear the spear entirely. Pain exploded in my thigh as the spiked wood sank into my leg, ripping through skin and nerves. I heard a howl echo off the walls, sure it was mine, but I no longer felt attached to my body.

Everything went in slow motion, as though I could watch each drop of my blood slowly hit the dirt, wetting the earth with my essence. A buzzing sensation rolled over me like I was being given more energy while numbing me of the agony freezing my limbs.

My gaze lifted to hers, my nose wrinkling in a snarl.

I turned feral and plucked the stick from my leg, huffing and snarling. Whatever she saw in me, she must have known something had changed as well. Her eyes widened as if she'd seen a monster crawl out of a cave.

Darting to the side in a blink, I whipped around her, causing her to glance about. That was what I strived for. To move so smoothly and fast, they lost track of me.

Slipping in, I rammed my fist into her throat with all my weight. With a garbled choke, she grabbed her neck, curling over, her mouth open, gulping for air. Swinging the stick at the back of her knees, whacking her off her feet, she thudded to the ground, the impact snatching what was left of her air.

All strength seemed to flee her body while mine buzzed with life.

I stood over her, staring down at her. Inhaling sharply, her throat bobbed as blood streamed down her face, her dark eyes locked on me.

Defiant.

Proud.

She didn't say anything, accepting her death as she watched me twirl the stick in my hand, still dripping with my blood. The crowd screamed and chanted for me to finish it. I knew there was no other way. One of us lived, and one of us died. That was the game.

Looking her in the eyes, I gave her the respect she deserved in the end. My arm went up; the broken staff she almost killed me with was her end. Acid swished in my stomach, shooting up my throat like lava, but I knew there was no stopping now.

With a grunt, I drew it down with all the strength I had left, the point spearing through her throat. It made a sick sound of flesh tearing, cartilage snapping as blood spurted out and sprayed my face. She gasped, choking on her own blood, air funneling out of the hole in her throat, spewing up red liquid like a blowhole. She fought for air for a while before her body went stiff. Then life abandoned her in one violent spasm, her figure going limp.

I heard nothing but the sound of my own breath. My mind pulled back from the harshness of what I had just done, the spear stuck in her throat, piercing the ground. Adrenaline soared through my muscles, shaking me with excessive energy.

I had killed her. Brutally.

But I was alive. I survived.

Wiping the blood from my face with my arm, I stepped back, my sight catching the jarring movement in the crowd before my ears finally synced with it. Bursting me from my bubble and crashing me back to Earth.

"Fish!"

"Piranha!" another yelled out over the rest.

"Piranha! Piranha! Piranha!" The mass chanted, jumping up and down, their fists in the air rocking back and forth with their mantra.

I scanned the haze of people in a daze, sinking under the overwhelming energy of the crowd, drowning in their lust for blood.

I felt a subtle tug in my gut—a flutter, drawing my gaze

to the side. Eyes seemed to glow like beacons in the darkness, grabbing on to me, yanking me back up, filling my lungs with air. I jolted as our gazes collided.

Warwick sat in his usual place, leaning back and angled to one side, his hand propped underneath his chin like he was watching a dull movie, but his gaze was sharp, burning into me.

My lids shut briefly, and I swallowed against the feeling that he stood right in front of me, his aura circling, touching me.

"Glorious." I twisted around toward the voice behind me. Zander stood there with his expression blank, but his eyes were twinkling. "Your stomach is full. You took." A smile hinted on his face. "You prevailed."

"I prevailed."

"Good." He moved past me to Mio's body. I watched him for a second before my gaze snapped back up the king's spot in the stands.

Empty.

Leaving me feeling as if I had imagined the whole thing.

Strolling out of the arena, covered in blood, the cries of my new moniker against my back, I slipped down the dark tunnel away from the exhibition.

Mio's death revealed one thing to the masses.

This fish had become a piranha.

The guards escorted me to a healer for my leg wound, who cleaned it and gave me medicine before I headed to the showers where a fresh uniform waited for me—a perk for winning.

Under the spray of water, blood swirled pink around my

feet, slipping toward the drain. The blood churned, Mio's and mine together, before disappearing. My arms shook as I pressed my palms to the tile, trying to keep myself up, the ringing in my ears and buzz of adrenaline receding dramatically.

My body responded fully to the night's events, falling from the high, but my mind was still numb to the fact I murdered Mio. It was for survival. It could easily be her bleeding in this shower instead of me, but the idea of killing a fellow human to entertain crowds coiled my heart and stomach in disgust.

"Two minutes!" A guard yelled at me, the same one who retrieved me from the hole. Scar Lip, I called him in my head. He seemed particularly fond of the shower shift. "Come on, fishy." He leered at me. "Need help getting dressed this time?"

Wrapping myself with my towel, I strolled assertively over to him, staring up without a hint of fear. He sucked in at my proximity, still trying to keep the smirk on his face. His eyes tracked down my figure, the water dripping and sliding over my bruised and broken skin.

"Piranha," I said, leaning closer. "And you ever touch me again, I will tear the flesh from your bones and use them to pick your remains from my teeth."

He blinked, shocked at my words, but quickly shoved it away, pressing in closer to me. "You think because you killed one weak human, you're invincible now?" His eyes ran down me again. "I could do anything I wanted to you right now, and not only could you not stop me, no one else would either."

"Your deep insecurity about your manhood is showing," I replied, ignoring the cold fear his words set in my bones. He was probably right about no one helping, but I would never show him he could break me. "Guess it's not just a human male trait." Comparing a fae to a human was a great insult.

The fae believed themselves so far above such follies, but the longer the worlds mixed, the more each took on attributes of the other.

"You bitch," he seethed, lurching for me. My fist rammed into his Adam's apple, his body stumbling back as he clawed at his windpipe.

"Tsk. Tsk." I clicked my tongue. "You know the rules. You can't touch me." It was something Tad told me. Once you were in the Games, no guard could rough you up. They wanted their fighters to be at their prime to put on the best show.

"No fun watching a fighter who's already beaten to a pulp in the ring, giving no fight," Tad had said. "They want the prisoners so distracted by the spectacle to not think about the fact they are doing their dirty work for them. Killing fellow inmates, keeping down the numbers, while they cheer you on to do it again is really sick, but people love it until it's their name thrown into the ring."

The guard hissed at me, his lids lowering to slits. With a leap, he grabbed my throat, squeezing down, blocking the air from my lungs. Abhorrence curved his scarred lip, death filling his eyes. "You filthy piece of…"

"Boyd!" A voice boomed through the room, bouncing off the tiles. Zander's frame filled the doorway. "Let her go."

The guard, Boyd, sneered at me, squeezing tighter.

"Boyd. I. Said. Let. Go."

Boyd's nostrils flared, and he shoved me back. Bending over, I drew air into my lungs with a burning cough.

"Watch yourself." Boyd pointed at me before stomping out of the room, glaring at Zander.

Zander watched me as I straightened, my hand rubbing my throat.

"Get dressed." He nodded at the pile on the table. "I will be right outside to escort you back to your cell."

He retreated, leaving me to get dressed. Shakily, I drew my pants on, the spike of fear collapsing down around me again. Overwhelming emotions built behind my crashing adrenaline. I finished dressing, slipped back into my boots, and headed out to find Zander waiting exactly where he said.

He gave me a quick but warm smile before he took off down the corridor, passing other cells. My eyes locked on one of them.

"Stop," I said to Zander, stepping up to the cage, peering at the person behind the bars. I knew the Games were still going, and almost all the cells were still empty.

Except this one.

I wasn't the only one who no longer wanted to be part of the show tonight.

"Can you open this cell?" I looked at Zander, my voice empty.

He nodded, not questioning my reasoning. Using a master key on his belt, he slid the metal gate open with a shrill bang.

Tess got to her feet, her eyes tracking every movement I made. Her jaw was locked, showing me no fear, but also no fight. Her watery gaze held no sign any actual tears had fallen for her friend. You didn't do that here until deep in the night when no one could see, and your cries were absorbed with the others.

"My blanket." It was an order, not a request or question.

She hesitated for a second, clearly battling the urge to fight. Begrudgingly she bent down, picking up a blanket from the nest she created on the ground.

"Both."

Her cheeks twitched, rage flaring through her face, but she grabbed the other one as well, holding them out for me.

She knew the game inside and outside of the arena. This was how it worked, and I could not show leniency. Otherwise, I was weak.

Taking the blankets, I headed out of her cell, and Zander closed her back in.

"She died well," I said.

"Fuck you."

"No more, Tess," I commanded. "Your war with me is done. You threaten me or even get in my way, and you join your friend." I walked away before she could respond. Zander scrambled to catch up with me, keeping stride with me to my cell. Walking into it, I turned to face my guard.

"You are…" Zander shook his head in awe, sliding my door closed, grabbing the bars the moment it locked, staring at me. "Something."

"I'm something all right." I snorted, dropping the blankets to the ground.

His silence drew my attention back, his brown eyes watching me. His expression made nervous energy flush through my body.

He watched me boldly, his intention clear. But different from so many other men, Zander's focus wasn't leering or lustful. He wanted me, but his look was softer, almost longing. Sweet. In a place filled with violent death and cruel torture, it was jarring. Unsettling.

I didn't know how to handle it. Staring down at the floor, I nervously licked my lip.

"There's not a word I could find in this language that could define you."

A curt laugh drove up through my mouth. "Don't worry. I've heard *cold-hearted bitch* in almost all languages."

"That is not at all the description I had in mind." His gaze stayed intently on me until he peered off to the side, finally breaking the contact. "You have stirred something here. From the moment you walked in, you have changed the dynamics, the order. It's as if everything is about to topple."

"What do you mean?"

"I don't know. I just feel it." His attention came back to my face. "And I feel myself being caught up in your current. I can't seem to stop myself."

I gulped, his declaration stirring both flames and ice in me, passion and fear.

He tapped the bars, stepping back. "Be careful of Boyd. He has a weak character, a lust for power and blood, and no conscience," he said before marching away as if nothing personal transpired between us at all.

Wow. I shook my head. Tonight had been an extreme roller coaster, and I wanted to get off.

Lowering myself onto my blankets, I curled up, the extra padding feeling better than any luxury bed I'd ever slept in.

Distant cries and cheers from the games filled my ears with white noise, pulling me into a deep sleep. My body gave over to the first full night of sleep I had since arriving, probably thanks to whatever the healers shot me with.

In spite of that, Zander's claim wound through my dreams. My sleep was haunted by images of HDF toppling, pieces crushing Caden and those I loved, while I stood in the middle… watching.

Chapter 19

Two weeks passed in a blur of sameness. The one difference I noticed was most stepped out of my way or nodded at me with respect, the name "Piranha" circling the prison. I still had to fight to get any "real" food, but toast with butter was available for me every morning. Still, more weight slid off my bones, leaving me weak and tired.

I wasn't ready to fight tonight, but when death awaited you, time had a funny way of speeding up. In a blink, the day of the Games was on me again. I had no idea who I'd be fighting, but there was no question they would make it harder, my chances of survival dimming.

"You will win tonight." Tad set down his coffee cup, studying me. The mess hall buzzed with more intensity than normal, excitement for a night of blooding and the thrill of looking around the room wondering who wouldn't be with us tomorrow.

"You don't know that, old man." I tossed my toast down, suddenly not hungry.

"Eat *every* bite." Tad nodded at the three slices of bread. "You need your strength."

Glaring at him like a nagging parent, I made a show of shoving half a piece into my mouth all at once.

"Oh, good. Choke to death first." He shook his head with a sigh, going serious again. "You can do this, girl. I have never seen someone fight as you do. The way you move?" He tilted his head. "Like a ghost. You are magic out there."

"Yeah, against a slow-moving human," I snorted, swallowing my bread, feeling it lump in my gut, "I'm lightning."

"No." Tad's bushy eyebrows blended into one long fuzzy caterpillar. "It's more than that. You actually remind me of—"

Tad's sentence was cut off by commotion at the doorway. Chatter and people turning to look drew my attention. My gaze landed on the guard who had checked me in, "cleansed" me on the first night, and showed me to my cell. He stood with a new prisoner, dressed in gray.

Human.

My eyes latched on to the new fish.

The world tipped to the side. With a gasp, my cup fell from my fingers, spilling over the table, whipping everyone's attention to me for a moment, including the new prisoner.

I blinked several times, not understanding what I was seeing. There was no way.

His eyes widened, taking me in, and filled with a mix of joy, relief, and shock.

"Oh. My. Gods. Kovacs?" He shook his head, not believing what he was seeing either, his form already moving toward me. "Shit. We all thought you were dead." he wailed, my brain taking in the form running for me.

Aron Horvát.

My comrade at HDF, the asshole who took my virginity, the guy I loved beating up. All that made sense out there, but seeing him here? My mind couldn't make sense of it, a puzzle piece being forced into the wrong spot. What was he doing here? How?

"Brexley, I can't believe it's you." He was suddenly there in my face, his arms slinging around me. "Fuck, Kovacs, I can't tell you how good it is to see you. Markos would flip if he knew you were alive."

Caden's last name and mine seemed to break away from the rest of his words, booming off the walls, echoing in surround sound like a jackhammer, slamming me back to the present.

Holy. Fuck. He had just said my name—one of the cardinal rules broken.

Dread filled my stomach, panic walloping my lungs as my eyes darted around. Some faces were blank, but most stared at me in disbelief, their brains trying to place the name, filling with awareness. Shock. Hatred.

Prisoner 85221 or Laura Nagy was safe. Unknown. Brexley Kovacs, ward of General Istvan Markos, daughter of Benet Kovacs, was a target.

It was something Istvan drilled in Caden and me, to keep our identities secret at all costs if we were ever caught. We had to be extra careful because we would be used as ransom, blackmail, and punishment to Istvan.

In seconds, Aron had crushed the foundation out from under me.

He grabbed my face, his eyes watering. "I-I can't believe this. Kovac—"

"Shut the fuck up, you idiot," I hissed under my breath, standing up from the table, breaking our connection.

"What?" He stepped back in disbelief, his eyes going back and forth between mine. I could see he was trembling, fear tossing out years of conditioning. I knew he didn't mean to pitch me under a train. Seeing me alive, a friend in a hostile place, took over his actions. But he still destroyed my safety net.

"What are you doing here?" The hostility around me grew, eyes drilling into me from all angles.

Most of all, I could feel *his* attention cutting me like glass from across the room. The king of Halalház. Nothing good came from Warwick Farkas's attention on you.

He had left me alone for weeks, acting as if I didn't exist. Now I could sense his eyes burning the back of my head, his eyes peeling at my skin.

"Caden's totally lost it."

"Jesus," I growled, grabbing Aron's shirt. "Stop talking." I tugged him out of the mess hall. No one moved toward us, but I sensed that would soon change. Marching him around the corner, I slammed him against the wall. "What the fuck is wrong with you?"

"I know. I wasn't thinking. I saw you…" He glanced away. "I can't…" He broke off, a sob tearing up his throat. "I can't die here. It was just a silly dare. I shouldn't be here."

"What do you mean?"

"Caden," he cleared his throat…"since he saw you die, or I guess thought you did, he's been on a bender. Lost it. Drunk and doing stupid shit. He's on some sniper mission to kill every guard at the fae train depot across the river."

The one where he watched me die.

"Caden has gone off the deep end. He dragged some of us with him in his pursuits. I was caught while trying to run away this last time." *Dragged, my ass*. Aron, with his big ego, would be the first in line, claiming he could kill the most.

"I can't believe this." Aron gazed at me in wonder. "We all thought you were dead."

"No, not *yet*." Though with tonight looming over me and my real name painting a bright target on my back, it probably wouldn't be long.

Another small sob hiccupped up his throat. "Fuck, Brex,

help me. I don't want to die. Not like this. This wasn't supposed to happen. I shouldn't be here."

The arrogant boy in the training room was gone. Cocky in his environment, but at the first signs of true horror, he was blubbering like a baby.

"You think any of us want to be here?" I shoved him harder into the wall, whispering hoarsely. "You don't think I want to go home? See Caden again? This isn't a fucking holiday, but here we are. The faster you accept it, the better."

He rubbed his hands roughly across his face.

"You are not gonna get any sugarcoating from me. This place is everything you imagine, if not worse. I've been beaten, tortured, starved, assaulted, threatened, demeaned, and locked in a hole for days. But you show weakness, and you're dead, Horvát. And as much as I've thought you were an asshole back at HDF, you are still my comrade. My team member. We protect each other. So get it together."

He nodded, his head dipped toward his chest, his hands shaking. I understood how overwhelming it was when you first arrived to find yourself in a place from which no human had ever returned. But it wasn't in me to give up and accept the end so easily.

Tonight I might die. But I would go out fighting.

The bell declaring the breakfast hour over, time to get our asses to work, trilled through the air. Aron jerked his head at the loud sound, his throat bobbing, his eyes leaping to the doorway, watching figures start to emerge from the room.

"What's going on?" he asked, reminding me of someone high on drugs: paranoid and jumpy.

Instead of answering him, I pushed him back into the wall again, demanding his attention back on me.

"You do not speak my real name again. Keep your

mouth shut. Out me one more time, and I will kill you myself. You understand?"

He nodded at my demand, though it really was too late.

"Being a newbie, you will go as *fish*. Don't tell anybody anything about yourself. Keep your head down, stay close to me, and do what the guards tell you." Aron was scared now, but I feared that as soon as he got a tiny bit calmer, his swaggering nature would start to show, which would not be good for him. "You want to live? You keep to yourself and follow the rules." *Unlike me*. "You understand?"

"Yes," he replied, flicking up his chin, a touch of the old Aron in his voice.

"Come on." I twisted around, feeling Aron was some younger bratty brother I had to show around at a new school, let him know the rules and unspoken laws of the place. "Unless a guard tells you differently, you can come with me to work. There is no training, so observe everything; pick up everything as fast as you can. Don't assume other humans are on your side here, because they are not. Whatever decrees we go by on the outside *do not* apply here. They will be the first ones to slit your throat. Demons are in red, fae in yellow, half-breeds blue, humans in gray."

"Then who is the guy in black?"

I stopped so fast Aron slammed into the back of me. My stomach plunged into my boots as I stared forward, feeling the side of my face burning.

Warwick stood in the doorway. No one moved behind him, waiting for the king to decide what he was doing.

"Who the fuck is he?" Aron sounded arrogant.

"Shut up," I muttered, keeping my head straight.

"Why? Who is he?" Aron's male insecurities were rising to the surface, the only person clueless to the power billowing off the man in black.

"Listen to her, *fish*." Filled with disgust and threat, Warwick's deep voice rumbled through the space, plucking the air from my lungs and running shivers down my arms. Sauntering to us, his long legs ate up the gap in a blink, gliding right up to Aron. Towering far above him, he leaned down into his ear, taking over his personal space. "Shut. The. Fuck. Up."

Aron stilled, finally sensing the dominance emanating from him.

"You just put a target on your back." Warwick sneered in Aron's face, his gaze snapping to mine. "And *hers*."

Air tore through my nose, my lungs tripping over the gush of oxygen. His threat felt like lead weights were dropped on my back.

I stared back at the man, not showing any emotion. His blue-green eyes rolled like a storm crashing through me. He tilted his head, watching me for a long time as if I were a science experiment until he stepped up to me, sending my pulse tapping wildly against my neck.

As his gaze rolled over me, his nose flared, the heat from his body colliding into mine. My head spun. Arms folded, he tipped closer.

"Watch your back now, princess." Rough and deep, his voice felt like it poured through my veins and down my throat. "Everything's changed now." His mouth grazed my cheek. "*Kovacs*," he whispered before brushing past me, his arm knocking into me purposefully as he strolled on, leaving me rooted to my spot, wheezing for air.

His departure sent the horde pouring out of the mess hall. Figures bumped and brushed by, whispers, snarls, and glares of death all centered on me.

"Who *was* that?" Aron grabbed my arm, snapping me out of the bubble Warwick seemed to always put around me when he was near.

"Remember on nights Sergeant Freeman got a little tipsy and would tell us old battle stories of the Wolf?"

"Yeah. That Farkas dude." Aron's forehead wrinkled. "The legend of the guy who came back from the dead after being killed in the Fae War, becoming neither human nor fae. It was said he could move like a ghost and hunt like a wolf, killing hundreds in minutes all by himself with his bare hands. But he's just a myth. He's not actually real. Bakos said he was made up to scare people."

"Bakos was wrong. He's *very* real. The legend and myth are true." I bit down on my lip. "The man who just threatened you? The man in black…" My gaze went to Aron's, feeling the power of saying his name. "Is Warwick Farkas."

Aron stumbled after me, trying to refute what I had just confessed to him, but the more he tried to deny it, the less sure he sounded. So many stories about the fae our parents or grandparents grew up thinking were fables were *our* reality, the fae having shown themselves when the barrier fell. But Warwick Farkas was one we still put in the Santa Claus or zombie category. No one rose back from death as if nothing happened and was neither fae nor human. Necromancers and Druids were said to do it, but it was black magic… wrong… and it came with bad consequences. The person was not right. Hollow, soulless, and angry, they were slivers of their former self, forced to live but not actually alive, their bodies cold and awkward.

Warwick was not any of those, his blood ran hot, his presence so full of life it choked you.

I was sure the part of him about being brought back to life was highly exaggerated; the man was real. So real, he caused everything in me to vibrate violently. I felt lost and found at the same time. He was everything I imagined a legend would be: overwhelming and on another plane, high above us mortals.

"85230," a familiar voice yelled out for Aron. Boyd's figure moved toward us. My stomach twisted at the sight of him. Boyd's eyes dipped to me, a sneer curling up his lip. "Awww, little fishy, I see you already found another fishy friend. How adorable." To Aron he said, "You are in the laundry room."

Aron's shoulders rolled back, his nose wrinkling with disgust at the fae guard.

These two were so much alike—a very bad thing for Aron.

"Just hold her hand, and she will show you." Boyd puffed up, getting into my face. "Isn't that right, smelly little fish? *You* know how it is here. Who's in charge." He nudged me, making sure I felt his threat pressing into my hip. "Though I still need to break you in, put you on your knees." His insinuation spread smugly over his face.

"Be careful," I replied coolly. "Piranhas have sharp teeth and are known to bite… hard."

"You do, fucking bitch, and you'll know how it feels to have your intestines pulled out and stuffed down your throat."

Aron lurched for Boyd, but I quickly moved in front of him, his chest smacking into my shoulder. Boyd's gaze tracked our movements, his head tipping back in laughter.

"You are dumb as fuck." He snickered at Aron. "Not a surprise with you humans. You better stick with her. She seems a bit smarter than you." He stepped back. "Better hurry, you don't want to be late on your first day." He motioned for us to move. "After you."

Taking a deep breath, I strode past him, catching sight of

Lynx watching me from the door before stepping inside. I could never tell what she was thinking. Her gaze was always intense but neutral. I sensed many layers beneath it.

I went directly to my table, pulling out my pile of mending, not looking at either Lynx or Tess on either side of me, while Boyd heaved Aron over to Hexxus.

"85230," Hexxus snarled at the new human, his gaze roaming over Aron like he was putrid food. "Station behind the other fish." He pointed to a recently empty spot behind me, a victim in last week's Games.

"What are those? Sewing machines?" Aron snorted. "Isn't that women's work?"

Holy fuck. Holy fuck. My teeth clenched together, my lids squeezing briefly at the silence following his statement.

The Aron I knew was back, his ego shoving common sense and everything I told him out of the way. He had never been truly opposed in his life and was the epitome of entitled—praised, coddled, and rich and only getting reprimanded with a stern voice or his back to a mat. All things he could walk away from and nothing really threatening. He had no common sense in the real world.

"I mean, isn't there something more useful for me to do?" He glanced around, as though his comment was perfectly reasonable. "Build shit. I *don't* sew."

Hexxus watched him, expressionless, tension growing as Aron seemed to realize the shocked silence was pointed at him. His Adam's apple bobbed, and his gaze fluttered to me.

Then Hexxus's head tipped back, and he released a howl, the kind of laughter that set my teeth on edge. Not one of us moved or breathed. Hexxus's hand slapped down on Aron's shoulders, shaking his head with humor. A smile twitched on Aron's face, and he joined in a little on Hexxus's laughter.

"Right?" Aron motioned toward the machines, chuckling with Hexxus. "I'd be better doing something physical. Us guys don't have a clue how to use those."

"Oh, Boyd, you didn't tell me our new guy here was so funny. He thinks this place is some kind of retreat where he can pick his own activities." Hexxus patted Aron's back.

It happened in a blink. Everything shifted.

Hexxus's eyes became black, his skin turned white and paper-thin, stretching over his bones, his teeth snapping. He shoved Aron forward, his fury discharging like tangible particles in the air.

Crack!

The lash of the whip snapped across Aron's back, knocking him to the ground with a scream.

Crack!

The sound of cloth, flesh, and muscle splintering apart ripped through the air. Aron's screeches tore through my eardrums as he tried to crawl away.

Fury burst from Hexxus, his body vibrating with energy. The demon was fully in control; any sliver of humanity was gone. His arm lashed down over and over brutally with raging passion. With every strike, my skin echoed in understanding, recalling the unbelievable pain.

Strike after strike, Hexxus didn't relent, and I wanted to scream for him to stop, to save my comrade. Bile filled my stomach, shooting up my throat, tears clouding my eyes.

Aron's shrieks turned into full sobs, blood spurting and spilling from the wounds. "Brex," he whimpered, his eyes pleading with mine. The survivalist in me told me to keep my mouth shut, not to get involved. My head twisted toward Lynx, her dark eyes meeting mine.

I got it—what she had done for me.

"No." She shook her head, but I was already standing.

"Please, stop," I begged, trying to swallow back the vomit in my throat. "Please don't kill him."

Hexxus's arm stopped midair, his black eyes turning on me. Nerves down my neck twisted and jerked, feeling his anger turn on me.

"You dare stop me in the middle of my lesson?" Hexxus's arm dropped, and blood splattered all over his face and clothes. "You think because you are in the Games, you are untouchable?"

"No, master." I bowed my head. "I would never deem myself that high."

"Good." Hexxus nodded, his eyes shifting back to yellow. "Because you aren't. You are nothing."

An agonizing moan came from Aron, shifting Hexxus's attention back down to his limp body. "Get this thing out of sight." He kicked Aron's ribs, glancing over at Boyd.

Boyd stared at me, a cruel smirk on his face, not moving. Hexxus's eyes flipped between us with mystification.

"Boyd," he spat. "Am I missing something?"

"No, sir." Boyd kept his sleazy gaze on me as he strolled over to Aron, a leer twisting at his lips.

"Play with your pets on your own time," Hexxus growled. "Get this piece of shit out of here. I'm sick of dealing with stupid, arrogant humans."

"Don't worry." Boyd squatted down, grabbing Aron and easily lifting him over his shoulder. His gaze found mine again. "I know the perfect place for him." His cruel smile widened as he carried Aron out of the room.

My throat tightened, fear poking between my ribs, sensing something more behind Boyd's sentiment. Before I had time to analyze it, Hexxus was standing before me, his expression back to neutral.

"For what you just did?" He leaned in, Aron's blood

dotting his skin like freckles. "I should lash you until your muscles could be used as floss." His hand wrapped around my throat, his thumb pressing into the pulse at my neck. He licked his lips, loving my terror. "But I have bets on the Games tonight, and feeling your fear as you get brutally torn apart in the ring?" With his free hand, he wiped Aron's blood off his cheek with his finger, sucking it off. "It will be such a high. It's like the best fuck in the world. And I will *get off* on your death tonight. Enjoy it like a sweet wine." He shoved me back, my ass knocking back into my chair.

He whirled around, his arms going up in the air.

"Everyone back to work. And thanks to your colleagues' interruptions, there will be no breaks or food."

Daggered glares and hisses shot toward me. Tess shook her head in loathing.

"Danger and violence," Lynx murmured for only me to hear. "They follow you."

I couldn't disagree.

Relief eased down my shoulders as I started to work, but the sneer on Boyd's face haunted me.

Whatever respite I got today, I would pay for later.

Chapter 20

"Pir-an-ha. Pir-an-ha." The crowd's chants dove into my bones, oscillating through my body, violently thumping my heart and lungs. The sharp smell of my fear, dirt, blood, and sweat clung to the tunnel where I stood, the light beyond the gate cutting through the bars.

"Blood-ing! Blood-ing!" Piercing calls exploded around for my life or for me to end my opponent's. It didn't seem to matter.

My stomach pirouetted with nausea, my teeth chattering against each other. The terror hadn't ebbed any. It shook me deeper to the core. I understood what was out there, what would happen, and how tiny the possibility was I would step away this time with my life.

"You ready?" Zander's hand reached for the gate, his brown eyes finding mine through the dark shadows.

"No." I rolled my jaw. "But I don't really have a choice, do I?"

Zander's hand dropped away from the handle for a moment, touching my arm lightly, moving close to me.

"I can't tell you everything will be all right," he said quietly, turning my head to his and forcing me to concentrate on his words, drowning out the cries from the stands. "You are fast and clever. Use *everything* you can to your advantage. And fight like as though your life depends on it."

"It does," I replied, feeling my chest falter at his proximity, his beautiful face blurring out everything around me.

"It does," he repeated. His features were serious, but his deep brown eyes were soft on mine. "Dirty. Cruel. Unforgiving. Do whatever it takes. You cannot die. You don't understand." My brows wrinkled at his last statement. He swallowed, his fingers pressing firmer into my jaw. "The fact that you are human and a woman means nothing here. Use it. Be smarter, quicker. Just win."

"You sound the same as my training instructor." A sentimental smile hinted on my lips while grief cracked through my heart.

Zander stared down at me, his intensity reserved and quiet, but I could feel so much from his eyes. He leaned in, his mouth inching closer to mine. "What is it about you? I can't fight it. I am drawn to you—"

"Come on!" A bang hit the gate, jolting us away from each other, my attention snapping to the figure on the other side.

Damn it.

"Well, well… Now I see why you were so protective over the human, Z." A malicious smile curved up on Boyd's face as he leaned into the gate, his gaze darting between us. "Breaking in this one for yourself?"

Zander didn't answer as he stepped toward the door, pulling out his keys.

"Thought we shared around here." Boyd salaciously licked his lips. "Though I guess it's pointless now." Boyd's eyebrows wiggled. "She won't be making it out of this one alive."

Zander unlatched the lock, and Boyd tugged the bars open.

"Come on. The people demand your presence for the fish fry."

"She's still fighting the human prisoner, right? The one picked from the lottery?" Zander's hand grasped my wrist as I stepped forward.

"Oh, did they not tell you?" Boyd parted his mouth in false surprise, reaching for my other arm. "The order has changed. She's proved she can fight at a higher difficulty. She did win her fight last time."

"What?" Zander's fingers gripped harder around my bones. "When did this happen?"

"Just a little bit ago." Boyd smirked, tugging me from Zander's grip. "Did you miss that discussion? Oh, right, you were busy getting her." He shrugged. "So eager to volunteer to get your filly here."

Boyd slammed the gate back on Zander's face, gloating.

"Who is she fighting?" Zander's head flicked up in irritation, his foot stamping at the ground.

"Why ruin the surprise?"

Boyd walked me several steps, leaving me in the middle of the arena before heading over to another gate. A shadowed figure stood behind it—the person who would either kill me or die tonight.

The mob cheered louder at seeing me enter the arena.

Use their energy. Focus, Brex. Survive.

Boyd wrenched open the other gate, letting out my adversary.

Fear crashed down on me, dulling the crazed cheers, stomping feet, and excitement from the crowd jumping and moving in my peripheral as the fae strutted out.

No. Nononono.

Oxygen evaporated from my lungs, acid rushing into my throat.

My opponent strode in with arms wide open, pumping up the crowd; his arrogant sneer tugged up his lip.

"Bull! Bull! Bull!" The crowd switched allegiance in a blink, their fickle devotion going with the strongest player. Ruthless and cold.

My head whipped back to the tunnel. Horror filled Zander's eyes, his head shaking in denial.

"No." He pushed to open the door.

"Uh-uh." Boyd wiggled his finger at him. "You know the rules. Once they are in the ring, we can't intercede."

A bray huffed from Zander, and for a moment, I thought he was going to come through the gate and rush Boyd, but he stepped back, his sorrow-filled gaze telling me he could not help me.

Snapping back to Rodriguez, I licked my lips, trying to calm my frantic heartbeat.

Fear got you killed.

The bell declared the fight was on. I could feel the bloodthirsty fans salivating for violence and my death.

"Bull! Bull! Kill! Kill!"

Rodriguez smirked, strolling over to me with bored arrogance. "Wow, not really fair, is it?" He winked, pausing about five feet from me. "Guess it will be an early night for me. Shower and back in my cell in what… twenty minutes?" He moved in closer, lowering himself to attack, his nose flaring, his feet scraping at the ground.

Countering his moves, I peered around me, trying to find items I could use as weapons. They had changed the setup since my last fight, taking away some, adding others.

"*Brexley Kovacs*." Rodriguez purred my name, his tone twisted with disgust and desire. "I won't lie; I'm really gonna enjoy goring you, spilling your guts on the ground." His nostrils puffed with excitement. "Just think, this whole time, the HDF princess has been under our nose. General Markos's pet bitch. A rich, entitled, spoiled human girl. You will be glad I killed you tonight. Consider it kindness, as the inmates will pick at you until you're a bag of bones."

"You fae keep telling me that." I offset his progression, my boots sliding over the dirt. "But yet, here I am."

"Not for long." He lurched for me, setting off the crowd, his head tilting as the cheers descended on him, a smile curling his lips. A showman. He thrived on the attention. Lived for the spectacle.

Use it, Brex. Use his ego against him.

The problem was how to do that. He was an excellent fighter, brutal even, feeding off the crowd's energy.

"You are like a bright red cape dangling in front of me." He padded the ground, ready to come for me. "And soon you will cover the ground in the same color." He stepped closer. "Your people killed my sister. It's only fair I kill you."

I didn't respond, but my eyes darted to his, making his evil smirk grow wider.

"Yeah, you have a lot of enemies here now, human. It's why I asked to fight you tonight. My sister was just a calf, but they had no problem kidnapping her, experimenting on her, and then taking her life." He spat at the ground.

Experimenting? What the hell was he talking about?

"And I will have no problem doing the same to you."

The information barely sank in before he leaped forward, his bulk barreling into mine, the back of my head smacking the ground with a painful blow. He grappled for my arms, trying to pin me beneath him.

Forcefully I bucked my hips up, tipping him forward, getting him off-center as my teeth bit down on his arm, loosening his grip on my wrist. Shoving my palm into his face with all my might, he fell off me, his face hitting the dirt.

I rolled out from under him, climbing to my feet. He twisted back for me, his fingers digging into the back of my leg. I kicked out, my foot cracking across his cheek, flinging him back into the ground with a grunt. After I stomped my boot into his side, his hand clamped around my ankle, twisting and pulling my leg. My knee popped as I turned, my face hitting the ground as I dropped, leaving my back exposed and vulnerable.

Get up! I screamed at myself, hearing him get back to his feet. Rushing forward, he pounced on my back, his fingers curled around my neck, crushing down on my throat.

A gasp choked out of my mouth as my lungs searched for air, his hand clamping down harder. Ringing filled my ears as my vision blurred, my lungs burning for fuel.

He seethed in my ear, but my mind couldn't pick up on words, trying too hard to breathe, panic swarming me like a cloud of flies.

A haze built around me as my gaze landed on the one clear thing before me, as if he were in high definition, while everything else was smeared in fog. Warwick stood up from his seat, his body rigid. His azure eyes sliced through the fuzz, zeroing in on me.

Fuck, he was viciously sexy. Terrifying. Cruel.

And pissed.

Rage and abhorrence heaved up his shoulders, all directed at me. His lips curled, hands rolling into fists, as if the way I was dying wasn't inhumane enough.

Something about his reaction vibrated through me, sparking a fierce fury. He was probably mad he wasn't getting to kill me himself. I was sure he'd love to be the one who exterminated the well-known ward of General Markos.

It was a flicker of time. The lack of oxygen caused a glitch in my brain. Even though I laid on the ground, I felt myself right next to him. His rich smell mixed with sweat and grime, the heat pulsing off his skin.

"*Fuck you,*" I sneered in his ear. Then in a blink, I was back.

He jolted, his head glancing over his shoulder, then shot back to me in the arena.

His nose flared, his head slanting to the side, his glare narrowing.

"*Fuck you back,*" his voice scraped the back of my neck, the feel of his lips brushing my ear. "*Now fight.*"

What the hell?

A charge zapped life into my chest, clearing out the cobwebs, bringing me back to myself as my mind emptied of everything except the sensation of Rodriguez's grip and the lack of air sputtering in my chest.

"Die, fucking HDF bitch!" Rodriguez tried to push my face into the dirt. "How are you not unconscious yet?"

With more energy than I thought I had, my head slammed back. *Crack!* The sound of his nose breaking snapped in my ears, his cry as his grip loosened, allowing oxygen to enter my lungs.

Heaving in, I swore I could feel Warwick next to me, yelling at me to move, to get my ass up. Gods, I must have lost a lot of brain cells.

Ramming my elbow into the bull's stomach, he pitched to the side, grabbing his nose and his middle. Rolling the opposite way, I scrambled back up to my feet, my lungs still working to greedily fill themselves as I backed away from him.

I really didn't feel any pain, only adrenaline pumping through my veins, all my energy settling down on one emotion.

Anger.

Rodriguez shot for me, and I darted to an overturned box, one side propped up on a stick. Diving for the spike, I yanked it from the ground, my body skidding across the gravel, tearing into my flesh. I rolled back up.

Rodriguez's head still peered around as if he was searching for me. *Hello? Over here!* Did he not see me move?

Taking advantage, I leaped back for him. Before he moved, I was able to pierce his shoulder with a sickly crunch with the wood spike. His head reared, and his back arched as a loud moo bellowed from his throat. His body jerked as I yanked the spike back out.

I was not going to lose my weapon to him. Plus, this left him bleeding. Weaker.

He whirled around, nose flaring with wrath, his eyes dark as night, his shoulders expanding.

This was no longer sport. He lowered down, kicking his leg back. Bulls did that when they were about to attack. It was his nature, but his nature was also his weakness.

His reveal. He gave me plenty of warning before he charged for me.

Twisting, I vaulted to the side, spearing him again as I twirled around him, blood spurting out of his side. He roared with pain, twisting back for me. Snorting and pawing the ground, he stormed for me again.

The dance of the bull and matador.

Holding out until the last moment, I leaped to the side, but his arm jutted out, catching me across the neck and slamming me to the ground. Blinking back pain, I managed to spin over, making sure to keep him in my sights. His feet hit the ground as he charged for me, death glaring from his eyes.

I realized it wasn't just Bakos's training that had

equipped me for this, but Istvan's as well. He'd obsessively pressed Caden and me to study the history of all regions, plus their customs and civilizations. From Tibetan monks high in the Himalayas to Spanish conquistadors. And traditions like bullfighting.

I remembered reading how matadors waited until the last moment to strike. The beasts, no matter in animal form or human form, had one real way of fighting, their bodies unable to stop and pivot as fast once they got speed.

I stayed on the ground, appearing hurt, watching him come for me, my heart thumping in my ears.

Hold, I ordered myself as Rodriguez sprinted for me, billows of dirt puffing off his boots with every strike to the earth. The instinct to get up and run wailed like a banshee in my chest.

I gritted my teeth.

Hold.

Closer. Closer. His boots quaked the ground under me.

Rodriguez grunted, his boot stomping down for my face at the same time I rolled. His boot hit an empty spot as I drove the spike into the side of his knee.

He bellowed like a wounded animal, collapsing from the pain in his leg. Scuttling to my feet, I slammed a heel into his chest. Then I leaped down on him, yanking the spike from his leg. He gurgled in agony.

The mix of boos and cheers raked up my vertebrae as my spear hovered over his heart. Blood leaked from his wounds, wetting the dirt. His expression was defiant and angry, but his throat bobbed with fear, his eyes tracking me.

"What are you waiting for?" he sneered. "Grow a conscience suddenly? You are no better than us, human. You do what you need to do to survive too. To protect your own."

Chants whirled around us, but nothing soaked in. I didn't

want to kill him, just as I hadn't wanted to kill Mio. I'd been trained to kill or be killed, but I'd never fully gotten that lesson, even though I was taught fae had no empathy, no morals.

Don't hesitate.

I was hesitating.

The bang of a gate jerked up my head, my defenses on alert. The guards weren't supposed to intervene before the fight was done.

I saw Boyd shove a figure out of a nearby gate, the guy stumbling to stay on his feet, brown eyes meeting mine with terror.

No.

Please, no. This couldn't be happening.

"Brex?" Aron's head jerked around like a scared bunny, his feet moving toward me. He moved as if he were still sore, but he shouldn't even be moving. He wore a new uniform, and the deep cuts showing on his arms were wrapped up.

He'd been patched together and probably given a numbing agent so he could fight.

"Don't worry. I know the perfect place for him."

Boyd had planned this.

Standing up, the spear tumbled from my grip, my eyes snapping to the figure behind the gate. Boyd smirked at me with triumph, lapping up my reaction like it was cream.

Fuck.

The receipt for my reprieve was up… and it was time to pay.

Chapter 21

"No!" I shouted, twisting around to Zander. "No, you can't do this."

Zander's eyes dropped, his grip on the bars tightening.

"Zander?" I tried to keep my voice even.

"He can't do anything, *Kovacs*." Boyd strung out my name as if it were a dirty word, letting me know this was about much more than a hurt ego. My name inspired vengeance. Power. Control. Blood. "He has no authority once players are in the arena; we can't intrude." He shrugged with a malicious grin. "Rules are rules."

"I'm not doing it." I glared at Boyd, shaking my head.

"Only one walks out, or none do." He winked at me. "Guess it's up to each one of you to decide who wants to live bad enough."

"No." I stepped back farther away from both men. Rodriguez climbed slowly back to his feet, his hand gripping his side, his skin pale, blood leaking the color of life from his skin.

"Well, I guess that made it easy. She volunteers to die." Boyd gestured to me through the bars, his eyes moving between Rodriguez and Aron. Panic and fear shook Aron, his eyes darting around, taking everything in before landing on me.

"Brex?" He whispered my name, pleading with me to explain what was going on.

"You can't do this. I've already fought!" I screamed back at Boyd, exhaustion skewering fury through me, my body drained and trembling. "This isn't fair."

"Fair?" Boyd's head fell back, howling with laughter. "Oh, poor little rich girl, used to being bubble-wrapped. Humans are so weak. Fragile…" He waggled his head. "*Fair*," he scoffed. "Sweetheart, look around you. You're in *Halalház*. It's feared for a reason." He pointed up to the crowd, which was booing and hissing. "Better decide soon. None of you have seen when a mob turns vicious." He stepped back, dissolving into the darkness of the tunnel.

Facing the new triangle, my gaze shifted back and forth between Aron and Rodriguez. I wanted to sit and curl into a ball as my soul shredded into pieces. Rodriguez, I would have killed due to survival and all, but Aron was different. He was my colleague. Someone, even as cocky as he was, I cared about. I knew him. Had grown up with him. He didn't deserve this. The only reason he was put in the Games was because of me.

The crowd rumbled their displeasure that no one was bleeding or dying as they were promised. Disgusting. The core of people, human or fae, when peeled back to the basic form, was violent and ruthless.

Unless they were in the ring.

The standoff lasted a moment before Rodriguez smiled grimly at me, his hand on his wound, bleeding out. He swiped the dagger off the ground, whirling for my friend.

"No!" I leaped forward, barreling into Rodriguez, causing him to stagger to the side. Aron's leg swept out in an arched kick, knocking the spike from Rodriguez's hands. As I moved in, my fist crashed against Rodriguez's already broken nose, more bits of cartilage snapping under my knuckles.

A bellow tore from Rodriguez, fresh waves of red liquid dripping down his face.

Wordlessly, Aron and I moved around the bull, stepping back into our training. Many times, Bakos not only had us fighting each other but also working together to take down others in groups. It was like a choreographed dance, which felt natural because of the countless hours we were drilled in it. Aron was never someone I had "danced" well with, but in this moment, I put all that aside. There could be no egos.

Just survival.

Rodriguez crashed back down to the ground, blood draining quickly from his wounds. His lungs heaved in and out shallowly. I knew death would come for him now no matter what, but the Games demanded us to take it.

"Aron, toss me the spike," I yelled, jumping down on Rodriguez.

Nothing.

"Aron!" I screamed again, my focus moving to him, watching him roll the wooden spear in his hand, not responding to me. "What are you waiting for? Give it to me."

His fingers wrapped around the chunk of wood. "I'm sorry, Brex." His brown eyes peered over at mine, no longer filled with fear or confusion.

Ice slid down my vertebrae to my belly.

"Only *one* of us can walk out of here." He flipped the stake in his palm with just a hint of sadness. "I regret it has to be this way, but there is no choice. I will not die here."

"Aron…" I tried to swallow the lump forming in my throat. "Don't do this. If we both refuse…"

"Right." He chuckled. "What kind of idiot do you take me for? You will happily stab me in the back the moment I turn around. Kill or be killed, right?" He moved toward me, his jaw twitching as he gripped the dagger firmer. "It's our final match, Kovacs, and this one *I* win."

Shifting off the dying man under me, I stepped away from Aron.

"Aron. Please. Don't do this… We are teammates. Friends."

"Friends?" he sputtered. "You treated me like shit under your boot. Not once did you look at me as if I was worth your time. You couldn't hide the disgust after we slept together. You didn't care about my feelings. I was your filthy secret. It was *always* Caden. He was all you could see or care about. So, no, Kovacs, we were never friends." He shook his head. "The only reason I'm even here is because of you and Caden. It's always about you two. I shouldn't be here. Die here. If killing you keeps me alive…" He took another step to me, glaring. "I don't want to. Shit, Brex, I was fucking in love with you… but this is the only way. Or we both die."

"In love with me?" Laughter burst from my lips. "You simply loved yourself."

"I wasn't the selfish one. You were so caught up with Caden you couldn't see anything else. Give anyone notice. And when you did? It was in the hopes Caden would observe it and get jealous." Aron darted to the side, and I easily spun out of his way. "Everyone saw it but you. He didn't care enough to step up. If Caden *really* loved you, nothing would have gotten in the way. No Romanian prince, his father, or any other girl who walked by."

"You don't know what you're talking about," I hissed. Caden and I lived in a world even our friends didn't understand. Things weren't so easy for us.

"You just don't want to face it." He stabbed the bloody dagger toward me, but I moved easily away. We knew each other's moves too well. "Did he fight for you? I mean, we all know what that sick Romanian fucker does to women. But Caden didn't put up a single fight for you, did he?"

"Shut up." I bobbed and weaved away from his attacks.

"No. He didn't. What does that tell you?" Aron slipped in closer. "He did mourn you. Completely lost his mind in alcohol and grief. That's true, but I didn't tell you everything. He's already moved on. Already fucking someone else."

"Aron." I batted away the weapon, trying to reset things.

"I'm telling you the truth, Brexley. If you had given me just a moment of your time instead of looking at me like I was your most vile mistake…"

"You were," I hissed.

"Blind to the end," he growled, leaping for me.

Our familiar dance was one we could do for hours. Kicking, punching, wrestling. We moved around each other, sweat sliding down my face, my energy weaning, allowing him to dart in. His foot hooked mine, tossing me painfully onto my back, knocking the air from my lungs. Jumping on me, grief in his eyes as he primed the weapon at the soft spot in my throat—a weak point for humans and fae alike.

Once again, I could feel a presence move around me, poking and prodding at me, as though telling me not to give up. My gaze darted to the stands. Warwick hadn't moved. His expression was even angrier, swirling around him like a storm. He snarled, turned and stomped away, disappearing in a tunnel near his seat.

Returning to Aron, the sparks of rage built through my bones again. Instinct was feral. Wild. It didn't think or care. It wanted to live—by whatever means necessary.

Aron's arm went up. "I'm sorry, Brex." He dropped his

arm like an ax, ready to take off my head. With all my might, my legs swung over, flipping him to the side.

Thud!

Aron smacked into the ground as I rolled him over, the wooden spike falling from his hand. Clawing and digging into his skin, I climbed on him, pinning him down. A crazed noise echoed from my lungs as I understood what I had to do.

Gripping the dagger, I only hesitated for a split second. The sheer terror and anguish in Aron's eyes imprinted on my mind as I swung down with a guttural cry.

"Brexley! No! Pleas—" His scream was cut off as the sharp point drove through his neck, ripping through his skin and muscles, blowing a hole in his esophagus. His eyes widened in horror as his mouth gaped and wheezed for air. His body lurched and jerked as his hands went to this throat.

Sliding off him, a cry wracked out of my chest at the sounds of my comrade gurgling and choking on blood, his body in the throes of death.

His wide eyes looked at me once with torment, shock, and anguish. Then his pupils glazed over as his life leaked out in a final shudder.

Aron was dead.

He was the first guy I'd ever been with, and we had fought each other on the mat countless times. I never imagined this would be our end. That I would be the one who took his life.

Guttural emotion swirled in my chest. I had killed my comrade with savage brutality and little hesitation. "Oh, gods...I am so sorry." The words dribbled over my lips, my breath heavy as I curled over him. At that moment, I just wanted to bring him to life to go back in time. "Aron…"

Suddenly his eyes bolted open, his mouth opened, and a hiss of sound—my name—came from his lips. His hand reached for me, and I jerked back with a cry. The moment I moved away, he went limp, falling back, his head rolling to the side, his dead eyes open and blank.

What the hell was that? Like some horror movie, the killer came back for one last scare. Was it the last bit of life leaving him?

I blinked at his motionless form, still and very dead, wondering if I had imagined it.

"Kill! Kill!" The onlookers in the stands clapped and chanted, bringing my attention back to the moment, their voices scraping against my skin. "Kill the bull! Kill the bull!"

I lifted my head and peered over at the figure feet away from me. Rodriguez's chest barely moved, his body shivering as his life leaked from him.

Fuck these monsters. Hadn't I given them enough? The man was dead anyway, but they wanted me to put in the final stake. Their lack of empathy and respect for life wrenched me up to my feet with a snarl.

Rage gurgled in my gut, my face twisting with rage as I peered at the faceless crowd, stepping closer to Rodriguez, escalating their cheers.

The wood spike dripping with Aron's blood hung at my side.

"Dooo iiiittt," Rodriguez hissed through his teeth, coughing and choking.

"No," I sneered. "I'm not giving them what they want. This is fucking disgusting."

"Do it for me. Don't let me die slow. Pathetically. Let me join my sister." He choked out every word, his forehead wrinkling with agony. "Wouldn't you want the same? A hero's death." He swallowed, his eyes pleading. "Give them what they want. Take the victory."

"I will do it for you. Not for them." I went down on my

knees. For the first time, I saw the person in his eyes, the life I knew nothing about. Friends, family. "Why are you in here?"

"Sister." His voice was barely louder than a whisper and broke over the syllables like a wave breaking against rocks. "Tried to save her from… testing… Savage Lands… there's… don't trust…" His eyes fluttered closed, his face streaked in agony.

"Don't trust what?"

"Kill. Me." The demand barely made it to my ears.

My chin wobbling, I covered his mouth and nose. He tried to jerk his head, but it didn't take much for him to drift into a forever sleep, his limbs going lax.

Sitting back on my heels, surrounded by dead bodies, I heard the boos of the mob, the viewers clearly unhappy with the way Rodriguez died. It wasn't cruel or violent enough to be considered entertainment.

Blood covered the arena, drenching my clothes in death. But it wasn't enough.

"I'm sorry." I leaned over him, my hands touching him.

His bulk jolted under my palms, his lashes fluttering. *Fuck me!* I jerked away, air clipping the back of my throat, but when I peered at him, he laid still, empty of life, as if I imagined it.

Death took a while for the body to understand, but it still had my heart thumping.

Slowly, I stood, but my muscles struggled to hold me. Tossing down the stake in revulsion, I turned around and marched to the tunnel, ignoring the crowd booing and hissing at me.

If you didn't come in a murderer, this place turned you into one.

"Prisoner 85221!" A man's voice formally called for me down the passage as I moved out of the tunnel to the main prison area. Footsteps pounded behind me. "Stop."

"Leave me alone." I could feel myself breaking with every step, the reality of what I had done tearing into my soul.

"I can't." Zander caught up with me, his hands clutching my arms and halting me. "You are still a prisoner." Zander stepped closer. "And not a very popular one right now."

"Why?" I exclaimed, tears clamoring up my throat. "I gave them everything they wanted. I killed *two* people tonight. One of whom was a close acquaintance of mine. What more do they want? Just because I didn't dagger Rodriguez? I still killed him."

"You are also General Markos's daughter."

"I'm not his daughter."

"Doesn't matter. You are close enough. You are important to him, which makes you important to his enemies. Markos's name is venom within these walls. You are not safe anymore."

"Was I ever?" I lifted my head, my gaze challenging his. "From the moment I walked in, I have been singled out far more than anyone else."

"That's because there is something about you. Good or bad. Admiration or hate. You are a magnet for them both." One hand dropped away from my arm, cupping my dirty and bloodied cheek gently. "The instant you walked up, I felt it. A lure. The scales tipping one way or the other. I just didn't expect the side I would end up on."

He was so close, his warm consoling hand on my face while the sounds of cheers and chants came from the pit, signaling the final fight of the night. Lost, grieving, and barely standing, I longed for safety. Comfort. To not feel or think.

He leaned in closer, his breath grazing my lips. I wanted

him to kiss me, to lose myself in pleasure. To forget all the pain and ugliness. He was a warm body who seemed to care about me.

"Brexley," he whispered my name, his mouth touching mine.

The clang of a cell door closing wailed down the corridor, jolting us back. Reality dumped down on me, the realization of what I was about to do to forget the horrors of the night.

I had sex with Aron, let him be my first because of heartbreak and longing for someone else. I'd known him since the age of thirteen, and I had brutally killed him, even as he pleaded for me to stop. And here I was, his gore still warm on my clothes, about to make out with my guard. What kind of person was I?

Suddenly, all I tasted was my victims' blood. All I felt were their spirits clinging to me, my skin itching so badly I wanted to crawl out of it.

"I need a shower." Emotions flooded my eyes and heart. I turned away, heading for the bathroom. Zander followed me, where another two guards waited.

I shot Zander a glance.

"Extra protection." He answered my unspoken question. "What better time to attack you."

Me, naked in the shower, was the most vulnerable time.

"Can I have a moment?" I asked, the walls around me thinning. "Can you stand outside the door?"

"I'm sorry." Zander shook his head. "You can't be left unattended anymore."

My lips squeezed until I knew they blanched, holding back a sob that swirled on the back of my tongue.

I moved for the shower. A new uniform and undergarments were laid out, with a less worn towel, unused soap, and shampoo *with* conditioner in it. Those were my perks for killing.

Conditioner and fresh soap for two lives.

Undressing, I let my soiled garments fall to the floor and stepped underneath the stream of water, trying to ignore the eyes on me. I resented them for peeling away another layer in a moment I needed to myself.

The water streamed down on me as I pressed my forehead against the cool tile. I fought back the sobs working up from my gut. I wouldn't let the guards see me break down, not even the horse-shifter, Zander.

I couldn't find the energy to move, to lift my arms to my hair, or scrub the blood off my skin. The dirt and stain went so much deeper.

Energy prickled at the back of my neck.

"Get. Out." A deep timbre thundered through the room, jerking my head around with a jolt. My heart and breath came to a stuttering pause.

Oh, my gods…

Warwick, covered in blood and dirt, stood a few steps inside the door. His dark hair was down and wild around his face, an open wound slashed over his cheek, dried blood at the corner of his mouth. *What was he doing here?* His fight had started less than ten minutes ago, but by the dirt and red liquid glinting off his uniform, it was already over.

Meaning he had killed one of the top fighters… in minutes.

His presence in this room also confused me. He had never been in this bathroom before. As far as I knew, he had his own. So why was he here? Asking me to leave?

The guards pushed off the walls, but none of them said a word, staring at him cautiously.

"I. Said. Get. Out." His intense gaze was on me, but his demand was intended for the guards, not me.

"Prisoner—" A guard stepped forward to argue, but Warwick snapped his head toward him, and the guard slunk back, swallowing nervously.

It was as if the world flipped. A prisoner had more power over the people guarding him.

"Farkas, you know we can't—" Zander stepped up to him.

Warwick puffed out his chest, crossing his arms, not bothering to respond, his power throbbing through the room with domination.

The two lesser sentries looked to Zander for direction, my alarmed gaze also on him. I waited for him to say no, to protect me as he said he would.

Conflict flashed over the horse-shifter, but then he sighed, putting his hands on his hips, and dipped his head in acceptance.

What?!

The three guards filed toward the door without a single word. My mouth dropped as I stared after Zander, unable to find my voice.

"We'll be right outside." Zander glanced back at me, concern wrinkling his forehead before he turned around and departed. Leaving me alone.

What the fuck? What happened to the guards protecting me?

Fright held me in place like a cornered animal. Did he plan to assault me? Kill me? Finish the job two others couldn't? Was that why he was so irritated earlier?

Brexley Kovacs was still alive, which must be rectified.

Emotionless, Warwick watched me for another moment, tension billowing through the room. His gaze never lowered down my naked figure, though phantom fingers touched my skin like they were tracing over my curves, sweeping down my legs and up to my breasts, my nipples hardening, my breath snagging.

Brexley! Anger at myself burned in my throat. This man was probably about to harm me in some cruel way, and I was fantasizing about his touch.

Keeping my chin high and jaw locked, fatigue shook my legs, but I didn't cower, just faced my death head-on.

Instead of lunging for me, his hands went to the bottom of his shirt, ripping the filthy battle-worn fabric over his head, tossing it onto the ground.

Holy. Shit.

I blinked, my insides locking up. Fear. Shock.

Desire.

He wasn't some pretty boy type, and I'm not even sure he would be grouped in the rugged category. Warwick Farkas was in a whole league of his own, everything about him severe and overwhelming.

His thick, corded shoulders and arms were the kind you could picture bending a car in half or wrapping around you like a shield. His torso and chest were carved with muscle and decorated with deep scars and tattoos, a timeline of his life. Symbols and pattern tattoos scrolled down his arms, and one started at his side and slipped below his pants line. I couldn't decipher the meaning of any of them, but there was no denying they were sexy as hell. He was brutal and sensual, terrifying and captivating.

His cool gaze remained on me while he shoved his pants down, kicking them to the side, along with his boots. Completely naked, he straightened to his full height with no hint of inhibition, displaying his *massive* physique.

The tattoo on his side curved over his ass and down to his thigh, drawing my gaze with it.

Fuuuuckkkkmmmmeee.

My mind blanked.

He stood fully erect. My gaze couldn't stop from moving to his deep V-line, my eyes trailing down. Even full of terror, my body responded.

I had seen a lot of naked guys at the academy: fit, toned, ripped, and in all shapes and sizes. I thought I had seen it all—but nothing, I mean nothing—prepared me for Warwick Farkas.

Chapter 22

He sauntered toward me, my body and eyes tracking him as my heart thumped in my chest. But I couldn't move. Couldn't breathe.

He strode right up to me, his toes nudging into mine. Craning his neck down, he loomed over me, the heat from him slinking over my skin, wrapping around it, dipping between my legs. He watched me for a moment before he stepped past me, his shoulder grazing mine as he dipped his head under my shower stream, his hand brushing the water off his face, running through his hair.

"Wh-what are you doing?" I whispered, my voice breathy and nervous.

"What does it look like?" he rumbled, tilting his head back. The water trailed down his face, over his lips. Every word he spoke, no matter loud or quiet, raked over me like gravel until it turned into liquid, dripping slowly down my limbs, seeping under my skin and into my bones.

Hot and burning.

I had never met anyone like him, who held the world in his palm. No fae or human could resist his lure, and I knew it wasn't magic. Not in here. It was just him.

I forced my eyes forward, away from him, terrified of why he was here, but I couldn't deny how aware I was of his naked body moving next to me. My skin screamed with his nearness, fixated on the way the water dripped down his physique. "Don't you have your own shower?"

"Yes." Dunking his head under the cascade again, his arm brushed mine, jolting me. A touch from him was similar to lightning ripping through my nerves. He grabbed the shampoo off the shelf, his gaze lowering as he poured the creamy gel into his palm and peered over at me.

"Your fight is already over?" I stared at the drops of water clinging to his long, thick lashes, which were so dark they almost appeared like eyeliner. "You can kill that fast?"

"When I need to." His tongue slid over his bottom lip, swiping up drops of liquid.

I swallowed. "You needed to?"

He peered at me, not answering, handing me the bottle of shampoo. The beads of water glided over his mouth, taunting me as they rolled over his shoulders and chest, to his stomach, moving lower, inviting me to catch them with my tongue, to taste the salt on his skin. The urgent need to rise up on my toes and suck off the water, skimming my mouth over every inch of his skin, to take him into my mouth and taste him on my tongue, wracked through my muscles, pulling me to him like a magnet.

I jerked back.

What the hell?

His brow furrowed with confusion, but the expression cleared before I even could decipher it. Running his soapy hands through his hair, he tipped his head under the cascade.

I watched him for a minute, realizing I had no fight left in me. Not for this. Switching off my brain, I gave in to the bizarre moment. Dumping the soap in my hand, I followed the same actions, our forms moving around each other as we cleaned the blood and dirt from ourselves, reddish water pooling at our feet, sliding down the drain.

We didn't touch, but I swore I could feel him glide and slither over my skin, sparking desire through my nerves. Losing myself, I shut my eyes, my senses heightening as the water pummeled my skin, the heat from his body skating over me feeling like hands.

Somewhere in my head, I knew I should be disturbed that this brutal and enigmatic legend was giving me comfort, soothing and centering me without a word or touch. His nearness made me feel I wasn't alone. He was someone who might really understand what I was going through.

I opened my eyes, staring up at him. He watched me with a guarded expression, his chest heaving like he had been running.

"Why are you here?" I muttered.

"Because…" he muttered, his gaze heavy. "I know where you are about to go. The darkness will seep into you, blackening your soul if you let it." His voice was rough, oozing down my neck, making me shudder. "What you had to do out there? Death demands payment from you as well. Compensation for living." His words pierced my chest with truth, a truth few of us comprehended.

No one left the arena without paying in some way.

"He was your friend?" he asked gruffly.

I was fucking in love with you. Aron's voice echoed in my mind, his pleading expression at the end.

I nodded, my throat closing. I wouldn't have exactly called him my friend, but I had a bond with Aron that no one else had. He hadn't been the only guy I had been intimate with, but he had been my first.

Without warning, my walls crumbled. The grief I had

been holding back surfaced with a wretched sob, curling me forward. My hand slapped over my mouth, but the dam had broken, letting my anguish flow out.

Not many had ever seen me cry, only Caden after I lost my father and a few times when the teenage emotions got too much. But the last man in the world who should see me break ripped at my barrier, and I let it fall.

Silent sobs sucked out the air in my lungs. Grabbing for the wall, my spine curved as heartache ripped and clawed at my chest. Trapped behind my ribs, it couldn't burst through and relieve me of the agony.

The misery, guilt, grief, disgust, and hate swallowed me whole. I slid down the wall and wrapped my arms around my legs. I let the agony plunge out of me and down the drain.

"I can't..." I gasped for air, my nails scraping at my chest, needing to release the pain, sensing the darkness slipping into my head like fog. He was right; death had come to claim another huge chunk of my humanity.

His enormous physique crouched in front of me, consuming every inch of space around me, my gaze not able to avoid his massive cock, mingling thick desire along with my sorrow. He clutched my chin, pulling it up so I had to look at him, forcing me to suck in sharply. In that moment, I felt no panic or grief.

Or pain.

It was instant. Relief and serenity poured down on me like honey, soothing and thick, balancing my tipped universe.

"You can," he growled. "And *you* will."

The water rained down on us, his gaze drilling into me. Not a flicker of emotion showed on his face telling me what was going through his mind, but his aura pressed into me, engulfing and oddly empowering.

"You heard me earlier? In the pit?" The question

stumbled off my tongue without thought, my tone curious and vulnerable, my gaze searching for something I couldn't even name.

His jaw twitched, his forehead furrowing. His fingers slid from my face as he abruptly stood. Turning, he strode out of the room, completely naked and wet.

I sat there under the cool stream, staring into the vacant space he left. Zander and the two other guards rushed in, taking me in.

"Are you okay?" Zander started to walk toward me, but he stopped right at the shower line, anxiously shifting from foot to foot.

Was I all right? Far from it, but not for the reason I had walked in with.

I had the most disturbing sensation of feeling centered with him near and then off kilter the moment he left, a fear that something was coming… and I had no idea how to fight it or how to prepare.

"Die, HDF bitch." A hiss crept up the back of my neck, and I jerked my head over my shoulder. Nothing but blank expressions met me, the regular morning zombies staggering forward, no one looking suspect. Blinking, I faced back around hearing another threat murmured near me, lacing fear down my spine. As I limped through the entrance of the bathroom, the figures bottlenecked at the doorway, where we shuffled in like sheep, and suddenly stopped. Bodies slammed into me, shoulders ramming me, elbows knocked me around with force as whispered threats muttered in my ear.

"I will kill you, *Kovacs*."

"Stop!" Still aching from the fight, I bobbed around,

trying to stay upright, panic curling in my throat. Yellow, blue, red, and gray uniforms danced around my periphery. Hands grabbed for me, touching me while some yanked painfully at my ponytail, bouncing me around.

Grunting, I tried to shove through the throng with any energy I could muster, my bones screaming in protest. I needed a rest from the abuse of the night before. The crowd only crunched in closer, getting angrier and braver.

There would be no special treatment for winning; my identity changed everything. Now I would be the prize. Kill the ward of General Markos—you win.

A hand crawled into the space, wrapping around my wrist. I tried to tug out of the hold, but it yanked me forward with unbelievable strength.

"She said stop!" Kek's voice drove through the mob, pulling me beside her, eyes black as night. "Do as she says or deal with me."

Growls and snarls echoed through the group, but begrudgingly they listened to the demon, huffing away with glares and promises of later.

I sucked in a deep breath, my barriers still wobbly and fragile since being in this very room the previous night with Warwick.

"Jesus, little lamb." Kek stepped in front of me, crossing her arms. "You have them clamoring for you, even without brushing your teeth." She winked. I stared. "Your performance last night? I have to say, I'm impressed, awed, slightly frightened, and *totally* turned on."

My lips pressed together, not responding. Speaking cost far more energy than I had to give this morning. The surge of adrenaline was already plummeting to the ground. I slept very little, and only because my mind and body gave in to the fatigue. Besides the mystery of Warwick's visit, my mind looped with Aron's declaration, Rodriguez's cryptic words, and Mio's eyes. They haunted me, their cries of death echoing through my mind, bolting me up during the night with a gasp.

On top of it, I hated to admit the absence of Opie and Bitzy this morning stung. Many days they weren't there, and I never really thought about it. But this morning I wanted to see them. I had grown used to their visits, adding a bit of reprieve to the horrific days. Even Bitzy was growing on me. I couldn't help wondering if they stayed away because they learned who I was. General Markos was known to be very anti-fae, killing sub-fae as if they were rodents. Did they think I was the same?

"Seriously, lamb, you gave Tad and me a heart attack."

I moved to my locker, grabbing my pouch of toiletries, and ambled for a free sink.

"You didn't hope for my death?" I questioned dryly, pulling out my toothbrush.

"Hope for your death?" Kek leaned on the counter, lifting a blue eyebrow. "Seriously?"

"I'm Brexley Kovacs, General Markos's ward, daughter of the renowned Captain Benet. As far as I can tell, most here consider those two associations as bad as the worst crime you could commit. I'm worse than a murderer."

"Well, since you've done that too…"

I shot a glare through the metal mirror.

"Too soon?" She met my gaze in the reflection.

"What do you want, Kek?"

"Nothing."

"I don't believe you. Everyone wants something." From the moment Warwick stalked away, my mood had turned foul.

Confused.

The anguish crept back in, taking over my mind.

Though the darkness didn't consume my soul as I thought it would, something about him beside me had made me feel balanced. Then the moment he left, I was… What was I? Unbalanced? Tangled? I couldn't explain the odd mix of feelings fluttering in my stomach. All night my mind had twisted the memory of him so much I wasn't even sure it happened. It could have been just a bizarre dream.

"I want mind-blowing sex, a very strong cocktail, a rare steak, and a great massage, but not sure you can provide any of those." She followed me over to a vacant toilet.

I tugged down my pants and sat down, ignoring the guy next to me muttering under his breath in disgust at my presence.

Funny, I no longer had any concern about how many had used the toilet before me. Germs covered everything we touched and ate here. How quickly priorities and hang-ups changed when survival was your only goal.

"I have no doubt you'd be excellent at the first, but I don't think I'd be your first choice. Plus, I think you *need me* more now." She motioned to the room. I glanced around, the space full of glaring looks and sneers. "What are you looking at, asshole?" she snapped at a man in a yellow uniform on the toilet next to me.

His eyes widened.

"Move," she ordered.

"Bu-but… I'm not done."

Blackness rolled over her irises again, her lip snarling, her skin bleaching out. "Move."

With a yip, the man grabbed for his pants around his ankles and ran off.

A smile curved over Kek's face, her eyes returning to normal. She grinned, clearly delighted with herself, taking the empty toilet to do her business.

"I can take care of myself," I grumbled, pulling up my pants and heading to the sink, washing my hands.

"I know you can. Anyone watching you last night would realize that. You were unbelievable. Sometimes I swear I didn't even see you move. But they won't come at you one on one." She stuck her hands under the same faucet I was using, scrubbing hers before we headed out, matching my slow steps taking us to the mess hall. "Doesn't hurt to have a demon on your side."

In one sentence, I realized how much my life had changed.

A demon on my side.

At HDF, that would be heresy. And just a few months ago, I would have shunned anyone suggesting I would work with not only fae, but a demon.

So much had changed.

How much of the girl who walked into this place was left in me now?

Chapter 23

"Do you like it?" Opie twirled around, showing off his new outfit. "I found some food coloring in the kitchen."

"It's… *colorful*." I leaned against the wall, rubbing the slumber from my eyes after getting a few solid hours of sleep. *Hmmm, I wonder why*, a voice taunted in my head. I rubbed my eyebrows, trying to push away the memory of the night before, pretending it was a dream.

"Just colorful?" Opie circled his arms in the air and down his figure. A smile wobbled my mouth, my eyes burning at the brightness of his new creation. His shorts and tank, which looked the same as a onesie, were cut from cheesecloth and stained a bright tie-dyed rainbow. He added a pink loofah as a hat.

"I like it."

Chirp!

"Shush. She said she liked it." Opie huffed, glancing at the huge-eared creature clinging to his back. "Why would she lie about that?"

"I wouldn't." I shot Bitzy a glare. "I *love* it."

Bitzy flipped me off.

I flipped her off back.

A strange warmth filled my chest. A burst of laughter gripped my chest at the amusement Opie's crazy costumes and Bitzy's middle finger brought me. Waking up to Bitzy shoving her finger in my nose gave me a feeling I probably should seek help for.

Pulling my knees up to my chest and placing my chin on them, I watched Opie strut around like he was on a runway, displaying his new creation. They were my one real joy in this hell, and I was so happy when they showed up again. Nothing changed in their eyes.

It had been two hellish weeks since I killed in my last Games. Every day the threats grew more severe. Bolder. From both inmates and guards. I had fresh bruises and scratch marks on my skin from those seizing a private moment to strike. Besides Tad and Kek, no one was on my side, and Kek wasn't around to help me except in the mornings in the washroom, and Tad couldn't physically do anything.

I was alone—an island by myself.

The fae and half-breeds I understood, but humans despising me was a shock. I mean, I expected a little bitterness from the Savage Lands dwellers because of my station. But it seemed like a deep-seated hatred causing them to choose fae over their own leader, which stirred an uneasiness in me. I didn't understand how they could go against Markos, who was trying to fight for them. He was a formidable person and a tough general, but not malicious.

My ideas of him had changed since being here. What I used to think of as cruel behavior was the way he showed his love. He fed me, raised me, and made sure I received the best education. I had been lucky and so spoiled I didn't even realize it. I would take his tough love in a heartbeat now and gobble it up like it was dessert.

I had no doubt if he knew I was alive, he would do

anything in his power to get me out. He had never laid a finger on me and always talked about wanting better for the human civilization. Peace and fairness among species, improving things for everyone. They just couldn't see it through their resentments and misery.

The fae and human tormenters weren't what bothered me. Even the threats and physical violence against me were manageable.

Being ignored pissed me off the most.

Warwick kept his distance from me since the night in the shower, giving me a *wide* berth, hardly showing up for meals. When his gaze did find mine, it was brief and full of abhorrence so thick it clung to me the rest of the day like a death threat.

This morning his aura clung to me in a different way—one I despised more than his hatred.

Last night three beautiful women dressed in expensive clothes were escorted through the prison. Two blondes and one redhead, all tan, curvy, huge-breasted, groomed, and manicured. Clean and shiny, and they probably smelled of flowers. I had no doubt where they were going and who they were here for.

"Guess we know his type," I muttered to myself.

The complete opposite of me. Not that I cared.

But I couldn't stop myself from peering down at my baggy uniform and stringy hair. Stripping off my shirt to my sports bra, my hands roamed over the protruding bones and rough scars now carving my skin. He would be touching their flawless plump skin, his mouth exploring their full, healthy figures.

I had always been thin with no boobs, but now I was sickly and gaunt; even my muscles had dissolved. Sweaty and dirty, I wore a week-old uniform, which had butter, sweat, and bloodstains all over it.

The girl who wore party dresses, with shiny hair and a perfect manicure, eating lobster imported from Japan and Scotch from Scotland... The girl who was secretly kissed in dark corners by handsome leaders and princes... She no longer existed.

Even the memories of my old life felt as if someone else lived them.

Lying down on my blankets and closing my eyes, I couldn't stop myself from imagining my body being touched. Kissed. Wanted. It had been so long. Happiness was so foreign here that you craved it like a painkiller. To ease the agony for a while. To feel good for a moment. Breathe easily another moment.

When the cries came, echoing through the prison, it was not grief from fellow inmates. It was uninhibited bliss. Wild, loud, and fierce, all three women screamed like they had no control, the pleasure too much for them to handle.

My body reacted, nipples hardening, my pussy wet and pulsing. Wanting. Desire formed like thick webs along my nerve endings, tugging and vibrating as though it caught its prey. My skin tingled, demanding to be touched. Slowly, my hand moved down my ribs, pushing under my pants, moving below my underwear, my fingers dragging through my wet folds. *Oh, my gods.* My back arched. The need was overwhelming. I was starving.

I attempted to ignore the voices coming from inside the prison, the name they were moaning with ferocity. I tried to imagine Caden, visualizing how things could have been up on the roof of HDF if he chose to kiss me instead. This time he'd forgo everything that had stopped him and choose *me*. For one moment, I let myself believe we had come together rather than farther apart. The city lights sparkled below our entangled bodies, the train we were going to rob rolling by as he made love to me instead.

My fingers went deeper inside me, and I bit down as electricity flamed through me. The scene I set evaporated like smoke, Caden's image weak and distant, my mind struggling to hold on to it as another moved in.

"No." I ground my teeth in a snarl. I wanted Caden. Wanted to believe this version of our story had happened.

But the women only shrieked louder, making grunts and bangs that rallied the convicts with hoots and hollers. Warwick controlled our moods and actions as he always did, turning us feral and vicious. Energy sparked the air with animalistic lust. Groans from other cages joined the women, inmates pleasuring themselves under Warwick's influence and power.

"Fuck you," I whispered to him, despising how he invaded everything in this place—even my sexual fantasies.

Squeezing my eyes, I focused on Caden, my legs opening wider. As if claws shredded through my best friend's likeness, another physique surged through the remains, crawling between my legs. "Fuck you back." A feral smirk hitched his lips. Dominant. Brutal. Warwick's image took over with sharp clarity, his fingers tracing down my form, a tongue flicking my nipples.

I gasped, a groan curving my back higher.

The weight of his build, the wetness of his mouth, his hair tickling my bare stomach. It felt *so* real. My imagination craved relief so intently I could *really* feel hands caressing my skin, fingers shoving my underwear over, pushing inside me, curling.

"Gods," I hissed, squeezing my eyes tighter. Letting myself fall into the fantasy, I no longer cared it was Warwick who completely dominated my thoughts. I didn't focus on his face, but I could feel his presence, the muscular arms and hands, knowing exactly where the tattoos covered his skin.

His insanely huge physique pressed into me like he was really there. As if his lips were grazing my skin, his teeth nipping, his fingers pumping faster. My hands no longer were in my control, knowing better than me how to seek my pleasure. Pulsing and squeezing, a moan emerged between my stunted breaths, his name rolling softy from me. My imagination was so good, I could almost feel him open me wider, his hand taking me to the extreme until I cried out, the desire almost turning painful with sheer bliss.

I heard the women bellow in the distance, their pitches bleeding together, tearing through me as I hit my peak, as if all of them were one voice. Mine.

My mouth parted, an explosion rocked me, and I no longer felt I was in my body but soaring through the prison, slipping through the bars of his cell to him, like he was calling for me. I could feel myself skating over his body, licking and biting, my tongue wrapping around him, taking him into my mouth.

A deep voice boomed, rattling the bars on all the cages. The sound of him roaring his pleasure sent more desire through me, tensing my muscles and holding me captive for several moments before I plummeted back to Earth.

Gasping for air, I blinked up at my own ceiling.

Holy. Shit.

This certainly was not my first or even hundredth time pleasuring myself, usually thinking about Caden, but it had *never* felt like this. Not even close. Maybe the deprivation of joy or sexual connection here heightened it, and the fact that the entire place was getting off together multiplied the energy.

I would take any explanation except the one nibbling at the back of my head.

Warwick.

It wasn't merely because I imagined him… but because he had been here with me.

"You okay?" Tad shuffled behind me in the breakfast line, his lids narrowed on me curiously, drawing me out of my reprieve. My cheeks burned with what I had been just thinking about.

"Yeah, why?" I grabbed two trays, handing one back to Tad, clearing my throat.

"Something's different."

"More dirt, maybe?" I shrugged one shoulder.

"No." He tilted his head, his gaze zeroing in on me like he was trying to peel back my soul. "It's strange, but it's as though I can almost see an aura. I can definitely feel it right now. Like it's buzzing and glowing." His bushy brows strung into one long caterpillar. "It's the most bizarre thing I've ever experienced before. Reminds me of auras after sex."

Oh.

Shit.

I twisted around, shoving my tray at the fae serving the watery oatmeal. Twice this week I had been denied food, so Tad shared his toast with me. But tonight was my next fight so I hoped they would allow me to eat.

Maybe it would be my last meal.

Survival was a strange thing. You learned the one way to keep going, to endure, was to compartmentalize. The memory of Aron was tucked away in a box in my mind, where I filed all the torture and torment too. I took every moment as it came, not thinking about anything except the present moment.

Even though my life was on the chopping block again, I behaved normally. I got up, peed, washed my face, and now was going to have breakfast.

Or was trying to.

The fae woman serving the food flicked up her nose, her head wagging.

"We don't serve your kind here," she spat.

"And what kind is that?" Fury sparked up my spine, and my patience flipped at the thought of another day eating crusts of bread. "I didn't realize there was a ceiling on who you served in a place full of murderers, thieves, criminals, and rapists."

"And they're all better than the entitled daughter of General Markos," she sneered, already motioning me to move. People bumped against me to move out of the way. She scooped up the diminishing food, putting it on their plates.

Fury ignited, my belly lined with bile, burning up my throat.

"No!" I slammed my tray down on the metal counter, my eyes watering.

Everyone stilled as I shoved the tray at her.

"Fill my bowl!" I seethed, leaning over the counter.

"No," she insisted, her voice strained. She looked like a peacock, all sharp features, her beady black eyes staring down her long beak at me.

"I. Said. Fill. It." Fury rattled through each word. I whipped out a hand and grabbed her by the throat. Her eyes widened with shock and fear, not seeing or expecting my move. "Now."

She picked up her ladle, her hand trembling, and shoveled a scoop onto my dish.

"More." I tightened my fingers, hearing the guards yelling at me, moving toward me. "For the Druid too."

She filled his dish before I released her.

"Thank you," I replied tartly, turning toward our table. I felt proud I'd stood up for myself.

It lasted for one pure blissful moment.

Slam!

My tray flipped, smashing into my face, oatmeal pouring down my front, burning my skin as everything tumbled to the ground with a loud crash.

"You think you can get away with that here, HDF bitch?" A huge man moved in on me, his friends stepping into my periphery. Tattoos covered his neck, face, and arms, a ring through his nose, and his hair brown and wavy resembled buffalo fur. His wide chest and shoulders and smaller legs told me he was probably exactly that.

Rodriguez's group stood around me, almost all Bovidae-shifters, inching closer, puffed up and angry, their noses flaring with revenge.

Shit.

"You think you own the fuckin' place now?" The buffalo widened his shoulders, stepping into me. "You cheated. There's no way some scrawny human HDF rich bitch killed my friend."

"If it helps you sleep at night." My voice came out low, but louder than it should in the silent mess hall. Everyone, including the guards, stared at us like we were theater, tension and suspense threading through the space.

The buffalo-shifter inched closer, puffing up, threatening, and knocking into me. At the same time, his buddies moved in, bouncing me off them like a ball. They weren't going to truly harm me. The rules stated I was to be untouched for the Games.

"I will kill you." He shoved me again.

"Volunteer tonight then," I growled, not caring how large and strong this fae was. "If you're so sure your friend lost to this scrawny human HDF bitch by *tricks*, then step into the ring with me."

What the fuck are you doing? Logic screamed at me. I didn't know, nor did I seem to care.

"Or are you a coward?" Oohs and hisses sounded around my challenge. I lifted my lip into a sneer with confidence. "All talk? I think you just prance and put on a show but don't have the guts to actually step into the ring."

A gruesome smile edged his mouth, his hands stretching and rolling. "Why wait?"

It took only a second, a blink.

The buffalo's hand wrapped around the back of my head and slammed me into a table with an agonizing crunch. Blood burst from my nose as my face knocked into someone's food tray, scattering the contents across the room.

Shock and pain froze me. My certainty he wouldn't touch me had blinded me, leaving me vulnerable.

I crumpled to the floor while cheers and hoots echoed in my ears as the buffalo grabbed my legs, yanking me away from the table, his fist coming down on my temple as sets of boots kicked into my body from all around.

Pain exploded through me. I was unable to catch my breath or get to my feet as six of them beat and stomped me. The agony was so overpowering, my brain started to shut down. This was not the way I thought I would die. I had already accepted one on one in the arena… but not this way.

But fair or right did not exist in this place. Not one guard stopped them, not one person tried to break them up. Not for me.

Darkness seeped into my mind, pulling me away from reality, detaching me from the excruciating agony, blood blinding my vision and choking my throat.

"STOP!" A voice thundered through the room, the vibration rumbling deep into my bones, yanking my soul back to the surface, forcing my eyes open with a gasp.

Warwick.

The herd halted, twisting around, their brutish egos flipping off like a switch.

"Shit!" Three of them scrambled back, horror streaking their features.

The main guy stood still, folding his arms, but I could see his jaw shifting, his shoulders rising in defense.

Footsteps hit the floor, and I heard gasps and movement as people got out of Warwick's way, letting the Wolf cross the room.

Warwick parted the crowd, stepping up to the new buffalo leader. Emotionless, he stared at the man, but I noticed the tightness in his shoulders, a twitch under his eye. Signs that rage boiled under the surface.

The buffalo man was huge, but Warwick's frame towered over him. The shifter gulped.

"You have the right to touch her?" Cold. Detached. His gravelly voice was somehow calm and threatening at the same time.

"Uh—well—I mean, she is HDF. Markos's daughter." The bull motioned to me. "And she cheated. Rodriguez's death was not a fair fight."

"You're right; it wasn't." Warwick tilted his head, his words feeling like a trap.

"I must avenge my friend. And this bitch walks around here like she owns—"

Warwick's arm darted out, his hand clamping down on the man's neck, baring his teeth. "I didn't say why it wasn't fair." He squeezed, the shifter gasping and pawing at Warwick's hand. "Rodriguez was completely outmatched. She was by far the better fighter, killing two people in the arena while your friend pranced around like it was a pageant." He yanked the man's body closer to his face, their noses knocking together. "You are the one dishonoring his death by being a bully and coward," he seethed, spitting in his face. "You touched her. Breaking the rules. You know what happens when someone starts acting as if *they* are in charge here?" The buffalo's skin turned a deep purple, his mouth open, his eyes bugging. "They are shown the error of their ways quickly."

"Hey! He can't breathe!" A buddy tried to step up, but Warwick glared. The guy stumbled back behind the others, hiding.

Warwick snorted. "Do you see anyone coming to save *you*? The fear pumping in your veins knows not one guard, not even your buddies here, are going to stop me. I want you to feel that. I hope it is your last thought." Warwick squeezed harder, and the man's legs bowed. "You get off while *six* of you try to beat a tiny girl to death? Did it make you feel like a man?"

Tiny? I am not tiny, you asshole.

His gaze darted to me for a second.

"This is what I do to sad, insecure men like you," Warwick snarled, clamping down harder. The shifter tried one last struggle, but his fingers dropped from Warwick's grip, the whites of his eyes bursting red, a snap of his neck, and his jaw went slack.

Warwick let go, and the man's lifeless figure fell to the ground with a thump.

Holy. Shit.

He killed him—without hesitation or effort.

"That's a lesson for all. Do not *test* me, or you will join him." Warwick boomed to the stunned room, anger seeping through his statement. "And if I hear one more of you touches her, or so much as breathes in her direction?" He paused, circling to all the inmates. "You will be next. And I will not be so generous in how I kill you." He glanced down at me, his eyes rolling coolly over me. "*She's mine.*" He paused for a moment, our gazes locking at his words before a cruel grin twisted his mouth. "My *kill*…"

The brief moment my heart fluttered into my throat was ruined by the ball of lead that entered my stomach, smashing my last bits of hope.

He crouched down, leaning in close to me.

"It's you and me in the ring tonight. Your life is now mine, *Kovacs*."

Now I understood why he had stepped in and saved me…

To kill me himself.

Chapter 24

The excitement from the crowd buzzed far down the corridor, lighting the air with sparks. Terror weaved deeply into my bones, and I struggled to breathe or even stay conscious.

"You'll be fine. You can do this." Kek strode beside me, nipping at her nail. Soon she'd have to leave, as only Zander could escort me into the tunnel used for the fighters.

"Really?" My tone escalated a few pitches, my lungs pumping in and out rapidly.

"No, sorry, you're totally fucked." She cringed, running a hand through her loose braid as we stopped at the gate. My body swung to hers, my mouth gaping at her.

"I'm sorry!" She tossed out her arms. "I'm not good at this whole consoling thing. Not in my nature."

Zander unlocked the gate, the metal squealing as it opened, death shivering through my heart.

Kek's words were brutal, but it wasn't something I didn't know. Everyone knew. I had received nothing but smirks and pitying eyes all day. The only time people were nice to me was on the eve of my death: a shake of the head, a pat on the shoulder, even from those who had threatened me all week.

I was a dead girl walking.

Warwick had demanded healers to mend me for the fight tonight so he could kill me properly.

"Did I not warn you?" Lynx had said to me as we left the laundry room earlier today. "This time, there is no going back."

Despondency filled my eyes as I peered at Kek. At this moment, I realized she had become a friend. In a place of violence, death, and cruelty, she, Tad, Opie, and even Bitzy had become sources of comfort.

"Brex—" Zander cut himself off, clearing his throat. "85221. It's time."

I pursed my lips, my throat thickening as I grabbed Kek's hands. "Thank you," I whispered, trying not to cry, "for having my back. I still don't understand why, but I appreciate it."

Kek twisted her head to the side, her lids blinking rapidly, her nose twitching.

"And tell Tad the same. I never got to say goodbye."

"Then walk out of the arena and tell him yourself." Ire flared over her brow. "Do what you need to do."

A sad smile curved my mouth, her fury inflating instantly. We both knew I would not be walking out. No one, especially a bony, weak human girl, could win against the Wolf.

He was a legend for a reason.

The man who came back from the dead took lives like he was death himself.

Not one for sentimentality, I spun away from her, stepping into the dark tunnel. My jaw locked down when I heard her call my name. I didn't look back, cutting off everything and everyone who made me human and tucking it behind my heart.

Caden.

My father.

Hanna, the only real girlfriend I had growing up, and the rest of my comrades.

Istvan and Rebeka. They had taken me on as family and raised me after my father died. They loved me in their way.

I gathered all their faces and memories and closed the lid. If I let myself think or feel, I would collapse, fear and grief immobilizing me.

My boots crunched across the gravel as it took us lower into the earth. The drumming and chants from the stands echoed through the corridor. They all knew General Markos's ward would be dead soon, my blood watering the dirt. They'd be carrying the true knowledge: I didn't die months ago but was cut down in front of them. They'd probably put my head on a spike and take turns parading me around the cell block in pride.

My feet stopped, a woeful sob wrenching from my chest, my spine bowed over. Zander's hand touched my lower back, his fingers circling in soothing motions. "Brexley." My name barely grazed his tongue, his voice soft and laced with sorrow.

"Don't," I whispered. "Don't say it will be all right or I can do this." I looked up at him, agony snaking up my chest to my face.

His brown eyes filled with emotion as his gaze dove into mine. "Stay alive. Not everything is what it seems." Then his hands gripped my face, pulling me to him, his mouth capturing mine. Soft, but full of need, his lips moved over mine. My heightened emotions seized on his desire, consuming the last moments of kindness and pleasure.

I took his hunger and passion like it was a charging station, sending fire down my spine. I was not kind or gentle, but rough and demanding. I pushed for more, my teeth biting, my tongue licking. He tried to keep up with me, but I knew I demanded too much.

I always needed more. No guy I had been with ever seemed to leave me quenched. I thought it was because I truly longed for Caden, but maybe it was just me.

Never satisfied.

Zander broke away, his head tipping back, his eyes round as he stared down in awe.

"Brexley…" He said my name with reverence. "I need to tell you—"

"Now I know what was taking so long." An icy timbre wrapped around me like a boa constrictor, jerking me to the huge figure on the other side of the gate.

Fuck.

Warwick's gaze burned into me, dread punched my lungs, and I stepped away from Zander.

"Did I interrupt your final goodbye with the donkey?" Warwick sneered, leaning his shoulder against the bars casually, rolling a toothpick in his mouth. His body seemed relaxed, but his eyes oozed with threat as he glared at Zander.

"Horse," Zander snipped back.

"Same difference. Both an arse." He shrugged, his eyes catching mine again. "Little surprised at your choice, Kovacs. You think by fucking a guard, you would have gotten better treatment in here. Started too low on the totem pole."

"Shut up." Zander stepped forward, his jaw tightening with anger. "You think you own the world… think yourself so mighty. But you are a prisoner like the rest. I can't wait for someone to take you down a few pegs. Someday someone will kill you, and you will be forgotten. No fanfare, no one to mourn or care."

"Someday I will probably die, that's true, but I guarantee the world will mourn as though they lost a god." Warwick's confident blue eyes slid to mine. "And *someone* will definitely care."

"Your mother doesn't count." I glared at him, my fear replaced with irritation. What was he even doing out there already? It didn't seem his style. He didn't wait. He came, he killed, and he left. Why was he waiting for me?

He snorted, leaning his back fully against the gate, motioning to the stands, causing them to go wild. "Soooo… we're all here waiting for you. When *you're* ready, princess. You are the star of the show, after all."

"You are such an asshole." I churned with indignation, toppling the debilitating dread I held minutes ago to the floor.

He barked out a laugh, crossing his ankles, still staring out at the crowd, his fingers rotating the pick between his teeth as if he were enjoying a relaxing afternoon. "Is that all you got? Pathetic. My grandmother used to call me worse."

My legs moved before I could even think. I slipped my hands through the bars, fingers sliding up his skull, and knotted them in his hair, yanking back.

His head slammed into the bars with a bang, pinned in place, my mouth close to his ear. "I have *a lot* more, *Farkas*. Want me to show you?"

He curved his head to the side, showing me his profile, a hungry grin on his lips, his eye glinting with fire as I pulled harder on his scalp.

"I would like nothing more, *Kovacs*," he growled, his voice seeping over my skin and between my legs. "Ready to stop fiddling with your toy pony in there and come out and play with someone who might actually challenge you?"

His energy revved through me. My belly burned, heat scorching down my limbs.

"You think very highly of yourself." My mouth brushed his ear. His nose flared, his eyes darkening, energy puffing both our chests. "Like most men, you are probably all talk and very little action."

"Come find out for yourself. But unlike your boyfriend, I won't be gentle." His one eye met mine. "And from what I just saw… rough is *exactly* what you are aching for."

I shoved him forward, thunder crashing in my chest. "Open the gate," I ordered Zander. Warwick chuckled, stepping back from the entrance, tossing his toothpick to the ground and opening his arms in a "come and get me" motion.

"Brexley." Zander reached for my arm, his head shaking. "You don't understand…"

Already out of patience, I snatched the keys from his hand, unlocking it myself, not even looking back as I strode out, hearing him cry out my name again. I could feel nothing behind me anymore, my entire focus on the man in front of me.

The mob went insane when I stepped out. Whistles, chants, stomping, claps all blended together like music—the soundtrack of my epic battle with Warwick Farkas.

"Finally." Warwick winked at me. "Been looking forward to this."

"Me too." I sneered maliciously.

Living. Dying. Neither were thoughts crippling my mind. Somehow Warwick had removed those and only filled me with the need to fight.

To be his greatest challenge.

The dirt crumbled under our boots as we slinked around each other, our eyes locked.

Predator. Prey.

The bellows from the stands throbbed off my skin, my

heartbeat pulsing in my throat. Every seat was filled: prisoners, guards, even the medical and kitchen staff were all in attendance. Not one person wanted to miss the show tonight.

"War-wick! War-wick! War-wick!" His name clanged in the air, scraping my eardrums.

I stepped closer, but instead of meeting my dare, Warwick sidestepped, his gaze darting up into the stands. Usually, he didn't put on a show; he killed and got out. Why was he stalling? Playing with me?

"We going to dance all night?" I jeered, my gaze sweeping over the scene, trying to find anything I could use as a weapon.

Nothing. They had cleared out everything, leaving it bare of anything I could turn into a weapon.

"The only thing I do all night is *fuck*." His throaty voice looped around me, flushing heat into my veins as if he was actually touching me.

"Stop it." I brushed my arms, the demand bouncing from my mouth.

"Stop what?" His head slanted to the side, his gaze plunging down my form, and more tingles rushed through me. A violent shiver jerked my bones as warmth spread between my thighs. The intensity made me roll my shoulders and shake my legs to dislodge the sensation.

"That," I growled. "How are you able to do it? No one is supposed to have powers in here." I shook my head with a scoff. "Guess the great Warwick Farkas is even above that. No rules could possibly apply to such a legend, right?"

A smirk twisted his full lips. "Calling me a *legend* without my even touching you? Just think what you will call me when I do."

I glowered at him.

He lazily reached for me, and I pirouetted away, his

fingers grazing my skin, sending excitement through the crowd.

Through me.

"But I have no idea what you are talking about," he replied. As we circled each other again, his gaze drifted up to the stands before snapping back on me. "I'm not doing anything." He lifted an eyebrow. "*Yet.*"

"What I would give to wipe that smug grin off your face," I snarled, my ankles crossing as I sidestepped him.

"You think you have the ability to do it?" He slid in closer. "Please… be my guest. No one has before, but give it a go, *tiny human.*"

"Fuck you."

"I'm open to that as well." He darted in so quickly, I didn't have time to move. "Show me what you got." His mouth grazed over my ear as he brushed by me, overloading my system with fire, down my neck to my breasts, sizzling me down to nothing.

Chuckling, as if he knew what he did to me, he strutted past, leaving me vulnerable. Exposed.

Angry.

In a blink, I whirled around. His back was to me, his focus on the crowd again. Snarling, I kicked, smashing my foot into the back of his legs. The giant man stumbled forward, his hands shoving off the ground, but he quickly scrambled back to his feet.

The horde roared with excitement, dispensing energy into me.

Warwick turned, his eyes bright, a snarl on his face.

"Stop wasting my time." I lifted my chin. "So far, *all talk*, Farkas, and very little action."

A sneer glinted his features, his broad shoulders twisting around to face me.

"Fine." He grabbed the hem of his shirt and ripped it over his head, tossing the fabric to the side.

Fuck.

Like when we were back in the showers, the effect his body had on me was almost debilitating. And by the smug look on his face, he knew it.

He lowered himself, clapping, his gaze set on me. "Let's do this."

Hunter. Prey.

I grinned fiercely back at him. With a swish, I pulled my top over my head. He stilled as I tossed the shirt next to his on the ground. The throng of viewers screamed and pounded their feet in approval.

I winked at him, owning the moment. "Only fair, right?"

"Take off your bra, then we can call it fair," he rumbled, stepping closer to me, his gaze burning.

"Come and take it," I dared. He wanted to fight with fire? Fine. *Bring it.*

A sound came up his throat, and then he was moving for me. This time I was ready. As he charged for me, I stood in place until the last possible second. Diving out of the way, keeping my legs out, his boots hooked on my leg, thrusting him toward the ground. He barely hit the dirt before he was back up, his huge physique defying the law of gravity.

I jumped to my feet and continued our dance. Darting. Swiping. Dodging. For the next ten minutes, we moved around each other as though we both knew what the other would do by instinct.

The crowd grew restless, jeering as we hopped around each other.

"You're boring your fans," I heckled him. "And here I thought you were going to actually challenge me."

He scoffed, his hand rubbing his chin. He grinned

hungrily, then in a blink he spun, his leg swiping mine, dropping me to the ground, stirring the throng of viewers with energy. He leaped for me. Rolling out of his way, my boots jutted out, smashing into his face. A gasp echoed from the crowd as Warwick stumbled back, his hand going to his face.

It was as if the world paused. Everyone went silent as he wiped the blood from his nose and lip, staring down at his palm, shocked I was quick enough to strike.

His eyes rose, meeting mine.

Fury.

Wrath.

Fire lit his eyes. He'd gone easy on me before. Not anymore.

A spike of adrenaline rushed through my veins, and I popped back up to my feet. He moved with such haste I barely had time to respond. Jumping to the side, his hand crashed into my torso, slamming into my kidney. Falling sideways, I hit the ground, rolling through the dirt.

Pain chomped down on my nerves, but my adrenaline smoothed it out like a numbing gel, letting me leap back up to my feet.

He had every advantage. He was bigger, stronger, and possibly even faster.

Use your weakness as an advantage. I could hear Bakos in my ear. I was weaker, smaller, and bony… not easy things to use as an advantage.

Warwick darted for me, his huge frame dwarfing mine.

Smaller. Use it! Bakos yelled in my head.

Instinct dropped me to my knees, shrinking and bending my form to fit under his legs. My fist plowed into his crotch. A roar exploded through the arena, his body toppling over, crashing to the ground clutching himself. It wasn't the most respectable fight move, but this was to the death. I would use what I could. "You must also use what you don't have to your advantage," Bakos used to say. So I had. A punch to the dick.

Getting up, trying to find anything I could use, my gaze landed on a single lit torch hanging by the gate where I had come out.

Racing across, my legs and arms pumping, I reached out for the torch as a hand clamped down on my shoulder, yanking me back.

Crunch! My bones hit the ground, shoving air roughly out of my mouth.

Fuck. He really was similar to a wraith, sneaking up silently and quickly.

Standing over me, glaring down, he watched me, not moving to finish the job or take advantage of my position. What the hell? What fighter didn't take advantage of an enemy's vulnerable moment?

My lids narrowed. He could snap me in half right now. Game over. But even as the crowd chanted for my death, his gaze subtly went back up, like he was searching for something. What was he waiting for?

And what the fuck are you *waiting for, Brex? Get. Up,* I yelled at myself.

Confused at his lack of action, I clambered to my feet and backed away. The viewers disapproved of my escape, but my focus was entirely on Warwick, blocking out the rest of the world.

He plucked the torch from its clamp, twirling the flaming stick in his hand like a baton. "Want this?"

We stared at each other, his nose and mouth still bleeding; a gash cut across his eyebrow and over his nose.

"Come and get it, then." He held it out enough for me to grab. Not moving, I tried to work out different scenarios in my head and predict what his move would be.

Everything felt off—like he was trying to stall. "What's going on?"

"What do you mean?" It sounded more like a taunt than a question. "I'm offering you a weapon against me. Even after you punched me in the nuts." He grabbed himself, flinching as he adjusted himself. "Level out the playing field."

"No." Warning prickled the back of my neck. "You're not. Now fight me. Stop playing."

He leaned forward. "I haven't even *begun* to start playing with you."

Air sucked up my nose, and I stepped back, feigning a dash to the side, but he seemed to know exactly my move, matching it.

He started chuckling. "Try again, Kovacs." His breath brushed down my neck. "Now, really *run*."

I didn't hesitate, I took off, once again trying to find anything to help me.

There was nothing.

"Surprise your attackers. Catch them off guard. Do something unexpected." Bakos was back in my head.

Unexpected.

I halted, Warwick right on me, his eyes taking in my stop too late. Swiveling around, my hand smashed into his face, knocking his head back, pain through my nerves. No time to hesitate, my elbow stabbed the soft part of his throat. He roaring doubled over, coughing. Taking the gain, my boot cracked across his chest, his ass hitting the ground, puffing dirt clouds around us, the torch rolling away from him, extinguishing the flame.

I could hear the masses react, but it was a faraway sound as I leaped for the torch, the end shaped into a spike.

A punch slammed into my temple, exploding behind my eyes, knocking me to the side, rolling me over him to the ground. He dove for me, seizing my arms, pinning them to the dirt. His body covered mine, every bit of him pressing into me. Blood covered both of us, our panted breaths knocking our chests together. His bare, sweaty skin pressed into me, and though he was probably about to kill me, my body reacted on its own, opening for him.

I was suddenly furious at myself, at the thrill of feeling him between my legs, at my awareness of his erection burning into me. Kicking and wiggling, I tried to break the hold, my teeth clenching with ire.

"Stop, Kovacs..." he muttered, his mouth so close to mine, I froze. "I'm trying *not* to kill you."

What? Confusion webbed through my head. Did I hear him right? This was to the death. There was no other way out.

"What is taking so long?" he muttered, his gaze going up again, taking his attention off me.

His mistake.

Slamming my head forward, I felt and heard the crack of his already sore nose. Blood spurted on me as he reared back with a bellow. Wiggling from under him, I went for the torch. Fingers circled my ankle, yanking me back, my face hitting the packed dirt with a painful crack. Blood burst from my lip and nose, coating my tongue, dark drops hitting the ground. Pushing through the pain, I crawled for the spike, the tips of my fingers skimming it.

My skin screamed as he dragged me away, raking me over the gravel, the weapon slipping through my fingers.

"Fuck." Warwick rolled me over onto my back, crawling over me again, covering me like a weighted blanket, smearing blood over my torso. "You are *actually* making this fun. Challenging me more than I figured."

"You think this is fun?" I snarled, trying to buck him off me. "You're a sick fuck."

"What does that make you then?" His nose dragged up the side of my neck, causing goosebumps to bloom over my skin. He tipped up his head, smirking arrogantly. "You are getting off on this too, princess. Makes you feel alive, doesn't it?" He clutched my thigh, tugging it up, rocking into me, kindling sparks through me. A moan formed in my throat, my body greedy to feel more. The energy in the arena pulsed and bled over us, heightening my emotions to the extreme. Death. Sex. The air vibrated, twining round the raw depravity of both, the mass yearning for the primal act of either.

Feral and crude.

I lost all civility, craving him to take me right here, feeling the high of his hands wrapping around my throat, stealing the last drops of my life as he thrust into me. I even liked the idea of everyone watching. The energy pulsed through me like a drug.

I curved into him with the impulse. He sucked in, swearing under his breath, his grip on my leg digging into my skin, his eyes blazing. He felt as if he were everywhere over me, inside and out. Taking over. And I pushed the same sensation out, wanting to consume and be consumed.

"Gods. Fuck." He jerked his head back with a hiss, making me aware of the surroundings, his eyes tracking mine. "I can feel it. Your body is crying for more."

I bit down, locking everything down, my nose flaring, terrified of how much I wanted him, and hating the fact that he sensed my desire.

"Get off me." I snarled, trying to wrestle out of his grip. "If you're going to kill me, do it already. Or is this wolf all bark and no bite?"

"You want me to bite?" In a blink, his hand came around my throat. "Like this? Is this what you want? No safe word. Want to feel the extreme? Push the line?" His thumb pressed down on my windpipe. It was instant, the rush of blood, the tingle of desire bolting across my heart. "Life and death. Love and hate. Such a thin line between them."

"Kill her!" someone screamed.

He watched me, a cruel grin hinting on his mouth. The pad of his thumb circled the skin at the base of my throat softly before pressing down hard, strangling the air from my lungs. I jerked, the instinct to fight for life flexing my muscles. Clawing and kicking, I tried to thrash against his hold, but I couldn't move. It felt like imaginary hands held me down, sliding and skimming over my skin, between my legs and over my chest.

"Blood-ing! Blood-ing!" the audience demanded, not liking his choice for my death.

He snarled, his eyes going up to the stands again.

Darkness ebbed around my eyes, slipping me further into the murky water, pulling me under. Death beckoned me to take its hand. I reached out for his bony hand, my fingertips touching his.

BOOM!

Death didn't take me quietly into the night. No. It detonated around me, shaking the ground, heaving the earth, and plunging the world into disarray and darkness.

Chapter 25

"Brexley." My name carved through the dark, yanking me from the nothingness. The deep voice wrapped around me, roughly pulling me back. "Kovacs!"

My lids flung open as oxygen zoomed into my chest. My lungs expanded, sucking in ravenous gulps. Bright aqua eyes stared down into mine, holding me like an anchor, pulling me to shore. Inhaling a shuddering breath, debris swirled down my throat, making me cough and wheeze more. I curved onto my side, hacking and panting.

"We have to go," Warwick growled, his voice snapping the world into sharp focus, overwhelming my senses into panic.

Chaos.

Pandemonium.

A shrill alarm screeched through the air, shredding my confused mind. Chunks of dirt rained down from the ceiling, the arena only lit with a few backup generators at the top, the place otherwise submerged in darkness.

And collapsing.

Piercing screams, stomping feet, and shouts echoed off the walls as the stampede of prisoners knocked and crashed into anything that stood in their way, weaving through the clumps pummeling down from the ceiling.

"Come on." Warwick yanked me up to my feet, my legs wobbling under me. I wanted to ask what was going on, but nothing made it to my tongue as I stumbled after him. Reflex and intuition guided me to follow as madness wailed and boomed around me, fear shooting my survival instinct up to the top.

Act first, question later.

Covering my head from the ceiling pelting us, he herded me toward the tunnel, his hand on my lower back steering me within the pitch darkness, reaching the exit that not too long ago Zander had brought me through. To die.

Warwick held up his hand when we reached the other end. Stopping, he peered out, then waved me on, jogging down a corridor and upstairs, the dim lights from generators eerily smearing the place in greenish-brown color, hiding everything but outlines. The shrill alarm and yells from the prison echoed through, shivering up my spine and setting my teeth together. Dust filled my nose, choking my throat, forcing my tender esophagus to hack violently.

Red, blue, yellow, and gray uniforms swarmed everywhere, most heading for the main tunnel, which led to the exit. Freedom. They rushed the guards trying to block the exit, attacking whoever stood in their way. The guards were quickly losing control.

Pure anarchy.

"No. This way." His large paw wrapped around mine, tugging me another way, going the opposite way as everyone else. His shoulders were tight, his muscles flexing, ready to attack or be attacked at any moment.

"Freeze!" Guards rolled after us like bowling balls chasing pins, knocking into the back of my neck. "I will shoot!"

Warwick's grip clenched down on my fingers, shoving and pushing us through prisoners swarming for the exit, resembling schools of fish making their way upstream. But his huge size couldn't get lost in the sea, standing like a beacon above the rest.

"Halt!"

Gunshots rang out, blasting through the prison over the warning bell, whistling by my head.

"Stop!" More shouts and pounding feet from soldiers came from behind us.

Warwick slipped us around a corner, hauling me into a pitch-black tunnel, yanking me down into the darkest corner. He crouched, pulling me into him. His heat wrapped around me, shielding me, his breath trickling down my neck.

The sound of footsteps tapped the dirt, slowing when they reached the tunnel. Silhouettes of four guards stepped into the passageway adorned with guns, whips, and knives.

"Where did they go?" One grunted, his boot crackling gravel under his heel, the noise snapping at my psyche. "They couldn't have gotten far."

"We *can't* lose them," a female guard said, her legs moving faster through the tunnel than the rest. "Everyone else, but not them."

Two others quickened their pace, rushing with her until the first one stopped. Warwick tensed next to me. Panic jackhammered my pulse as I froze, a knot lodging in my throat, my legs quivering under me.

The guard sniffed the air, his nose going up as if he were trying to pick up on our scents. He took a step closer to us, inhaling in quick puffs.

Fuckfuckfuck.

Terror slammed my heart against my ribs, pounding in my ears. Afraid he would be able to hear it, I bit down on my lip, trying to control my breaths.

Every sense seemed heightened. I was more aware of my surroundings than usual.

Of him.

Warwick's hand slid over my thigh, strangely calming me and adding to the frenzy in my chest. Without knowing how, I could feel him, feel his reassurance that if this guard found us, we would take him out.

Together.

The guard sniffed a few more times, a growl humming in his throat before a gunshot echoed down the way. Jolting forward, the guard hunted down the location of the shooting, exiting the tunnel.

A relieved exhale dropped my shoulders. Far too close.

"Come on—" Warwick started to stand when an explosion tore through the prison, rippling the earth underfoot.

Booooom!

The ground shivered, and more rubble poured down on us. Warwick dove for me, his body covering mine as the cave crumbled around us. His warmth and weight pressed into me as his scent filled my nose, devouring me, tingling every nerve and lighting me to life. A combo of sweat, dirt, and a deep woodsy smell ignited a hunger in me. It was irrational to feel this desire in the middle of escaping, but I couldn't seem to fight it. The sensation grew more intense when he tucked me tightly against him until the underground building quieted, our heads popping up. We coughed at the film in the air.

"Shit," he grumbled. "They're early, or we're late." He peered down at me, our eyes connecting for a moment, his intense regard burning into me. He felt familiar. Like I had known him forever. A piece I didn't know I was looking for. The feeling scraped at my mind and chest.

His eyebrow tipped up. "You okay?" Gruff and almost angry, he peeled off me, standing up. Clearly not at all feeling the odd link I did. Only able to nod, I stood next to him, shaking my head, trying to clear it.

"Fuck." Warwick ran his hand through his dusty hair, his knuckles curling angrily into his scalp, his attention on the now blocked tunnel exit. Pacing for a second, he hit his fists against his legs before stomping past me. "There went plan A. We'll have to get there another way." Warwick nudged me to move, traveling back the way we came, muttering under his breath.

"Plan A?" My gaze shot to his. "Another way?"

He didn't answer, slinking us up another set of stairs and down a vacant hallway. The stillness after the last explosion was melting away to gunfire and screams of death, icing my chest with fear.

Winding us up a spiral staircase so narrow his shoulders brushed the walls, we came to a landing. I had no idea where we were going, but to me up meant freedom. The notion coated my tongue, making my mouth water with hope.

"Farkas…" A voice came out of the murky shadows causing me to jump, a figure stepping in front of us, blocking our way. Disappointment gripped my stomach like a vise. We were so close; I could feel it. To be caught now? "You are late." The voice set me back on my heels. I recognized it.

"*Baszd meg.*" *Fuck off,* Warwick snarled.

"You have her?"

"Yes."

I squinted, taking a step forward, his face becoming clearer through the shadows. What the ever-loving hell?

"Zander?"

He smiled at me. "So glad you are all right."

"What's going on?" I shook my head in confusion.

Bang. Bang. Bang. Gunshots recoiled down the corridor.

"No time," Zander replied, waving us forward to a door, unlocking it. "Hurry!"

"Is everything set?" Warwick paused at the door, addressing Zander as a begrudging ally.

Zander nodded. "Yes. Head southwest of Gellért Hill. Behind the tree in the old garden."

Warwick dipped his head in understanding as Zander opened the heavy metal door. Zander's brown eyes peered over at me, a woeful smile curling his lip, his hand brushing over my cheek.

Another round of pops cracked through the tunnel.

"Take this. You might need it." He withdrew his gun from his belt, handing it to Warwick.

"You ready?" Warwick shoved the gun in the back of his pants. "Not that I won't enjoy this."

Zander nodded, pushing up his chin. Without hesitation, Warwick's fist cracked across his jaw. A cry broke from my lips as Zander flew back, body hitting the stone, splaying over the ground. Out cold.

"What did you do that for?" I screeched, moving toward the horse-shifter, my heart leaping up in my throat.

"Had to. Needed it to look real." Warwick grabbed my arm, heaving me away from Zander and pulling me through the exit, the door slamming behind us. Spiral stairs led up to another door, reminding me of the tunnel Sloane and the others brought me up the first day. "But fuck, I really, really enjoyed it."

Had to? What was going on? Zander helped us flee? It was more than him just turning his head while we passed. This had been planned. Zander was left unconscious on the other side to appear as though he had been ambushed and beaten.

"Kovacs," Warwick hissed, motioning to me to keep moving. "You can cry about me hitting your boyfriend later."

I jolted forward, my boots slapping against the metal steps as Warwick broke through another door, letting us out into the night.

Into freedom.

Fresh air ballooned in my chest, hitting my face with an energetic slap. I inhaled the delicious onslaught. Tears filled my eyes as I greedily sucked in more, starving for the fresh wind coming off the Danube, full of the warmth from being soaked in summer sun all day. I could taste the musky river on my tongue, sour and earthy. Like a food I used to eat as a child, it brought back a joy I never thought I'd have again.

Liberation.

Life.

We slipped farther out. Warwick's head whipped around, checking out the situation as we both flattened against the wall, keeping us low and in the shadows. Shouts and gunfire blasted in front of us from the main entrance to the prison.

The statue of the lady and the feather was now a pile of rubble, along with the ground around it. The explosion put a large hole in the Citadel and entrance to Halalház, allowing prisoners to gush out of the wounds, fleeing for the wild park only yards away.

"Halt!" a man boomed out into the night, jolting my head up to the catwalk near me.

Throngs of silhouettes bolted for freedom, hoping to slip into the night and disappear.

Bang! Bang!

Several running figures hit the ground, blood splattering out like black ink over the cobblestone. One of them was a woman with a braid. My breath caught between my teeth, panicked at the thought it might be Kek. Was she out? Was Tad? Getting this far and dying at the door was heartbreaking. Though, at the very least, if they died now, they fell with one last breath of fresh air in their lungs.

The Liberty Bridge's lights glinted from the Danube far

below. Back before we split from the King and Queen, my father said tourists and locals could freely enjoy the grand views of the Pest side, having a picnic at the maintained and beautiful Gellért Hill Jubilee Park. Now nature claimed the area like a once domesticated pet, forsaking the rules to survive and flourish in this feral country.

"Come on," Warwick whispered, hunkering down his massive frame, scouring across the road to the heavily wooded area.

"*Állj meg!*" a voice yelled, sounding right above us. "Stop!"

My head cranked back as I scurried after Warwick. An officer pointed a pistol at me from his perch above.

Panic drove my muscles to move faster, a blast hitting the cobble by my feet.

"I said, stop!"

Click. Bang!

Pain sliced up the back of my calf as a muffled scream tore up my throat, my leg dipping under me, agony clinching my lungs, locking down my jaw.

No! Don't stop. A voice inside pushed me forward, tapping into the horrendous fear of being caught.

"I found them." A whistle shrilled in the air, calling attention to his location. "Hurry! I found them."

"Fuck!" Warwick hissed, suddenly by my side, helping me, both of us slipping into the brush. More bullets zipped by us, all low to the ground like the guard didn't want to kill us, but immobilize us.

Shutting off my mind, numbing the pain in my leg, Warwick and I trudged through. Branches and thorns sliced at my exposed arms and torso, my heart thumping madly to keep up with my blood loss and pain, hoping adrenaline would keep me going. Warwick tried to clear the path, taking the brunt, his hand constantly reaching back for me, pulling me along.

Sweat trickled down my back, huffing as I tried to bite back my whimpers. Gunshots, cries, and shouts discharged through the night sounding like a messed-up symphony. The chorus of death, the notes they cried out, grew more distant the farther we ventured into the park.

Warwick's hand went back, stopping us, his head jerking around.

"What?"

He held up his finger, and then I heard a crack of branches.

"It's not just the guards out here who want to kill us," he muttered. "Fae have filled this area with large game for their leader to hunt. But what is hunted also hunts. The game will gladly eat any of the escaped prisoners."

"Great." I peered behind me and stiffened at the sound of another snap of foliage rustling in the distance.

Animal? Guard?

"Farkas, I know you're out here. I can hear your heart beating. And I can see in the dark," a woman's stern voice called out. "You will be found. Don't do this."

"Don't make this harder for yourself," a man shouted right after her. "You had it good. Don't destroy that."

Warwick silently moved in front of me, his frame pressing into mine, pushing us back into a hedge. He gripped my arms, taking the pressure off my hurt leg. As his frame engulfed mine, he blocked out all light.

My lungs contracted as his scent curled around me once again, his bare chest rubbing against mine, blotting out all my thoughts.

"Don't think for a moment you are safe with him, Kovacs," another male guard yelled out. "You'd be better off coming with us now. He's not who you think he is."

As a trained soldier, I understood their tactics. They were playing with my head, trying to create doubt, but I already believed I was not safe with him. Especially given the way my body reacted to his. His erection cut through his thin pants, burning into my stomach. My thighs twitched with need. The desire to open for him and feel him sink deep into me rocked headily through my core.

His gaze shot to me, the pristine ocean color turning stormy as if he could feel my need. His nose flared, his hands sliding slowly down to my elbows, his touch oddly fierce and soft. Everything about him felt like yin and yang. Conflicting. Challenging.

Life.

Death.

His stare scorched so strongly into me, I dropped mine, which was even dumber. My vision seized on the tattoos inking his ripped stomach, his chest knocking against mine, the outline of his cock pressing into me, the tip of it almost pushing out of the top of his pants.

Fuck.

No, seriously… fuck.

Really, Brex? Right now?

But as if the world outside no longer mattered, the feel of his skin on mine cut a craving through me. The back of my neck tingled as the guard's footsteps got closer, spinning my head with adrenaline. Everything was peaked. Danger. Fear. Life. Death. They all came together in a tempest.

"They're close." The woman spoke to her comrades.

"Normally, Yulia, you can pinpoint from yards away," a man retorted.

"I know. Something's messing with my senses tonight. There are a lot of animals and fae moving around out here tonight, maybe that's why," the woman, Yulia, replied.

"Comes in handy not having an aura sometimes. Harder to get a reading on." Warwick rumbled into my ear, my eyes popping up to him.

"I'm going to shift." The girl spoke again. "Cover me."

Warwick's form went rigid, his fingers pressing painfully into my arms, yanking me out of my stupor. He leaned down, his mouth sweeping across my ear, "We need to run. Yulia's an owl-shifter. She will find us in seconds." His deep voice sent shivers down my spine. "Can you run?"

I nodded. I had no choice. Owls had the best night vision and hearing of all the animals and could locate prey at a half-mile. Perfect for hunting.

"One."

A squawk screeched through the air.

"Two." His lips skimmed my earlobe.

Wings flapped as the owl soared into the sky.

"Three." In a blink, he peeled away from me. My body registered the loss like a drug withdrawal, but I had no time to mull it over. I moved in step with him, blocking out the pain.

A screech filled the air.

"Over there," a guard yelled as Yulia cried out again, heading for us instantly.

I forced my weak leg to move, limping more than running, trying to keep up with Warwick as we weaved and darted through the foliage, knowing the owl-shifter would be able to see us like it was daytime.

Over the profuse panting of my breath, I could vaguely make out more shouting. Breaking through a hedge, Warwick headed directly for a large, old tree standing high above others.

An old motorcycle leaned against it.

That's what he and Zander had been talking about. Our escape *had* been planned.

Warwick jumped on, his foot slamming down on the kickstart. With a roar, the motorcycle came to life, giving away our location. The bike lurched forward, taking off. For a split second, I feared he was going to leave me, but he paused the bike as I came up to him.

He handed me the gun Zander gave us. "Don't hesitate."

I nodded, took it from him, and swung my bad leg over with a cry, my pants saturated with blood.

"The owl will follow us," he said over the roar of the bike. "Shoot to kill."

The motorcycle lurched forward, my arms wrapping around his waist so I wouldn't fall off. A handful of guards breached the foliage, their guns pointed at us.

The bike tore off, Warwick weaving away from them.

Bang. Bang. Bang.

Bullets hit the ground, splintered trees, and zoomed by my ear, zinging off the metal of the motorcycle. Warwick flinched as blood spurted out of his bicep, pushing the bike harder, tearing across the land. Ammunition volleyed after us, but we quickly escaped their reach as he took us down the hill. Nature had consumed the old paths with tall grass, brush, and debris, forcing us to make our own.

The roar of the engine cut off the gunshots and commotion from the prison break, the motorbike taking us farther away. Bouncing and sliding, I gritted my teeth at the violent jolts. I dug my legs into his hips, my shaky arms holding him so tightly I could feel his heartbeat through his chest. I practically became his backpack. My hands skimmed his bare torso, curving over his muscles.

Finally, the bike hit a paved road at the bottom, skidding. Warwick curved for the bridge. For a moment, my shoulders sagged in relief. The Pest side was so close I could taste it.

Home.

Freedom.

Screech! The owl dove down for us. I wasn't afraid it could overpower us, but I knew it would follow us, find out where we were going, leading the entire Halalház team to us.

"Holy shit." My eyes widened, noticing the harness the owl was wearing. A live cam. Yulia was reporting our whereabouts straight back to the prison. They probably already had guards coming for us.

There was no choice now. She had to die.

Locking my knees tighter against him, I felt one of his hands reach back, clamping down on my thigh to keep me steady as I held the gun with both hands and aimed it at the bird. My arms shook, and shadows started to line the edges of my vision. *Do. Not. Give. Up.* I pointed the gun at the owl. She swooped and weaved, making it almost impossible for me to target her.

Bang! The gun recoiled, and the bird screeched but dipped clear of the shot.

Warwick gripped me harder, his thumb digging high into my inner thigh, close to the seam of my pants, shooting another wave of energy into my bloodstream. His touch jumped my body, giving me focus. Peering down the barrel of the gun, I waited.

She hooted, circling us.

The end of the bridge stood only yards away to the road leading straight into the neutral zone, where both sides could hide.

"Kovacs," he muttered my name, his fingers squeezing my leg.

Ignoring him, I held. *Wait... wait... Now!*

Boom.

A painful shriek shrilled the night air, sounding almost the same as a woman's cry, and the bird's form plunged into the icy river below with a splash.

With both relief and sadness, I lowered my arms, my grip sweaty and slippery on the gun. It had to be done, but different from what I used to believe in training, I didn't enjoy taking a fae's life. I had seen too much to think them all evil and worthy of death. She was doing her job. But our survival was more vital… to us

Warwick didn't say anything. Letting go of my thigh, he gripped the handlebars and revved the bike faster. Just like that, we crossed to the other side.

Into the Savage Lands.

Chapter 26

The smell hit me first.

Dirt. Shit. Urine. Gasoline. Animals. Body odor. Rotting garbage.

Sour.

Heavy.

The bouquet of animals and people living together in squalor and filth filled my nostrils and my mouth with a bitter taste. The warm summer night baked the odors into the pavement, ballooning it to nauseating levels.

The paved road quickly became cobbled, loose and crumbling under the bike tires, rattling our bones.

The streetlamps disappeared the moment we crossed over to the Savage Lands, leaving us in thick shadows, only a handful of dim lights from windows cascading down softly on us.

As my sight adjusted to the dark, I took in collapsing buildings teetering on unstable foundations. Vandalized, decaying, or destroyed, few held a hint of their former glory. Boarded-up shops, cafes, and businesses looked as though they had been looted and abandoned long before, leaving a sad feeling in the darkened doorways of the old stone buildings. The former life of this place was now merely shadows and ghosts.

Our ride started off quiet, a handful of figures dotting the streets or sleeping on the cracked pavement, with only strips of cloth or boxes to sleep on. No one ventured out for an evening stroll in the temperate night, enjoying a night with friends. But the longer we drove, the more people I saw. Most of them were skin and bones. Drunk, dirty, dressed in rags, their frames sagged as if they had given up on hope a long time ago. A few slept with the livestock, now fenced on empty parking lots and in old squares.

The unbelievable smell of piss and feces permeated the streets. Human. Horse. Sheep. Hog. Most cars were picked clean and vandalized. Some were barely shells and were being used as homes for the lucky ones who procured them. Despair reeked in the atmosphere, my skin itching with the destitute and polluted air, stabbing at my heart. Did Istvan know how bad it was here? He couldn't possibly realize the extent. He'd never let his own people wallow in this filth without trying to do something.

Now I realized how much had been kept from us within Leopold's walls. The news shaped and painted a picture that did not match what my eyes were taking in, and night hid most of the true horrors. Poor, yes, but this was beyond that.

"Stay close to me." Warwick's voice jolted me from my thoughts. "This place is dangerous."

"We just broke out of the Halalház." I leaned closer to him to speak, our mouths only an inch apart, our bloody skin pressing into each other, sticky and dirty.

"Halalház is civilized and orderly." He tilted his head so I could hear him, his loose hair tickling my cheek. "It has rules. This place doesn't. Gunslingers, gamblers, outlaws, and prostitutes with nothing to lose. They will shoot you in a blink for just looking at them wrong."

"What?" I blinked.

"There are no laws here, princess." He gave me a side-eye, like *how adorable you still believe in fairytales*. As a soldier, I guess I still believed there were laws in a society we *all* followed.

We turned down another road, the Hungarian name still visible on the side of the building, *Király u.*, meaning King. The narrow street was lined with worn and ramshackle neo-classic stone buildings, their glory days forgotten. It was suffocated with people, buildings, and makeshift structures erected on roofs or crammed in places they should never have fit, choking out any sense of space. It felt like a jungle—reedy, dense—making my lungs palpitate.

He slowed down to almost a crawl as hordes of people milled everywhere, closing in the narrow lane. There were a surprising number of horses tied randomly to posts or moving freely around, adding to the intensity of closed space and putrid smell.

When the curtain fell between worlds, the rulers in the West were quick to adapt and modernize, using the magic in the air to power devices and automobiles. Not here. Only the ultra-rich could afford to buy these innovations, and most of our country reverted to simpler times. Horses did not break down under magic. Even Istvan used a horse when he was in the city.

Magic-friendly motorcycles were the lone motor vehicle being manufactured in the East. Russia and Ukraine had cornered the market, which added to their power and dominance over other countries.

Brash laughter, talking, yelling, and music streamed down an alley where Warwick slowed the motorcycle to a stop. Torches lit up the outside of the pedestrian lane, people stumbling in and out, women and men, fae and human. The amount of loud and unruly people caused my lungs to pulse with anxiety. Gunshots echoed through the lane, making me jolt with a cry, clenching the gun I was still holding.

"As I said. Stay close." Warwick got off the bike and turned toward me, taking the gun from me and stuffing it into the back of his pants before reaching for me. Blood still leaked down his arm from where he'd been shot, but it looked like the bullet had grazed him—lucky him. I was only in my sports bra, my gray pants so soaked with blood they were sliding off my bony hips, the weight pulling them down.

Both of us were shot, bruised, wounded, covered in dirt and blood, and not one person gave us notice as we entered the lane.

Walking through the entryway was like passing into another world—a dark fantasy and a terrifying circus. It was unlike anything I had ever seen. Overwhelmed, I stopped in my tracks, my mouth parting. My senses were inundated with stimuli. The stench of body odor, liquor, smoke, vomit, and food slammed up my nose. The boisterous noises had me darting my head around the pedestrian lane packed with bars and restaurants. The air reverberated with the sound of high-pitched laughter from scantily clad women, coupled with music from pianos or live bands. Tables were filled with people drinking and gambling, people kissing or fighting, passed out, dancing, or doing drugs right in the open. One fae had partially shifted into her fox form, alluring everyone who passed to come watch her dance. Most customers were dressed in simple cotton trousers or skirts with shirts and jackets in muted, dull colors, as if they had been washed and worn for so long they'd lost all pigment. The insipid fabrics emphasized the shirtless men and painted women strolling around, their eyes empty, but salacious smiles curved on their mouths.

Women in racy fantasy costumes dangled from the ceiling on hoops and swings. A hammock high up was filled with multiple naked forms—groaning, touching, licking—not hiding one bit of their ecstasy as they openly fucked each other.

"Full house!" A man's voice bellowed, drawing my attention to a group gambling at a table inside one of the bars. All the doors and windows were open on this balmy night. "My reward. Come." The old man curled his fingers at one of the young men near him, beckoning him over with a lustful sneer. The boy couldn't have been older than fourteen. I turned away, feeling sick to my stomach. I wasn't naïve, but my world had none of this depravity. Not in the open anyway. We kept our sins hidden.

I hobbled forward, the pain in my leg screaming louder with each step, but I was still caught up in the debauchery around me. Feeling overwhelmed and uncomfortable, the lane seemed to tighten around me, figures knocking into me, pushing and touching my emaciated frame with ease, forcing me to tuck closer to Warwick.

We reached an intersection in the path. A building on the corner boomed with activity, my skin shivering with the extra energy and shock. Women draped out of the windows above, motioning to the men walking by as music streamed out, enticing the people below. Men paraded in and out, some not even bothering to proceed up to a room, their pants down around their ankles as they fucked against the wall, right under a sign that read *Kitty's House.*

Feeling revolted, but unable to stop watching, my stomach twisted, my innocent world crashing in around me as my gaze caught more lewd acts among the shadows in the alley.

"Here." Warwick turned me toward the whorehouse.

"What?" I yanked back on his arm, almost falling, realizing I had been leaning on him much more than I wanted, my leg barely able to hold my weight. "Here?"

"You gonna get righteous on me, Kovacs?" His brows furrowed as he tugged me forward, my feet stumbling to catch up.

"Warwick!" A woman yelled down, her smile growing into elation, her eyes turning hungry.

"Warwick! Warwick's back!" More women joined in from the windows waving down, pushing each other out of the way to see and call down to him.

Why was I not surprised he was well known at a whorehouse?

"Gods, Warwick. We've missed you. It's been so long. We thought something happened to you." A stunning dark-haired woman blew him a kiss. "Madam is going to be so happy to see you." Her voice was like velvet, a song in the air. Alluring. An inkling, a tiny voice, told me to follow her, to be near her, a hook drawing me in.

"Hey, Nerissa. You know I'm not that easy to get rid of." He winked up at her, his eyes glinting, only making her lids lower with desire. Suddenly the voice inside my head flipped. I wanted to punch her in the face. "Been held up elsewhere for a bit."

"Well, we've missed you. Me most of all." She curled her finger at him. "Come upstairs and let me show you… like old times."

I didn't even know I moved until I felt Warwick's arm wrap around my torso, tugging me back, a snarl curling my lip.

Where the fuck did that come from?

"Whoa there." His deep voice vibrated against my neck, my attention still on her.

Nerissa's smile parted, an enchanting laugh falling over my skin, but I could easily brush it off. "You can certainly join us, human." She stared at me, curling her finger. "Come, pretty one."

"Nerissa…" Warwick warned.

"I think I'd rather be whipped and locked up in the hole," I snapped at her.

Her head jerked back, puzzlement creasing her forehead.

Before she could say any more, Warwick picked me up, taking me up the stairs and through the door. He placed me back on my feet the moment we crossed the threshold, staring at me.

"What?" I sighed. My adrenaline was leaking from me; the blood loss and pain from my calf was catching up. I suddenly felt the exhaustion of the entire day weighing down my bones.

"She's a siren." His eyes rolled over me like he was trying to figure out something.

Siren. I had heard about them but never encountered one. They were supposed to have the magic to lure any man or woman to their death with a song.

"So?" I shrugged. "We're not in water."

"Doesn't matter," he snorted. "Sirens are deadly in water but are almost as alluring on earth, *especially* to humans. No human can turn them down as they tap into human and fae sexual desires. They are extremely powerful." He lowered his lids, standing fully. "She focused her charms on you. You should not have been able to ignore her call."

"*Warwick.*" Low and precise, his name had us both turning to the figure gliding toward us. The woman was tall with broad shoulders and a narrow waist. Somewhat masculine, but still delicate in the way she held herself. Her skin was a rich chocolate, and her curly hair was left wild around her face, setting off her hazel eyes. Her tall heels made my feet ache just to look at them, but they made her even more formidable, her black dress tightly fitting her slim frame. She was beautiful, striking, but something felt off. "It's been far too long." She outstretched her hand, her voice deeply baritone, though she tried to soften it.

"Kitty." Warwick took it, brushing his mouth over her knuckles. The madam herself watched him with a mix of adoration and weariness. After being around him, I completely understood. She pulled back when she spotted me, her nose wrinkling at my half-naked, cut, bruised, bloody form. "I see you brought a friend this time. That's a first. Bringing your own meal into a restaurant?" She arched a plucked eyebrow.

"I'm sorry to intrude on you like this. I was hoping—"

Madam Kitty held her palm up, stopping his words.

"Warwick, darling." She sighed, her head shaking subtly. "I don't recall a time you haven't come here shot, stabbed, and covered in blood, needing my assistance. I have never turned you away. You know you are always welcome here." Her painted lips pursed. "I swear, violence and danger follow you like a shadow, my love."

Her sentiment caught my attention. Lynx had said the same thing to me. Odd.

"Follow me." She swung around and sauntered for the stairs. Every swing of her hips was controlled with sensual movement and purpose. With the grace of a drunk cow, I cursed and hissed at every step, trying to follow. With Warwick's help, I made it up the four flights of stairs and down a corridor, trying not to puke or pass out.

Women and men lingered in the hallways and in doorways of bedrooms, all dressed in very little: bodices, silk robes, and sexy underwear. They greeted Warwick as an old friend, both sexes shimmering with desire as he passed, not at all shocked to see his condition, some even peering at me with interest.

Kitty stopped at a door, grabbing on to the doorknob, and opened it. "I had your room prepared for you."

"Even if it's been years, you seem to know when I'm coming." He wagged his head, looking at her with adoration.

She shrugged, a hint of a smile on her lips. "You're a powerful force, Warwick. Hard to ignore. Even more so tonight." Her gaze dipped to me before motioning for us to enter.

Stepping in, my gaze drifted around. The space was simple—a bed with a nightstand, a fire lamp casting the room in a rosy color. A threadbare chair stood in the corner next to a dresser with a scuffed mirror over it and a bowl of water and towels stacked on it. The curtains were pulled back from the two open windows overlooking the lane below, music and voices roaring up into the room. "I will have someone bring you healing supplies, food, and clothes."

"Kitty, thank you. Once again, your kindness is unparalleled." He bowed his head to her. It was unsettling to see him be pleasant to someone. Kind. It was a side I never thought he had.

She exhaled, and a thin layer of fake annoyance swished her hand, revealing how much she and everyone else adored him here.

"I'm glad to see you, Warwick. There have been a lot of rumors." She grabbed the handle, pulling the door closed. "Good night."

The door clicked shut, leaving us alone in the tiny bedroom. A bedroom with only one bed.

In normal circumstances, this might cause some awkwardness, but upon the closing of the door, I felt I was permitting exhaustion and pain to command me. I bent forward, bracing myself against the wall.

"Sit down." Warwick pointed at the bed, his tone cold and angry again. He tugged the gun free, setting it on the nightstand, moving to the dresser.

There's the guy I know.

Plopping on the bed, the frame squeaked under me, my bones aching with exhaustion, my calf on fire. I knew adrenaline had kept the pain at bay, but now I was keenly aware of the excruciating ache of my muscles and the fire of my bullet wound. From the fight, the explosion, being shot, and escaping—there wasn't a cell in my body not screaming in pain.

Breathing heavily and trying not to throw up, I heard someone knock. Warwick answered the door, mumbled to someone, and closed it. I zoned out, biting back the agony.

He stepped in front of me, setting down the bowl of water, rags, pliers, gauze, and other instruments I didn't want to think about. He opened one of the bags, pulling out a jug.

"Drink." He thrust the bottle in my face. The brutal smell of really cheap palinka burned my nostrils, and I turned my head away. "Sorry, princess, I don't have the premium stuff you're used to. This is going to have to do."

Scowling, I swiped the bottle from him, my tender stomach rolling at the harsh smell.

As his hands moved down my leg, pain lit up my nerves. I poured a swig down my throat, hacking and coughing as the liquid scorched my gullet. I took another huge shot right after, flinching at the severe liquor.

Far cry from the palinka Caden and I shared our last night together.

Caden.

My head shook at the memory. That was another lifetime—another girl.

"Sounds like you are a regular here." I shivered at another swig.

"I was."

I waited for him to continue. He didn't.

"How do you know her?"

"Kitty and I go back a long time," he answered coolly.

"I'll bet," I snorted, feeling fire course down my throat. He ignored my comment. "Did you know *Kitty* means chaste and pure?" I sniggered, staring at the light brown shitty liquor. "Ironic, huh?"

"Take off your pants," Warwick ordered, sitting back on his heels.

I peered up, staring at him.

"Seriously?" He rolled his eyes, annoyance heaving from his nose. "You think escaping from that hellhole and getting you shot was all simply my grand plan to see you in your knickers?" He tilted into me, his mouth so close. I inhaled sharply, the alcohol already buzzing my mind. "Plus, I've already seen you naked, princess. Nothing special. Far too bony for me."

I frowned, huffing with embarrassment and irritation. "Screw you."

"Now look who is trying to get into whose pants."

I turned my head, afraid of the fury boiling up in me. The whiskey had numbed my pain enough to hate him.

"Take them off, or I will." He stood up, looming over me, his hands on his hips.

Exhausted and incensed, I sat glaring up at him acting like a stubborn child.

"Fine." He shrugged, reaching for me, his hands curling around the waistband, his fingers grazing my hips, igniting the skin where he touched me. He slowly dragged the pants down my legs, gently at the spot where my pants stuck to my wound, and tossed them on the weathered floorboards with a slap.

Wearing only a bralette and prison-issued underwear, I peered down at myself, blinking the tears from my eyes. How fast Halalház changed me. A few months were nothing to most, but inside there, it was years.

I had always been thin from training, but fit and muscular. Healthy skin, hair, and nails. A glow in my cheeks. My skin before had been smooth and creamy, Rebeka insisting on facials and spa days along with a healthy diet. Prison robbed me of those qualities. Now, I was unhealthy and gaunt. Every inch of my pallid, dry skin was covered with purple, yellow, and green bruises, my ribs poking through. Veins tinted my translucent skin a greenish-blue color. Deep scars from lashings, beatings, and being knifed hacked my skin like rough terrain.

I hadn't looked in a real mirror since the night of the party so long ago, and this girl staring back at me over the dresser was no one I recognized. I had seen my face beat up many times. This one held the burden of what I went through internally as well as externally. I was covered in dirt, dried blood, cuts, and bruises. Dark circles underlined my eyes. My usually shiny, long hair was tangled in greasy knots; strands had been falling out more than usual.

Vain or not, I couldn't stop the sob collecting in my chest at the loss of myself, my youth, and beauty. I turned away from the mirror and took another sip of liquor, my shoulders curling forward in defeat.

"Hey." Warwick lowered himself in front of me again, his hand tipping up my chin to him. "We're out. Alive. We made it, Kovacs. That's better than most."

"What happened? How did we get out… and Zander—"

"Not right now." He shushed me. "Let's worry about one thing at a time. We're out. Besides your leg, everything else can wait. Okay?"

I nodded, knowing being free was by far the most important thing. I should have been elated, but I couldn't seem to feel anything. My gaze latched on to his aqua irises like he was the one thing anchoring me to the earth, the feel of his fingers holding my face.

He held my stare, neither of us breaking away. A sensation scratched at my consciousness, something crying out to be recognized, but I couldn't decipher it. The noise from the outside world dimmed. The only thing I saw was him; the only thing I felt was his touch. There was that awareness again—he was everywhere, inside and outside of me.

His lashes lowered, eyes falling on my lips before they snapped back up, his hand falling away.

Suddenly the noises from the outside world flooded back in with a harsh stab. I inhaled, peering off to the side.

"Drink more." He cleared his throat, picking up a towel and pouring alcohol on it. "There's no posh hospitals in the Savage Lands."

"You know what you're doing?"

He snorted. "Yeah."

I didn't argue, pouring more liquor down my throat. I knew we had so much to discuss, but it could wait for tomorrow. Right now, I just didn't want to lose my leg to infection.

"If you can't get it out, leave it." I downed another swig, no longer coughing over the burn.

"Not my first rodeo."

"Not shocking." I heard my words slur and trip over themselves, and my body swayed to the side. Weary, I was giving over to the alcohol, to the utter exhaustion and trauma, my lids drooping.

"Lie down." Warwick helped me roll onto my stomach on the bed, putting a towel under my leg, propping up my calf.

"This is going to really fuckin' hurt." The alcohol-soaked rag grazed over my wound.

A scream tore from the depths of my gut, tremendous agony bowing my back before everything went fuzzy.

Then black.

Chapter 27

Pain.

So much.

It engulfed me so tightly I couldn't decipher the source of it. From my head to my toenails, it drove me awake with a brutal lashing. Lying on my stomach, my face mushed into a flat pillow, I blinked, my blurry vision slowly clearing on a wall with a painting of a pinup model dressed in only a leather harness, covering nothing, whipping a tied-up man.

What the hell? Where am I?

Pain jerked my head up, and the sudden movement shot bile up my throat, my head swimming with agony. I heaved over the side of the bed, right into a bowl placed on the floor. Puking up mostly bile with nothing much in my stomach, the violent action made me more nauseous. I collapsed onto the pillow with a whimper, already spent of energy.

But curiosity pricked the back of my neck. I slowly looked around. Filtered light seeped into the room, making it hard to decipher the time of day. The daylight unmasked the room, showing how much grime had been hidden in the magic of darkness and shadows the night before. Not that I was complaining. The lumpy bed and pillow felt heavenly compared to sleeping on the ground. And being here meant we had truly escaped Halalház. It wasn't a dream. We were free.

"Warwick?" My voice came out weak and gritty, sounding like a scratched record, as pain slicing down my throat.

Raw. Sore. As if I had been strangled or had screamed until it gave out.

Oh right. Both happened.

Twisting to look over my shoulder, I saw my leg was wrapped up with gauze and propped on a pillow, blood staining the discolored whitish towel. Warwick Farkas had tended to me. What a bizarre idea when just a few days ago he was going to kill me.

Where was he?

Strangely, I felt unsettled waking up without him here.

"Warwick?" Pushing up, every muscle, nerve, and joint complained, telling me to lay back down, my head spinning in retaliation. Inhaling, I placed my feet to the floor, my knuckles curling into the duvet, trying to hold back the urge to vomit again.

A soft knock tapped at the door before it swung open. A pretty woman looking to be in her late twenties or early thirties with bright red hair and blue eyes poked her head in. She wore a corset, half-slip, and silky kimono.

"Hi." She smiled, wrinkles lining her mouth, her teeth slightly yellow. Those things told me she was human, instantly easing my tension. "Thought I heard you." A light British accent glazed her words like icing.

I watched her, my brain feeling slow and groggy as she stepped in, carrying a bowl and more towels. She trotted over to the dresser and set them down.

"Who are you?" I croaked out.

She moved to me, taking my face in her hands, peering

at it from different angles, cringing as her thumbs moved down my bruised neck.

"I don't mean to be rude, luv, but you look like hell." She clicked her tongue, shaking her head as she backed away from me. "Nothing a nice bath and soap won't help with. Lots and lots of soap. Maybe some disinfectant? I hope we have something that can handle this." She motioned over me, her eyes opening wider at my bloody sports bra and prison underwear. "Oh, my… good thing I'm here."

"Who *are* you?"

"Oh, sorry, luv." She batted her hand at me. "I'm Rosie." Curtsying playfully, her voice was suddenly heavy with accent. "The English Rose."

"You're from England?" I couldn't imagine leaving the glorious Western countries to be here. In hell. "And you left?"

She let out a trill of laughter. "Oh lord, no. I'm not English at all." She put her hand on her chest, winking at me. "But they love the accent, and we all have our roles to play here. With some people, accents are their kink."

I stared at her in confusion, my brain working through fog.

"I was an actress before this. Have an exceptional ear. I pick up on brogues easily, but now I've been playing this role for so long it's become part of me. Sometimes I forget I am not British." She laughed, switching back to me in a blink. "So, let's get you a bath, fresh clothes, and some food. Sound good?" She talked so quickly that my fuzzy mind struggled to keep up with her.

"Rosie?" I rubbed my head. "Where is Warwick?"

"You mean that virile, intense, dangerously enticing man?" She sighed heavily, fluttering her fingers across her breastbone. "He has to be part beast or something. Hell, could you imagine him in bed? Oh lord… He's one I would *not* charge." She fanned herself. "Oh, I'm sorry, is there something going on with you two?'

"No—"

"Oh good." She cut me off. "That would be terribly awkward. He's been a patron here before I even started, which feels so long ago. But I have yet to get him in my bed. I will, though. I am determined." She shimmied her shoulders. "Grrr. Just to have one night with *that man*."

"Rosie."

"He's terrifying and so sexually charged. Gods, he must know how to fuck… He makes my brain melt. He has to be fae, right? There's no way he can be human."

"Rosie!"

She exhaled, shaking her head. "See? That man fries my brain."

"Do you know where he is?"

"No." Her back-length, dyed red hair slid over her shoulders. "He left a couple of hours ago, saying he had something to do. Practically demanded Madam post one of her guards at your door to watch over you. He was *very* insistent. You do not order Madam in *her* house, though. They were about to have a brawl when I volunteered." Her lids tapered, and she paused for a moment. "You sure there is nothing between you?"

"No." I scoffed, my head waggling. "Fuck no. Definitely not. Absolutely *definitely* not."

She tapped a painted fingernail against her teeth, her gaze rolling over me, her lips puckering. "Mmmm-hmm."

I glanced to the side, feeling chagrin flame my skin—good thing no one could see it through the dirt and blood.

"What is that smell? Ohhhh." Her nose wrinkled as she bent down to pick up the bowl on the floor. "I'll take this out, get the bath ready, and come back for you, all right?"

"You don't have to do that." I tried to stop her from retrieving my vomit. "It's my mess."

"Please, luv." She rolled her eyes, stepping back with the basin in her hands. "If you think a little vomit even fazes me, you have *no idea* what I've had to clean up here." She arched her perfectly curved eyebrow, winking at me before her heeled boots clunked across the floor as she headed for the door. "I'll see if I can scrounge up a painkiller. I'll be back in a few."

The door clinked after her exit, and my shoulders dropped with fatigue. My frame curled back up on the bed, needing to sleep and hide from the pain.

Shutting my eyes, my mind buzzed with the information she told me.

Warwick and I had been free barely a few hours, so what had him running out of here so early? Weren't we supposed to be hiding? What was he doing?

The questions swirled around in my head, falling down the black hole as my body succumbed to sleep again.

Tipping my head back, the cool water lapped just below my breasts as the liquid slowly sloshed around the old claw tub. I had been in here for at least an hour. Rosie already changed the water once because of the blood and dirt that had come off me the first round. Plumbing worked for the most part in the Savage Lands, but only cold water came out of the pipes and not always frequently, according to my new friend. She brought buckets of hot water up from the kitchen to get it warm enough to scrub my body and matted hair before leaving me to soak.

She had let me sleep most of the afternoon, stirring me around four so I could get the bath before the house woke up.

This world woke with the darkness. Fae were naturally nocturnal but had conformed to rules of human society, fitting into our world unnoticed at one time. It was still this way in most places, but in this seedy world, they clearly preferred the darkness to veil their deeds. Opening their arms and curling their fingers, they beckoned the disheartened folks coming off their shifts who wanted to escape from life.

"It's hard to resist the call of the night when the day is so brutal and cruel. Getting lost in the pleasure of flesh, drink, drugs, and greed is a mistress no human or fae can resist," Rosie had told me before she left. "Be careful, luv, it is an easy hole to fall down, especially with that man around." She blew me a kiss and shut the door.

Rosie was a lot, but she had been very kind to me. I kept forgetting what she did for a living. Where I was. In the daylight, the house was still quiet, most still sleeping, slowly coming to life again.

It was a struggle to be here without judging everyone I saw and not being grossed out or acting above such things. In Leopold, there were no prostitutes or whorehouses. Those were for the poor class, the vile and depraved. Though I heard murmurings from Leopold soldiers about slipping over here. I had never witnessed it or talked about it. It was shunned and deemed disgusting and lowbred by the elite.

Instead, the rich just opened their legs for power and dominance. Games of deceit and treachery while dressed in finery, sipping expensive liquor. Weren't arranged marriages the wealthy's version of a whorehouse? Selling your daughters and sons to the highest bidder? Were we any better than the men and women here trying to survive?

Not wanting to answer the question, my mind jumped to Caden. The notion I could get back to him, go home, filled my thoughts. I had to be close, about a mile from him. A smile crept over my face, my lids closing as I shifted in the tub, imagining Caden's expression when he saw me again.

Alive.

His shocked face turning into pure elation, his smile lighting up the world as he ran to me, folding me up in his arms and spinning me around. His lips crashing against mine.

"You're alive," he would breathe against my mouth, taking them fiercely again. "They told me you were dead."

"I know." My lips would seize his, unable to break from his for a second.

"I can't live without you again. I won't. It's always been you and me, Brex. I should have fought for you that night. I will never make that mistake again. I want *you*. I *love* you."

The words rained down on me, bubbling in my chest with joy, sliding tears down my face.

"I love you too."

My mind quickly switched to my bedroom, Caden laying me down on his bed, his mouth on me, his body crawling over mine. I wanted so badly to actually feel him; my mind tried to make it real, like that night in the prison.

"Brexley…" His vision whispered my name, sounding like a plea. Desire. Want.

Falling into my illusion, I shut off the outside world, committing fully to my fantasy. My hands moved down through the water, ignoring the scars and bumps trying to bring me back to reality. I pretended my hands were his, caressing me, undressing me.

Touching me.

My fingertips squeezed my nipples, the pleasure opening my thighs with need, drowning in thoughts of Caden and me exploring each other.

"Is this what you want, Brexley? Me?" Caden murmured in my ear, his imaginary kisses soft down my neck.

"Yes." My back arched.

"No, it's not." A deep gravelly voice skated over my skin, the man over me suddenly changing. A smirk covered his mouth, his aqua eyes glinting. Long, dark hair played through my fingers, a massive form pressing down on me, sparking fire in my veins. I could feel his weight. His wet skin against mine. His heat and excitement pressing into me.

Damn, he feels so real. So good.

"You don't want tender or sweet. You want to be fucked. Hard. Feel alive." Warwick's mouth skimmed my throat, electricity sizzling through me, filling me with desperate need. *"You think you still want him? Think he's the kind of man you should end up with? You hold on to him because he's safe. But it's not you. Not anymore, princess. You are feral and dangerous. A monster that can't be caged. There is a wildness inside that won't be tamed. And that's all he'd want to do. Break you of your savagery. Tame you."*

His words felt like arrows, each digging into my soul.

No! I yelled at myself. *Get out of my head. I don't want you. I love Caden.*

I tried to clear my mind, reset it.

"You've tried that before. Didn't work then," Warwick growled against my ear. *"Just like I tried not to think about you while fucking those women. I want you out of my head just as much."*

Every word was a threat. They dripped with hate, but his hands moved down my body, sending tingles over me, parting my mouth, my pulse thumping through my nerves.

How did this feel so real? Like he was really here with me. Fear rang in the back of my head when I knew my hands were at my sides but could still feel fingers glide down my sternum, a moan growing in my throat.

What the hell! Stop it, Brexley. My eyes jolted open,

yanking me out of my dream world with a gasp. Alone in the tub, I peered at my limbs as if they would explain to me how they could feel him. My imagination wasn't that good.

Out of the corner of my eye, I noticed a huge silhouette in the doorway. I jolted up with a croaked cry. "Holy shit," I cried. Pain stabbed through me as my muscles tweaked, water swishing in the tub. Seeing the real man who had been so *vividly* in my head twisted me with confusion and humiliation. It was as if he had jumped from my head to where he stood.

Warwick leaned against the frame, his arms crossed, eyebrows furrowed. He lowered his eyes on me, a clouded expression drifting over his features.

"What the hell? What are you doing in here?" Mortification flipped to anger as I tried to sink deeper into the water, covering myself, but it was too low to fully hide. How long had he been there? Did I say anything out loud? Did he watch me? "Get out."

He didn't answer, staring at me as if he was trying to figure something out. His presence didn't just fill the room, he overtook it, flooding it until I couldn't breathe. Angry and brutal.

"He's terrifying and so sexually charged. Gods, he must know how to fuck." Rosie's sentiment rushed back into my head before I shoved it out.

My arms crossed over my breasts, glaring at him, the serene moment of my fantasy now gone, though energy pumped through me, sparking the air, drumming down my thighs.

"What?" I growled, my throat still raw.

He watched me for another beat, the intensity of his gaze making me fidget. He shook his head, the unreadable expression turning to his usual smug sneer.

"Enjoying yourself in there?" His cheek twitched, his tone leaving no doubt he had been watching me.

My nose flared. "Get. Out. Perv."

"You sure, princess? I think you really would like me to join you." Self-assuredness purred from him. "Remember, I've already seen what you have to offer." His eyes moved down to my mostly exposed body. The feel of his gaze slipped down my skin, adding more flames to my fire. "I'll pass."

He'll pass? Irritation wiped out all notion of modesty or prudence. The need to challenge his claim. Provoke. Push.

Forcing myself up, I gripped the edge of the tub. The sound of swishing water crashed off the walls, my skin prickling with awareness as he went rigid, his eyes rolling down my figure. Putting weight on my good leg, I stepped out, moving until I was flush to him, my head tipping back. The water slipped down my naked figure, dripping onto his pants, my bare toes hitting his dirty boots.

Clean. Dirty. Naked. Clothed. Wet. Dry.

Yin. Yang.

He inhaled sharply but didn't move, his gaze cautious and defensive like I was a wild animal. Feral and unstable. His chest moved in quicker pulses.

"Really?" My voice stayed low, husky, causing a twitch in his jaw. "For someone who declares I disgust him, you seem to find me often when I'm naked."

A twitch flicked at his temple, but he kept his face emotionless, tipping up one shoulder. "It's like being around a naked *boy*."

"Have a lot of experience with that, huh?" I curved an eyebrow, inching closer, his T-shirt absorbing the water from my body. "I should have known. All makes sense now."

He snorted, his eyes glinting with rivalry. "Glad you have me all figured out." His tone was condescending, but he tipped forward until his mouth lingered just a breath from mine. I forced myself not to move, his nearness setting off alarms in me. "I feel so much better now."

As if his words could physically touch me, I could feel the sensation of hands sliding everywhere over me, curving up the back of my thighs, skimming my ass, tracing my spine, across my collarbone.

I sucked in, freezing in place.

At my reaction, he went still, his head jerking back, his eyes widening slightly.

"You felt that?" he muttered so low I barely caught it.

"What?"

"Nothing." He pulled back, his face turning aloof and cold. "Get dressed," he ordered. "I need to bandage your wound, which is probably infected from the dirty water. And you need food," he snarled, his gaze briefly going to the ribs showing through my skin as if they had insulted him. He rubbed his heavy scruff, swearing under his breath. Fury rode his shoulders, disgust for me choking the air from the room.

What the hell was his problem? As if being starved, beaten, and tortured in prison had been part of my plan to utterly piss him off.

"I don't need your help," I snapped back. Pulling my hair over my shoulders, I covered my front the best I could, feeling vulnerable and insecure. "Actually, I'd be better without you. I can't wait to get back home and leave this whole horrific time behind me. Especially you."

It was a second—a blink.

He grabbed my shoulders, shoving me back into the wall, igniting sparks through me, flushing my skin with energy. Adrenaline slammed into my bloodstream, spiking my senses. His enormous physique flattened against mine.

"You *aren't* going back home, princess." He glared down at me as his legs pressed into my thighs, the fabric of his cotton pants and T-shirt rubbing across my bare skin. My body responded with want, curving into him, greedy for more, which only made me angrier.

"I am," I seethed. "You have no say over me."

"Really?" he gritted, moving in closer. On purpose or not, the movement scraped his clothes against my core and nipples, filling me with blinding need. *Stop, Brexley. You don't even like him.*

Clenching my jaw, I funneled everything into hate. "Get. Off. Me."

He smirked, his hand coming to my throat, the pulse of his erection rubbing into me, spinning my head like a whirlwind, shooting out all my logic. His thumb grazed over the black and blue bruises he put there yesterday. His jaw twitched as he ran over them, fury lighting up his eyes.

"Let me go."

"No." His fingers trailed down my throat, firing another shot of adrenaline into my blood. With everything I had, I swallowed back the moan clawing up my throat. "You need me, Kovacs." He pushed me into the wall harder, wetness slicking my core.

Fuck, did I like this? What was wrong with me?

"You would be still in prison if it wasn't for me. Or dead." He loomed even more fiercely.

"Need you?" I spat, lifting my chin. "I don't need a man who wants me dead."

His thumb ran up my neck. Slowly. Sensually. Threatening. "If I did, you would be. That was just me playing with you. Bought us more time."

"You choking me was just a little game?"

His thumb sank down into my collarbone, and once

again, I was overcome with the sensation of hands grazing up the back of my thighs.

"Yes," he replied. "And you liked it."

I sucked in sharply, feeling my body answer with an eager yes.

"But make no mistake, I saved you. Your life is mine now. I *own* you."

"*Nyasgem.*" *Fuck off.* I felt my voice vibrate against his palm. "*No one* owns me." I realized how easily I let Istvan give me over to the disgusting Romanian asshole. I didn't fight, sensing it was out of my control.

Owned. Weak. Submissive.

I had been beaten, stabbed, starved, tortured, locked in a hole, whipped, and almost raped. I had survived it all.

I wasn't some little doll anymore.

I was now a killer.

Going in innocent, considering myself tough, but I came out of Halalház as the monster they created.

Feral and dangerous.

And I wouldn't be tamed.

Adrenaline masked the pain in my body, so I curled my good leg around his, wrenching it hard. Warwick dipped to the side, giving me a moment to shove him back.

"That all you got, princess?" He laughed, his frame barely registering my hit, which spiraled frenzy in my chest.

A growl vibrated in my throat as I barreled forward. As if I was siphoning energy from him, I rammed into Warwick with a force I knew my fragile frame was not capable of in its condition. Warwick's eyes widened slightly as he stumbled back, his arms flailing, his massive build dropping back.

Splash!

A wall of water sprayed into the room like stormy ocean waves, roaring and breaking as they came crashing back down, dumping on his head, spilling over the floor. His form folded into the bathtub.

Holy shit, how did I do that?

There was a pregnant pause as liquid dripped down his face, drops sticking to his lashes. His livid blue eyes shot up to mine, glinting with fire, his nostrils flaring. Slowly, his tongue slid out, sweeping up the water from his lip.

Heat and terror flushed my stomach with hot and cold, but I kept my head up, holding on to my façade of strength.

"I'm not property," I snarled, keeping my voice low. "And if you try anything like that again, I will stab you in the throat. I've done it before… and I will do it again."

Before he could respond, I whipped around, going for the towel on the hook but seeing it was drenched with the water sloshing around my ankles. *Damn it.* With a grunt, I flung the door open, the prudish voices in my head screaming to cover up my bits when several people passed by.

Pride won out. Plus, I doubted nudity even registered here.

I stormed out of the room with my head held high, my message clear. Okay, I limped out, terrified of his retaliation, but I didn't pause as I went to the room and slammed the door.

Fuck Warwick Farkas. The moment I could get out of here, I was going home.

Back to where I belonged. To my life and the man I loved.

Chapter 28

A few moments after entering the room, there was a knock on the door just before a figure burst through. I grabbed the bedspread, tugging it over me, building myself up for another attack from the Wolf.

"Hey, luv." Rosie sauntered in, her arms full of clothing.

I exhaled, my shoulders sagging with relief, thankful it wasn't Warwick slamming back into the room for revenge. I was far too exhausted to fight him again. I still had no idea how I had been able to push him over. He was a mountain, and in my weakened state, I shouldn't have been able to move him at all.

"Thought you might need something to change into." She dumped the pile on the bed. I reached out, picking up a tiny silk tank, which had to be more of a nightshirt. "Went around to find someone more your size." I guessed she meant bony, no curves, and small breasted—the complete opposite of her.

I peered at her, feeling a stab of envy. Rosie was everything most men would desire. Stunning face, voluptuous in both hips and boobs. She rouged her cheeks a deep rose color, false eyelashes making her blue eyes pop. Their English Rose. The perfect sweet seduction.

She was exactly the kind of woman I could see Warwick inviting into his bed. *Surprised he hasn't already. Probably just working down the list.*

I had never been insecure before. Most women in my world were envious of my slim figure. The skinnier, the better was the motto of the elite, who were entitled enough to starve themselves purposely. They lived in a place that had plenty of food, but they wanted to be thin. Here, people were starving; curves were worshiped.

No one would envy how I looked right now. I wasn't sexy in the slightest. Nor should my emaciated figure be envied. This wasn't because I refrained from eating the biscuit at teatime, trying to hold on to my figure. This was a prisoner's body.

"Sorry there aren't more options around here. Clothes aren't important at Kitty's, especially normal, everyday items." She lowered her head as though embarrassed. "I'm sure you are used to much finer stuff."

"What do you mean?" I sat on the bed, my leg throbbing, my energy tanking.

"It's obvious you aren't like us." She shrugged a shoulder. "You are a proper lady."

"Proper?" I snorted. "What gave you that idea?"

"A lot of our job is observing, figuring people out. It's how I know what they want, even if they don't. I can tell their ultimate desires. We pick up on even the tiniest of nuances." She motioned to me. "The way you sit with your back straight, your hands in your lap. The way you talk. Hold yourself. You came from money, grew up educated and with decorum. These are all qualities you don't find in this part of town."

I blinked, my gaze dropping to my hands folded in my lap. Etiquette had been drilled into me from an early age, and

I didn't even think about it. Pulling my hands apart, I reached for a piece of clothing, picking up a slip, which normally would go under another skirt. The thin white cotton was worn and frayed, but it was clean.

"This is perfect, thank you." I pulled the skirt into my lap, seeing the lacy undergarments beneath. I was a cotton-bikini-bottoms-and-sports-bra kind of girl. Swallowing, I picked up the black scraps of fabric. They were only for decoration; there was nothing to them, no support.

"Sorry, no granny pants here." Rosie snickered, winking at me. "If you'd rather borrow a bodice..."

"No." I shook my head firmly. I had worn dresses with bodice tops—they were worse than any torture device Halalház could think up. "This is fine."

"Thought so. I'm so used to them now; I feel naked without it." She smiled, tugging the top of her bodice and stuffing her plump breasts back inside it. I tugged on the delicate lace thong, frowning at how little it covered. "Sooooo." Her playful tone flicked up my head. She tapped her lip, her eyebrows curving. "I couldn't help but overhear you and Warwick in the bathroom—"

The door creaked open, stopping the rest of Rosie's sentence, our eyes swinging to the entrance. Warwick stomped through, filling the space, loading the air with energy, causing shivers to run down my back. Commanding. Dominating.

I knew I wasn't alone in feeling it. Rosie inhaled, her hand going to her breastbone, goosebumps prickling her skin. Her feet twitched like she was nervous, but she licked her lip, her chest puffing out like a peacock, not able to fight her nature.

Not against him anyway.

Soaked from his voyage into the bathtub, his clothes

clung to his physique, forcing my gaze to roam over each place they stuck tightly to him, curving over his muscles and… gods, the man's cock was even indecent fully clothed. Nerves fluttered in my stomach, forcing my head to the side.

"Warwick," Rosie said his name as if she were addressing a god, her mouth open in awe as she took in how the fabric clung to him. "We have never officially met, though I feel I know you. Your reputation precedes you. And I have to say, it's been greatly minimalized. You are even more impressive up close." She bit her lip, her gaze moving over him like a cat stalking its next meal. A part of me wanted to knock her across the head, another part totally understood her reaction, and yet another part wanted to tell those two parts to shut up. She could have him. I didn't care.

His heavy gaze met mine, not responding to Rosie. He kept his expression neutral, but I could feel the pulse of his fury radiating off him like a tangible object. Even with the bedspread covering my chest, I felt stripped bare as his eyes burned into me.

"If you need anything… *Anything. At. All.*" She continued to talk, but not once did his eyes flicker to her.

"Rosie, is it?" he rumbled, still watching me.

"Y-yes." Her face bloomed with elation. "The English Rose at your service." She winked, her eyes heated, her robe open, allowing him to see her ample breasts, which practically fell out of the bodice.

"Thank you for watching over her." His attention narrowed on me.

"Oh, you are so welcome. She was no problem. Anything I can do to make your stay here bet—"

"Rosie," he cut her off.

"Yes?"

"You can go."

Her shoulders jerked at the dismissal, but she quickly gathered herself, nodding.

"Of course." She turned back to me, her eyes darting between Warwick and me before she took off for the door, trying to slip quietly out.

"Thank you, Rosie."

She paused, looked at me with an impish smile, then closed the door with a click.

Leaving me alone with him. I could feel him glowering, a weight pressing down, and with every second of silence, it grew heavier. I realized quickly trying to out-stubborn him was a losing battle. Warwick did not have the normal responses to awkwardness and tension most people did.

"I'm not going to apologize if that is what you are waiting for," I grumbled, folding the blanket firmer against my chest.

Silence.

I turned my attention back to him, sucking in as if he had plucked the air from my lungs. Was I always going to have this response to him? Wet, sexy, intense, brutal. He was too much—overwhelming and dangerous. Someone who would drown you. Take all of you.

Gritting my teeth, I shoved against his intensity, glaring back at him. "Is someone pouting 'cause he got a little wet?" I taunted, wanting to stand up, but my leg wasn't having it. "Or because a human girl got the better of him?"

His focus didn't relent as he took measured steps toward me. Nerves collapsed my lungs, my backbone going rigid, but I didn't flinch as he lowered his head to mine, his mouth a breath from mine.

"You think you got the better of me?" Raspy, his words went through me like Scotch, burning and heating my muscles, his breath snaking down the thin sheet covering me.

"Yes." I tipped up my chin, not backing away from him.

A smirk pulled up the side of his mouth. "You think that was a real fight between us?"

I glowered, hating my betraying eyes as they dipped down to his mouth.

"I held my own against you in the pit."

His patronizing smile grew.

"Believe me, when it's a *real* match between us, you'll know how easy I was on you. You'll be begging for me to relent."

Once again, his words grazed me like fingers tracing my skin, threatening me with other things besides battle. The line between danger and ecstasy was very fine.

"Now drop the bedsheet and flip over." He tilted his head as if he was going to kiss me, but I heard a deadly menace in his tone. "Now."

"What?" I jerked back, slamming into the bed frame, my fingers gripping the comforter to my chin. Heat swarmed my veins, my damp skin prickling with stimuli.

His eyes dropped down to my body, pausing over my lips as they came back to my glare.

"How many times do I have to tell you? Seen it. Not at all interested." He stood up to his full height, peering down at me, adding to the raging mortification I felt. "Your leg, Kovacs. I need to wrap it up. It's bleeding all over the sheets right now."

My head snapped to my calf. True enough, the wound had reopened and was leaking down my leg. I hadn't felt a thing.

Shit.

Humiliation colored my cheeks, knowing his presence was the reason I didn't notice. It was hard to notice anything with him around. He overpowered. Consumed.

As he returned to the dresser to grab the first aid supplies, I slipped on the silky tank, forgoing the pointless lace bra, covering myself up as much as was possible. I rolled over, acting like the thing they considered panties exposing all of my ass was no big deal. This guy had seen me naked. Twice. This should be nothing… but it didn't feel like nothing. The strip of lace and loose, silky tank falling off my shoulder were almost worse than if I was completely naked. These items were meant to entice.

Seduce.

Invite.

He strolled back up to me, setting the gauze and antiseptic on the bed. The sensation of him over me locked my muscles down. When I was in the bath, it was as if I could actually feel his weight on me, feel his wet clothes rubbing against my skin. I gulped, tension coursing through me.

He didn't move for a long time, and the silence in the room blasted out the voices and movement stirring in the building. The sun was lowering, coating the room in shadows, fashioning an intimacy.

Finally, his fingers wrapped around my calf gently, his other hand gliding down my leg, his palm coarse, spouting shivers over my skin. My teeth ground, and it had nothing to do with pain. Though that quickly changed.

As a damp cloth glided over the wound, a gargled cry broke from my lips and made my stomach churn. "Ahhh!" My fingers rolled into fists.

"Oh yeah, it's gonna sting."

I shot him a look over my shoulder, wishing he'd melt into the rug. He only smirked. He was enjoying this.

"You really are a bastard," I snarled, gripping the comforter harder, the alcohol sizzling my leg.

"Actually, I am."

My head yanked back over my shoulder, my forehead scrunching down.

"If you believe in that shit." He concentrated on cleaning my leg. "If a piece of paper between two people declares their offspring legitimate or not."

"You don't believe in marriage, I gather."

"A deed issued by the government should not determine the nature of a relationship. Who are they to tell you your love is valid? Your child is valid?"

"So… you believe in the fae way?" I bit down on my lip, huffing through the pain stabbing up my leg. His fingers were surprisingly gentle, but it still throbbed as he finished cleaning it.

"Seems more honest to me." He shrugged, tossing down the rag and grabbing the gauze. "Fae don't need a marriage license to prove they're together. When they meet their mate, they know it. Don't need a flashy leash."

"Flashy leash?" I burst out laughing. "You mean a ring."

"Same thing. A collar around your finger is no different from a collar around your neck or dick."

"Wow. Tell me how you really feel."

"Let me guess, princess… you dreamed of your wedding since you were a little girl. Fluffy white dress, glamorous party, perfect cake, the envy of all society… even though the wedding is a total fantasy, and reality wakes up next to you the next day snoring and farting in his sleep. Will you even like the wanker when the glitter is gone? Then you start popping out kids to avoid actually being with each other."

"Damn." I shook my head, my mouth parted. "What the fuck happened to you to be so jaded?"

"Not jaded." He tied off the wrap, patting my leg, which made me wince. "Just honest."

"I'm gathering you never met a girl who made you want

to be with just her." I twisted, sitting up, facing him. "Or guy… I'm not judging."

He snorted, his head shaking, traveling back to the dresser. A brown bag I hadn't noticed was perched on top. He tugged out a bottle of brandless palinka, cracked it open, and downed a huge gulp.

"Not for me."

"Which one? Women or men?" I smiled coyly. From the female guests he'd had in prison, and the sounds of their moans piercing the walls, I had no doubt of his first preference.

He shot a look at me, taking another drink. "Relationships. Being with one person." He leaned over the bed, handing me the bottle, his voice going low. "I can't imagine *anyone* being *enough* for me. So far, *three* don't even meet the challenge."

A strange tightness gripped my chest, but I swished it away, taking a drink. The cheap, harsh brandy attacked my throat, and I coughed and hacked. It tasted like someone produced it in their home bathtub.

"Oh, right, you can't drink with the commoners." He reached back for the palinka. I yanked it out of his grasp, glaring at him as I took another drink.

"Don't presume to know me."

"What's not to know?" He put his hands on his hips. "Grew up inside Leopold as General Markos's ward, only daughter of Benet Kovacs. You got the best education and training. Everything money can buy. Parties, dresses, food, top-shelf alcohol." He nodded at the bottle in my hand. "Rich, pampered, and entitled."

Anger rolled my shoulders up, and I scrunched my face, parting my lips to tear into him.

"What part is false?" He folded his arms over his chest.

"Maybe nothing." I strangled the bottle. "But you say it's an insult to you. I didn't choose to be born into that world. I was one of the lucky ones, and yes, I had an excellent education and got to sleep in a safe, warm bed, and food was never scarce. But don't act like you know me or know what I've gone through. The wealthy play different games, but they are just as ruthless and cruel."

"What? No mint on your pillow at night?"

"Fuck you." I got on my knees, wobbling a bit, moving closer, poking his bare chest. He leaned his head back at my nearness. "Don't patronize me or make me less. I've had men do it to me most of my life. Don't forget that I endured Halalház… the attacks, the starvation, and torture. I didn't have the luxury of being 'king' there, having everyone, even the guards, at my beck and call. I survived the Games. *I* murdered three people. Two at once, if you recall," I seethed, our chests pressing together. "I killed one of my *own friends*. So get off your high horse. In there, *you* were the pampered and entitled one."

His eyes tracked me, darting and moving over me as he slowly inhaled through his nose. Not responding felt like a victory to me, and I wasn't about to let go of my seat.

"Now, before you can have another sip of this," I wiggled the bottle, keeping it out of his reach, "you are going to answer some of my questions."

"Really?" His brows went up at my audacity.

"Really," I replied, settling back on the bed. "Starting with what the hell happened last night. I know the escape was planned. So sit your ass down and start explaining."

Chapter 29

"I don't need to explain anything to you," he replied coolly, glowering at me.

"Hmmm." I sloshed the potent liquor around in the bottle, taking another drink. "Suit yourself."

His lids narrowed into slits, a nerve in his jaw twitching. "You're blackmailing me?"

"Guess it depends on how bad you want this." I forced down another large gulp, doing it more to piss him off than for the enjoyment. "It's only coercion if you want this more than being a stubborn ass."

A low rumble came from him, his hand sliding through his damp hair and scouring at his face. "You are a conniving little bitch."

"Thank you." I downed another sip, warmth moving through my limbs. On an empty stomach, it sank into my bloodstream like melted butter. "Now explain to me how you knew the jail would be attacked. Why Zander helped us escape? Why you helped me and where you've been all day?"

Warwick's chest expanding in anger, using his build to loom over me. His lip rose, and he shook his head. "Fuck this." He whipped around, heading for the door. I knew I lost my leverage, my clout over him oozing out like air from a popped balloon.

"Wait." I started to climb off the bed. "Warwick, stop." I stepped down and my leg gave out, sending me crashing to the floor with a thud, my tailbone smacking the floor.

"Jesus." He flipped back to me, crouching down and grabbing my arms. "You realize you were shot in the leg, right? Try not walking on it for at least five minutes." He heaved me back on the bed, scolding me like a toddler.

"What?" I opened my eyes up wide. "I was shot?" I did a dramatic double-take, looking down at my bandaged leg. "Oh, my gods! When did this happen? Why didn't you tell me?"

He grunted, rising to his full height. "You are hilarious," he said, unsmiling.

Taking the palinka, I sucked more down, in real need of numbing the aches stabbing me like a voodoo doll. Knowing I lost the first round, I sighed, letting out my frustration. "Okay, how about we start easier."

"Like?"

"You." I motioned up to him. "I've heard about you since I can remember. What's true? What is false? Are you fae? Human?"

"You ask a lot of questions."

"Can you answer any of them?"

"Yes." He tilted his head. "And no."

Collapsing my face into my palms, aggravation gurgled from my throat.

"What? I answered your question."

"Yes and no? How is that answering it?"

"I'm human…" He reached for the bottle tucked between my thighs.

"What?" My mouth dropped open. "You're human?"

"And fae." He smirked, tipping the bottle into his mouth, his eyes glinting with mischief. "I'm one of those degrading mixed breeds. Someone tainting the purity of both races." The derision crawled thickly over each word. "Part of the group that doesn't fit in anywhere."

Half-breeds were only accepted in the Savage Lands. Pure humans lived in Leopold, the elite looking down on those who would mix with the enemy, finding it vile and gross to be friendly to a fae, let alone bed one. The fae side felt the same about mixing with humans.

"But why weren't you in a blue uniform? How come no one could figure out what you are?"

"Because I don't belong there either," he muttered before consuming half the bottle.

"What?"

"At one time, I was a half-breed." He wiped at his mouth.

"One time?"

He shrugged, moving away from me, his fingers going to his wet pants, peeling them down his body, making my pulse skyrocket. His bare, perfectly sculpted, firm ass was so round I wanted to bite into it like a juicy apple.

"What are you doing?" Unable to tear my gaze away from his lower half on display, my heart pounded in my ears. The night in the shower together, I had been so distraught, I didn't fully take in his physique. Damn, this man…

He peered over his shoulder as if he could sense my craving, catching me ogling his rear, roasting my cheeks into a deep char.

"They're chafing because someone got them wet." He lifted an eyebrow. Everything he did seemed to be doused in sex and danger, tapping into this deep feral need.

He stripped off his shirt, his muscular back flexing and

twitching under his skin. A bandage covered one arm where he'd been shot, his tattoos and scars demanding my attention.

Fuuucck.

Turning away, I took in clipped breaths, trying to act as if he didn't affect me, that his body didn't make mine respond with raw need. My act was more for myself than him. His smirk told me he saw right through me.

"What did you mean?" I cleared my throat, my gaze sliding and darting back to him as he took a minuscule threadbare towel off the dresser, wrapped it around his waist, then moved to the window. He flung his pants and shirt near the open frames to dry, then dropped down into the chair, propping his feet up on the bed, bottle in hand.

"You probably know more about me than I do." He settled into the wingback.

He was not going to make this easy for me.

"One of the rumors is you died then came back to life."

His mouth pinched together, his finger rubbing the lip of the bottle.

"True or not true?"

"Is there a third option?"

I rotated to face him, confused by his non-answer. "No."

He adjusted, glancing out the window.

"True."

My eyes bugged, ready for him to respond the opposite way.

"W-what? How?" That was the one thing neither human nor fae could escape. Death was death. "Was it only for a few moments?" It was possible to restart a heart within a reasonable period of time.

He squirmed again, clearly uncomfortable with this topic.

"No, I was dead." He rubbed his temple, flinching as

though he was reliving it. "I was stabbed, shot, gutted, and burned alive before someone snapped my neck."

A small gasp caught in my throat.

"They really wanted to make sure I was dead."

I didn't move or breathe, not wanting him to stop.

"It was the night of the Fae War. Right before the final barrier fell, I was jumped by many enemies at once. A hunting party." He stared out of the window, taking another drink.

"How is that possible?"

"*Az en sotet démonom*," he muttered so low I was pretty sure I imagined him saying "my dark demon."

My neck prickled at the name. I folded my legs to my chest. From what I heard and read of the Fae War, the night the barrier fell, battles raged throughout the world between those who were on Queen Aneira's authoritarian side—who wanted to turn the humans into slaves—and those against her dictator reign, wanting to end her rule. The fae crashed through the holes in the barrier as she tore it down, killing and attacking anyone on the other side, the flood of magic taking out millions of humans. One of those was my mom.

The day I came into this world was filled with death and blood.

"That's my birthday."

His gaze snapped to me.

"I was born the moment the final wall dropped. It was a very difficult birth… and I guess between me and the magic flooding in, my mother couldn't take it." I lowered my chin on my knee. "I killed my mother."

He stared at me. For a second, I thought I sensed a taste of alarm and confusion, but quickly it disappeared. He pulled his eyes off me and turned his attention back to the bottle, guzzling more. He abruptly stood, strolling for the door.

"Are you leaving?" A panic I hated hearing in my voice

called out to him. He ignored me, his hand on the knob. "Like that?" I motioned to his barely covered physique.

"It's a whorehouse, Kovacs. I think I'm overdressed." He ripped the door open. Rosie stood there with her hand up like she was ready to knock, a bag in her other hand. Her eyes widened at the sight of the mostly naked man, the towel not hiding the hard outline of him at all. Her gaze slowly moved down him, a sensual smile glowing her eyes as she stopped right on his package.

"Wow," she breathed, biting her lip.

"Thanks."

"If you need any assistance with that…" She nodded at his cock, chewing on her lower lip.

"Really?" He leaned against the doorjamb, his eyes sliding back to me so fast I didn't know if it happened.

"I mean, *I am* a professional." She grinned up at him.

Irritation bloomed in my chest. I had the strange urge to slam the door on my new friend.

"Did you need something?" Clearing my throat overtly, Rosie's attention snapped to me, her head shaking like she was stepping out of a trance.

"Oh, right." She held up the bag. "Madam wanted me to bring this up to you. She figured you'd be starving and needing more to drink."

Pushing off the frame, Warwick took the bag. "Damn, that woman is psychic. I was about to ask for someone to bring dinner."

"It's why she is where she is. She anticipates people's needs before they do." Rosie twirled her hair, her glazed eyes dreamily looking at him again. "We all do here."

"Well, tell her I said thank you." Warwick dipped his head at Rosie, stepping back, taking the bag over to the table.

Rosie sighed, inspecting his backside, practically drooling on the floor.

"Rosie," I called her name, but it was as if she didn't hear me, lost in him. "Rosie!"

She jumped, head whipping to me, her eyes going wide, looking bewildered. She motioned to him that he was at fault. Mouthing "sorry" to me, she gestured to her head, acting out like her brains were melting on the floor. I couldn't help but chuckle at her theatrical pantomiming at the door, the actress in her showing.

"Anything else?" Warwick swung back around. Rosie stood straight, pretending like she wasn't about to swoon to the floor.

"No. I'll leave you two… *alone*." She looked back and forth between us with a grin, reaching for the door. "Oh right, Madam also said it would be better if you didn't venture out tonight. Some guests coming in tonight might be *very keen* on knowing you two are here. Guess there is a high bounty for you both."

Warwick's head dropped in understanding, the space between his eyes wrinkling. "Thank her again for us."

Rosie dipped her head and shut the door.

"Guess we should be honored we already have bounties on our heads." I rubbed my arms, a chill running down my skin. Spending all day recovering in this place made me forget about what was going on outside these walls.

"Yeah, when I went out earlier, the streets were swarming with fae soldiers."

"Many of us escaped last night, right? There must be a lot of criminals they want to recapture."

Warwick huffed, turning his back to me. He pulled out the items in the bag, and the smell of noodles and sauce curled in my nose, my stomach clenching with hunger pains.

"They are only after us."

"Us?" I repeated. "Why just us?"

Silence.

"Where did you go today?"

"Got rid of the bike," he said, opening one of the cartons and sniffing.

"It took you all day?"

"No." Warwick turned around, handing me a carton of noodles, my mouth watering at the container of pad thai, forgetting everything else.

"Oh gods, this looks so good." Not waiting for him to hand me a utensil, I scooped up the noodles, dumping them into my mouth, half of them hanging out, dripping down my chin.

"Go slow." He tossed a fork on the bed next to me. "Your stomach is not used to a lot of food, and it will retaliate if you try to stuff it too fast. Believe me."

I heard him, but the taste of the delicious noodles spurred me to eat more. It felt like years since I had proper food.

"I warned you." He grabbed a new palinka bottle out of the bag, his carton in the other, and fell back into the chair, digging into his meal.

"Shit, this is so good." I moaned, thinking I would actually orgasm right there. His gaze drew up to mine, his lids narrowed. "What?"

He grabbed the liquor, pouring it down his throat until it was a quarter gone.

"Jesus. Who is the one who needs to slow down?" I stuffed more food into my mouth, another groan escaping my lips.

He muttered so low I couldn't hear him and shifted in his chair like he was uncomfortable.

"Why do you think they are only after us?" I garbled through the food in my mouth, getting another huge bite ready.

"I just know." He rammed a full fork into his mouth.

"What else did you have to do earlier?"

He continued to eat, not answering me. This seemed to be the theme tonight. Switching tactics, I went back to the topic he seemed open to.

"Why did you say you *used to* be a half-breed? That doesn't make sense."

He stabbed at his noodles, taking a deep exhale. "I died, and when I came back, I was different."

"Different? How?"

"It's complicated."

"Try. My *human* brain will attempt to keep up." I rubbed my stomach, feeling it gurgle.

"Just different. Can't really explain it."

"Wow, you're right, I will need it dumbed down for me."

He shot me a look, then turned back to the window. Darkness was creeping into the room. The activity in the street and in Kitty's was picking up, music and voices flittering through the thin walls and windows. This seedy part of the city was coming to life.

The wall he kept slamming between us like a drawbridge had gone up again. I knew when I was losing a battle.

"Last question tonight." I moved, my stomach squeezing with discomfort, nausea flooding over my tongue. "What was the reason you got locked up in Halalház?"

The side of his lips pulled up as he leaned his head back in the chair. For some reason, a spike of fear licked at the back of my neck.

"Repayment."

"And that means?"

"I tracked down all the people who had killed me… one being the fae king's right-hand man. In the end, he fell just the same as the rest. They got to feel everything I felt."

"You did the same back to them?" I sucked in, the wavy

sensation in my stomach slouching more. Stabbed, shot, gutted, burned, and a broken neck.

"And strung them all up as a warning." His eyes burrowed into mine as if he was seeing if I'd run from the room.

I didn't. "It took you twenty years?"

"No, it took me five. It took the guards twelve to track me down."

He had been locked away in Halalház for three years. And survived. I probably should have feared him, but I felt strangely calm. Serene in his presence.

My stomach had other ideas.

"Oh, gods…" My hand went to my mouth. "I'm gonna be sick." Not even feeling the ache in my leg, I tore off for the bathroom. I heard his laugh follow me down the hall.

"I warned you."

Asshole.

"It's hot, right? I'm hot." My mouth moved without much input from my brain. Everything felt toasty and happy.

My stomach ejected the food quickly but settled once it was back to being empty again, forbidding me to add anything except liquid. I lay on the bed, suckling on the mostly empty bottle, mourning the waste of my tasty dinner, while Warwick finished off his meal and the rest of mine. At least I had a nice buzz, a really, really nice one, taking the edge off the pain, worry, and most of all, him.

Nighttime was in full bloom, the house and passage below thriving with activity. Music, laughter, glasses clinking, smells of food, body odor, perfumes, and cigarettes crammed through the open window, battling for dominance.

I could hear the girls already shouting down at pedestrians passing by, encouraging them to indulge in their wildest fantasies.

"What do you want, pretty boy? Fae, half-breed, or human? Male or female? On top or underneath? Against the wall or over a table? Chains or feathers? Any way you want it," a woman purred down above us.

"How about all my friends and me? It's his birthday," a youthful boy's voice hooted up.

"Ugh." I swallowed, no longer feeling the burn of the shoddy liquor, each sip glossing the room in a haze.

Warwick scoffed, pouring back his own shot, his attention out the window. He began to slump down more into the chair with every chug he took.

"What?" I struggled to push myself higher against the headboard, my muscles limp and floppy.

"You really are uptight and prissy, princess."

"Stop calling me that."

"Stop being so judgmental."

"About a bunch of boys wanting to chain bang a girl?" I flung my hand toward the window. "Sorry, I really am awful."

"No." He shook his head. "About the fact she fucks for money."

"I wasn't."

"Please. I can feel—" he cleared his throat, gesturing to me. "See it all over your face. Your nose wrinkles every time you hear them in the hallway or calling out."

"Didn't know I was being monitored so closely." My ears heated with guilt. Did I do that? I couldn't deny I was uncomfortable being around prostitutes. Meeting people such as Rosie, who made this place feel so normal, was kind of unsettling.

He flicked his eyes, peering back outside. "Guess you

can't help it. Though really, as someone coming from prison, who are you to judge?"

"I'm not." *I so was*. "Prostitution is *severely* frowned on in my world. I'm sorry if I'm having trouble adapting instantly. Plus, prison wasn't a choice. This is."

"You think what they do is a choice?" he snapped back. Wagging his head, he returned to the window, quietly drinking, his attention feeling far away and haunted.

Picking at the label, his silence curled around us, choking the air. Several minutes passed before he spoke.

"I was born in a whorehouse," he muttered, making me freeze with his admittance. "Nothing as nice as this one. Back then, life was even more cruel and unkind to women trying to survive. Especially those who didn't come from money, weren't married, and had been abandoned and pregnant. It's not a choice. It's survival."

My teeth dove into my bottom lip, not sure how to respond.

"I was ten when she died of syphilis."

"I'm sorry." I curled my good leg closer to my chest, understanding the effects of losing a parent.

"It was a long time ago."

"How long?" I tried not to slur, my mouth not working as fast as my head. I was curious about how old he was. To humans, age mattered, to fae it didn't. I wasn't sure how half-breeds aged.

His blue eyes slid to mine, his lip curling up. "Subtle."

"What?" I feigned innocence, but a wicked smile hinted on my lips. Damn, he was so sexy. Was the room humid? Why was it tilting?

"You think you're the first to try and figure out how long I've been around?"

"No," I retorted, really feeling the alcohol cloud my

head. "But for some reason, you have this unexplainable need to tell me."

I was flirting, wasn't I? What the hell was wrong with me?

His head tipped back in laughter, and goosebumps vibrated my flesh. He rubbed his brow, chuckling to himself.

"I'll just say I'm a lot older than you." He smirked. "You should get some sleep. You're drunk."

"Am not."

"Go to sleep, Kovacs."

"Is that an order, Grandpa?" I narrowed my lids, swaying as I took another drink in defiance.

"If you want it to be." His tone was neutral, but I felt the implication race up my thighs. "They have a lot of whips, handcuffs, and rope here." His gaze burrowed into me then roamed my barely clad form. "If it's the only way you will listen."

Yes!

Nooo!

Brexley, I chided myself, pulling my gaze down to the bedspread. *You are lonely and drunk. Go to sleep.*

Annoyed he thought he could tell me what to do, I almost kept drinking just to vex him but knew I was simply hurting myself. My head already flinched with tomorrow's headache.

"Then you should too." *Oh yeah, stick it to him, Brex.*

"Was planning on it."

"Fine," I said, very maturely slamming the bottle on the nightstand. I rolled my hair into a bun and curved onto my side away from him. I could feel his eyes on me. Squeezing my lashes together, I attempted to block him out.

It didn't work.

Opting for another strategy, I switched off the lamp on the table, plunging the room into obscurity, feeling the need to hide. Lights from outside stretched shadows across the room like ghosts. If I thought the dark would shield me, I was sorely mistaken. His presence in the corner seemed to grow. The night only emphasized the sound from inside and out.

Sleep, Brex. I curled into myself, trying to clear my mind.

I heard him exhale, the chair creaking as he shifted. Minutes passed, and every second the need to look over at him intensified.

I fought. I really did.

Giving in, I glanced over my shoulder. His silhouette sat in the chair, his head tipping to one side, his massive frame not fitting the decrepit, small wingback.

"You're sleeping there?"

Half hidden in shadows, his head turned to me.

"Figured the princess of Leopold would prefer the bed to herself."

"*Stop* calling me that." I gritted my teeth. "Plus, I'm not so uptight and prudish as you seem to think I am." My alcohol-influenced tongue spoke before my mind could tell it to shut up.

"*Really?*" The simple word licked up my spine, twisting my stomach, making me wonder what the hell I was doing. It held so much implication in six letters.

I had "slept" with Caden all the time. We did it a lot as kids, and it never really stopped, especially after I lost my father. He was my anchor. His nearness and warmth kept me from drowning in agony. It ebbed when other girls started taking my spot, but every once in a while, he'd climb in next to me, curling up like we were kids.

If I could handle sleeping next to Caden, who I was in love with, I could certainly deal with someone I felt nothing for.

"Whatever," I huffed. "If you want to stay in the chair, I'm perfectly fine with taking up the entire bed." I flopped back down on my side, pulling the blanket over my shoulder. The seconds ticked by. Nothing happened. A stupid feeling of disappointment and embarrassment pricked at me, arousing anger in me. I tucked deeper into the lumpy pillow.

Only at the sharp creak of the chair, followed by the sound of his footsteps, did my eyes snap open, my pulse leaping into my throat. Forcing myself not to peer over my shoulder, acting as if I were either asleep or didn't care, my muscles locked down.

The mattress dipped, and the frame groaned under our weight as he moved down on the full mattress, his enormous build consuming more than half of it, so close I could no longer breathe. His knee brushed my ass as he settled on his back. In one second, I was sober. Awake. Alive.

Danger, my mind yelled as my nerves purred with the contact. I squeezed my eyes shut, pretending I didn't feel his presence or his heat smacking against my back like a whip.

He exhaled loudly, the bed shifting again.

Fuck me.

Go to sleep, Brex.

Letting out an exhale, I tried to relax, letting my mind retreat, concentrating on my exhaustion, forcing my mind on Caden again.

Thump. Thump. Thump. The noise hit the wall, and my lids lurched open with alarm and dread.

"Oh shit! Oh shit," a man's voice moaned loudly.

"You want that, don't you?" a woman asked.

No. Please. No.

"Yesssss," he hollered louder.

"Fuck me harder, bad boy. Spank me… yeah, that's it." A woman wailed dramatically through the wall as slaps and the sound of a bed creaking filled my veins with heat. "Oh, gods! Oh, gods! Yesssss!"

Oh, my fucking gods… Frozen, I couldn't even breathe.

The pounding against the wall vibrated our bed like a quake.

A giggle tore down the hallway, followed by men hollering back at their friends, then a door slammed on the other side of our room.

In a whorehouse, sex was going to be rampant, but I didn't think about it seeping into this space, crawling up my thighs, and shredding through the fragile bubble I was in. Not while I laid barely dressed next to a man who wore only a towel and was so sexually charged, he could light up an entire country.

Pinching my lips until it hurt, the sliver of oxygen going into my lungs stumbled and fell, causing me to suck in sharply. I could barely breathe.

Warwick hadn't moved, to the point it was unnatural, only adding to the tension between us.

Sweat beaded along my spine. I wanted so bad to kick off the covers but didn't want to show I was being affected. Especially when noises started in the room on the other side of us.

"Fuck! Yes! You want my big fucking cock?" The man in the first room grunted like a pig, frantically banging against the wall.

"Yes! Oh, gods, yes," she cried out, sounding more like a bad actress, but he didn't seem to notice, nor did my body. "I've never had this big before."

Lie.

A bedframe from the other room thwacked against the wall, along with loud moans.

I wanted to cry. Perspiration pooled between my legs and breasts, need aching my core.

"Oh, gods!" The woman in the first room shrilled as he bellowed, their release flooding our room.

Warwick shifted, his leg grazing me again, my body jerking at his touch.

"Bed's small." His voice was gruff and thick.

"Yeah." Mine squeaked. "It is."

While the one room went silent except for the sound of them exiting, a thump hit the ceiling from the room above us. Warwick mumbled something under his breath, modifying his position, tucking his arm under the pillow, his arm gliding against the skin of my shoulder. Flames scorched the area he touched, spiraling down my nerves before he jerked away like I had burned him.

"Call me Daddy. That's right, little boy. Suck me. Harder!" Men's grunts and groans came from the room across.

I was in hell. I had to be.

My side ached, forcing me to twist onto my back, my frame restless and hot. But I now could see his bare chest out of the corner of my eye, his hardness almost breaking through the thin towel.

Damn. If I thought prison was cruel and evil, now I was about to beg for them to take me back. Days in the hole felt like nothing compared to being stuck in a small bed with Warwick Farkas and surrounded by sounds of kinky sex.

I closed my eyes, demanding the liquor or fatigue take me away. I wanted to turn him and all the thumps and groans into white noise and make them disappear into my head, But his presence pressed against me, scratching at my wall.

Nooo. I shoved back the sensation of him, needing to breathe. Blocking him out, I turned over again, coiling into a ball.

Compelling myself to leave my consciousness, I dug

deep into the darkness. After a while, the alcohol finally took me under.

As I drifted off, I swore I heard Warwick mutter, "Fuck! This is hell."

Chapter 30

Filtered sunlight streamed through the curtains, shooting through my eyes and into the back of my skull. Groaning, I slammed them shut, feeling my brain splinter in half.

Damn palinka. Though, it was more than my head throwing a tantrum. Inhaling through the agony, my muscles screamed and spasmed. In training, it was always the second or third day when your body really responded to a brutal workout. There were days I struggled to even sit on the toilet and pee. Today my body suffered everything it had gone through during our escape.

A louder moan parted my lips as I tried to stretch out, my legs aching, feeling tight, as though I hadn't moved all night. Locked in a ball resembling a pill bug, I had been too afraid to venture out of my protected space.

Every memory of the night before swept in, some slightly fuzzy, but all rocking my stomach like the ocean waves. I really needed to stop drinking my meals.

Lifting my lids, I found the room empty again. After the night before, I thought I'd be relieved to not face his intense presence this early, but instead, my shoulders deflated at his absence. Where was he going every morning? I thought we were supposed to be in hiding. He only had one motorcycle to dispose of.

Slowly, I rolled up, pausing to take a breath several times on the way. Placing my feet on the ground, I clutched my head, leaning over my legs. The idea of scrubbing my teeth and drowning in a shower sounded like heaven.

I stood, bones cracking, and shuffled to the door, feeling decades older than my not even twenty years. My birthday was coming up in a few months, the day fae celebrated Samhain all over the world, an ancient Celtic festival. Another reason I never wanted to observe my birth—it was a sacred day for fae.

Caden always threw me a party, trying to cheer me up, but I would have been happier ignoring the whole thing. To me, my birthday represented my mother's death. Millions were murdered and killed that night. Our world crumbled into chaos, never to be the same again. And for us in the East, nothing but hardship came after. The day the wall fell was filled with hate, sadness, heartbreak, and blood.

"They really wanted to make sure I was dead. It was the night of the Fae War. Right before the final barrier fell." Walking down the quiet hallway, I rubbed the space between my eyes, recalling Warwick's admission the night before. He had died when I had been born.

Life and death.

"Oh, gods." I groaned at the reflection in the mirror. My pale skin appeared almost blue under the dim lighting, my veins showing through my thin skin. My cheeks were gaunt, my eyes bloodshot, and my body was covered with bruises and marks.

Once, I had been the perfect bait for powerful leaders, a lure for generals and delegates. Heads of state had courted me for my unusual beauty and wit.

Now? I looked haggard and beaten down by life.

Washing my face and teeth, taking care of business, I headed back to the room, halting in shock at the person leaning against my door.

"What are you doing up?" I tilted my head at Rosie. Dressed in her silky negligee and robe, her makeup smeared under her eyes, hair in tangles, she still looked better than I did. "Shouldn't you be sleeping for another six hours?"

"I should be, yes. But thanks to your man, I haven't gotten to bed yet." She trailed me into the room, her throat husky and low.

"What?" I spun to her, regretting my quick movement as a brick of dread plummeted to my stomach.

"Oh relax, luv." She swished her hand, tugging at her robe with the other. "It's not what I meant. Though I won't lie to you and say I wish it was for that reason." She winked at me. "But because we're friends, I could never do that to you. Plus, he doesn't want me…" She arched an eyebrow at me.

"I have no idea what you mean." I rolled my shoulders back. "And he's not my man. You have full permission to go after him."

"Right." She snorted, twisting a strand of her hair, not believing a word I said. "I was ushering my last customer out when he was leaving. Told me to tell you to stay put."

"He said what?" I blinked at her.

"Think his exact words were, 'Make sure she doesn't step a fucking foot out the front door.'"

"Oh really?" I folded my arms. "He leaves each morning but orders me to stay put like a dog? He has no say over what I do."

"Funny, he knew you'd say that. He told me, quote 'hogtie her if you have to, use your cuffs, but she doesn't leave.'" She curled her fingers in quotes.

Indignation detonated inside, breaking my hangover into tiny pieces, leaving only rage and obstinacy. "He said I couldn't leave through the front door. Did he say anything about the back one?"

"Oh, I know that look." Rosie grinned wickedly, rubbing her hands together. "I mean, I wasn't against tying you up. You are seriously sexy, but once upon a time, I was married to a controlling man. I'm all for putting them in their place."

"You were married before?" The peek into her life, the realization she was completely human with a life before this, punched me in the gut. As much as I pretended I didn't judge people here, I did. But they were people with lives. Families, mothers and fathers, husbands, wives, kids.

"Yeah." She wrinkled her nose. "He saw me in a play, came to the back door every night for a week with flowers and promises. He was charming, and I was young. Thought it was love. I was looking for an escape from that penniless life and thought he was it." Her gaze went to the floor, agony slicing over her expression. "He was the opposite."

There was a moment of quiet, her past life haunting the room, stinging my heart.

"I'm so sorry."

She let out a shaky breath, forcing a smile on her face. "No worries, luv. He's long gone, and I couldn't be happier."

"He's dead?"

"One can hope." She shrugged one shoulder. "He disappeared years ago after one of his business deals went bad. He was into a lot of shady shit, always trying to find the quick, easy way to make money, which usually went the opposite way. Had a lot of enemies. Left me with a lot of debt from really bad men. Madam Kitty took me in. Saved me."

"Saved you?"

"She paid them off so they wouldn't kill me. I slowly

work off what I can each month." She smiled through a twinge of grief. "I'm a lifer here."

Would my life have been so different if I married Sergiu? I would have luxury, but I'd be trapped, paying off my debt in sex and abuse. At least here, Kitty protected her girls.

"Warwick and my husband shouldn't even be in the same sentence. Your man is *nothing* like him."

"Not my man." I gritted my teeth.

She ignored me, continuing, "His type of dominance is something most of us dream about: feral, rough, *passionate*. He could make you explode into a million blissful particles. But I'm still all for causing trouble."

"Good," I replied. "Because I have no notion of staying put." I put my hand on my hip. "Just a few things I need: water, painkillers, breakfast, and an outfit that won't make me stand out."

Rosie's smile grew slowly, mischief glowing her face. "Oh luv, you came to the right woman."

"Be careful," Rosie whispered as she peered out the back door first, checking the alleyway for people. "Causing mischief is one thing, but Warwick actually wanting to kill me is another."

"I promise." I tucked back into the hood. The late summer weather heated the air and soaked into the buildings, causing beads of sweat to pool under my garments.

Rosie was able to track down enough clothes left from customers to allow me to disappear into a crowd. Faded colors of blacks, dark greens, and grays. The cargo pants, cotton tank, and hooded cotton jacket were loose, submerging my identity under the clothing.

"It's a little warm for this, but you won't stand out," she had said earlier when she pulled me into her room. She peered down at my lacy underwear and silk tank I had worn to sleep, her mouth pursuing information about Warwick again. "Wore that to bed? Small bed with such a *huge* man. Wasn't he only wearing an itty-bitty towel?"

"Shut up," I growled, not wanting to think about the night before. I would stuff that memory back into a box, never to see the light of day again.

She sniggered, tossing me a handful of clothes. "Get dressed and come down to the kitchen. Painkillers, water, and food await."

Once fed, dressed, and medicated, I felt a little better. I still ached, and I had a noticeable limp, but my plan was set, my determination locked to go.

I wasn't going out of my way to be a brat to Warwick by leaving. I was taking *my* life into my own hands. I was going home.

In prison, I learned trust was not something given freely, if at all. You looked out for yourself. And to a man who was riddled with mystery and secrets, no matter what tiny insight he confided, in the end, trust didn't amount to much. He wouldn't even tell me why he aided in my escape, which meant he was hiding something. He was looking out for himself as I needed to do for me. As he was disappearing each morning and up to something, and it would be very naïve of me to think the Wolf suddenly had my best interest at heart.

We couldn't be far from the wall dividing Leopold and the neutral zone. Any soldier on patrol along the wall would know my face. I was good at melding, slinking up on people. If I kept a low profile, I could get home. I had no doubt the moment Caden and Istvan heard I was alive, they would turn the world upside down to get me back.

"You are returning, right?" Rosie's expression tightened, as though she suddenly realized maybe there was more to my plans than I'd let on. Rosie had no idea who I really was, and I wanted to keep it that way—keep her innocent of my true plan.

"Of course." The false smile I pinned on my face hurt deeper than I thought. I liked Rosie, and the idea of never seeing her again upset me more than I imagined it would after such a short time.

I clutched her to me, hugging her tight. "Thank you for everything."

"Why do I feel I should have hogtied you?" She pulled back, searching my eyes for truth. "That I'm never going to see you again?"

"You will," I lied again.

"Be careful out there. Savage Lands is not safe, day or night. And if you are hiding *here*, people are certainly looking for you out there." She stared at me, her brows furrowing. "Why do I feel so devastated? I don't even know your name."

"Better that way."

She chuckled sardonically, her head dipping. "Now I know I should have tied you up. Guess he knows you better than I thought."

"I will miss you." I dropped the pretense, squeezing her arm. "I better go." I didn't want him to return before I escaped.

She pinned her lips together and brought me in for a quick hug before looking out into the alley again. "Go."

I touched her arm one last time before I slipped out the door and into the passage, going out the way she suggested to the main road.

Caden. I will see you soon. A butterfly of excitement fluttered in my chest at the thought. I missed him so much.

I slunk out to a heady mix of stale alcohol, vomit, and

burned coffee thick in the passage. Half the world was already up and working, the other half sleeping until the night brought their world to life.

As excited as I was to get home, to see Caden again, I couldn't deny the twist in my stomach at just walking out on Warwick. He had saved my life, but he of all people would understand. In this dog-eat-dog world, I had to look out for me.

Making it to the end of the corridor, I peered out into the daylight and saw people milling in the streets, urging my defenses up. When we arrived, it was in the dark, and I had been less than coherent, so I had no real idea where we were in the city. That changed the moment I stepped out.

My eyes locked on a structure in the distance, a choked sob hiccupping in my throat.

I could see a six-story wall about a mile from me, and behind it, the great dome of HDF. Like an old friend greeting me with shimmering brilliance.

A symbol of wealth and strength to some, but to me, it was home.

Chapter 31

From what I could tell from maps of the past, Budapest had been a much different city. The once famous districts had crumbled away in a quick slaughter after the fae wall fell. Reformed in shape and use, Leopold was half of what it used to be, a thick wall separating it from the rest of Pest. It was its own walled city.

Twenty years was a blip in history books, but for those of us living now, the decision to distance ourselves from the Western monarchy, having no personal connection to what was best for our country, turned quickly to devastation. The fae nobles in charge then hadn't cared about humans, only power, slicing our city in a constant tug of war between human and fae control, similar to a dictatorship. Civil battles between the two sides have been going on in Budapest my whole life. Since the devastating fight when my father was killed, the two sides had gone quiet. But you could feel the rumbling under your feet, the unrest growing louder, ready to break through again.

People do not respond or act when things are satisfactory or good. They react to fear and danger. The magic that filled the world after the fall plunged a country already deeply seeded in communism into chaos. Hungary hadn't been free of communism all that long, and many of the older generation still remembered the time far too well, while their children just knew freedom. The clashing of all the opposing ideals sank us deeper in turmoil.

Now there was another group of us, one who only knew this world—when fae and humans fought to rule. Suppression came from all angles. Universities, museums, cafés, streets of boutique shopping throughout the city were no longer. They either crumbled in decay or were being used for something else. I certainly hadn't realized the level of decay and despair on this side.

I was one of the lucky ones. I lived behind the walls of privilege and power. Savage Lands felt a world away. In reality, it was just blocked from our bubbled world, most of us having no real notion of why it was called Savage Lands.

Now I did.

"Get out of the fuckin' road!" A man bellowed at me as his horse almost careened into me, its hooves crackling at the broken lane, puffing debris into my face. I jumped out of the way as the man glared down at me with a snarl. "*Kibaszott idióta*." *Fucking idiot*.

Noise and smells attacked me, activity bustling around and jarring my nerves. My mouth parted half in shock and half wonder as I pressed against a wall, taking everything in. This was a completely different beast from what I saw coming in. In the daylight, I could see the buildings were more decrepit and neglected than I first thought, the darkness covering their wounds and blemishes. Planks of wood or tarps were used to cover up holes, broken windows, and doorless entries. Spray-painted designs and sayings were tagged on most of the lower stories.

Women, men, children, fae, human… dozens and

dozens of figures darted and weaved through the small lane, winding between the transportation. There was a mix of motorcycles and mopeds, but mainly horses trotted up and down with people on their backs, some pulling wagons, carts, or small gutted cars.

The air swelled with dust, horse shit, the stale smell of body odor and chemicals. A building in the distance pumped out smoke, clotting the atmosphere with haze. The monarchy in the West was big on making everything environmentally friendly. Savage Lands had no such regulations or concerns.

Bang!

At the sound of a gunshot, I jerked around and saw the same rider who almost hit me shooting into the sky, forcing the horse and cart ahead of him to pull over so he could ride past. My gaze darted around to watch most people not even take notice of the incident.

What the hell? Was shooting a gun the same as honking a horn?

Panting, I tried to calm myself, realizing how quiet and calm my world had been in Leopold. Ordered. Clean. Simple. There were lots of people around, but I only had interacted with a handful daily. Most I saw just in passing or at parties.

Even Halalház had been structured. An orderly hell.

This place was utter bedlam.

Come on, Brex, you are so close.

Hope propelled me forward. I darted down another lane, weaving through streets and alleys. Keeping my head down, my shoulder cracked into someone.

"Watch yourself, bitch," a woman grumbled, shuffling by.

Keeping close to the wall, my gaze locked on the dome in the distance. *Caden, I'm coming.*

Turning a corner, bricks packed my stomach, the weight

halting my feet. Down the lane, two figures progressed my way, punching fear into my lungs.

Guards.

"When I went out earlier, the streets were swarming with fae soldiers."

"They are after us."

Shit.

Stopping every person who passed, holding up something for them to look at, their belts dripped with guns, cuffs, and walkie-talkies. Terror gushed in my stomach as my gaze landed on one of them, his familiar scarred sneer lifting his lip.

Boyd. The man who took delight in hurting me. Zander had protected me in Halalház, but out here, there would be nothing to save me from Boyd's depraved power trip.

Panic lobbied through my entire body and sweat beaded down my spine as I swung around, returning the way I had come. My heart thumped in my ears as I tried to keep my pace steady, my head down, hoping to blend into the crowd of pedestrians.

Zigzagging through the throng on motorcycles and horses, I glanced up. Horror made me stumble, dread thrumming my nerves like a fiddle. Another set of guards headed my way, stopping every person who went by, holding up the same paper. From here, I could make it out enough to understand.

It was a picture… of me.

Fuck. Fuck. Fuck.

My gaze darted around, searching for an alley or doorway—any way to escape.

"Hey!" Boyd's voice boomed from close behind me, the sound stabbing the back of my neck. The bitter taste of adrenaline coated my tongue.

The guards in front of me looked up, and I froze in place.

Oh, my gods.

The team that had collected me at the door at Halalház and taken me down into the prison stood only a few yards from me. Zion and Jade. Their eyes were pointed in my direction, feeling like they were burning through the hood drooping low on my face.

"What the fuck?" A hand came down on my shoulder, Boyd's harsh voice right in my ear.

Everything stopped. My breath, my heart… my life. A deep sob balled up in my chest, ready to burst at the idea of going back to Halalház, especially this close to home. I wouldn't make it out a second time. They would make sure.

"What are you doing here?" Boyd shoved me out of the way, stomping up to Zion and Jade not unlike a bulldog. The other guard, who had been his sidekick in prison, trailed after him like a puppy.

I gaped, a sliver of air making it into my lungs.

"I was gonna ask you the same thing." Zion folded his arms. "This is our terrain."

"No, it's not." Boyd lifted his head higher. "Who called you fuckers in anyway? We got this handled."

"Looks like it." Jade smirked, lifting an eyebrow, motioning to Boyd's partner. "Oh wait, that's your bitch, not the prisoner."

"Fuck you, Jade," Boyd huffed. I knew the longer I stood there, the more noticeable I would become, but I was afraid to move, to call attention to myself. My pulse thumped against my neck. I had a talent for being sneaky and ghostlike, but right now, I was afraid they could hear my heart thump like a loud drum.

"He decided after two days of you guys sitting on each other's dicks, to get people who will actually find her."

Her.

Me.

"And have you found her?" Boyd motioned around the pair. "I have every inch of the wall covered lying in wait for her. She gets anywhere near it, and we'll know. I also have men combing this whole area. I *will* find her." Why did it seem they were only after me?

Biting on my lip, I slowly turned, hoping to blend in with the activity around me, and slipped down the street.

I now realized the extent of my naiveté. I hadn't even thought about the wall being watched by enemies ready to grab me before I could claim sanctuary. They were lying in wait, knowing exactly where I'd go. If I hadn't overheard them, I would have been caught today and returned to prison.

Turning down an alley, I hunkered against the wall, peering back out at the group from under my hood. The four of them still conversed in the street, unaware the very person they sought had slipped under their nose.

Oxygen heaved out of my lungs, dropping my shoulders with relief, and I sagged into the building.

A huge hand slipped around my mouth and yanked my body back. A muffled yelp tore from my chest, my head whirling. My world dropped through the ground as an arm wrapped around my waist and spun me around, slamming me back against the wall, pinning me in place.

"Look what I just caught."

Fevered cerulean eyes sparked with rage, shoulders reaching up to the sky, his form completely encompassing mine.

"Warwick," I whispered against his palm, almost crying

with relief. He dropped his hand from my lips. For such a massive guy, he was damn stealthy.

His fingers wrapped around my arms, pushing me harder into the wall, his lip rising. "Shut. Up."

My mouth opened to speak.

"Warning you, Kovacs," he snarled, his muscles trembling with fury. "You open your mouth right now, and I will hand you over to them."

"No, you won't." Ignoring his warning, I pushed into him, ignoring the fierceness of his presence, glaring back at him. "First, that would be giving yourself up as well, and second, if you wanted to do that, you would have already done it. You didn't break me out just to hand me right back over."

His cheek twitched, his nostrils flaring. "Didn't I?"

"No. Though I am curious. Why did you break me out? What is your plan, Farkas? Do you want to use me as leverage as well?"

His eyes moved down me, his mouth close to mine, pulling my eyes to them. He rolled his lips together.

"This is not the time." Grunting, he pushed off me, peering around the corner, spotting the guards. "We've got to go." He huffed, spinning the opposite way and hurrying down the passage. "They're heading back this way."

Jogging down the path, I followed him. The paralyzing fear of getting caught didn't return even after his comment. I felt strangely calm, like together we could take on anything. Which was stupid. We weren't a team. We weren't anything.

I hadn't traveled far from Madam Kitty's, but with the fear of guards patrolling, it took us longer to sneak back.

"They're stationed at the front and back entrances of the alley." Warwick waved me to follow him into a decrepit building, the white stone painted with the sayings:

"Sarkis will lead the resistance to the future!"

"Markos the murderer!"

"Sarkis is our light to a new way!"

What? I knew Istvan had made many enemies, but he was fighting *for* the humans. To make us equal. It was Killian who was oppressing. Killing.

Istvan told me this Sarkis guy was nothing more than a thug. A guerilla army wanting to become the resistance in Prague, the Povstat, trying to find their piece of the pie.

"Kovacs," Warwick hissed, gesturing me to follow. Touching the quotes stirred up questions in the back of my mind. "Come on!"

Following Warwick out the back of the building, we made it back to Kitty's, where we ran up the stairs to our room. With every step, his body tensed with rage.

"Uh-oh! A lovers' spat already?" Rosie leaned in a doorway, smoking a joint.

"You!" Warwick growled, storming up to her. Her eyes widened in fear. "I told you to keep her inside the fucking house, tie her up. Not help her escape."

Rosie stumbled back, swallowing nervously.

"Hey." I jumped between them, my palms pressing into his chest, trying to push him back. "She's not your minion. We're no longer in Halalház; you don't get to order people around."

"Oh really?" He tilted his head, his face barely a sliver from mine, his fury smashing against me, encouraging mine. His gaze scoured over me, hacking into my skin. "Want to test that?"

Yes.

No.

"I'm not afraid of you." My toes hit his. "She was being a friend to *me*. If you want to be mad at anyone, be mad at me… not her."

"Believe me. I am." He stepped even closer, his voice low, caressing my throat. "That was the most foolish, idiotic, dangerous—"

"Enough." I put my hand up to his lips, stopping his words, but the feeling of his lips against my flesh made heat rush through me. His gaze leveled with mine, the intensity in it pounding my heart. My body flamed to life at the touch. Dropping my hand, I stepped back, taking in a breath to speak.

Nothing.

Words wandered off, losing their way from my head to my tongue. I rolled my fists, marching into the bedroom, needing to put distance between us.

If he wanted to yell at me, he could leave Rosie out of it.

Following behind, Warwick grabbed the door, flinging it shut behind him. Right before the door closed, my eyes found Rosie's. Her pressed lips curved into a smug smile; an eyebrow arched in a knowing expression.

I glowered at her before the door slammed, her laughter trailing into the room.

Warwick gave me no time to regroup, barreling for me. I stumbled back, my ass hitting the wall. My chin jutted up, my nose flared as he closed in on me, and his chest knocked into mine with heavy breaths.

"Do you know how reckless it was?" He pressed his hand into the wall by my head, anger straining his shoulders.

I rolled my jaw, not answering.

"Were you trying to get caught?"

I glared at him.

"Because that has to be the only reason." Derisive, he loomed in closer, his mouth almost grazing mine. But it was neither seductive nor sweet. He was taunting, batting at a toy. "You couldn't possibly be stupid enough to try to get home… in the middle of the day? While you are being hunted? You think I've been going out every day to enjoy a nice walk? I've been out there spying on the scouts covering this city for us. I thought when I said the streets were swarming with fae soldiers, you would have taken it to heart."

"Seems they were looking just for me," I countered, my voice low.

He leaned on his forearms, bringing his threatening presence in closer, crowding me. "Anyone with a brain cell would know you'd try to go back to Leopold. They were watching out for you at every section along the wall, waiting to get you before you could make a move. You have a bounty on your head so high commoners on the street are frantically searching for you so they can get the reward. So… please tell me you weren't actually heading there." He cocked his head like he was waiting for my answer. Embarrassment sizzled up my spine. "HDF does train their soldiers to have an ounce of common sense, don't they?"

"Fuck you," I snarled. His scorn burned my cheeks with chagrin. He was right. I had acted purely on emotion, tossing all my training away in a blink over the need to get home. I hadn't thought about how extensively I was being sought, foolishly thinking I could easily dissolve in the city, getting to the gates without a problem. Home was within reach.

With his free hand, he tugged off the jacket hood covering my head. It felt as if he were stripping me bare, his lashes lowering to my lips before popping back up. "Without even a goodbye, huh?"

I could see my chest lower and rise with my breaths, the need to shove him back, slam him back into the wall and…

My gaze dropped, running from the feral thoughts coming into my head.

"I didn't threaten Rosie to keep you here because I get off on toying with you."

"Don't you?" I jerked my head up, my teeth grinding together as he boxed me in with his other hand, his gaze like razor teeth, gnawing into me. His mouth was so close to mine, and I could feel the heat of his breath. I dug my nails into my palms. "Seems exactly what you enjoy."

He watched me.

"What do you want with me, Warwick?" I pushed my chin even higher. "You won't tell me anything. Even how we got out. It was planned. By who? Why? Why did you save me?" He kept his lips secured together. "You're not keeping me around because you care about me. Are you any better than the men outside hunting me?"

We stared at each other, an emotion I couldn't decipher clouded over his face for a moment.

"Be ready after sundown." He abruptly turned away, flipped up his hood, and sauntered to the door. "I'll be back."

"What?" I lurched off the wall, coming after him. "Where are you going?"

"We can't stay here any longer." He stared at me accusingly. "I need to handle a few things first. Ready at sundown," he repeated before storming out the door, leaving me rattled and confused.

Flopping down on the bed, I let out a frustrated exhale. *Asshole.*

"Oh, luv…" Rosie clicked her tongue from the open doorway, looking between where Warwick went and back to me. "If you two don't fuck soon, you're going to combust."

"Rosie." I rubbed my head. "It's not like that. We hate each other."

Laughter howled through the room, her hand going to her throat. "If this is what hate looks like, then sign me up."

"We are nothing but a forced partnership for the time being. That's it."

"Luv, *my marriage* was a forced partnership. What you two have… you guys could ignite the Eastern Bloc with your sexual energy. You two have a connection; I feel it in my bones. Anyone alive could."

"No." I shook my head, rejecting her theory. "I have someone at home I love. He's *everything* to me."

"I don't doubt you might genuinely think that." She leaned against the door, still dressed in her negligee. "But take advice from someone who's seen a lot. There are very few people who find someone who challenges them, makes them feel alive, fights and loves with the same passion."

"How do you know I don't have that with Caden?" I folded my arms.

"Because I've seen you with Warwick."

Chapter 32

"Stay close," Warwick sniped, his foul mood infusing the weight of the shadows as he headed out the back of the alley. The night-kissed air colored the path in dusk, the sun's exit painting the alley in various dark blues and purples. His surly temper had not ebbed since finding me on the street. If anything, it had only gotten worse.

After another goodbye to Rosie, the madam of the house watched us, expressionless, from her doorway as we departed the protected walls of Kitty's. She neither looked relieved nor sad by our departure, making me even more curious about what Warwick's connection was to her. I didn't sense any sexual vibes between them, but at the same time, there was something between them, something that had made her willing to hide the two most wanted criminals in Budapest. Especially since money was awarded for our capture.

"Where are we going?" I demanded again, gathering in close to his tall form and using him to shield me from the people stuffing the lane, melting us into the sea of activity.

Smells, music, and sexy costumes with feathers and colors brushed around me, women whispering enchanting words in my ear. Glamour tickled my skin, taunting me to try their goods. Half-naked women and men with wings, animal ears, and glowing eyes dangled from the swings and hoops attached to the overhangs. A man blew fire from his mouth into the air as a stunning woman twisted the fire into forms that seemed to come to life. Her features were split down the middle, dark hair on one side, blonde on the other, her eyes two different colors, which was even a rarity in the fae world. The circus environment was set to tempt and seduce people to open their wallets in their establishment.

Wearing similar clothes to many others, dark and hooded, we slipped through the spectacle. I constantly gazed behind us, while Warwick kept his eyes ahead. His sudden need to leave, not even waiting for the middle of the night, had me asking over and over where we were going.

"They'll expect us to move at night, have more eyes out looking," he had said when we were moving into the street. "Twilight tricks the eyes, the world between day and night, shadows and light."

With nothing but the clothes on our backs, which weren't even ours, he took us through the backs of buildings, coming out on a side street and going directly to a motorcycle tucked into a side alley.

"Hop on." He motioned to our newly acquired bike, suggesting what he might have been up to after he disappeared earlier. I peered up at him, his gaze not meeting mine, aggravation twitching his limbs.

A flutter of doubt wrinkled my forehead, but I shoved it back. I didn't have much choice. Warwick and I were in this together for the time being. Both of us were wanted and on the run.

My list of friends was almost nonexistent in my life: Caden and maybe Hanna.

My willingness to trust people and let them in was something I always struggled with.

Warwick saved my life. Got me out of Halalház. Protected me. And yet, I still didn't trust him. But going with him now was my only choice.

My hesitation drew his attention to me, his eyes finding mine.

I'm trusting you. My lids narrowed on him. His head dipped like he understood me perfectly.

His Adam's apple bobbed, his jaw grinding together. Then he spun around, settling on the bike, and kick-started the engine to life.

Rolling my shoulders back, I swung my leg over the back, wrapping my arms around him as it lurched forward down the lane.

I clung to his back, the warmth and firmness claiming me and making my heart jump like it was on a trampoline.

Speeding away from the area, the indigo of evening gobbled up all the light, curtaining us in this private world where I actually felt safe and free as the wind blew my hair back, skating over my face. He kept to side streets, the buildings growing even more dilapidated and covered in graffiti the farther we went. We passed several huge factories, smoke chugging out of chimneys at the top. Both the fae and humans had factories in the neutral zone, the products needed to export and keep this city afloat were all made here. Maja's kids worked in one of these.

Bang!

My thoughts vanished at the sound of gunfire, jerking my head as four men riding horses came galloping out of an alley, as if they had been hiding there in wait, their guns pointed at us.

"Shit!" Warwick hissed, racing faster and weaving the bike in a curved line.

A bullet whizzed by my head. The shot meant to kill. Glancing over my shoulder, I saw the figures race toward us, the horses keeping up with the bike better than I thought. The men's hoots and hollers echoed over the roar of the motorcycle.

"Who are they?"

"The Hounds," Warwick yelled back. "A gang of thieves who would kill their own mothers for money."

They were dressed in black clothes and black cowboy hats with guns and knives hooked on their belts or aimed at us.

"Are they fae?"

"Doesn't matter here. There are no sides. When you are struggling for food, what species you are doesn't matter. Especially because so many here are mixed. A bunch of people who have nothing to lose and no morals left," he responded, his hands clutching the handles. "Hold on."

The warning was all I had before he turned sharply, tearing down a road, his shoulders tense, the alley snug with people and carts.

Bang! Bang! Bang! Gunshots tore down the lane, clipping the back of the bike.

Screams broke out from pedestrians, causing them to scatter like confused squirrels.

"Get out of the way!" I screamed, but no one listened. Warwick skillfully wove through the chaos, but the people in our path forced him to swerve down another smaller alley, the walls almost grating the handlebars.

His shoulders tightened, but he punched the bike faster.

Shouts hurled down the corridor after us. Peering behind, I saw the lead horseman galloping toward us, the alley making us a perfect target—like a bowling lane with no gutter. His arm was raised, the gun glinting off lights from the building above us.

"Warwick." The warning ground from between my teeth as the sound of a gun popped off behind us.

Warwick's arm darted back, yanking my body around his torso, and ducking me down right as a bullet struck his shoulder blade. Right where I had been.

Holy shit. That would have been my head.

His fingers dug harder into my skin, a tiny grunt huffing his chest, but it was his only response to the shot burrowing into his flesh. He tore the motorcycle out of the alley, skidding back onto a main street, the large road giving the bike freedom to hit top speed.

Glancing back, the gang struggled to catch up, disappearing gradually into the darkness.

I exhaled with relief, the tension in my stomach ebbing. Twisting back, I noticed blood dripping down Warwick's arm onto my knee, the new wound not far from the one he'd gotten the night of our escape.

Rolling and wadding up his shirt, I tried to slow the bleeding, my hands saying the thank you my mouth couldn't seem to find.

He had taken a bullet for me. Once again protected me.

The infamous and feared Warwick Farkas, the man who killed without thought or conscience, appeared to have one after all. At least for me. The guy who could so easily snap a man's neck in prison, but gently cleaned and attended my wounds. Who shared a bed with me, but did not take what I did not offer. Shared food and drink. Spilled memories and secrets.

If it was the adrenaline or gratitude for him saving my life, I didn't care. I felt the feeble wall I had kept up against him bend. My opinions on him sharpened with chaotic emotion.

As if he felt every confused emotion, sensed every

messy thought, his chest expanded, his spine stiffening. It didn't stop me. I flattened my palm against his taut back, my hands caressing his glorious body, even as his muscles tensed under my fingertips.

With one hand, I kept pressure on the laceration, while the other explored, drinking in the heat and firmness, curving around his sides.

A strange ache started throbbing in my shoulder blade, as if I had been shot too, but I shoved the sensation away, concentrating on him.

He sucked in, his eyes darting to my hand, then back to the road. Not encouraging, but not discouraging either. My touch moved under his layer of clothing, electricity snapping at my chest as my fingers touched his skin. He went rigid, his breath hitching.

"Kovacs." I heard my name. A threat. A warning. A question.

My hands moved farther over his ripped abs. Fuck, he felt good. Like I was drunk and clearheaded at the same time, dreamy and sharp. I stopped thinking… only feeling, everything around me disappearing.

"Brexley…" He curved his head to me, breathing shallowly. Hearing my name on his lips, the way he drew my name through gravel, husky and deep, shredded every fiber of my will.

My gaze met his. I had no idea what he saw in my eyes, but his head snapped around. Every moment the tension between us thickened to painful levels. The desire I'd shoved away now broke free, spilling everywhere, and I couldn't seem to wrap it back up.

"Fuck," I heard him snarl, the bike coming to a skidding stop. He stayed facing forward, boots on the ground, his grip tight on the handlebars. I watched his shoulders rise and lower with his heavy breaths, more blood soaking into his cotton jacket.

"You saved my life again," I whispered, my hands once again moving up his spine, pushing up the fabric.

He made a gurgling sound in his throat. "What would be the point in saving you if I let you die now?"

My thumb traced his vertebrae. His knuckles gripped the handlebars until they were white. Right then, I noticed how I affected him. My touch controlled him. It was heady and powerful. Addicting. And my pull to him was a force I couldn't fight.

"What do you want me for?"

"Doesn't matter." Every muscle was tense. Every syllable rough. Thick. "Not anymore."

The adrenaline pumping in my veins had me feeling out of my body. I couldn't deny I was extremely attracted to him. Of course, I hadn't met anyone who wasn't. But this was consuming. Burning me up. "Why is that?" Impulsively, I leaned forward, my breath grazing his skin.

"Jesus," he growled, but didn't pull away, a vibration rattling his lungs. "Kovacs… stop."

I wanted to tip this man over, the ghost, the Wolf, the legend, making him as needy as I felt. My mouth brushed up his spine. "Thank you. For saving me. Helping me. For all of it."

A guttural noise came from his chest, his hand clamping down on my thigh, his thumb rubbing over the crotch of my pants. Desire flooded me; I was throbbing and aching for more.

"Warwick," I breathed. What the hell was happening?

I could feel his hands on my body, his breath gliding between my breasts, the heaviness of his erection pressing into me without him moving a muscle. Even more, I could feel his desire filling me. It wasn't an idea or the way he gripped me, but a presence… entering me like a ghost, hitting every erogenous nerve, bursting pain and pleasure so blissfully through me, my breath stuttered.

"Fuck." His thumb pressed through the material, rubbing along my folds. My mouth parted in a moan. I knew only one hand touched me, but he was everywhere.

My heart thumped against my ribs, an alarm ringing in my head, knowing this was not right. This couldn't actually happen. But desire swallowed up my thoughts, a deep need overtaking me. Nothing about this was normal, but for some reason it felt right.

He curved around, his nose flaring, his eyes flicking over my shoulder before locking on mine like he was clawing at my skin to let him in.

In the distance, I heard a noise, but I was so hyper-focused on the man in front of me, all I could see was him.

"Kovacs—" I could hear a pinched note in his murmured voice. "I'm sorry."

It was like someone cut a cord, the connection between us snapped, the sensation of him vanishing, leaving me cold and off kilter.

"I had no choice." He turned away, climbing off the bike.

"What?"

A door slammed, jerking my head to the side.

In one second, the earth ripped out from under my feet. Confusion and terror flung me out into the atmosphere with no rope.

A man ascended elegantly out the back of a shiny, black Mercedes SUV, stepping forward. With a gasp, I scrambled off the motorcycle, my gaze taking in what my brain didn't want to accept.

I had grown up seeing his likeness on statues, in paintings, and in fae society papers.

In person he was even more deadly handsome than claimed, and every bit the high fairy, with violet-blue eyes and sharp, chiseled features.

Killian, the leader of the Budapest fae, stood in front of me.

He had challenged the noble leader before him, the one who voted we part from the UN, and won. He was said to be so brutal and cruel, no one dared contest his seat since.

Tugging at the cuffs of his expensive dark suit, his eyes pierced me through the darkness. My lungs hitched; his power and looks forced me to step back. He was tall and built, with dark brown hair slicked back and a light scruff over his jaw. He appeared to be in his early thirties, but his aura held centuries of knowledge and experiences.

Beautiful. Elegant. Perfect.

And deadly.

Killian's gaze found me, and I could have sworn his eyes widened for a second, but then I blinked, and it was gone. He again wore a composed mask of dominance.

"Warwick." Like butter melting over a juicy steak, Killian's voice was rich and smooth. "Glad we could finally make this deal. You made the right decision."

"As if I had a choice," Warwick spoke, my head snapping back to him. He stood near the front of the bike, his expression hard and angry, his jaw locking down.

"You could have turned her over to my men. Prevented all this fuss looking for you both." Killian took a step, sliding his hand in his slacks. "I was beginning to think you had forgotten what was important, Farkas." His gaze glided over me. "Or maybe your priorities changed."

"Nothing's changed." Warwick's hands rolled into balls. "Your men are imbeciles. I wanted this between you and me."

"Took you three days to come to that conclusion?"

"I'm here now," Warwick growled.

My head spun with their words, not able to take in what my gut already sensed.

"What's going on?" My lungs clipped with fear, my gaze darting from Warwick to the fae ruler, then finally at the three men around Killian.

The three guards who had taken me to Halalház.

Sloane, Connor, and Vale.

Killian's personal guards?

Sloane took a step toward me, and instantly my gaze went to Warwick with confusion. I didn't understand. Why wasn't he trying to get away? They wanted him too. He was an escaped convict as well.

Warwick stared at me, not a shred of emotion on his face.

"What's going on?" I asked again, my feet retreating a few steps.

Warwick grabbed my arm, yanking me back. "I brought my part of the deal. Now where's yours?"

Deal?

"I am a man of my word, Farkas. You should know by now." Killian's voice ran over my skin, cooling and soothing, making my shoulders want to ease back in relaxation. I fought against the instinct. That was what fae did. They used their powers to trick humans, to make us their prey.

Not me. Not ever.

"Deal? What deal?" My head swirled, trying so hard to grasp what was going on.

"His freedom for yours." Killian lifted a brow, his gaze rolling over me like I was an insect.

"Wh-what?" I snapped to Warwick, daggers of pain knifing my chest.

"That wasn't all of it." Warwick sneered at Killian, a nerve in his jaw twitching. He was a wall, not one single emotion I could gather from him.

"I-I don't understand." My voice came out almost like I was begging. Hoping this was all a mistake. "Warwick…?"

Betrayed. I felt the word more than heard it in my head, wrapping around my throat and squeezing out all my hope and trust. My lungs deflated with disbelief.

"Why?" I croaked. He wouldn't meet my eyes.

His grip crunched down on my arm, his head twisting away from me.

"Warwick has been secretly working for me." Killian tipped his head at him. "After he brutally hunted down, tortured, and murdered seven of my men, one of them being my right-hand man. We made a little deal, didn't we?"

Warwick rolled his jaw, his lids lowering on the fae leader, but he didn't refute this claim.

"Warwick?" I stared, trying to rip down the fortress he put between us, not wanting to believe it, while my stomach twisted with the truth. This didn't make sense. Getting me out, Zander helping, and then turning me back over to Killian? This had all been a setup?

"It's been a very fruitful relationship."

"For you maybe," Warwick grumbled, his nose wrinkling.

I felt I had been dunked in ice water until everything froze, keeping out reason and logic. "But… he was a prisoner."

"He was. He was also the perfect spy." Killian smiled at me, but his eyes went to Warwick. "Though he was not as communicative in the last couple of months. He was keeping a very big secret from me." Killian's attention locked on me like I was the reason. "I never thought a human woman could have such power over you."

"She doesn't."

Killian's eyebrows rose.

"She's here, isn't she?" Warwick snarled, yanking me with him, stepping closer. "Now, give me what I asked for, and I'll be on my way."

Killian dipped his head, his guards reacting, moving for me. Instinct drove my feet backward, trying to free myself from Warwick's grip. His fingers squeezed harder, his voice only loud enough for me. "Kovacs—"

"Fuck you," I snarled like a feral cat, thrashing against him. "I can't believe you."

Sloane, Vale, and Conner circled me, clasping down on my arms, but Warwick didn't let go, his gaze still digging into mine as if he wanted to communicate something. I no longer gave a shit.

"*Szétbasz az ideg!*" *The nerves are fucking me apart!* The old Hungarian curse flew from my lips.

"Brexley…"

"Don't you dare say my name. *Baszd meg magad!*" *Go fuck yourself*, I wailed, anger turning me wild and violent. "Get him off me!" I screamed at Vale, yanking at my arms like they were my saviors. "You vile piece of shit. Let me go."

"Farkas," Sloane said, his name sounding like an order.

Warwick lifted his chin, a deep growl shuddering the air. Sloane stepped up to him, his stature a little smaller than Warwick's, but both were threatening and challenging.

It was a full beat before Warwick snarled and dropped my arm and stepped away. Vale and Connor took me, cuffing my arms behind my back. A sick sense of déjà vu filled me, choking me with misfortune.

"This ends my debt," Warwick barked at Killian. "I'm free of you for good."

"Sure." Killian grinned smugly, picking up a large envelope off the seat. "And as I promised."

Warwick stepped forward, grabbing it from him and

opening it, peering in at the contents. He exhaled, his shoulders slouching in relief. Folding it into his pocket, he swung back for his bike, not even looking at me.

He got what he wanted and fucked off.

Anger. Hurt. Sadness. My soul felt sliced into pieces as I watched him walk away, grief burning the back of my eyes and throat. How could he do this? I had been so blind. A fool to trust…

Connor and Vale pushed me forward, forcing me into the back of the SUV, sitting on either side of me, guns primed, seeming to recall I was a little more dangerous than I appeared. Killian slipped into the passenger side, Sloane taking the driver's seat.

The SUV squealed as we pulled away. I hadn't even noticed where we were until now. The old abandoned commuter train station not too far from Leopold.

I had been so close to home once again. To my family. To freedom.

But that wasn't what hurt the most. My gaze went outside the darkened windows. Warwick straddled the bike, ready to take off, his eyes on the back window like he could sense me, piercing the darkened glass and pinning me in place. His face was blank and defensive, but I swore I could feel raw emotion slam into me: Hatred. Anger. Confusion. Guilt. Doubt.

But it disappeared as he started the bike. He circled us once before the bike tore off into the night, leaving me gutted.

Betrayed.

Alone.

Staring straight ahead, the fae castle in the distance, HDF glittering in the night like stars, I felt something shift inside me.

Whatever was ahead, whatever Killian had planned for me, I would come out alive.

Whatever it took, whatever I had to do, I would survive. Live.

Because right there, I made a promise to myself.

I would kill Warwick Farkas.

It was a promise I would not break.

I would become the very monster Halalház created.

TO BE CONTINUED IN WILD LANDS BOOK 2

About the Author

Stacey Marie Brown is a lover of hot fictional bad boys and sarcastic heroines who kick butt. She also enjoys books, travel, TV shows, hiking, writing, design, and archery. Stacey swears she is part gypsy, being lucky enough to live and travel all over the world.

She grew up in Northern California, where she ran around on her family's farm, raising animals, riding horses, playing flashlight tag, and turning hay bales into cool forts.

When she's not writing, she's out hiking, spending time with friends, and traveling. She also volunteers helping animals and is eco-friendly. She feels all animals, people, and the environment should be treated kindly.

To learn more about Stacey or her books, visit her at:

Author website & Newsletter: www.staceymariebrown.com

Facebook Author page:
www.facebook.com/SMBauthorpage

Pinterest: www.pinterest.com/s.mariebrown

TikTok: @authorstaceymariebrown

Instagram: www.instagram.com/staceymariebrown/

Goodreads:
www.goodreads.com/author/show/6938728.StaceyMarie_B
rown

Stacey's Facebook group:
www.facebook.com/groups/1648368945376239/

Bookbub:
www.bookbub.com/authors/stacey-marie-brown

Acknowledgements

Besides the *Winterland Tales*, which is more a fairytale retelling, this is my first PNR in 2 years. I've been terrified the entire time writing it, scared that it wouldn't live up to the DCL Saga. It's always hard starting a new series. Even though its set in the same world, it's takes place in a different part, which required much world-building.

I fell in love with Brexley and Warwick and hope you guys will too. Hope you will give these new set of characters a chance!

Kiki & Colleen at Next Step P.R - Thank you for all your hard work! I love you ladies so much.
Jordan Rosenfeld at Write Livelihood - Every book is better because of you. I have your voice constantly in my head as I write.
Hollie "the editor" - Always wonderful, supportive, and a dream to work with.
Jay Aheer - So much beauty. I am in love with your work!
Judi Fennell at www.formatting4U.com - Always fast and always spot on!

To all the readers who have supported me: My gratitude is for all you do and how much you help indie authors out of the pure love of reading.

To all the indie/hybrid authors out there who inspire, challenge, support, and push me to be better: I love you!

And to anyone who has picked up an indie book and given an unknown author a chance. THANK YOU!

Printed in the USA
CPSIA information can be obtained
at www.ICGtesting.com
LVHW012142070724
784867LV00033B/1194